H. F. Samman

Monograph on the Cotton Fabrics Of Assam

H. F. Samman

Monograph on the Cotton Fabrics Of Assam

ISBN/EAN: 9783742812810

Manufactured in Europe, USA, Canada, Australia, Japa

Cover: Foto ©Andreas Hilbeck / pixelio.de

Manufactured and distributed by brebook publishing software
(www.brebook.com)

H. F. Samman

Monograph on the Cotton Fabrics Of Assam

MONOGRAPH

ON

THE COTTON FABRICS OF ASSAM.

H. F. SAMMAN,

SUB-DIVISIONAL OFFICER OF CHUADANGA, NADIA.

FROM

    H. F. SAMMAN, Esq.,

        SUB-DIVISIONAL OFFICER OF CHUADANGA,

To

    THE SECRETARY TO THE CHIEF COMMISSIONER OF ASSAM,
                              SHILLONG.

        [Through the Director of Land Records and Agriculture, Assam, Shillong.]

                Dated Chuadanga, Nadia, the 21st August 1897.

SIR,

    I HAVE the honour to submit herewith my Monograph on the Cotton Fabrics of Assam.

                        I have the honour to be,

                            SIR,

                    Your most obedient servant,

                      H. F. SAMMAN.

MONOGRAPH

ON

THE COTTON FABRICS OF ASSAM.

In Assam, as in most other parts of India, cotton cloth is the chief material used by the people for their dress, their satchels, their bed sheets and their rugs. From time immemorial the inhabitants of this Province have spun cotton thread and woven cotton cloth. The homespun thread and home-made cloth are now giving way before those imported from the West, but as yet they have not been entirely driven out. The cloth now woven is nearly all ornamented in greater or less degree, very little is absolutely plain. The fabrics and the ornamentations they display vary widely over the Province—the fabrics in texture, the ornamentations in design, and both in quality. One of the main causes of this wide variety is the immense mixture of tribes and races found within the Province.

The cotton fabrics of Assam have thus a three-fold interest, commercial, artistic and ethnological. The scope of this monograph is, however, mainly industrial, and it is, therefore, only the commercial aspect that is here developed.

The subject has been divided into four parts. The first deals with the cotton spinning and weaving industry, the manner in which this industry has been affected by imports from abroad, and the trade in the home-made fabrics; the second deals with the materials used; the third with the process of manufacture, and the fourth with the fabrics themselves.

The information has been derived from several sources. First and foremost come the reports received from each district and sub-division, secondly, the Provincial Returns and other literature on the subject, and thirdly, personal observation. The reports from the Brahmaputra Valley are generally exhaustive, and those from the Hills, while briefer, are full of interest, but those from the Surma Valley are, with some exceptions, meagre, owing to the insignificance of the industry in that valley. The returns have been of great service for the first part of this work and articles by different writers, most of which are published in the Journals of the Asiatic Society, have afforded much additional information concerning the cotton fabrics made and worn by the Hill Tribesmen of Assam. Personal enquiry has been, of necessity, somewhat limited. The only sub-divisions in which any such enquiry has been made are those of Golaghat and Goalpara; neither of these is greatly celebrated for its weaving, and while both exhibit peculiar varieties of the process of manufacture, the close inspection of these processes has been rendered practically impossible by the timidity of the weavers, and by the limited time available for such enquiry. A collection of cotton fabrics, however, has been made, comprising specimens from nearly every district, and all these specimens and many others in the Indian Museum have been carefully examined and described at some length in the last part of this monograph.

PART I.

Of the industry itself, the influence of competition from abroad, and trade in the home-made fabrics.

The total number of professional weavers in this Province censused in 1891 was 213,950, of whom 109,842 were males and 104,108 females.

The following statements show the distribution of these persons, first, among the various weaving castes and, secondly, over the Province.

TABLE No. 1.

	Males.	Females.	Total.
Chhipa (Hindu).	30	5	35
Jolaha (do.).	109	83	192
Do. (Mahomedan)	1,105	883	1,988
Jugi (Hindu).	90,282	87,464	177,746
Kapali (do.).	652	470	1,122
Koshta (do.).	7	7	14
Mehra (do.).	48	23	71
Pan (do.).	10,659	8,984	19,643
Do. (Animistic)	313	150	463
Pator (Hindu).	428	392	820
Patwa (do.).	401	318	719
Samosi (do.).	48	65	113
Tanti (do.).	5,755	5,247	11,002
Tatwa (do.).	5	17	22
TOTAL	109,842	104,108	213,950

The Kapalis are almost exclusively confined to Sylhet and Goalpara, and all the other castes, except the Jolahas, Jugis and Tantis consist mainly of immigrants from other provinces. This table does not include the Dhunias, a class of Mussalmen, whose traditional occupation is cotton-cleaning.

TABLE No. 2.

	Males.	Females.	Total.
Surma Valley	57,908	54,567	112,475
Brahmaputra Valley	51,863	49,523	101,386
Hill Districts	71	18	89
TOTAL	109,842	104,108	213,950

The above figures classify people according to their professional or rather traditional occupation only. The Census Report gives statistics also regarding the present occupations of the people. The accompanying table shows the numbers of those connected with the cotton industry in its different branches.

TABLE No. 3.

	Males.	Females.	Total.
Raw cotton dealers	2,571	2,627	5,198
Cotton spinners, sizers and yarn beaters	2,407	10,979	13,386
Cotton weavers and sellers	11,970	21,673	33,643
Others	173	144	317
TOTAL	17,121	35,423	52,544

Thus, 52,544 persons, or rather less than 1 per cent. of the total population of the Province, returned themselves as employed in the cotton industry. Of these, nearly half, viz., 24,449, combined this occupation with agriculture, and more than two-thirds of the total number were women. The actual spinners and weavers numbered only 47,029, i.e., only about 22 per cent. of the number of professional weavers in the Province. The distribution of these persons among the plains districts of the two valleys and the hill districts is shown in the accompanying table.

TABLE No. 4.

	Males.	Females.	Total.
Surma Valley	11,683	19,580	31,263
Brahmaputra Valley	2,176	11,030	13,206
Hill Districts	518	2,042	2,560
TOTAL	14,377	32,652	47,029

From this table it will be seen that, whereas in the Surma Valley the number of women is less than double that of the men, in the Brahmaputra Valley and the Hill Districts it is approximately five times as great. Another striking point is that the total number of weavers and spinners in the Surma Valley is considerably more than double that in the Brahmaputra Valley, whereas the total population of each valley is nearly the same. The number of spinners and weavers in the hills is in about the same proportion to the total population as in the Brahmaputra Valley.

It might be thought that these figures would throw some light upon the extent and distribution of the industry, but they do not. The reason is not far to seek. Throughout the Brahmaputra Valley weaving is not a profession, nor is it, strictly speaking, an industry. It is carried on by women and girls alone, but by those of every family, rich or poor, high caste or low.[*] Weaving among the Assamese forms part of a girl's education and part of a woman's ordinary household duties. The women of the family are expected to make their own clothes and those of the men as well. In former days they certainly did so, but now a change is coming over the country. Cotton fabrics imported from Europe and India can be purchased ready-made for a moderate sum, and these, though less lasting, are much finer in texture than those usually made by the Assamese. Accordingly, among the richer classes, the women have given up weaving cloths for ordinary wear and confine themselves to the production of fine cloths delicately and tastefully ornamented with borders and patterns of silk or gold or silver thread. The middle classes, too, have now taken to wearing imported clothes and it is among them, at the present day, that weaving is at its lowest ebb. The poorer people, especially those living in the interior, still, to a large extent, make their own clothing, as they cannot afford to purchase foreign goods, and in most cases, too, prefer their own productions.

It must not be supposed, however, that the art of weaving is looked upon with much less favour now-a-days than in the past. Skill in the art is still held to be one of the highest attainments of a woman, and gains for those who can acquire it such complimentary epithets as *Hipini* and *Kaji* ; in fact, almost all the terms expressing excellence of attainments in a woman have at their foundation this idea of skill in spinning and weaving. When a proposal of marriage is made, the first question asked about the bride is whether she knows *boakata*, *i.e.*, whether she is skilled in spinning and weaving, and as a proof of her skill the guardian is expected to produce some cloths of the girl's own handiwork. One of the most usual and most acceptable of wedding gifts is a cunningly embroidered cloth woven and worked by the donor herself.

It is not difficult to account for this high value set upon weaving as an occupation for women in Assam. Here there never was that marked division of the people into castes or guilds that is so characteristic of many parts of India. In days of old, it is true, there were a few professional weaving castes such as the Tantis and Mohamedan Jolahas; but the Jolahas have now almost entirely disappeared, and the other weaving castes have long since abandoned their professional occupation for trade or agriculture. But even in the days of their prime these weaving castes did not supply the masses with their clothes. They were engaged rather in weaving the finer fabrics required by the Royal Family and others of high estate. These Royal Weavers received a grant of rent-free land and other favours in return for their services. They rarely, if ever, sold the products of their looms. Thus the masses were left dependent on themselves alone for the supply of clothing for the family, and it was upon the women that this important duty devolved. The women wove and weave for themselves, and for the men and children of the household. In some instances they weave also to oblige their neighbours, friends and masters, but they do not take their clothes to market. They can seldom be induced to weave for an outsider. If they do consent to weave a *khania* or *borkapor* in return for a few powas of cotton, they will dawdle over the work and while they could, if they chose, finish a cloth in 8 or 10 days, they will prolong the work for several months, and in the end try to back out of the agreement, saying the cotton was not sufficient for the cloth and bringing forward every imaginable excuse for the delay. •

For, while weaving as an art, a household duty or a pastime is looked upon with high respect, weaving as a means of livelihood is considered derogatory to almost every class of people (except in Mangaldai). It is only the Katonis, a low weaving class whose products are coarse and rough, and the hill tribesmen settled in the plains, who make cloths for sale and take them to the market. A few old Brahmin widows who have no relations to support them and no other means of livelihood are driven by dire necessity to sell the clothes they weave in order to eke out a bare subsistence, † but .even they dispose of their goods as privately as possible.

Such is the nature of the industry in Assam Proper, the districts of the Brahmaputra Valley. Among the hill tribesmen weaving occupies much the same position. As the Deputy Commissioner of the Garo Hills remarks, weaving is hardly more of a

---

* There is an exception in the case of the Tantis (a professional weaving caste) of Sualkuchi in the Darrung District, but their numbers are very small and their productions of no importance. In Jorhat, too, there are a few Tantis, but, with them, the men help the women in weaving only in the case of silk and not in that of cotton cloth.
† In Kamrup the earning of a livelihood in this way is termed *Katani katikhowa*.

profession than cooking. Here, however, there is not the same feeling against earning an honest penny by the sale of home-made cloths. Whatever surplus there is in the family is either disposed of to a neighbour or some member of an adjacent tribe or else taken to the nearest *hát* and sold or bartered for the necessaries or luxuries in demand. With the exception of the Hill Miris and possibly the Akas, all the hill tribesmen are acquainted with the art of weaving, though some are very backward in the art. Among them all it is the women who spin and weave, the men have no knowledge of the processes.

In the Surma Valley the nature of the industry is entirely different. Weaving among the plains-people of this Valley never was a household industry, but was confined only to the Tantis and Jugis (or Naths), professional weaving castes. Among the Tantis men and boys only, and among the Jugis both men and women engaged themselves in weaving, but among all other classes, except the hill tribesmen, the occupation was considered derogatory for men and women alike. The finer clothes were woven by the Tantis and the coarser by the Jugis. The nature of the industry is the same now as it always has been, but the industry itself has become almost extinct even among the professional weaving castes, who have been driven to agriculture and other occupations now that their own has been rendered unprofitable by the influx of cheap imports from abroad.

About the spinning industry there is little to be said. Those who do spin, spin for themselves ; they are the weavers as well as the spinsters. The only exception to this has been noted elsewhere, *viz.*, the case of widows in the Surma Valley who used to supply the Jugis with their thread in days gone by. At present spinning is an almost forgotten art, it lingers only among the Hill Tribes and in the most remote villages of the plains, and even here imported thread is daily gaining ground, and now raw cotton is practically only used where the thread required is coarser than any that can be bought. In Nowgong, however, raw cotton is still used to some extent for the manufacture of *bor kapor* and the coarse cloths woven by the Lalungs. It is a significant fact that it is these very cloths from Nowgong which have been most successful in holding their own against imports from abroad.

Slight as it is, the importance of the cotton industry in Assam is, owing to its wider range, relatively greater than that of any other industry carried on by the natives of the Province ; for Assam is essentially an agricultural country and peculiarly devoid of industrial occupations. In Dhubri, however, the manufacture of gold and silver, brass and iron, is more important than weaving, and in the Surma Valley it is impossible to compare weaving in its present forlorn condition with any of the other local manufactures. Formerly, however, the spinning and weaving of cotton occupied the foremost place among the indigenous industries.

No part of Assam has yet felt the wave of industrial activity that is passing over India. Nowhere have any spinning mills or power looms been established, * and nowhere has any attempt been made to produce cotton fabrics on a large scale. There are hardly any native capitalists in Assam, and such as there are, are foreigners who prefer the safer investments of trade to embarking in any speculative industrial enterprise. Government, too, have made no attempts to create a cotton industry of commercial importance. In the jails, weaving has been carried on to some extent, but attempts to effect production on a large scale have resulted in failure. A short description of the cotton manufactures of the Assam Jails will be given hereafter. [*cf.* Appendix I.]

Seeing that weaving is no longer carried on as a profession, there is very little use in calculating the average earnings a weaver can make. As a matter of fact they are generally almost nil. The Subdivisional Officer of Sonamgunge, however, reports that, considering the time taken in manufacture, weaving of the cloth called *gilap* does not, in all probability, give a profit of more than six annas a day. But he says that it is very difficult to say how much is earned, owing to the work being done only during leisure time. It is, therefore, almost certain that this estimate of six annas a day is far too high.

In Moulvie Bazaar it is reported that the time and labour spent in their manufacture are out of all comparison with the price of the cloth, but no figures are given to show the amount of profit earned. Beyond this there is no information on which to calculate the profits from cloth weaving in the Surma Valley at the present

---

* Several attempts have been made to introduce the modern cotton gin into the Province. Mr. Darrah, in his 'Note on Cotton', describes the result of experiments with such gins at Doboka and Tura in 1885, and another gin was worked about the same time in the Goalpara look-up. But in neither case does the experiment appear to have proved successful, as all three gins have ceased to work. The subject of ginning being hardly within the scope of this monograph, it is not proposed to discuss it further.

day. Mr. Ware Edgar in his "Report on the History and Statistics of the District of Cachar" for 1865-66 gives some interesting figures. He says the raw materials for a piece of the coarse cloth made by the Jogis, 1½ yard long and one yard wide, cost about one rupee, and the cloth sells for R2-4. It is not said how long this cloth takes to make. The Manipuris, however, are calculated by him to earn six annas a day; the calculation is as follows:—

		R	a.	p.
Cost of making one Khesh 2¼ yds. × 1⅓ yd.		1	4	0
viz., Raw cotton, one seer	10 annas.			
Dye, two seers	10 annas.			
Ordinary sale price of ditto		3	0	0
	Profit . R	1	12	0

To make a *khesh* of this size takes five days, but from the profit something must be deducted for the proportion of the cost of manufacture of the loom and spinning wheel which are both home-made. Their cost is very trivial and their durability great.

A mosquito curtain is said to have given the Manipuri makers a profit of R2-10, its sale price being R4-0-0, but these curtains were generally made in Manipur and thence brought down to Cachar.

Mr. Edgar shows that the *puri* or rug made by the Kukis of Cachar was at that time a profitable article of manufacture. A rug 2½ yards long and containing 14 seers of cotton sold for R20. The price of the cotton being only R8-12-0 and the time taken in manufacture being twenty days, the average daily earnings work out at the high figure of nine annas. From this must be deducted a very small sum for the wear and tear of the loom. The total original value of this in labour is estimated at R20, but it is not stated on what daily rate of wages this calculation is based.

In the Brahmaputra Valley and in fact throughout Assam at the present day the difficulty of calculating the daily wages earned lies chiefly in the fact that so few cloths are sold that it is difficult to assign any market value to them. Figures have been received from many districts, in which the price of the home-made cloth is fixed at approximately the same figure as that of an imported cloth of a similar nature. From these figures it appears that the wages of the weaver average about half an anna a day. In Dhubri and Mangaldai the calculation gives a daily profit of 1¼ anna, but in Goalpara and Barpeta the profit when bought thread is used is *nil*, while in Golaghat the cost of the thread itself is said to exceed the cost of a machine-made cloth. The explanation of this is that a home-made cloth contains considerably more material than an imported cloth of the same dimensions owing to the threads being woven closer together. The consequence is that the former cloth is much more lasting than the latter. From the figures received it appears that the daily earnings are greater when the thread is home-spun than when bought thread is used. This would indicate that spinning is a more profitable occupation than weaving.

The accompanying table shows, for certain places in the Brahmaputra Valley, the cost of making a man's loincloth out of (1) raw cotton and (2) imported cotton thread :—

	RAW COTTON.					READY MADE THREAD.				
	Price of raw cotton.	Sale price of cloth.	Profit.	Number of days' labour.	Daily wages.	Price of thread.	Sale price of cloth.	Profit.	Number of days' labour.	Daily wage.
	R a. p.	R a. p.	R a. p.		R a. p.	R a. p.	R a. p.	R a. p.		R a. p.
North Lakhimpur	...	...	...	...	...	0 6 0	0 8 0	0 2 0	4	0 0 6
Golaghat	...	...	...	...	...	0 15 0	0 12 0	Loss	of 3 annas.	
Nowgong	0 2 3	0 8 0	0 5 9	10½	0 0 7	0 6 0	0 8 0	0 2 0	4	0 0 6
Mangaldai	0 2 0	{0 10 0 to 0 12 0}	{0 8 0 to 0 10 0}	8	{0 1 0 to 0 1 3}	...	...	...	...	...
Barpeta	0 4 6	1 0 0	0 11 6	20	0 0 7	1 0 0	1 0 0	*Nil.*	...	...
Goalpara	...	...	...	...	...	0 9 0	0 9 0	*Nil.*	...	{0 1 2
Dhubri	...	...	...	...	...	0 5 0	{0 8 0 to 0 9 0}	{0 3 0 to 0 4 0}	2½	to 0 1 7}

The man's loincloth has been chosen, because it is similar throughout the Valley and because, in many cases, figures have been received regarding this and no other fabric. In cases where figures regarding other clothes have been given, the result is approximately the same; but, among plain clothes, the *borkapor* (or *dangoria kapor* appears to be more profitable to make than any other.

It is clear, therefore, that from a pecuniary point of view the manufacture of ordinary cotton cloths is wholly unprofitable. The case is different with those cloths that contain elaborate designs, for here the profit depends considerably on the skill of the weaver and the rapidity with which she can work. Thus in Barpeta a *paridiya kapor* is worth R200 to R300. It takes six months to make one from the raw cotton, of which only 2½ seers, value 7½ annas, are required. If ready-made thread be used the cloth takes 4 months to make and the thread (1 seer) costs R1-8-0. The cost of the gold lace is R150. Thus in the former case six months' labour results in a clear profit varying from R49-8-6 to R149-8-6, giving a monthly wage of R8-4-1 to R24-14-9; and in the latter four months' labour produces a profit of R48-8-0 to R148-8-0, giving a monthly wage of R12-2-0. to R37-2-0. Similarly in Golaghat a *gutibulua kapor* costs twelve annas in white thread and R1 in gold thread total R1-12-0 and is worth as much as R50. It takes 15 days to make. Hence its manufacture results in a profit of R48-4, giving a monthly wage of R96-8.

These figures are, it is believed, approximately correct.

For the Hills no figures have been received. Here, however, it is, as a rule, only coarse cloths that are made. The cost of raw cotton is probably much less and the cost of imported thread slightly more than in the plains. The calculations of daily earnings will be modified accordingly, but the result will, it is believed, be, in the main, the same as for coarse cloths in the Assam Valley.

The weaving industry being of the nature above described, it is not surprising to find few or no persons or places specially renowned for weaving in Assam. It is said that in days gone by, the Ranis of Darrang in Mouzah Hanlimohanpur and some ladies in Mouzah Banagorah were famed for the manufacture of very fine *khania kapor*, but nowadays it is very difficult to procure such fine *kahnia*. So, too, the Ahom Rajas kept skilled weavers to supply the royal wardrobe with clothes, and it is related how, in the reign of Purandar Rajah, one Madhuram Tanti excelled all the other weavers of the day and was, for his services to the Royal Family, granted land rent-free by the King. The family to which Madhuram belonged used to live near Badlipar in the Golaghat sub-division, but none of their descendants are now to be found there.

At the present day there is no person or place in Assam specially noted for its weavers. In North Lakhimpur the Kacharis of the Kadam Mouzah are considered the best weavers. In Golaghat and Jorhat the Miris are celebrated for weaving a kind of rug called *mirijin* which is not made by any other persons in the sub-division. A description of this rug and its manufacture will be given hereafter. In Jorhat, too, some Norahs make a sort of bag (*thung*) unlike anything made by the Assamese, and some Mussalmen of Jorhat town make a peculiar kind of embroidered shawl. In Nowgong the only weavers of any particular note (Mahomedan women of Puranigodam) confine their exertions to the manufacture of silk cloths. In Kamrup, Sualkuchi and Kamarkuchi of Hajo, Lashkarpara of Rangia and North Gauhati are said to be famed for the manufacture of fine and skilfully embroidered fabrics. Kamarkuchi is famed for the finest kind of cotton cloth made with locally-made thread called *surakata suta*, but nowadays this thread has ceased to be employed. In Nowgong, too, this thread was made in the time of the Rajas of Assam for weaving into cloths used by the Royal Family. Nowadays there is no Royal Family and no *surakata* thread.

On the whole, of the sub-divisions in the Brahmaputra Valley, perhaps those most celebrated for artistic skill in weaving are first Jorhat and next North Lakhimpur, but there is not much to choose between most of them. In Goalpara the Kachari women living on the south bank are skilled in making cotton cloths elaborately decorated with flowered borders. As regards variety of outturn, the centre of the cotton industry appears to be the Sadr Sub-division of Kamrup, and as regards quantity, the Sadr Sub-division of Darrang.

In the Surma Valley the Manipuris of Rupairbali and Lakhimpur in Cachar make *fanek*, and those of Ambicapur and Ramnagar mosquito curtains in larger quantities than their fellow countrymen residing elsewhere in the district. In the Sonamgunge Sub-division plain *gilap* ¸which will be described later on) are made chiefly in ¸Budharail and *gilap* striped with red in Dohatia. In Cachar and in the North Cachar Hills a few Kookies make more cloths than are sufficient for their own requirements. They also make a *pari* or rug somewhat similar to the *mirijin*. Among the Hill Districts there are no persons and places celebrated for their cotton fabrics, but the Manipuris far excel any of the other tribes in weaving, and the Khamptis and Singphos of Lakhimpur make most interesting and artistic cloths. The Phakials, too, who live in two or three small villages near Jaipur, still make very handsome cheque-patterned clothes, which find a ready sale among the Europeans in the district.

It is now time to examine more closely the extent of competition from abroad and its effect on the industry.

It has been already shown how the people of the Assam Valley are exchanging the ordinary clothes woven by themselves for those imported from the west. These imported fabrics have flooded the valley and are now to be found for sale even in the remotest villages. It is therefore only the poorest classes, who cannot afford the slight extra cost of these clothes, that still continue to weave their own.

In the Surma Valley the success of the foreigner has been even more complete. The Jugis and Tantis of this valley used in former times to subsist entirely by the manufacture of cotton clothes, and used to derive a fair income from the business. They had an extensive field of work, and the majority of the people used to purchase the products of their looms. The Jugis used to make clothes of coarser texture, buying the thread from poor widows of all classes who used to spin, or taking it off them and returning it in the form of cloth. The Tantis, as a rule, made clothes of finer texture, buying the thread or making it themselves out of cotton bought in the market. This cotton they would clean with the *charkhi* and then spin into thread by the *charkhá*.

Even in their best days, the weavers in Cachar were unable to supply the local demand for cotton fabrics. It is not known whence the remainder was obtained, but probably it was from Dacca or the adjoining districts of Bengal. Now for many years the industry has been almost dead. The locally made clothes are much coarser than those imported, and none but the Jugis themselves and still lower castes would dare to wear such clothes in public. The Tantis are not even mentioned in Cachar, and in Habigange there are only three families who still earn a living by weaving. In Sonamgunge the coarser cloths woven by the Tantis have been driven out, but the *gilaps* woven with imported thread are still prized as there is nothing like them among imported goods, and they are considered cheap. They therefore find a ready market, but the supply is very limited, and they do not therefore go outside the Pargannah in which they are made. So, too, the Jugis can now make little profit by weaving, their cloths being rejected or despised, and they have now turned to other occupations. They have not, however, as yet forgotten their knowledge of the art, for in South Sylhet where not a single person lives by weaving, and where the Jugis have thrown away their looms, they were still able to make new looms and weave some cloth before the Sub-Deputy Collector who was enquiring into the subject of cotton fabrics.

Thus the weaving of common cloths does not at all repay the workman for his time and labour; and the foreign substitutes for these cloths, though inferior in durability, are finer in texture and superior in finish. It is therefore found that, wherever weaving used to be carried on as a means of livelihood, *viz.*, throughout the settled parts of the Surma Valley and among the professional weaving castes elsewhere, the imported fabrics have driven the local manufacture entirely out of the market.

That this has not yet been effected in the Brahmaputra Valley and among the Hill Tribes, is due mainly to two causes. First, weaving is a domestic occupation and practised by women alone. The cost of labour therefore is in reality never taken into consideration when the cost of the cloth is calculated. The Assamese women, after their household duties are over, would, if they were not weaving, be sitting idle. They will not do manual labour for hire, and they have no other source of amusement than the loom. Weaving, therefore, is a pleasure rather than toil, and there is no reason why the time devoted to it should be priced or made a factor of the value of the cloths produced. Thus, on the score of cheapness and economy, the poorer classes still make the clothes they ordinarily wear, and will in all probability long continue to do so. But it is not economy alone that keeps the industry alive. There are other forces at work. The mere fact that an article is home-made gives it an additional charm, an artificial value, and not only that—to stamp out the industry means to change the routine of household duties, the daily round of life,—these are the sources of vitality in household industries, and weaving in Assam is no exception to the rule. But of late the pressure of competition from abroad has been severely felt. The women of the middle and richer classes have ceased to make the clothes they and their husbands and brothers ordinarily wear. Their love for the home-made goods has given way to a preference for the finer though less durable fabrics from the West, and these classes now look with some disfavour on the coarser cloths of Assam. This feeling is most marked among the progressive party of the middle class, but there are some places where the people are more conservative and still prefer clothes of their own make. Thus in North Lakhimpur the people have never fancied foreign goods, believing that they are not genuine, and these, though for a time they made some way, are now hardly holding their own. The home manufacture here has on the contrary sensibly increased during the last twelve years, and the quality of the fabrics has considerably improved. The local outturn of cotton cloths is at present, it is said, sufficient to supply one-third of the population. But North Lakhimpur is an exceptional case ; · it is, however, interesting as showing the possibility of a general reaction among the Assamese in favour of their own manufactures and the consequent revival of the industry.

The second obstacle which the foreign competitor has to meet is much greater than the first. It is the peculiar nature of many of the fabrics made in Assam. Among those of the Assamese themselves may be mentioned the richly embroidered shawls worn chiefly by women but sometimes also by men, the *Karsapi bunkara kapor*, the *gutibulua*, the *paridiya* and many others. It is to the production of these fancier and more delicate fabrics that the women of the richer classes now devote their attention and direct their skill. The cost of the materials for these cloths is very great, but as has been shown already, is nothing in comparison with the value of the cloths when made. Even now it is only a few people who can afford to make these cloths, and the number of those who could afford to buy them would be still smaller. The work involved in the manufacture of these fabrics is immense, and even by the aid of the best machinery, the foreign producer could never expect to turn them out at a price which would create a demand sufficient to repay him. It is doubtful indeed whether these fabrics could be turned out by machinery at all.

Then among the hill tribes, not only do the cloths of one tribe differ *in toto* from those of most others, but even among some tribes it is only a very small portion of the community that dresses alike. Thus, among the Nagas, each village or group of villages is distinguished by the colour of its cloths and the peculiar arrangement of the stripes, and similarly, among the Khamptis, each division of the tribe wears a different patterned loin cloth. The number of people, therefore, using one particular kind of cloth is so small that the demand for any of these cloths would never be sufficient to repay the foreigner for producing them. In many cases, too, the peculiar nature of the ornamentations on these cloths would render their imitation very difficult and comparatively expensive. The manufacture of these cloths is particularly suited to the hand loom, not the mill. But even the hand loom of the foreigner cannot successfully compete as has been shown by the failure of the Manipuris in their attempt to supply the Nagas with cloths of the patterns they require.

So long, therefore, as the hill tribesmen retain their national costume, it is certain that the art of weaving among them will continue to flourish in its present condition. But the hillsmen who have settled in the plains have almost entirely abandoned their national costume, and there is a similar tendency among those who visit or live near the plains. Every year, therefore, the costume of the people is becoming more uniform, and it is probably only the matter of a few more generations before the ordinary costume of the plains has spread throughout the hills. The change is, in some parts, taking place very rapidly. Nowadays, in the Garo Hills, "cheap English and Indian fabrics are largely imported and sold in every market ; for one man wearing a Jharwa cloth ten men can be seen in these hideous machine-made articles." These remarks by the Deputy Commissioner of the Garo Hills are corroborated by the following passage quoted from an article by "Esme" in the *Calcutta Review* of 1885 which will show that even then the foreign fabrics were making ground :— "Within the last few years there is a great difference observable in the Garos who live near Tura. A *hât* is now established at Tura itself, and a brisk trade carried on ; cloths of various kinds and colours, such as delight the eyes of all savages, are easily obtainable. Consequently the exceedingly primitive costume of the Garo is now frequently supplemented by a gay coloured cloth flung not ungracefully round the shoulders and neck." So with the Nagas. Writing of Cachar in 1866 Mr. J. Ware Edgar says : "I have remarked, however, that the Nagas of the villages near the plains have of late become very unwilling to appear in their customary dress before Europeans or Bengalis, and they are now seldom seen in the plains without a *dhoti* tied over the triangular *khes*."

This tendency to adopt more civilized clothing has not progressed so rapidly in Upper Assam. It would perhaps be a good thing if some of the Nagas who come down to the plains to do their shopping were a little more shy in appearing before Europeans and Assamese in their native garb; for a crowd of Nagas in the Sibsagar bazaar is often a sight hardly fit for a lady's eyes.

In their own hills the Nagas are very conservative in the matter of dress. In both Kohima and Mokokchang the industry has not been affected by cheap imports. In Mokokchang the local industry has improved during the last eight years since the sub-division was taken over, owing to the country being more peaceful and the people growing richer. The cloths made by the Nagas are remarkably strong, the Nagas will wear no others, and at the same time these cloths are worn by none but Nagas. The industry will, therefore, probably continue for some years to develop with the increase of population and prosperity, but it is never likely to assume large proportions.

Some tribes are more conservative than others, and the change will consequently take place more slowly among them, but the process will be none the less sure. And, as some tribes are more conservative, so some cloths are more likely to retain their popularity. An instance of this is the Manipuri *fanek* or petticoat described hereafter. It has been suggested that the Manchester and Bombay firms would do well to reproduce this cloth. It is probable that if they did so with success, the popularity of this garment would increase more and more and that the venture would be profitable for the mills and advantageous to the consumers, as the price of such cloths in the market is at present rather high. It is at the same time doubtful whether this cloth is one that could be produced at a reasonable price, owing to the nature of its embroidered borders.

On the other hand, some cloths are fast becoming obsolete, for instance, the *kadisil* of the Garos, a peculiar band of cloth that only he who had taken a head could wear.

The effects of cheap imports on the cotton industry in Assam is clearly reflected in the statistics of the imports and exports of the Province. The figures concerning twist and yarn will be discussed more fully in the second part, but it may be here remarked that the import of cotton thread into the Brahmaputra Valley is still on the increase, which goes to show that the weaving industry in that Valley is by no means dead. The figures concerning piece-goods, which will now be discussed, are equally instructive.

The external trade of Assam is divided into two parts, *viz:* — 1st, the trade between Assam and Bengal, and 2nd, the trade between Assam and the adjoining foreign countries.

The trade with Bengal includes that passing through Bengal to Europe and other parts of India. It is carried almost entirely by river. A very slight fraction, it is true, is carried by road, but the figures representing this traffic are so small as to form a negligible quantity. The trade with adjoining foreign countries is likewise of very slight importance. During the five years ending March 31st, 1896, this trade resulted in an average annual net exportation of 538 maunds of European piece-goods and an average annual net importation of 14 maunds of Indian piece-goods.

It is therefore only the river-borne trade between Assam and Bengal that requires discussion in detail. This trade is divided naturally into two parts, that along the Brahmaputra into the Brahmaputra Valley and that along the Meghna into the Surma Valley. In each case it must be remembered that the imports supply the adjoining Hills as well as the Valley itself. The accompanying table shows the imports and exports of the two Valleys separately for the two periods April 1881 to March 1886 and April 1891 to March 1896 :—

Brahmaputra Valley.

	1881—86.		1891—96.	
	European.	Indian.	European.	Indian.
	Mds.	Mds.	Mds.	Mds.
Imports	152,895	1,292	305,795	1,712
Exports	*Nil*	*Nil*	220	646
Net imports	152,895	1,292	305,575	1,066
Average net imports per year . . .	30,579	258	61,115	213

Surma Valley.

	1881—86		1891—96.	
	European.	Indian.	European.	Indian.
	Mds.	Mds.	Mds.	Mds.
Imports	222,436	5,688	355,747	11,979
Exports	2	52	6	288
Net imports	222,434	5,636	355,741	11,691
Average net imports per year	44,487	1,127	71,148	2,338

From this table it will be seen that the average yearly net import of piece-goods for the first period was 30,837 maunds in the Brahmaputra Valley and 45,614 maunds in the Surma Valley. The corresponding figures for the second period are 61,328 maunds and 73,486 maunds respectively. Thus, while the imports into the Brahmaputra have, during the ten years, nearly doubled in quantity, those into the Surma Valley have only increased by about 61 per cent. This is due to the fact that even at the earlier period the Surma Valley depended chiefly upon imports for the supply of its clothing, whereas in the Brahmaputra Valley it is only of recent years that imported cloths have been rapidly supplanting local fabrics. Another cause at work is that in the latter Valley the use of clothes made of the local varieties of silk is gradually being discontinued in favour of cotton fabrics; but the use of silk as a material for clothing even in the Assam Valley has always been small compared with that of cotton. At the present day it is probable that silk does not form a very large item in the wardrobe of the average Assamese.

Dr. Royle, in his "Culture and Commerce of Cotton in India," gives an estimate showing that the average amount of cotton clothing annually consumed per head by the adult population of India is about 2¼ pounds. Taking the extra demands of the well-to-do as balancing the lesser demands of the children and infants this average may be taken as a fair representative of the amount consumed per head by all classes, old and young. Thus a maund of cotton clothing would clothe rather more than 33 persons. Taking the figure at 33⅓ the calculation will be much simplified and the error, if any, will be slight. Thus it can be assumed that 3 maunds of cotton clothing are sufficient for 100 persons. The net imports of cotton fabrics into the Surma Valley during the last five years (73,486·4 maunds) would therefore suffice to clothe 2,449,547 people, and those into the Brahmaputra Valley (61,328·2 maunds) to clothe 2,044,273 persons. Now the total population of the Surma Valley (including the North Cachar and North Lushai Hills) was, according to the last census, 2,584,710; and that of the Brahmaputra Valley (including the Naga, Garo, and Khasia and Jaintia Hills) 2,892,123. Hence we find that nearly 95 per cent. of the population of the Surma Valley with the adjoining hills is clothed in imported cotton fabrics, whereas, in the Brahmaputra Valley, under 71 per cent. is so clothed. [It is here assumed that all the imported piece-goods are used as clothing, which, though not absolutely correct, is not very far from the truth.] Thus it is clear that, even when the proportion of silk clothes worn in Assam proper has been deducted, there still remains a considerable amount of cotton clothing locally made. In the Surma Valley, on the contrary, the manufactures of the hill tribesmen settled in the plains probably account for nearly one-half of the 5 per cent. of clothing made in the Valley.

To sum up, the cotton weaving industry in Assam, is, at the present time, in three distinct stages among the different classes of the people. Among the civilized inhabitants of the Surma Valley, the industry may be said to be extinct, and there is little probability of its revival, unless mills be established. There seems no particular reason why cotton mills in Cachar or Sylhet should not be a profitable venture, as the cotton is grown so near at hand, and, with the opening up of the country by the Railway, cheap labour should be easily procurable. Among the Assamese proper weaving still holds an important position, even in the manufacture of the coarser cloths. It will probably be long before these are altogether superseded by imported fabrics, and the weaving of delicately ornamented cloths will, no doubt, long continue to be a favourite pastime for the wives and daughters of the well-to-do. In the hills also and among the hillsmen who have settled in the plains, weaving is still largely practised. But here the industry is rapidly declining and there is little doubt that its decline will continue. The rough hillsman does not, like the Assamese, disdain to labour on the soil at a daily wage. More and more every year are resorting to the tea gardens, where both men and women can earn a wage far in excess of what they could possibly earn by the most assiduous application to the loom. Others, too, though not caring to work on the gardens, are turning to agriculture, which they find a more profitable occupation, and buying their scanty clothing from the bazar.

The large amount of European capital invested in Assam cannot have failed to affect the cotton industry. The influence has, however, been indirect. The investment of this capital has resulted in the rapid development of communications and enabled the foreign producer to land his goods in the markets of Assam at a price suited to the purses of the people. The imports have therefore largely increased, as already shown, but it must not be forgotten that a portion of this increase, by no means inconsiderable, is due to the increasing demands of the labourers imported to the tea gardens. The coolies on the gardens as a rule wear nothing but imported clothes, they buy few or none made by the Assamese. The only instance of such a purchase that has been reported, is that of 200 *borkapor* bought by the well-to-do coolies on the Brahmaputra Tea Estate in Golaghat in the cold weather of 1895. These cloths had been imported from Nowgong by a local Keya who sold them at a price of R1-8 each. They were used by the coolies as wrappers in the daytime and as blankets by night.

In Sibsagar, too, it is reported that the tea industry is beginning to give some impetus to the manufacture of cotton fabrics. The time-expired coolies who have settled down as cultivators in the district occasionally buy *churia* and *gamcha*, but sale is not large. They generally buy fabrics imported from India or Europe. In Nowgong it is said that an occasional sale is made to garden coolies of a coarse *gamcha* or *borkapor*.

The trade in the cotton fabrics of the Province is, as might have been expected, very insignificant. In the Brahmaputra Valley, Nowgong, Kamrup, and Goalpara are the only districts in which locally made cloths come to the market. Even here they do not find their way to the permanent bazars, the chief place of sale being the local weekly markets or *hât*. In several parts of the Province there are also annual trading fairs called *mela*, or in Kamrup *sobha*. Here some few cotton goods are found, but their numbers are very small compared with those of similar goods from Manchester and Bombay. In Goalpara I visited several *hâts* and looked about for cotton cloths made in the Province, but there were very few indeed, fewer in fact than cloths of Endi (or Eri) silk. On the other hand, in every *hât* there was the enterprising Marwari with his large stall full of every variety of cotton goods from Manchester and Bombay. Of the Assamese cloths the only varieties found were those of the roughest make, *borkapor* and *gamcha*, and the sole purchasers seemed to be the Garos.

In Kamrup the sales of cotton clothes at the *hât* are made both direct to the consumer, and also to the Naga traders who come to buy up local produce and sell imported goods. In this district, too, there is a class of men, called Phalengis, who collect cloths from the different villages and then hawk them about other villages for sale. Elsewhere the sales are always direct with the consumers.

The interdistrict trade is of even less importance. In the Brahmaputra Valley, Nowgong is the only district from which any considerable quantity of cloths is imported to other districts. From here cloths go to Darrang and the neighbouring hill districts. An instance of export to Golaghat also has been already mentioned. From Kamrup also there is a certain export trade to other districts, but it is quite insignificant. The interdistrict trade in this valley, such as it is, is carried on by the Keyas or Marwari traders.

In the Surma Valley the Jugis of Cachar import a certain number of coarse cotton cloths made by the Jugis of Sylhet, and sell them to men of their own caste and other low classes. They buy them chiefly at the Karimgunge and Badarpur bazaars and dispose of them at the different local bazaars or in the villages.

Cloths manufactured by the Tantis of Habigunge are exported to the Brahmanbaria sub-division of the Tipperah district in Bengal. The Tantis sell them to the cloth merchants who retail them to their customers; they also sell them direct to the consumers.

This is almost the only instance of export from the Province (except to the hill tribes), for the cotton fabrics of Assam find no demand among Bengalis or Europeans. The latter do occasionally buy a cloth, but it is usually bought as a curiosity or for collecting purposes. Many of the locally-made clothes however are not unsuited to European use; some, owing to their bright colours, make screens or hangings appropriate for an Indian bungalow; they would not, perhaps, be much appreciated as such at home. Miri *gamcha* are sometimes bought and used as cummerbands or sashes for flannel trousers, and they look very well when worn as such. In

Cachar the European residents used at one time to buy a fair number of Manipuri and Kuki cloths for use as table cloths or curtains, and also Kuki rugs, but the demand has greatly decreased of late.

The above account refers to trade in the plains. The trade in the hills is comparatively more important. The hill tribes take cotton cloths from the plains and occasionally find a market there for those they make themselves; but the bartering of cloths between neighbouring tribes is very frequent. This trade or barter is all in the hands of the hill tribesmen themselves. It may be mentioned here that the Miris act as middlemen, importing cloths from the plains and selling them to the Abors.

The demand by Garos for Assamese or Kachari cloths has been referred to elsewhere; according to Mr. Robinson, the Garos in turn sold a few cloths to the Mikirs. These cloths are described as usually striped and used for throwing over the shoulders. They are called *selu*. From this description it is difficult to understand what cloths are meant, but, in any case, the trade is no longer in existence.

The Mishmis, too, while they import the *borkapor* from Assam, supply both themselves and the Abors with clothing, and their textile fabrics, Captain Dalton says, always sold well at the Saikwa market. The Abors import not only from the Mishmis, but also from Thibet, as they wear coats of Thibetan or Chinese manufacture; but they are suppliers as well as customers, as they exchange their long-napped white cotton cloths with the Assamese who prize them much as rugs and quilts. These instances are taken from accounts written long ago; no information has been received to show if a similar trade still exists.

The following instances of trade in the hills at the present day have been reported.

The Megams on the Khasia borders supply the Garos not only with purple silk puggaris, but also with a kind of sleeveless cotton coat, having fringes round the bottom.

The Khasias, in their turn, import from the Kukis and the plains. From Nowgong come cloths described as *salang* or cotton *sari* which are largely used by the poorer women. The *cheleng* is probably the cloth referred to. From the Kukis of North Cachar they get a few cotton sheets, exchanging them for dried fish, etc.

Some of the Kukis of North Cachar also make the blue cloth so much worn by the Nagas. The Sub-Divisional Officer, however, does not report to what extent, if at all, the cloths are exported to the Naga Hills, and as the Deputy Commissioner of the latter district does not even mention them, it may be presumed that the interdistrict trade in them is insignificant, if it exists at all.

The Kukis in the plains of Cachar occasionally sell a kind of rug called *pari* to the inhabitants of the plains; and Europeans, it is said, sometimes buy these rugs for use as quilts.

But of all the hill tribes by far the most enterprising, as they are by far the most skilled in weaving, are the Manipuris. The cloths made by these people have always found a sale beyond the confines of Manipur.

During the reign of Choorjeet Singh (*i e.*, at the very beginning of this century) a very brisk trade was carried on between Manipur and the Burmese inhabitants of the frontier, through the Kubo Valley and cotton cloths were among the articles sent from Manipur. This trade, however, was discontinued, owing to a temporary misunderstanding between Manipur and Ava, and up to 1835, when Captain Boileau Pemberton wrote, it had not been renewed. In 1837, however, Mr. McCosh, in noticing the importance of the commerce of Assam with China and Ava, remarks that it was every day increasing and mentions among the articles sent to the markets from this side, the Manipuri cotton cloths of durable fabric and handsome patterns.

In 1866 Mr. Ware Edgar wrote that an inconsiderable quantity of cloth worked by Manipuris, Nagas, and Kukis was exported from Cachar.

The most interesting instance of Manipuri enterprise, however, is their attempt to supply the Nagas with their own peculiar cloths.

In 1882 the officiating Political Agent in Manipur wrote as follows: "A brisk trade has, within recent times, grown up in the sale and exportation of Manipur-made Naga cotton cloths. The greater knowledge of the Manipuris has enabled them to improve considerably upon the rude Naga loom, and now all the clan patterns of cloths are closely imitated and made so much cheaper, that the Nagas prefer to buy them rather than make them in their own villages. I observed that this influence has extended as far as Kohima. In fact, in a shop just opened there many Manipur-made

Naga cloths were exposed for sale." No figures are available to show the progress of the trade in cotton cloths between Manipur and the Naga Hills.· In 1887, however, the subject is again referred to in the "Report on trade between Assam and the adjoining foreign countries." The note is interesting and worth quoting. "A feature in the · Manipur trade, which is rising into prominence, is the part taken in it by the Nagas. These half-civilised people used formerly to wear their own coloured cloths, but of late years, recognising either the superior quality or cheapness of the manufactures of Manipur, they have taken to importing from this Principality. The Manipuris, on their side, have not been backward in taking advantage of the growing trade with the Nagas, and have met them half way by manufacturing cloths of the patterns most affected by their hereditary foes. Considering the natural enmity which usually keeps apart neighbouring half barbarous tribes, it is curious to see, as may be seen now any day in Manipur villages, coloured cotton fabrics of purely Naga designs growing into completion on Manipuri looms." From this time to the present day the industry appears to have attracted no further notice. The Manipuris think, however, seem now to have lost their hold on the Naga markets, for the Deputy Commissioner of the Naga Hills writes as follows: " A certain number of cheap cloths made up in Naga patterns are imported from Manipur by Angami traders. They are, however, thin and not durable, and are not much in request." The cloths made by the Nagas themselves are, as already mentioned, particularly substantial and lasting. The Political Agent of Manipur writes to the same effect: "Naga cloths are made by Manipuri women after the Naga pattern, and are sold in the two principal bazaars in the Capital. These fabrics are not so durable as those made by the Hill people, and their price is much below the average."

Speaking of the cotton-weaving manufacture generally at the present day the Political Agent writes: " The manufacture of cotton fabrics by Manipuris and hill-tribes-women is only sufficient to meet the local demand. Very small quantities of cotton fabrics are exported by Manipuris and outsiders to Cachar and Kohima. They, I believe, do not fetch sufficiently high prices to induce the people to trade in the articles, owing probably to Manchester goods being available at a lower figure. During the late scarcity of food grains in Manipur many Manipuris took down different kinds of petticoats, pagris, etc., to Lakhipur and Silchar for sale, but brought back their wares owing to less than half the prices realisable in Manipur being offered there.

The report received from Cachar, however, shows that the trade in cotton fabrics with Manipur is still prosperous. The Manipuris take down large consignments of their own cloths (chiefly *fanek, inaphi, ngoubong,* and *maihap*) to Cachar to sell them to Manipuri traders living at Lakhipur. Some of these traders, too, themselves go up to Manipur and bring down cloths which they hawk about in the Manipuri villages in the plains; they also find a ready demand for their goods among the Nagas and Kukis who are now exchanging the loom for the hoe.

The Manipuris living in Cachar make more clothes than they require for their own use, and sell the surplus at the nearest markets.

Manipuri *Khesh* have always sold in considerable quantities in the *mela* held annually at Silchar.

In the district of Sylhet, too, there are many Manipuris. They numbered over 30,000 at the last Census. Mr. Hunter, in his "Statistical Account of Assam" referred to a considerable trade in cotton fabrics carried on by the Manipuris in the town of Sylhet. At the present day the Manipuris throughout the district carry on weaving on a comparatively large scale.

The statistics given in the Provincial Trade Reports divide cotton piece-goods into two classes, *viz.,* European and Indian. The latter include, of course, goods made in any part of India, and there is nothing to distinguish · those made in Assam and those, for instance, of Bombay. The figures for export by river have already been given, and they are altogether insignificant. They are of no value whatever, as showing the amount of Assamese-made fabrics exported from Assam as they are so small that it is impossible to conjecture what proportion of them consists of goods from Bombay and other places out of Assam. It may be noted, however, that the exports of Indian goods are, as a rule, larger than those of European goods, whereas the reverse is the case with the imports. It may be inferred, therefore, that there is a certain river-borne export trade in Assamese cotton fabrics, but that this trade is of very small proportions.

The figures for the Frontier Trade are open to the same objections. It is of little use, therefore, to quote figures generally. The following figures relating to the exports from Manipur however are of interest, in view of the apparent discrepancy between the reports received from Cachar and Manipur, regarding the trade between those two districts;—

Imports of cotton piece-goods, Indian, from Manipur.

	Value in rupees.
1890-91	122
1891-92	*Nil*
1892-93	5,297
1893-94	*Nil*
1894-95	*Nil*
1895-96	1,284

These figures would seem to show that the export of cotton piece-goods from Manipur to Assam is very fitful, but that in two years it assumed comparatively large proportions considering the size of the State.

The only other point of interest in the Frontier Trade Reports is an increase of exports of various kinds of cloths, Eri, cotton and wool of both European and Indian make, from Assam to Towang in 1878-79, and the explanation of this furnished by Colonel Camber:—" A large portion of the cloths taken up this pass " (the Dhansiri pass) " are sent to North Thibet, and even to the inhabitants beyond Thibet, and I have no doubt that the sales at Udalguri are influenced a good deal by the tastes and fashions prevailing at the time amongst the actual consumers." The last two Frontier Trade Reports show a certain export of Indian cotton piece-goods from Assam to Towang, but for the six years the total value of this trade is only R1,286, so that after deducting the element of Bombay goods, the residue is very slight indeed.

The trade in mixed fabrics will be very briefly referred to in Part II of this monograph; it is wholly insignificant.

PART II.

The Materials used.

There is a considerable amount of cotton produced within the Province, the methods of cultivation are simple and inexpensive, and the cost of carrying it to the looms is nothing but the value of the time and labour of the carriers—usually hillsmen. It might naturally have been expected, therefore, that this cotton would form the chief material of the cotton fabrics made in Assam. In former times, when the weaving industry was at its height, this was undoubtedly the case. The weavers were, for the most part, spinners too. First, cleaning the raw cotton, they would spin it into thread and then convert this thread into cloth. In rare instances, as for example in the Surma Valley, poor widows would clean the cotton and spin it, and then sell the thread to professional weavers or give them thread in exchange for cloth. But at the present day, the state of things is entirely changed. The production of cotton is no less extensive than of old, but the effect of cheap imports has been to crush the spinning industry entirely, and we have the curious anomaly of raw cotton leaving the Province in large quantities, and equally large consignments of cotton thread being imported, the greater portion coming all the way from Europe. It would be extremely interesting to know how much of this imported thread is made out of the very cotton that had left the Province in its raw state, but there are no statistics by which this can be calculated.

Thus, at the present day, the amount of cotton grown in Assam, cleaned and spun within the Province, and there converted into cloth, is quite insignificant. An account of the total quantity of cotton grown, the method of cultivation and the way in which it is carried to the market, would therefore bear only indirectly on the subject of the cotton fabrics in Assam. Mr. Darrah, in a " Note on cotton in Assam," written in 1885, has discussed these matters at some length. The subject has subsequently been developed and brought up to date by Mr. Schofield in his " Note on Indian cotton " (1888), and by Dr. Watt in his " Dictionary of Economic Products of India " (1889). Little, if any, fresh information has been received, and the estimates of area under cultivation and outturn of cotton are still mere guesses. For these reasons the subject of cotton cultivation will not be here discussed.

Statistics of the River-Borne Trade in cotton twist and yarn are given below for the same years as those chosen above for piece-goods.

Cotton twist and yarn.

Brahmaputra Valley.

	1881—86.		1891—96.	
	European.	Indian.	European.	Indian.
	Mds.	Mds.	Mds.	Mds.
Imports	39,405	576	87,247	7,983
Exports	Nil	Nil	75	51
Net Imports	39,405	576	87,172	7,932
Average net imports per year . .	7,881	115	17,434	1,586

Surma Valley.

	1881—86.		1891—96.	
	European.	Indian.	European.	Indian.
	Mds.	Mds.	Mds.	Mds.
Imports	1,608	529	8,924	1,942
Exports	Nil	Nil	11	75
Net Imports	1,608	529	8,913	1,867
Average net Imports per year . .	322	106	1,783	373

These figures show that the importation of cotton thread into the Brahmaputra Valley far exceeds that into the Surma Valley, and that, in both valleys, the imports have increased enormously during the ten years. This increase is especially marked in the Surma Valley, where the total average import for the last five years is over five times what it was for the corresponding period ten years earlier. In the Brahmaputra Valley the imports have increased in the proportion of 12 to 5.

It has been shown above that imported piece-goods supply 2,044,273 persons in the Brahmaputra Valley and 2,449,547 in the Surma Valley. The adjoining hill districts being included in the calculation, there remains a population of 847,850 persons in the former Valley and 135,163 in the latter Valley to be clothed.

It may be assumed as approximately correct that cotton twist loses 2 per cent. in waste during the process of conversion into cloth by the hand loom. The net imports of European and Indian cotton thread now average 19,020 maunds in the Brahmaputra and 2,156 maunds in the Surma Valley which would be equivalent to about 18,640 and 2,113 maunds respectively of cotton cloth. According to the estimate already given, this would suffice to clothe 621,320 and 70,429 souls respectively, presuming, of course, that the whole of the cotton imported is converted into cloth.

This gives the following figures:—

Number of persons clothed.	Brahmaputra Valley.	Per cent.	Surma Valley.	Per cent.	TOTAL.	Per cent.
1. With imported cotton piece-goods .	2,044,273	71	2,449,547	94¾	4,493,820	82
2. With clothes made of imported cotton thread	621,320	21	70,429	2¾	691,749	12½
3. Otherwise, i. e., with clothes made of home-spun cotton thread . .	226,530	8	64,734	2½	291,264	5½
TOTAL .	2,892,123		2,584,710		5,476,833	

Thus, whereas over 21 per cent. of the total population in the Upper Valley is entirely clothed with fabrics made of imported cotton thread, in the Surma Valley only 2¾ per cent. of the population is so clothed. The number of persons clothed "otherwise" in the former Valley is 8 per cent. of the total population, in the latter Valley it is 2½ per cent. Thus, it appears that in the local weaving industry, raw cotton is used in a much larger proportion in the Surma than in the Brahmaputra Valley, though the actual consumption is, of course, greater in the latter than in the former, owing to the industry being of greater extent.[*]

This is fully borne out by the information received from District Officers. From all the plains districts of the Brahmaputra Valley the same replies have been received, viz., that the use of raw cotton is extremely rare if not extinct, the cheap imports having almost entirely killed the spinning industry. Among the Miris the raw cotton is indispensible for the manufacture of their *mirijins*; for ordinary cloths, however, imported thread is generally used. In the Jorhat sub-division the Deoris, Turungs, Morans and Nagas use raw cotton or thread made in Assam to a very limited extent. In Barpeta a little *dhemti* cotton is sold and made up into yarn. But in all these cases the quantity consumed is very small. The only place where raw cotton is used to any extent is the Nowgong District. Here the coarse cloths found for sale in the markets are, as a rule, made of home-spun thread. Here, too, however, spinning is fast falling into disfavour.

Then, in the hill districts of this Valley, imported thread has established a good footing. In the Naga Hills and in the Garo Hills both ready-made and home-spun thread are used. The Angami Nagas live at too high an elevation to cultivate cotton with any success. They therefore have to import whatever material they use. The majority of villages import raw cotton from the Rengma and Zhota tribes, but some import ready-made thread, and the use of this is steadily increasing. The Garo Hills, on the other hand, is a most prolific cotton-growing country. The district is, however, so readily accessible from the plains that imported thread is easily conveyed there and is largely used.

In the Surma Valley the state of things is different. Here, unlike the other valley, a large proportion of the clothing locally made is the outturn of the hill tribesmen. In the plains the Manipuris and Jugis of Cachar have almost ceased to spin, but the Kukis, Nagas and Kacharis have only partially abandoned that industry. In South Sylhet it is reported that the cotton used is locally grown by the hill tribes. In the other portions of the plains imported thread is used. In the hills, however, the thread seems to be entirely home-spun.

Thus the calculation, that nearly as much of the home-made fabrics of this Valley, is made from raw cotton, locally converted into thread, as from imported yarn, appears to be approximately correct.

[In his "Note on Cotton in Assam" Mr. Darrah has given an estimate of the cotton grown and consumed within the Province, and has compared this value with that of the imports of cotton as shown by the River-Borne Trade Report for 1884-85. Now the amount of cotton used in the Province for any other purpose than as clothing is very small, hence an estimate of the total consumption of cotton in the Province and one of the total amount of cotton clothing worn by the people, cover nearly the same ground. It will be interesting therefore to compare the two estimates.

Mr. Darrah's figures are as follows :—

	Value R			
Cotton grown and consumed in Assam	5,61,165 or	6 per cent. of total consumption.		
Imported cotton piece-goods, European and Indian	83,42,060 or 88¼	"	"	"
Imported cotton twist and yarn, European and Indian	5,33,885 or 5¼	"	"	
Imported raw cotton	4,209 or practically Nil.	"	"	
Total consumption	94,41,319			

---

[*] In the Brahmaputra Valley silk is worn to some extent and a few persons also use nettles and bark of trees as substitutes for cotton ; some tribes, too, go naked. In the Surma Valley the use of silk is practically unknown and that of bark and nettles entirely so ; and no naked tribes are reported. On this account the average consumption of cotton clothing per man might be expected to be less in the Brahmaputra Valley than in the Surma Valley, in which case the percentage supplied by foreign imports would be proportionately increased, and consequently the percentage clothed in fabrics made of raw cotton would be diminished. But owing to the difference in climate between the two valleys, it is probable that the average amount of clothing of all sorts worn in the Brahmaputra Valley is greater than that in the Surma Valley, and that the average consumption of cotton clothing per head is no less in the former than in the latter in spite of the larger use of substitutes for cotton.

This estimate is for a single year, and it is for values, whereas the estimate for clothing given above is based on a calculation of five years and is for quantities, not values. At best either of them is but a rough approximation to the truth. But the proportions borne by the several items to the total in each estimate bear a remarkable. resemblance to one another, considering the enormous increase during the last decade in the popularity of imported thread. It would appear from the increase in the amount of piece-goods imported, as shown by the figures in Part I, that the proportion of piece-goods in Mr. Darrah's estimate is too high—in my estimate it is probably too low.]

The statistics of River-Borne Trade show two varieties of material for cotton fabrics, *viz*, (i) imported thread and (ii) raw cotton produced within the Province. Each of these requires a closer examination.

The thread referred to in these statistics is practically all machine-made, the produce of the mills of Bombay and Europe. Comparing the popularity of the produce of the Indian and European mills, it is seen, from the figures given above, that whereas the imports of Indian thread have increased in a far larger proportion than those of the European article, yet the latter is still nearly ten times as extensively used as the former. At one time it appeared as if the Indian mills would carry all before them. In the River-Borne Trade Report for 1890-91 the following passage occurs:—It would appear as if Indian cotton twist and yarn are rapidly driving those of European manufacture out of the market. Three years ago the import of the former stood at only 1,500 maunds, while 15,500 maunds of the latter found its way into the Province. Since then country yarn and twist have advanced by rapid strides from 1,500 maunds to 11,500 maunds, while those of European manufacture have gone down to 9,500 maunds. The price of the former being only about half that of the latter, *viz.*, Rs. 32-8 against Rs. 60-8 the total value of the imports has naturally fallen off to some extent, notwithstanding the rise in total quantity." In that year, however, the popularity of Indian cotton thread had reached its zenith. The following year the imports fell to slightly over 6, 000 maunds, and in the year after to under 800 maunds. They remained at that figure for the succeeding year and then rose to 1,000 maunds, while last year they stood at 1,100. Meanwhile the imports of European thread had risen from 9,500 to nearly 23,000 maunds, so the precedence gained by the Indian article was purely temporary. The causes of these large fluctuations are unknown. The only considerable fluctuation in the relative price of the two kinds of thread was in 1894-95, when Indian thread fell to Rs.24-12 per maund, the price of European thread being R57-12. It was in this year that the quantity of Indian thread imported rose from 800 to 1,000 maunds. Last year the prices were R29 and R57-6 per maund respectively.

The preference for Indian thread appears to be stronger in the Surma Valley than in the Brahmaputra Valley. This is due to the fact that coarse thread is used more largely than fine in the former. As a matter of fact the Indian mills do not compete so directly as might be supposed with those of Europe. The thread made in the former is generally much coarser than that made in the latter and the recent falling off in the demand for Indian thread is probably due to a decline in the local manufacture of the coarsest cloths.

As regards the comparative popularity of Indian and European thread the Provincial Trade Returns are corroborated by the District Reports. In almost every district the imported thread is said to be of European make. It is only in the Naga Hills that Indian thread is used exclusively. In the following places both Indian and European are used, the latter more largely than the forms:—

Assam Valley : Dibrugarh, Mangaldai and Goalpara.
Surma Valley : Cachar.

The nature of the yarn imported into Assam and most largely used there is shown in the following figures which are all that have been received.

In North Lakhimpur the numbers of counts used, with their local names and prices per seer, are shown in the accompanying table.

No. of thread.	Local Name.	Price per seer.
		R a. p.
80	Saru (fine)	3 0 0
60	Saru majhalia (medium)	2 8 0
40	Bar majhalia (medium coarse)	1 8 0
30	Majhalia (medium)	1 4 0
20	Dangur (coarse)	0 12 0

In Sibsagar the counts most used are 20, 30, 40, 60, and 80 ; in Nowgong 40, 60 60 and 100 ; in the latter place the prices of imported thread are given, without particular reference to the counts as Fine R3, Middling R1-8 and Coarse R1 per seer.

In Cachar the following numbers are chiefly used :— Indian thread, Nos. 10, 11, 12, 13, 14 and 22; European, counts 40, 60 and 70. In former days it is said that the favourite counts were 50, 80, 100, 100, 110, 120, 130, 140, 150, 160, 170, 180, 190 and 200.

In Nowgong, as has already been said, the coarser thread is usually home made, hence the coarsest thread imported to any extent is 40s. In Cachar it appears that the coarser threads are obtained from the Indian mills. and that now-a-days no fine thread is imported. Before the disturbances in Manipur, there was a considerable demand by Manipuris for very fine thread, usually white, for the manufacture of their *Inaphi* and other delicate fabrics. This demand has now ceased, owing, it is believed, to the depression of trade and general scarcity in Manipur resulting from the disturbances of a few years ago. Even at the present day the finer counts imported are used chiefly by the Manipuris for making their *fijong* (waist cloth) and similar cloths. The absence of the coarser counts in former times is no doubt due to the larger use in those days of home-made thread.

The finest count of thread imported into Assam at the present day appears to be No. 100. But most districts have furnished no information on this point, and it is probable that much finer threads are used in the manufacture of the more delicate fabrics of the Assam Valley.

In Dacca the thread used for making the finest muslins is always home-spun, as the weavers can turn out thread really much finer than any now made in the European mills. This has been conclusively proved by Dr. Forbes Watson in his "Textile Manufactures and Costumes of the People of India." This does not however seem to be the case in Assam where the people are not particularly noted for the fineness of the yarn they can produce, and there instead of the cloths of finer texture being made out of home-spun yarns, it is only for the coarser cloths that home-spun thread is used. In former days a variety of thread called *nurakata* used to be spun in Assam by a special process described later on. This thread was exceedingly fine, but it is no longer manufactured, as its place has been usurped by the imported article.

It is not only plain thread that is imported from the mills. Coloured mill-made threads are now very popular, and Mr. Duncan in his "Monograph on Dyes and Dyeing in Assam" has recently shown that the practice of dyeing in Assam has now almost ceased.

The colours of imported yarn most largely in demand are red, blue, green and yellow in different shades.

The following interesting passage concerning coloured thread in Lakhimpur is extracted from Mr. Duncan's "Dyes and Dyeing":—

> "Cotton articles are sometimes dyed but the custom is dying out, as the fine Calcutta articles have taken their place. In some parts of the district, however, the home-made, coarsely-dyed yarns are preferred to the fine and well coloured Calcutta threads, which are sold at the Keyas' shops, but the merchants of Calcutta are now manufacturing coarse and badly coloured threads for importation into Assam, to compete with the home-made articles....... It is only the Phakials, Khamptis and Mataks that prepare dyes of their own."

Imported thread both plain and coloured, Indian and European, generally comes into the Province through Calcutta.

Concerning the raw cotton grown within the Province, a few remarks will suffice. In 1885 Mr. Darrah wrote as follows :—

> "The varieties of cotton are not numerous, but the names by which the crops are known differ from district to district, and peculiarities of soil, climate and method of cultivation, have, no doubt, produced divergencies from the original type. Roughly speaking, there are two well marked varieties :—
>
> (1) The large-bolled high-growing cotton, known as *dhal* (white flowers) in Lakhimpur, as *boga kapah* in the Majuli, as *khungi deva* in Cachar, as *kil* in the Garo Hills and as *bor kapah* (lit., large cotton) in Nowgong. Probably also the same as the *bhugai* of Sylhet. In Nowgong, this species is grown on level ground but has a smaller number of seeds than the second variety (mentioned below), can be ginned more easily, can be plucked twice a year instead of once, and bears for three seasons. The *kil* of the Garo Hills is very nearly the same, except that the crop is annual, that it is grown everywhere on the hill-sides and not confined to level ground, and that it can only be plucked once a year. The pods

are very large, sometimes as much as eight inches in length, and, when they burst, the contents come out in a cataract of cotton which gives the field the appearance of being covered with snow. This variety is, how-. ever, not as much in request for ordinary purposes as the smaller kind. The fibre is said by the trade to be harsh and to twist badly. It is better adapted for mixing with wool than for any other purpose.

(2) The small, round-bolled species, known as *shet* (reddish flowers) in Lakhimpur, as *thumsa* in Cachar, as a *kynphad* in the Jaintia Hills and as *horu kapah* (lit., small cotton) in Nowgong, possibly identical with the *chotsa* of the Angami Nagas. This species in sown annually, and can only be plucked once a year. The Lakhimpur variety has pale reddish flowers. That grown in the Jaintia Hills is said to be the best cotton produced in the Province. Its thread can be more closely woven than that of other kinds. The Naga Hills variety is rated lowest of all, being very short in the staple, and coming into the market in a very dirty condition.

*There is a pale *khaki* variety in Cachar and Manipur known as *kungajas* in the former, and as *tissing anguanba* in the latter district. The pods are not a uniform khaki but contain a few white threads here and there."

Concerning these varieties the following remarks are made in Watts' Economic Dictionary : —

" It is difficult to determine to what species all the above mentioned kinds belong. The large-bolled, high grown cotton, however is in most cases probably G. neglectum, *Tod.*; in the case of the Garo Hill cotton it certainly is so. Specimens which have been seen by the authors are perfect types of that species, and have the very large ovoid balls referred to by Mr. Darrah. The statement that the cotton of Lakhimpur (*dhal*) has white flowers is curious, and would suggest its being a form of G. neglectum with which we are not familiar. It may be noticed however that G. arboreum is said by certain authors to occasionally bear white flowers. The large-bolled cottons of Majuli, Cachar and Nowgong are probably all botanically identical with those of the Garo Hills.

Turning to the second form described by Mr. Darrah the difficulty is greater. The *Chotsa* of the Angami Nagas is undoubtedly G. Herbaceum, *var.* obtusifolium, the small cottons of Cachar, the Jaintia Hills and Nowgong are probably also forms of G. herbaceum or G. Wight, *Tod.*, while the *shet* of Lakhimpur would appear, from its reddish flower, to be a small round bolled form of G. arboreum. The khaki variety of Cachar and Manipur is probably indigenous cotton not Nankin."

In the Agricultural Ledger No. 8 of 1895, Mr. Middleton gives the results of some experiments with Assam cotton, and describes seven varieties. The following is extracted from this report.

Assam Cotton.

" I received samples of seeds from about a dozen different districts in Assam, and grew all of them, but the change from the climate of Assam to that of Guzarat was too great to permit of taking minute distinctions showing themselves, and I have, perhaps, failed to note differences between plants which may be marked in their native country ; *e. g.,* Mr. Darrah in his " Report " quoted in the Dic. of Ec. Prods. IV. 141, mentions a tall and a small variety, but in Baroda all the varieties are about the same size. The most interesting point about Assam Cottons is the particularly strong family likeness that runs through their group. The Assam region appears to have been the home of G. roseum or of a species that corresponds closely with Todaro's description of that plant, and it is probably from an Assam stock that the inferior but prolific *Varadi, Katil Balati, Mathia*, etc., have sprung. The deeply-cut leaves, large bracteoles, pale flowers, long bolls and coarse white wool are common to all these cottons."

The following varieties are enumerated by Mr. Middleton :—

(1) *Bungai Cotton* (In Dic. Ec. Pr. spelt Bhungai) samples of this seed were obtained from Karimgunj and Habigunj, Sylhet.

(2) *Bhoga Kapa* from Sibsagar. " The cotton is finer than that of Bungai."

(3) *Khanaa* from North Cachar " is another very similar variety with still smaller seeds, and with a much finer quality of cotton. Compared with the floss of the other Assam cottons that of this variety is quite silky."

D 2

(4) *Kunma cotton* from North Cachar. "Wool coarse and short-stapled."

(5) *Shet cotton* from Lakhimpur, "beak with white fuzz, and firmly adhering wool which for Assam cotton is tolerably fine, staple short."

(6) *Ukynphad cotton*, from the Khasia and Jaintia Hills, "fuzz very long, whitish brown; wool short, coarse and firmly adhering to the seed."

"*Ukynphad and shet* cottons are much alike except in the fibre."

(7) *Kil cotton*, from the Garo Hills, "wool white, but very coarse."

After the description of these varieties come the following concluding remarks regarding Assam cotton.

"In several of the Assamese plants and specially in the *kil* variety, the floss is matted so that the seeds are not readily pulled asunder. When the capsule opens, the cotton bursts out and hangs down several inches from the branches; against the dark green foliage the appearance is effective and most peculiar."

An experiment is now being made in the Tezpur Jail to grow *bhoka* or Garo cotton. A short account of this is given at the end of the last part of this monograph. [cf. Appendix I.]

The supply of cotton grown in Assam comes chiefly from the hills. The Nagas supply Jorhat and Golaghat; the Mikirs, Nowgong and Darrang; and the Garos, Goalpara and indirectly Barpeta and also Mangaldai. In the remainder of the Upper Valley there is practically no home-grown cotton consumed in the weaving industry, except by the hill-tribes who supply themselves. In the Surma Valley the raw cotton is similarly obtained from the adjoining hills. [cf. Appendix III.]

In North Lakhimpur the raw cotton used by the Miris for making their *jin* cloth is called *doopood*. "They spin coarse thread very loosely, keeping a portion for use as *doopood* and using the rest for the warp of the cloth. This description is not very clear, but probably the name *doopood* is applied only to the tufts of cotton woven in with the warp in this particular cloth.

Besides the ordinary cotton or Gossypium there is another kind of cotton used in Assam for making fabrics, *viz.*, the Simul or *Bombax heptaphyllum*. The use of the down of this tree for weaving purposes has long been known to the Assamese, but this down is not very well fitted for weaving purposes, in fact it is doubtful if it can be woven alone. At the present day it is sometimes woven up with ordinary cotton thread to form a soft cloth, but no mention of its use has been made in any part of the Province, except Mangaldai, and there, too, it is but little used. A fuller description of the fabric made of this kind of cotton is given in Part IV of this monograph.

Besides the materials included in the Provincial Trade Reports there are two others which deserve notice, *viz.*, (i) hand-spun but not home-spun cotton thread, and (ii) admixtures of cotton with other materials—

(i) Hand-spun but not home-spun thread.

At one time, comparatively large quantities of twist and yarn were imported from Hill Tipperah, but not for long. In the year 1884-85, 130 maunds, in 1885-86, 344 maunds, and in 1886-87, 367 maunds, were imported. None of this found its way out of the Province either Bengal way or to the hill tribes. There were, it is true, 5 maunds of Indian twist and yarn exported to Towang in 1885-86 and 8 maunds exported to the Abor Hills in 1886-87, but beyond this the export was absolutely nil and there is nothing to show whether this was Hill Tipperah yarn or yarn imported from the Bombay mills; in all probability it was the latter. It may fairly be presumed, therefore, that practically the whole of the yarn imported from Hill Tipperah was made up into cloth in Assam. During the seven years ending March 1884 only 7 maunds had been imported from this place, and after 1886 the imports again fell off. In the three years 1887-90 they averaged only 6 maunds a year, and during the subsequent six years they have amounted to 1 maund only.

Cotton twist and yarn are not imported in any appreciable quantity from any of the other adjoining foreign states. The Deputy Commissioner of the Naga Hills reports that a good deal of coloured yarn is imported into his district from Manipur, but, as it does not find its way into the Trade Returns, its quantity is probably very small. *

The only other instance of hand-made but not home-made thread being used is reported from the Jorhat Sub-division. Here, it is said, "the Khampties of the Lakhimpur district sometimes bring for sale a sort of rough home-made twisted thread of beauti-

---

* The Frontier Trade Report for 1890-3 shows that in 1892-3 cotton twist and yarn (Indian) to the value of R250 was imported into Assam from Manipur and in the Report on Native States for that year this trade was noticed, and it was stated that this yarn went to the Naga Hills.

ful red and blue colours, which is purchased by the Miris for making their *malegápe*
This kind of thread is very strong and is sold for Rs. 2 and Rs. 3 per seer, the price
of the red variety being higher than that of the blue.

(ii) Mixed materials.

In many parts of the Assam Valley, besides the cloths made of cotton alone,
there are a few mixed fabrics made by combining cotton with some other material to
form the body of the cloth. There are of course many varieties of materials used for
ornamenting cotton fabrics, but these will be discussed in their proper place.

The process of combining cotton with any other material in the formation of
thread appears entirely unknown in the Province. The only mixed-fabrics found are
therefore those in which cotton thread is used together with some other thread or
fibre in weaving. The only materials mixed with cotton thread in this way are silk
and nettle-fibre.

The silk so used is of three varieties, all locally produced. The best variety is the
pat or pure white silk. The combination of this with cotton produces a fabric very
closely resembling one of silk alone, and it is not uncommon for the maker to try and
impose on an unsuspecting purchaser by offering him cloth of this nature as a pure
silk fabric. It is only in Nowgong that cotton is combined with *pat*, the former
being used only in the warp and the latter only in the weft.

* The next best variety is the *muga* or khaki-coloured silk known as Assam silk and
much resembling tusser. This variety is far more often combined with cotton than
either of the others. In Nowgong it is used only in the weft with cotton only in the
warp, in other districts it is used in the warp, the cotton being in the weft. In Jorhat,
fabrics of this nature are made and used as *churia*, *riha*, *chadar* and longcloth
for coats, *chapkan*, etc. In Tezpur they are used only for making coats. In
Mangaldai fabrics of this nature are called *garbhasutia* and in Gauhati they are
called *mugabania kapor*, but it is not stated for what purposes they are used. There
is another method of combining muga and cotton, reported only from Jorhat, though
it is not unknown in other parts of Assam; this is to use cotton and silk alternately
in either warp or weft or both—the result being of course a striped cloth. Such cloths
are used as *chadar*, *gamocha* and *riha*.

The last variety of silk is that produced by the silkworms who feed on the castor
oil plant. It is called *eri* in Upper Assam, *endi* or *eri* in Lower Assam, and *randi*
in the Surma Valley. It is inferior in quality to either of the first two varieties, and
is seldom combined with cotton. In Nowgong it is occasionally so combined, being
used only in the weft, the cotton being used only in the warp. In Tezpur mixed-
fabrics of this description are sometimes made for use as *burkapor*, and in some parts
of Bornagar in the Barpeta Sub-division they are also made. In each of these two
places the warp is made of silk and the weft of cotton.

It will be seen from the above description that Nowgong is the chief seat of
manufacture of mixed fabrics made of cotton and silk, and that in that district all
three varieties of silk are used for this purpose. Nowgong is further distinguished by
the fact that it appears to be the only place where *pat* is combined with cotton, or
where the silk, of whatever description, is usually shot in the weft. In other places
the silk is usually laid in the warp and the cotton shot in the weft, and this would
appear to be much the most convenient mode of manufacture. The manufacture of
these mixed-fabrics in any part of the Province is slight, and in the Surma Valley and
the hills it appears to be almost unknown. There is one exception, *viz.*, North Cachar,
where silk is rarely mixed with cotton, but the method of combination has not been
reported. In Jowai also *sari* made of a mixed-fabric of cotton and silk (called *thosaru-
shuli*) are worn by the very poor women, but these are imported from the plains of
Assam.

A full discussion of these varieties of Assam silk will be found in two monographs,
one by Mr. Stack on "Silk in Assam", 1884, and one by Mr. Darrah on "The Eri
Silk of Assam ", 1890.

In his "Textile Manufactures and Costumes of the People of India ", Mr. Watson
in discussing mixed-fabrics made of cotton and country silk says: "Mixed fabrics of
this description are stated by Mr. Taylor to form the fourth class of the Textile
Manufactures of Dacca, the cotton yarn used in their manufacture ranging from 30*s*
to 80*s*. The silk—muga or munga—is imported into Dacca from Sylhet and Assam.
The cloths of this class are of considerable variety both as regards texture and pattern.
Some consists chiefly of cotton, with only a silk border or a silk flower or figure in
each corner; others are striped, chequered or figured with silk throughout the body of
the cloth. The different varieties may amount 30 in number, but the principal ones
are *Kulawroomee*, *Nowbulee Azeezola* and *Luchuck*.

These cloths are made exclusively for the markets of Arabia. Some, indeed, are occasionally shipped to Rangoon, Penang and places to the eastward, but the far greater portion of them is exported to Jidda, whence they are sent into the interior of the country. A considerable quantity of them is sold at the annual fair held at Meena, in the vicinity of Mecca. They are made into turbans, gowns, vests, etc., by the Arabs. They were formerly transported from Jidda to Egypt, and were at one time the principal articles of export from Dacca to Bassora, whence they were sent to various parts of Mesopotamia and to Constantinople."

No exportation of mixed-fabrics of this nature can be found to have taken place from Assam. There seems no reason why a trade in them should not be started, as many women who have left off weaving cotton appear to have now devoted themselves to the weaving of silk which is not altogether unprofitable. Whether the weaving of mixed silk and cotton fabrics would repay the workman or not is difficult to say.

The second kind of mixed-fabrics, which is far more unique, is found only in the Naga Hills. The Deputy Commissioner of that District describes it as follows :— " Nettle fibre is used mixed with cotton yarn to make cloths. This nettle is locally called *lone*. The fibre after being extracted is made into yarn, and the cloth is made partly of nettle and partly of cotton yarn, the warp is of nettle thread, while the thread used in the shuttle is of cotton. I have never seen a cloth made wholly of nettle thread."

The scientific name of this fibre is unknown to me. The fabric resulting from its mixture with cotton is very coarse, heavy and rough to the touch, but very warm and durable. These fabrics are used as warm sheets or wrappers. A fuller description of them will be found in Part IV. In his " Statistical Account of As m " Mr. Hunter says that the Nagas export large quantities of sheets made of this nettle fibre to the neighbouring districts of Nowgong, Sibsagor, and Silchar.

It has been already mentioned that the principal use of cotton fabrics is as clothing, and that the great majority of the clothing used in Assam consists of cotton fabrics. It will be interesting, therefore, to refer briefly to the materials used as clothing by the people of this Province in place of cotton.

Among the direct substitutes for cotton may be named the rhea fibre, yak hair, wool, and country silk. " The Chulikata Mishmis were probably the first people on this side of the Himalayas to discover the valuable properties of the *rhea nivea* and many others of the nettle tribe; with the fibre of one of these they weave a cloth so strong and stiff that, made into jackets, it is used by themselves and by the Abors as a kind of armour ". About the use of the rhea fibre no further information has been received, but it is certain that this fibre is not extensively used for weaving.

Yak hair cloth is said to be occasionally used by the Digaroos to make a coat or sack-like garment reaching from the neck to the bend of the knees. But this garment is more usually made of cotton.

Wool is very little used in Assam as a material for clothing. The Mishmis are said to make a few woollen articles with the fleece of the Lama sheep. These fabrics in appearance seem to possess great durability and the colours seem to be fast. No other instance has come to notice of woollen fabrics made in the Province. The Dofflas wear woollen cloths of Thibetan manufacture as well as the cotton goods they make themselves. The Bhutias also wear wool to some extent. Beyond this the use of wool appears to be confined to a few babus and menials attached to the Courts or similarly employed. Some of these may be seen wearing a chapkan or shirt made of imported flannel in the cold weather, but the amount of flannel so used is very small.

Of all the substitutes for cotton, by far the most important is country silk. The use of this is practically confined to the Brahmaputra Valley, though it is also found in the Surma Valley to a very slight extent. The extent to which this silk is used as clothing in Assam proper is often overestimated. It is actually very small, as will be seen from the following summary of the information received from different districts.

Lakhimpur.

Sadr Sub-division.—Women of the upper classes make use of silk in public and private, those of the lower classes use cotton for home wear, and silk on special occasions only. Men of all classes nowadays use only cotton.

North Lakhimpur Sub-division.—About 25 per cent. of the rich villagers, and 50 per cent. of women of all quarters use *muga* and *eria* as well as cotton. Gentlemen living in the town and babus on tea gardens, wear chiefly imported cotton garments, but also in some cases *muga* and *eria* cloth.

Sadiya.—Silk is not largely used in these parts and it is never likely to usurp the place of cotton.

Sibsagar.

Sadr Sub-division.—Cotton fabrics are gradually taking the place of those of *muga* and *pat.*

Jorhat Sub-division.—Among the women, those of the richer classes generally use silk, and those of the lower classes cotton. Men wear imported cotton, and the more advanced clothe their wives and daughters also in cotton saries. Among the conservatives and aristocratics, silk is still considered as a sign of respectability.

Golaghat Sub-division.—Muga is used for special and cotton for ordinary wear. Most women have a few cloths of *muga* for use on special occasions.

Nowgong.—Pat and eri are largely used instead of cotton, especially by the women.

Darrang.—The place of cotton is little usurped by that of *muga* or *eri.* Even respectable and well-to-do women hardly ever use silk.

Kamrup.

Sadr Sub-division.—The *rihu* and *mekhela* of the richer women for ordinary wear are made of *muga* or *endi*, and those for special wear of white silk. The poorer classes, both men and women, generally use cotton, those who can afford it wear *muga* and *endi* on special occasions.

Barpeta Sub-division.—Ladies of high rank seldom wear cotton *riha* or *mekhela ;* the latter are usually of *muga* or *pat.* The middle classes look with disfavour on articles made at home, but they use *eri* or silk wrappers instead of cotton *borkapor.* The poorer classes can hardly ever afford anything but cotton, and only 1 in 1,000 can afford to substitute an *eri chadar* for a cotton *borakapor.*

Goalpara.

Sadr Sub-division.—No silk is used.

Goalpara Sub-division.—About 30 per cent. of the women have a few *eri* or *muga* cloths for use on special occasions ; *muga* is very little used.

Summing up then, the use of silk in the Brahmaputra Valley at the present day may be said to be confined to the women, and even among these, the poor classes cannot afford it except for use on special occasions. It is, of course, only the Assamese that are here referred to ; the quantity of such silk used by foreigners of all classes is inappreciable.

In the Surma Valley country silk is hardly used at all. In Cachar a few Cacharis produce the *eri* silk, locally called *randi*, on a very small scale and weave it into a coarse and rough but durable fabric which they use themselves as *dhuti* and *chadar ;* but the use of cotton clothes is said to be not at all affected by silk fabrics. On rare occasions a rich Cachari or Manipuri may be seen wearing a *muga* waistcloth or turban. In Hailakandi *muga* silk cloths are worn on special occasions by the hill tribes and the well-to-do. Throughout Sylhet the use of silk appears unknown.

Lastly as to the Hills. In the Naga Hills silk is not used at all, in the Garo Hills it is practically never worn. In the Khasia and Jaintia Hills *eri* cloths are used to a very small extent by women, generally as *sari (thohsaru ryndia) ;* but the very poor women use *sari* made of cotton (*salang*) or of mixed fabric (*thosharu-shuli*), both of which are brought from Assam. In North Cachar *iri* silk cloths are used to a large extent by the more well-to-do Cacharis, Mikirs and Syntengs. In Manipur cotton cloths are generally worn, but silk *dhuti* are worn at the time of worshipping or divining.

There are other articles of clothing used by the hill tribes of Assam, which can hardly be called substitutes for cotton, but which, none the less, decrease the demand for that material. The principal of these is clothing made of bark. In the Garo Hills the bark of the Hamphak tree (Trema Orientalis) is used to make rough sheets for bedding. The Deputy Commissioner of this district gives the following description of its manufacture : " The trees are cut and the bark pulled off in one long strip ; the outer surface is scraped off with a dao and the under part is then beaten from 10 to 15 minutes with a stick to make it pliable ; it is then worked with the hands and feet to stretch it as much as possible and put out to dry in the sun. From 10 to 20 of these strips are sewn together and the sheets thus made are worth from 4 to 8 annas."

The Jharuas on the border land call this bark-cloth *jungfong* and bring a little of it down to the plains for sale in the Goalpara *hâts*. I purchased a poor specimen of it for 4 annas at the Dhupdhara *hât*. This piece measured about 8 feet by 3 feet. A specimen of this fibre was exhibited at the Amsterdam Exhibition of 1883 under the name of *phakram*.

The Garos are not the only people in Assam who wear clothing made of bark. In his "Memoir of a Survey of Assam and the neighbouring countries, 1825-8" Lieutenant Wilcox says : " The dress of the Abors consists principally of the choonga (Assamese name for dhuti) made of the bark of the Uddal tree. It is tied round the loins and hangs down behind in loose strips, about 15 inches long, like a white bushy beard. It serves also as a pillow at night." Unfortunately Mr. Wilcox gives no description of its manufacture and does not state what the Uddal tree is. Nearly fifty years later Colonel (then Captain) Dalton in his "Ethnology of Bengal," 1872, refers to this strange cloth, and says :—" The garment thus described by Wilcox is seldom now seen in the plains, but is still worn by the Abors of the interior."

Some tribes in Assam wear nothing resembling a fabric, some are clothed only in girdles of cane, some in belts of polished brass, some go absolutely naked. Nudity is also not unknown in the plains, large numbers of the children wear no clothes at all for the first few years, and generally the children of Assam are very scantily clothed, to a degree even of insufficiency, not only among the poor but also among the well-to-do.

PART III.

The Process of Manufacture.

The conversion of raw cotton into cloth consists of three main processes, *viz.* :—

(1) Cleaning raw cotton, *i.e.*, the removal of all impurities and extraction of the seeds.

(2) Spinning, *i.e.*, the manufacture of thread out of cleaned cotton.

(3) Weaving, *i.e.*, the manufacture of cloth out of thread.

It has already been said that no spinning machines nor power looms have been started in the Province ; but that attempts have been made to introduce the modern gin. It is proposed here to describe the indigenous instruments only and the methods of cleaning, spinning and weaving by those instruments.

There are, broadly speaking, two methods employed in Assam, the first by the plainsmen and the other by the hillsmen, but some of the hillsmen have already adopted the more improved methods followed in the plains. Each of these methods again exhibits several varieties on account of the different instruments used, and also the different ways of using the same instruments.

The process of manufacture followed in the plains is much more complicated than that used in the hills ; but either process is extremely simple compared with those of the West. There is no need to compare the simple instruments made in Assam with the complicated machinery of the English mills, but it may be well to notice some essential differences. In the first place, the cotton usually reaches the mills in England not in its raw state, but with the seed extracted, in any case the gin is never in the same building as the spinning mills. Thus the process of ginning is hardly considered a part of the spinning and weaving industry. On the other hand, the cotton generally arrives in bales packed by machinery, and in consequence the loosening of the fibre and cleansing it from all impurities form very essential portions of the manufacture and require very careful attention. In Assam the cotton is either raised by the very men who convert it into cloth, or else is brought down from the hills packed in baskets by hand and sold to these men in small quantities. There is, therefore, practically no loosening to be done and cleaning is a simple matter, but ginning is an essential branch of the manufacture.

In Assam there is no mixing of cotton, for the simple reason that only one variety is ordinarily available, no testing, no scutching, properly so called, and no carding, drawing or slubbing as these terms are understood in the cotton spinning trade. Another point worth noticing is the stage of development to which the art of weaving has been carried in England ; the number of different "weaves" now produced is very large, the plain weave, the twill, satin, spot, plush, cross-warp, double-cloth textures and many others. In Assam practically nothing but the plain weave is found — the plains-men can certainly weave nothing else on their four-poster loom, but curiously enough, with still ruder instruments, some of the hillsmen have advanced to the stage of weaving a four-shaft twill, *e.g.*, the Noras and Turungs of Jorhat, the Khamptis of Lakhimpur and the Manipuris.

The processes of manufacture followed in the plains will now be described, together with a short account of those used by some of the hill tribes.

Process of Manufacture in the Plains.

1.—Cleaning Raw Cotton.

The first step in the cleaning of cotton (*kapah* or *kapas*) in Assam is to free it from all the impurities with which it has got mixed on the tree, while being gathered, or on its journey from the tree to the market. The earthy and vegetable matter thus accumulated is picked out as far as possible by hand. This stage of the process is often dispensed with. In Barpeta it is called *kapah chandiowa* and takes 10 to 15 minutes per seer of cotton.

The cotton is next spread out in sieves, and exposed to the sun for three or four hours to dry. This stage is called *radiowa* in Barpeta. It is never dispensed with, as it is absolutely necessary to ensure a good outturn when the cotton is ginned. The sieve (*chalani*) is of bamboo and can be made by any Assamese. It is also purchaseable at from 1 to 4 annas. It lasts for one year.

The cotton is now ready to be ginned, unless it be required for making very fine thread, when it is first combed with a comb (*dar*) made of the teeth or rather jawbone of the *borali* fish (*Silurus boalis*). This combing effects a double purpose by removing not only the minor impurities left in after the preliminary cleaning, but also the loose and coarser fibres of the cotton. The jawbone of the *borali* fish is especially adapted to this purpose, as the teeth are small, recurved and closely set. The comb is not usually sold. It is said to last for two years.

This stage of the process is very tedious as it takes four hours to comb a seer of cotton. It is exactly the same as that used by the Dacca weavers in the manufacture of thread for their world-famed muslins, but in Assam it is only used in extremely rare cases, and never in the manufacture of thread for ordinary coarse fabrics. The names applied to this stage are *dariowa* (Barpeta) and *kapah bachha* (Tezpur).

The next stage in the process of cleaning is ginning, *i.e.*, the separation of the seeds from the fibre, which is performed by means of the gin which consists of two horizontal rollers one close above the other mounted on an upright stand.

This instrument is called by various names, *viz.*, neothani (Upper Assam), neothu (Lower Assam), netha (Mangaldai), jatari (Tezpur) and charkhi (Surma Valley). It is made of wood and is of the following description:—In a stand (*bahani* in Kamrup, and *bahuna* in Barpeta) consisting of a rectangular wooden board about 12 inches long and 4 inches broad, two holes are cut midway between the two sides, one near either end. Into these holes are fitted two upright posts (*khuti*) of equal size, *viz.*, about 11 inches long and 2 inches in diameter. These two posts, standing vertically, support between them two horizontal rollers (*pakara*) each about one inch in diameter between the uprights. The two ends of each are inserted in holes in the uprights tightly, but not too tightly to allow of their revolving. Generally one end of each roller is formed into a screw, the two screws fitting into one another and leaving an interval between the central portion of the rollers rather less than the diameter of a small cotton seed. In some cases, Mr. Darrah says, the end of one roller only is formed into a screw which catches a projection in the other. The upper roller (*opar pakara*) is 12 inches long, while the lower one (*talar pakara*) is 16 inches. To this lower roller is attached a handle at the opposite end to that formed into a screw. (In Barpeta the handle and screw are said to be both at the same end.) This handle (*hata* or *hatabari*) is nothing but a plain piece of wood 8 inches long and 2 inches broad fixed at right angles to the roller. In order to give the instrument stability, a narrow piece of wood (*bhandhara* in Barpeta and *salkha* in Kamrup), about 10 inches long and 2 inches wide, is fixed at right angles to the middle of one side of the stand. In some places too, *e.g.*, Kamrup, the uprights are strengthened by two cross-bars, *viz.*, flat pieces of wood, the ends of which are inserted in one large hole in each post about half-way up. These two cross-bars are of equal size in Barpeta, *viz.*, 9 inches by 1 inch, but in Kamrup the upper one is 6 inches by 1½ inch. The lower cross-bar is called *dola* in Barpeta and *chatibari* in Kamrup; the upper one *opar ghora* in Barpeta and *ghorapira* in Kamrup. These two cross-bars are close together, one above the other, and are kept firm by means of a wedge (*kumti* in Barpeta and *sal* in Kamrup) at each end. They form, however, a subsidiary part of the machine and are often dispensed with, *e.g.*, in Mangaldai

Goalpara and South Sylhet. In Tezpur instead of these two cross bars, there is one wooden bar and the wedges are between this and the lower roller.

This hand-gin is made by ordinary carpenters and sold for from 4 to 8 annas according to the quality of the wood. In Tezpur it costs as much as R1. In Barpeta it is said to last for ten years, in the Garo Hills, where the instrument is bought from the plainsmen, for only one year. This great variation in its durability is due probably to differences in the quality of the wood which form the rollers, and in the more frequent use of the machine in the Garo Hills. In South Sylhet the gin is larger than usual—the stand, for instance, is 18 inches × 6 inches × 3 inches, and more elaborate—the handle consists of a small flat piece of wood having a hole near each end by one of which it is fixed on to the roller, while in the other is inserted another small piece of wood at right angles to it, and consequently horizontal. Here the instrument is said to be home-made and to last for two or three years.

To work this gin, the operator sits on a wooden stool (*pira*) or on the ground, and places one foot, generally the left, on the projection from the stand to keep it steady. With her right hand she turns the handle of the lower roller, and with her left she takes up a small quantity of the raw cotton and applies it to the interval between. the rollers. The turning of the handle causes the rollers to revolve in opposite directions and thus to pull the cotton through the intervening space. The seeds being too large to pass through, are left behind. To prevent the posts uncleaned cotton from mixing with the cleaned, a piece of cloth is often hung against the upright posts between the rollers.

The process is very slow, for the machine can never be worked to its full power owing to the impossibility of feeding the whole length of the opening between the rollers at the same time. The ginning should be done as soon as possible after the drying of the cotton. Mr. Darrah says: " Experiments have shown that this machine gives a result of from one to two-and-a-half seers of cleaned cotton per diem. " In South Sylhet it takes a day to clean 2 or 3 seers, in Barpeta a seer (probably of raw cotton) can be cleaned in an hour. In Nowgong one seer of raw cotton can be cleaned in half a day.

Like the gin itself the operation of ginning is called by various names in different parts of the Province, e g., *kapah neotha* or *gutiguchuuwa* in the Assam Valley and *bichi tyag kara* in Cachar; the last two names mean simply the removal of the seeds, the first is derived from the name of the instrument.

The cleaning of cotton in Assam is never carried beyond the stage of ginning. The next process is that of spinning, but, before passing to that process, it may be mentioned that the seeds of cotton are hardly ever made use of in Assam. Mr. Darrah noticed this in 1885; he says: "In some places the seed is utilised as cattle food." In the parts of Kamrup near Gauhati it is a regular article of sale. Its price in the neighbourhood of Tura in the Garo Hills is 10 annas a maund. But this is not general. It is usually flung away as useless. If it were of more value in this country, it is probable that less uncleaned cotton and more cleaned would be exported. But, partly owing to scarcity and dearness of labour here, partly owing to small value attached to the seed, together with the fact that labour is comparatively cheap in Calcutta and the seed there largely in demand, cotton is exported chiefly in the uncleaned state." These remarks apply equally at the present day.

II.—Spinnig.

At the end of the cleaning process the loose fibres of cotton (now called *tula*)[*] are gathered up and taken to an enclosure surrounded and roofed with bamboo mats (*dhari*) and there the cotton is bowed. This mat-house, *tulaghar* or *tulaghara*, may be large enough to contain several persons working together, or it may be for a single workman only, in which case it is small enough to be roofed with one mat. The object of this mat-house is to prevent the fluff from flying about.

The bow used by the Assamese consists of a single piece of bamboo (*bari*) about 3 feet long, and rather wider in the centre than at the ends; to which is attached a string (*jor*) made either of a very fine strip of cane or of the midrib of a plantain leaf. It is nearly always home-made, but is occasionally sold in Barpeta for one to two annas, and lasts for three years. When home-made it is said to last for only six months. It is the men of the household who make it for the women. In Tezpur when sold it costs one anna or less and lasts for years if the string be occasionally renewed.

---

[*] In Tezpur the cotton is said to assume this name after being bowed.

The bow used by the weavers of Sylhet differs from the above in having not a single long piece of bamboo, but two pieces of about half the length, fitting one into each end of a hollow bamboo, which has a knot in the centre.

The names applied to those bows are *dhanu, dhenu, dhuni, jorbari, jor,* etc.

To use the bow a mass of cotton is thrown on a mat or the bare ground, and the handle of the bow is held in the left hand in such a position that the string almost touches the loose mass. The string is then pulled by the fingers of the right hand into the mass of cotton and let go. The vibration throws the cotton in all directions and loosens the fibres.

The process of bowing is called *dhuna* or *tuladhuna.* It corresponds to scutching. In Barpeta it is said that a seer of cotton can be bowed in 15 minutes, but in Nowgong the bowing of ¾ seer (the cleaned outturn of 1 seer of raw cotton) is said to take a whole day. The latter estimate is probably more nearly correct than the former.

A sufficient quantity of cotton having been thus bowed, it is picked up and placed in small handfuls on a smooth wooden stool (*panja bata pira*) measuring 1½ × 1 foot in Kamrup and 12 × 8 × 2 inches in Tezpur, or on a flat piece of wood with a smooth surface. The operator then places a small slip of bamboo or ekra on a handful of cotton, and rolls it with the open hand over the cotton, which is picked up and wound round the slip. This roll of cotton is then slipped off the slip and is ready for the spinning-wheel.

The slip used for this purpose varies in size over the Assam Valley from 5 inches to 9 inches, or even a foot. In South Sylhet it is only 4 inches long. It is home-made and has no market value. The following are some of the names applied to it : *panji, bata bari* (Golaghat and Mangaldai),*panji bata mari* (Tezpur),*tula bata bari* (Kamrup), *batti bari* (Barpeta), *panji kathi* (Nowgong).

Mr. Darrah says that the cotton is rolled upon the ground, but this does not appear to be the case, as a clean, smooth and even surface is essential to the process.

About 3 or 4 hundred rolls are formed out of a seer of cotton, and the process of working up this amount of bowed cotton takes about an hour.[*]

The rolls are called *panji* by the Assamese and *painj* in South Sylhet. The process of forming these rolls is called *panji bata.*

The next stage in the process of spinning is the conversion of these rolls of cotton into thread (*suta*), by means of the spinning-wheel, (*jatar* or *jautar*), which is of the following description :—

The stand is formed of two rectangular pieces of wood joined together by a narrow tie-beam, about 22 inches long, each end of which is fastened to the middle of one of the longer sides of each plank.[†] The one plank is 14 inches long and 4 inches wide, and in it are fixed two upright posts (in Tezpur flat pieces of wood 18 inches × 3 inches) to support the axle of the wheel which passes through a hole in each post about 15 inches from the ground. The other plank is smaller, being only 9 inches by 4 inches ; in this are fixed two small uprights, about 8 inches long (in Tezpur flat pieces of wood 6 inches × 1 inch), through the centre of which passes the spindle. In South Sylhet the spindle is supported on two loops of cane which are fixed into these uprights, and bound with string.

The wheel (*chaka* or *ghila*) which is 18 to 20 inches in diameter, is of two kinds : (1) a disc of wood, about one inch thick, with its circumference grooved, the groove being ¼ inch wide. This kind is called *sarei* in Kamrup, and *charia* in Tezpur ; (2) two separate frames, like cart-wheels, with flat wooden or bamboo spokes, generally 4 in number, and a circumference of twisted cane. The spokes (called *pahi* in Tezpur) radiate from a circular wooden disc (*dila*) about 5 inches in diameter. The circumferences of the two frames are united by a network of cane, called *chhak.* This species of wheel is called *chhatani* in Kamrup. The word *chaka* is applied to both kinds of wheel.

The spindle (*salakathi, batiya* or *sala*) is a thin piece of iron or bamboo like a skewer pointed at both ends, which project beyond the posts, that nearer to the operator length of nearly 4 inches. The portion between the posts is occasionally bound to a round with cloth to give the cord a better grip on it. Near the centre of the spindle are two small round beads (*mani*) about ¼ inch in diameter, to keep the cord in

---

[*] This is the estimate received from Barpeta, but in Nowgong it is said to take half a day ;to work up ¾th of a seer of bowed cotton in this way.
[†] This tie-beam is called *bharbari* in Kamrup *bharidhara* in Barpeta and *Sahowa* in Tezpur.

position. These beads are made either of wood or of gourd shell (*loakhola*). In Mangaldai a third bead like the other two, but larger, is fastened about half way between the centre of the spindle and the end next the operator.‡

An endless cord (*mal* or *jatarar batiya*) passes at full tension round the wheel and the spindle (between the two central beads). It is sometimes rubbed with the gum of the jacktree or waxed before use. To keep the cord in position a small upright post (*maldhara, batiya dhora khuti* or *satini bari*) 7 or 8 inches long, with a hole in the centre, through which the string passes, is fixed on the tie-beam near the smaller plank, *i.e.*, at a point about 4 inches from the spindle. This point is called *jatarar-nai*.

The axle of the wheel (*dilabari* or *salkha bari*) projects about 5 inches on the side nearest the operator, and to this end is attached a handle (*hata* or *hatabari*) consisting of a piece of wood about 8 inches long. In South Sylhet the handle consists of two pieces of wood; the one, 6 or 8 inches long, has a hole in each end; by one hole it is fixed on to the axle while in the other is fixed the second piece of wood, which is a plain rod, 5 or 6 inches long.

The dimensions given throughout are those received from Barpeta. The Tezpur spinning machine seems to be rather larger, but is practically the same in shape. .

To work this machine, the woman sits facing it, and with her right hand turns the handle, while with her left hand she takes up one of the rolls of cotton described above and applies the end of it to the point of the spindle nearest to her. The rotary motion of the wheel is communicated to the spindle by means of the connecting cord, and each revolution of the former produces 8 to 12 revolutions of the latter owing to the difference in their diameters. The rapid revolution of the spindle causes its point to pick up a fragment of the roll of cotton applied to it, and as the woman raises her left hand to its full length a thread is drawn out. A slight change in the direction of the extended arm causes this thread to roll up round the spindle; the roll being meanwhile gradually brought down to the spindle point. The same motion of the arm is then repeated till the whole roll is converted into thread, when another roll is taken up and treated in the same way. When the spindle is full the balls of thread (*sutalahi, sutalei, pakara* or *pakari*) are slipped off and are ready for the next process, *vis.*, weaving.

The thread thus spun is not often of very good quality. Its thickness and evenness depend on the way in which the roll of cotton is manipulated by the operator. If this be pressed tightly between the finger and thumb and the tension of the thread be kept firm and uniform, the result will be a fine and even thread; if the roll be loosely held a coarse thread is the result.

Compared with other instruments used by the Assamese, the spinning-wheel is rather expensive. In Tezpur it is sold at from Rs. 2 to 2-8, in Mangaldai at from Re. 1 to Rs. 4 In Barpeta it is, however, cheaper, the kind with a solid wheel costing Re. 1, and that with the double wheel only 8 annas. In Sibsagar the price of the two varieties is Re. 1 to Re. 1-8 and 12 annas to Re. 1 respectively. It is sold occasionally at the Naosali *hât* by Jolahas and Cacharis of Chapaguri. It lasts a considerable time, the estimates given in different districts varying from 3 to 12 years.

The spinning-wheel is still largely used throughout the Assam Valley, even by those who have given up spinning thread, as it is utilised for making the spools for the shuttle even when ready-made thread is used.

Concerning this instrument there is a very clever riddle, which may be translated thus: "I saw a curiosity just now. At first I took it for a thief, as it had a cord tied round its waist. But it was not a thief, the cord was rather an ornament. It had no neck, but yet wore beads. It hummed like a bee, but when I came close I found it was not a bee. It has no shame, for it cares not for men's society, but loves the company of women. 'Listen one and all', says poet Kankan, 'and tell me what it is'."

The humming sound of the spinning-wheel when at work is well brought out in this riddle, and it is interesting to note that the creaking sound of the ginning machine has given rise to a curious tale. One of the Ahom kings went out to hunt and on the roadside saw an old woman busy ginning cotton. He stopped to see how the gin was worked, praised the woman's skill and then passed on. Then some one came up to the old woman and blamed her for working while the king was passing by, for the king, he said, had been displeased at the sound of the machine. So the old woman oiled the rollers and went on working her silent gin. In due time the king returned and, hearing no sound, asked if the old woman was still at work. Finding that she was still working and the instrument had ceased to speak, the king took her

---

‡ For spinning, iron is generally used; for making spools, bamboo. (Tezpur.)

for a sorceress who could strike a person dumb. And so the old woman paid the usual penalty for witchcraft and lost her nose.

There is a variety of the spinning-wheel or *jatar*, called *mahura pakowa jatar*, reported from Golaghat, which is said to be used only for making the spools for the shuttle, but its description seems to correspond exactly to that of the *sarei jatar* of Kamrup.

The working of the spinning-wheel is called *suta kata*. It takes a woman three days to spin a seer of cotton by this machine if she be exclusively engaged on this work, but it would take her 12 days if she did her ordinary household duties as well (Barpeta). The same estimate has been received from Nowgong.

The total time taken in converting a seer of raw cotton into thread is given as 5 days in Nowgong, and as 4 days (of 5 or 6 hours each) in Jorhat.

The outturn of thread from a given quantity of raw cotton depends largely on the quality of the cotton. When the methods of cleaning and spinning just described are used the best cotton is said, in Jorhat, to give an outturn of half its weight in thread, the worst only one quarter. The average outturn is taken as ⅜. In Nowgong the average is given as ⅜, in Barpeta as ½, and in Mangaldai as much as ⅝, which would seem far too high.

Spinning of Norakata Thread.

There is a peculiar method of spinning thread called *norakata* reported from Nowgong, where it is almost obsolete.

The cotton is first cleaned, combed and ginned, and then very thoroughly bowed in the ordinary way. At this point the peculiarity of the process occurs, for the cotton is not formed into rolls (*panji*), but the thread is spun direct from the loose mass of cotton fibre. The spinning-wheel is used. The thread so spun is very fine. This method was used in the time of the Ahom kings for making thread for the clothing of the Royal Family. It has now almost gone out of use owing to the importation of the finer counts of thread (80s and 100s).

Before leaving the subject of spinning it may be of interest to describe the bow used by the Dhunias or Madaps. These people, who profess to be descendants of Khajeh Mansur, come from their homes in Arreh to Goalpara about September and return in February. They bring their bows with them and charge 2 or 3 annas per seer for bowing cotton for stuffing quilts. If the cotton be old or of bad quality they charge a pice or two extra per seer. This bow is not used by the Assamese, and is very different from either of the kinds above described. It consists of a straight, stout rod made of sal wood, about 4 feet in length, having at the right end a flat semicircular piece of wood fastened to it so that the curved surface is outside and the flat surface (about 6 inches long) at right angles to the rod. Near the left end is fastened another plank of wood larger than the first and in the shape of a quarter circle. One flat side, about a foot long, is firmly bound to the rod by means of catgut, the other of the same length being at right angles to it and the curved surface facing inwards. The string is made of buffalo gut and is very strong, it passes through a hole in the left end of the rod, thence runs over the corner of the larger plank straight to the smaller plank and round its curved surface, and is fastened by a peg to the right end of the rod. The gut is usually much longer than is actually required, the surplus being wound round the rod, and being utilised if the other portion of the string wears out or frays.

The larger plank is further strengthened by another string of gut connecting the round edge with the centre of the rod. This string is kept taut by three pegs driven into the curved edge of this plank. At that corner of this larger plank round which the string passes, is a small piece of leather which tightens or slackens the string according as it is moved outwards or inwards.

To the rod is attached a sort of handle made of a piece of rag rolled up, one end of which is fastened by a peg somewhere near the centre of the rod, the other being fastened 6 or 7 inches from the left end. This loop serves as a support for the arm when the instrument is being worked.

This instrument cannot be worked with the bare fingers. To make the string vibrate, it is struck with a kind of hammer made of ebony or other heavy wood. This hammer is shaped much like a dumb-bell, it is about 15 inches long and weighs about 3 pounds.

III.—Weaving.

The instruments used in weaving are very numerous but very simple. Some are so simple that they can be best described in the account of the process of weaving, others are ordinary household belongings, not made exclusively for weaving, and so need no description. The following list, therefore, comprises only the more important items of a weaver's outfit in Assam, and those only which are specially designed for weaving.

1.—The first kind of reel.—(Plate I, fig. i).

Vernacular names :— Latai (Golaghat and Tezpur), *Hatlatai* (Barpeta), *Bar latai* (Goalpara), *Letai* (Gauhati, Mangaldai, Sibsagar), *Netai* (Mangaldai), *Natai* (Gauhati), *Nata* (Goalpara), *Nathu* (South Sylhet), *Naotha* (Cachar).

This reel is constructed as follows :—Two flat bamboo sticks, each about 4 inches in length and half an inch wide, are fixed at right angles to one another at their centres so as to form a cross. Through the centre a hole is bored. A similar cross is made with sticks about six inches long. These two crosses are slipped on to the ends of a central rod, which is made of bamboo and is about 3 feet 3 inches in length and ¾ inch in diameter at the centre; the ends are, however, thinner, so as to allow of the smaller cross passing along to a distance of one foot from one end and the larger cross to 15 inches from the other end. These crosses are then tied firmly to the central rod by string or bamboo ties, so as to prevent them from revolving, and so that all the arms of one cross are parallel to the arms of the other. Next, four thin, flat bamboo sticks, each about 2 feet long are taken. One end of each is fastened to the end of one of the arms of the larger cross and the centre is fastened to the end of the corresponding arm of the smaller cross. The other ends of all four are bound tightly round the end of the central rod.

Thus the instrument is a conical framework not revolving on the central rod.

In Goalpara this instrument is of rather a different description. The central rod is fully four feet long and is provided with a handle at the end nearest the larger cross. The ends of the sticks forming the framework are also fastened differently. Both ends project a short way past the crosses and are fastened in the same way, *viz.,* by cane ties connecting the ends of two opposite sticks with each other and with the central rod. There are of course two such cane ties at right angles to each other, at either end,

There are intermediate varieties between these two kinds, but there is no difference in principle.

An instrument very similar to this is used in the Surma Valley. It is thus described in South Sylhet :—The *Nathu.* Some eight or nine fine split bamboos are arranged around a central bamboo rod. At the lower end they are fastened to a bamboo ring which is supported by two fine split bamboos placed crosswise. At the upper end they are all tied together to the central rod at a short distance from that end of the rod.

The essential object of this instrument is for forming skeins or handles. It is thus distinguished from the second kind of reel which is used for transferring the thread, after it has been formed into skeins, on to a reel or a spool. In Sibsagar eight or ten of these reals are said to be used, the skeins made on them are called *tatbati.*

This instrument is generally home-made, but can also be purchased occasionally for 4 annas or less. In Barpeta its price is only 4 or 5 pice. It lasts for many years with ordinary wear and tear.

2.—The second kind of reel.—(Plate I, figs. ii and iii).

Vernacular names :—Chhereki (general), *cherki* (Gauhati and Goalpara), *charaki* (Goalpara and Cachar).

In this reel the centre rod (*bharbari*) is about three feet long and is pointed at the lower end. For nine inches from the end the rod is thin and then comes a ledge where the rod widens out. On this ledge the smaller cross loosely rests. The two crosses are of about the same size as those of the first kind of reel. The larger cross is slipped loosely over the end of the rod and held so that each of its two cross-sticks is at an angle of 45° with each of the sticks of the upper cross. Then eight round slips of bamboo about 18 inches long are tied by their two ends to the upper and lower crosses in the following way :—Two sticks are tied at one end to one of the arms of the upper cross, the other ends being tied one to each of the two nearest arms of the lower cross. In this way each arm of each cross has two slips of the framework bound to it.

PLATE I.

Fig. 1.—The first kind of rod (latti).
" ii.—The second kind of rod (chkrki)—jack-screw.
" iii.— " into— small screw.
" iv.—The third kind of rod (aghli).
" v.—Karhani.
" vi.—The rod (roli).

This reel is used wherever a large revolving framework is required, *i.e.*, in the process of preparing the thread for warp and weft, and also in the making of the healds. In the former case it is used only for transferring thread. It is generally home-made, but, when sold, it costs 4 annas in Tezpur and only 3 or 4 pice in Barpeta. It lasts for several years.

The girth of the framework of this instrument is regulated by that of the framework of the first kind of reel, so that the skeins formed on the latter may fit on to it also. This remark applies only to those reels that are used for reeling home-made thread. The skeins of imported thread being much larger require a much larger reel This reel, which is called *bar chhereki*, is exactly similar to the smaller reel.

No such instrument appears to be used by the professional weavers of the Surma Valley.

3.—The third kind of reel.—(Plate I, fig. iv).

Vernacular names :—*Ugha* (general), *paghe* (Lower Assam), *paghai* or *pohai* (Goalpara), *ugala* (Cachar).

The only difference between this reel and that of the second kind is in its size and shape. The crosses are of equal length and very much shorter than those of the first and second kind of reel. The length of the central rod is about two feet. The shape of this instrument is something like an elongated barrel. It is constructed in the same way as reels of the second kind, and, as with them, the frame revolves round the central rod. It is used in the process of warping and is generally home-made. Its use is more fully explained hereafter.

In Barpeta the central rod is called *nal*, the crosses *chaki* and the slips of bamboos forming the framework *sali*.

No such instrument seems to be used by the professional weavers of the Surma Valley.

4.—The Karhani.—(Plate I, fig. v).

Vernacular names :—*Karhani* (general), *kanni* (Gauhati, Mangaldai and Goalpara), *karni* (Goalpara).

This is an instrument used for guiding the threads when they are being laid round the posts to form the warp. As several threads are laid at one time, it is necessary to keep them in their proper order and at fairly regular intervals from one another throughout. This is effected by means of this instrument, of which many varieties are found in the Assam Valley, where alone it appears to be used.

The simplest kind (from Goalpara) consists of a flat piece of wood about a foot long and half an inch thick, almost pointed at one end and widening out steadily towards the other to a width of 2½ inches. This end is roughly rounded off. Five holes are bored through the face of this piece of wood ; one is almost exactly at the centre, another is about an inch from the broad end and equidistant from either side. the other three being in a straight line between these two and at intervals of about one inch, though not very regular. This variety of the instrument is of the roughest possible description, the holes having been bored with a red hot skewer. The wood is *sal*.

The second variety (also from Goalpara) is quite as rough and crude as the first, but differs from it in being made of buffalo horn instead of wood. It is about 10 inches long and 1 inch wide, the five holes being about ⅜ inch apart.

The third variety (also from Goalpara) is far superior. The wood is carved into the shape of a dagger, with a sharp point at one end and a well-shaped handle at the other, the whole being about 14 inches long. Its width is greatest (1¾ inch) at the point where the blade leaves the handle. The centre of the blade is cut out, leaving a rectangular hole about 5 inches long by 1 inch wide, which begins about an inch from the handle. This hole is divided off into compartments by six parallel pins driven through one side of the blade across the hole, and into the opposite side. Each pin carries a small tube of reed or bamboo which revolves freely round it. At right angles to these tubes, four smooth pins are fastened, two above them and two below, one (on either side) near each long edge of the hollow in the blade. The ends of these pins fit into holes in the blade. Thus, there are five similar compartments each bounded at the two ends by revolving tubes of reed, and at each side by two smooth pins. There are also two more compartments, *viz.*, one at either end, but these two compartments have a revolving tube at one end only and are not made use of. This kind costs about 4 annas.

A fourth variety from Goalpara is on the same principle as the last, but of far superior workmanship. Instead of four pins running lengthwise, however, there are only two, which are both near one edge of the framework, one above and one below the revolving pins. These lengthwise pins do not revolve. This kind is about 18 inches long and gracefully carved at either end, the design at one end being a *fleur-de-lys*. It is also painted red, black and yellow and varnished. The central portion, corresponding to the blade, is about 9 inches long, 3 inches wide and ¾ inch thick. The point in which this variety is an advance upon those described above is that into the hollow in the blade are fitted eight small panels, four on each side, two lengthwise and two breadthwise. The long panels are of the same length as the hollow, and about ¼ inch wide; the short ones are about ¼ inch wide and long enough to fit in between the side panels. They are all very thin. These panels are glued in and painted to match the rest of the instrument. They add a finish to the whole and also form a safeguard against the pins falling out. This instrument was bought at the bazar for 4 annas and was cheap at the price; the wood however was rather soft.

A fifth variety from Goalpara consists of a frame of *sal* and other strong wood. The shape in the centre is rectangular, one end being rounded off into a handle (like that of a tennis bat) of about the same length as the rectangular portion. The other end is carved to represent some animal, flower or the like. The price of the instrument depends upon the nature of this carving. One of the designs at present in fashion is the *hangar-mukh* or alligator's head. This is a very effective piece of carving, the neck projecting from the end of the central blade, and the whole being really well executed. This instrument has nine tubes revolving on central pins running two lengthwise and seven breadthwise. They are fixed in the same way as the cross tubes in the third variety. The hole in the blade is a rectangle 5 inches by 1¼ inch. This is the highest form of *karhani* found in Goalpara. The threads pass through any of the spaces (except the end two which are very small owing to the two extreme cross tubes being quite close to the ends of the excavation in the blade), and can touch nothing but revolving tubes with very smooth surfaces, no matter which way the instrument be turned. Friction is therefore reduced to a minimum.

The sixth variety comes from Golaghat. It differs from all those found in Goalpara in being made entirely of bamboo, and in having a far larger number of compartments.

The outer framework consists of a single round piece of bamboo, about 21 inches long and ¾ inch in diameter. This is split down the centre for about 15 inches. At the end of the split it is firmly lashed with a binding of cane to prevent the split extending into the whole portion of the bamboo which forms the handle. Two holes are bored through the split portion at right angles to the line of fissure, one at 3¼ inches from one end and one at 3¼ inches from the other end (where the binding is). There are thus really four holes, two in each half of the split portion. These two halves are pulled apart and the inner framework inserted between them and fitted into the holes. The two free ends of the split halves are then brought together and firmly lashed with cane, string, or leather.

The inner framework consists of two end-pieces and two side-pieces to hold the revolving rods. Each of the two end-pieces is about 1¾ inch by 1¼ inch, and at the centre of each end is a short projection to fit into the holes in the outer framework. The two side-pieces are each about 7 inches by ¼ inch, the ends having similar projections, which in turn fit into holes in the end-pieces.

There are four long rods and no less than 16 cross rods. These rods are not thin pins carrying hollow tubes of reed revolving on them, but are small, solid cylinders of bamboo about ¼ inch in diameter, and they themselves revolve. At either end of every rod a portion about ⅜ inch long is of only half the diameter of the central portion. The thin portions of the long rods pass through holes in the end-pieces, and those of the cross-rods through holes in the side-pieces. The central portion of the long rods is 7 inches in length and that of the cross-rods 1¼ inch. The cross rods are parallel and so are the long rods which lie near the side-pieces, and are arranged as usual, two above and two below the cross rods.

This variety, though not so elaborate in design, yet possesses all the working qualifications of the best specimens from Goalpara, and excels them in the fact of its having so many more openings for the thread. Its rods cannot possibly drop out, as the holes through which their ends pass, though sufficiently large to allow of their freely revolving, are not large enough to allow the central portions to pass through; and all these rods, both long and cross, revolve. Its inferiority to the best Goalpara variety lies in the fact that the rods, unless their central portions are all cut accurately to length, are apt to stick instead of revolving, and their surfaces are not so smooth as those of the tubes of Belani reed used in Goalpara; moreover the instrument is not so durable when made entirely of bamboo as when the framework is of sal. The price of the Golaghat variety just described is four annas.

There are, doubtless, many other varieties of *karhani* to be found in Assam, but the descriptions received from other districts are in general terms and no other specimens have been collected.

5.—The Reed (Plate I, fig. VI).

Vernacular names:—Ras, rach or *rah* (general), *ra* (Cachar), *lachh* (South Sylhet and Habigunj), *hana* (Habigunj).

This instrument is thus described by Mr. Darrah: "This is a sort of comb. The teeth consist of very fine strips of bamboo, fastened at each end between two long pieces of the same material. The teeth are just far enough apart to allow easily of the passage of a thread". It is used during the process of shooting the weft, *i.e.*, the final stage of weaving, for a double purpose, first to keep the threads of the warp at regular and convenient distances apart, and secondly to drive home each weft thread as soon as it is shot. The interval between the teeth varies with the texture of the cloth to be woven. The finer the thread used and the more closely the cloth is woven the smaller is the interval between the teeth and the finer are the teeth themselves. And as reeds differ in fineness, so, too, they differ in length. The smallest used in Goalpara is about a cubit long and contains 350 teeth, the largest is about 3 cubits long and contains 1,000 teeth. The former is used only for making towels or other narrow cloths and the latter only for making large sheets or cotton shawls. Mr. Darrah's description is very meagre. The teeth (*kati*) are, in Goalpara, made usually not of bamboo, but of a very fine kind of reed, and it is from this that it derives its English name. I have never seen one in which the teeth were made of bamboo, but such are reported from Tezpur, Mangaldai and Barpeta. They are usually 3 inches long, but vary in length from 2 to 4 inches. Their length does not however depend on the length of the reed. The long pieces of bamboo (called *bao, kami* or *sali*) between which the teeth are fastened are about 2 inches longer than the actual length of the instrument itself. They are nearly flat, but slightly rounded on the side, the two flat sides facing inwards, *i.e.*, touching the teeth, and the two round sides facing outwards. Each piece is about ½ inch wide. Near their right hand extremities all four of these rods have deep notches cut in the edges, the two top rods having the notches in the outer edges and the two lower rods in the inner edges.

The two pairs of rods are parallel and about 1¼ inch apart, so that the ends of the teeth project a short way beyond each of them. These ends are, in Barpeta and Upper Assam, often thickly smeared over with cowdung. The teeth are bound to each pair of rods by a single length of string which passes once round the rods between each tooth and the next, the hitches being made alternately in opposite directions. Thus each tooth is separately lashed between the two rods of each pair, and the method of lashing described above forms a plaited ridge along each line of binding. This ridge is used as a means of counting the number of teeth; for after each hundred (*siya*) of threads, a slight variation in the method of lashing creates a break in the ridge, and each of these breaks marks off one hundred teeth. The numbering always commences from the right hand side, and it is marked on the binding of only the lower pair of rods. The number of teeth in the reed is not necessarily in full hundreds. This numeration system is referred to again later on. To strengthen the instrument, at each end of the main set of teeth is bound a flat bamboo of the same length as the teeth and about ½ inch wide; beyond that are four or five more teeth, and then another piece of bamboo like the last. These pieces of bamboo are bound to the long rods exactly as the teeth are; the numbering of the teeth begins, of course, from the inside of these bamboo sticks.

The reed is, perhaps, the most important of all the instruments used in weaving, for it is this, more than any other, that regulates the texture of the woven cloth. Without a fine reed it is impossible to weave as closely as is required for the more delicate fabrics. The reeds used and made in Assam are, on the whole, very inferior, and it is largely to this inferiority that ladies attribute their inability to vie with the weavers of Dacca in the quality of their work. I know of one Assamese gentleman holding a high appointment under Government, who quite recently got a friend to procure some superior reeds in Dacca and bring them back for his wife. On receiving the reeds he was very sanguine that his wife would be able to weave cloths far superior to any made with the aid of the Assamese reeds. I have not heard whether the result justified his expectations.

The reed varies in price with its size, fineness and workmanship. A common reed of ordinary size costs about four annas, while a fine reed may cost as much as R1-8-0. The reed, if used constantly, will last about one year. It is the only instrument of all those used for weaving that is invariably bought instead of being home-made. It is found for sale at most weekly markets, and is sometimes hawked round from village to village. It is not everybody who can make the reed. In North Lakhimpur reeds are purchased generally from the Katanis of Darrang and the Majuli. In Golaghat they are made chiefly by the people of Kaziranga and Marangi; in Kamrup by Mussalmen and Ganaks of Ellengidal in the Babjani mouza and Kardaitola in the Khata mouza, and by Ganaks of Barsaderi, Bhaluki, Bhogpur, and Boloigaon in the Bajuli tahsil.

A similar instrument is used in the Surma Valley.

6.—The Hook.

Vernacular names:—*Hakota*, *hatkota* (Goalpara), *kata* (Mangaldai), *rachh bharowa* or *rachh bharowa kuthi* (Sibsagar).

This is an instrument about 7 inches long and shaped like a bill-hook. It is made of buffalo-horn, deer-horn, brass, ivory or bamboo. The price varies with the material and workmanship. The ivory hooks are expensive, but others vary in price from two to eight annas.

The hook is used for drawing loops of thread through the intervals between the teeth of the reed.

Instead of this instrument a straight piece of bamboo with a pointed end is used in Tezpur and Goalpara, called in the former place *sala* and in the latter *sala kathi*. The instrument used in Sibsagar is rather of this nature than a true hook.

Then, again, in place of either of these, the spindle of the spinning-wheel, when of bamboo, is sometimes used for this purpose. This spindle has been already described.

The instrument used for this purpose in the Surma Valley is the *kathi*, which is described from South Sylhet as a bamboo needle having a point at one end and an eye at the other.

7.—The Brush.

Vernacular names:—*Kuchi* (Assam Valley), *kuchh* (Surma Valley).

This is a small brush made of sun grass in Barpeta, where it is sold ready-made for two annas; it is also often home-made. In Golaghat it is made of a kind of grass called *tabhanga*, and in South Sylhet with the roots of sugar cane tied on to bamboo.

It is used for smoothing the warp while the reed is being pushed along it in the process of warping, and again for sizing the warp the second time just before the actual weaving commences.

8.—The Loom (Plates II and III).

Vernacular names:—*Tantar sal* (Tezpur), *tantsol* (Mangaldai), *tatghar* (South Sylhet), *tat* (Goalpara and Cachar), *sal* (Gauhati and Sibsagar).[*]

In describing the loom it is well to keep in mind the three main purposes which this structure is intended to fulfil. The first is to support the warp horizontally at a moderate tension; the second, to hold the reed suspended in such a position that it may be readily driven backwards and forwards; the third, to supply an arrangement for working the healds.

To support the beams, four thick posts (i) are driven into the ground so as to form a rectangle, measuring 6 to 7½ feet by 2½ to 3½ feet, the former figures representing the

---

[*] In Gauhati the term *sal* appears to include not only the loom, but the whole collection of instruments used for shooting the weft, including, e.g., the shuttle and the temple, but excluding those that have been previously used during the warping process, e.g., the reed and beams. Another expression (*tantar sajali*) is used in a similar way in Gauhati to designate the whole collection of instruments used during warping and forming the healds, except the reels, which have already been used during the process of preparing the thread. There appears to be no expression, however, to designate the collection of instruments used during that first process.

(i) *Vernacular names:*—*Khuta* (Tezpur), *salar khuta* (Goalpara and Gauhati), *bihkaram khuti* (Gau.), *tantar khuta* (Sibsagar, Barpeta, and Goalpara).

PLATE II.

THE LOOM (Back View).

Fig. i.—4 Posts.
  „ ii.—Yarn beam.
  „ iii.—Cloth beam.
  „ iv.—2 Reeds.
  „ v.—3 Bars.
  „ vi.—Cross rod.
  „ vii.—Frame enclosing the reed.

Fig. viii.—2 Wooden pegs (one concealed from view).
  „ ix.—Shaft of braces.
  „ x.—3 Bachmis.
  „ xi.—Treadles.
  „ xii.—2 Wooden pans.
  „ xiii.—Shuttle.
  „ xiv.—Tunquis.

width of the loom, and the latter the distance from front to rear. These main posts are generally very rough and very stout, more or less cylindrical, and not less than 4 inches in diameter. The two front posts are of equal length, always about 5 feet ; the two rear posts are likewise equal in length, but this length varies from 4 feet to 5 feet. The yarn beam is supported by two loops of string (*garí dhara jarí*) hanging from the rear posts ; the cloth beam is sometimes supported in a similar manner by loops attached to the front posts. When so suspended, the beams are very near the ground, and the weaver, when at work, sits on a low stool, a plank of wood or the ground itself, in which case a hole is dug in front of her in which to rest her legs. More usually, however the cloth beam is not suspended from the front main posts, but rests on two shorter posts (i) (about 3 feet high) driven in close in front of the two front main-posts, and having their tops cut into the form of a ledge on which the cloth-beam rests between the shorter and main-posts. When thus supported the cloth-beam is, of course, about 3 feet from the ground, and the yarn-beam is supported by string from the rear posts at a similar height. In this case the weaver requires a raised seat ; sometimes an ordinary stool or a kerosine-oil box is used for this purpose, but sometimes a superior seat (called *bahapat*) is constructed for the occasion by laying a flat plank on 4 short posts or legs (*bahuna khuti*) driven into the ground.

The yarn-beam (ii) is a square bar about six feet long, with faces about 2 inches wide. A length of about six inches at each end is rounded off to a diameter of 2 inches or rather less. Along one of the faces runs a groove (*keoara*) about ⅓ an inch wide and deep, extending over nearly the whole length of the beam. Near one end of the beam two holes (*tatar kan*) are bored, one passing right through two opposite faces of the beam, and the other, which is 2 inches from the first and at right angles to it, through the other two faces.

The cloth-beam (iii) is exactly like the yarn beam, except that it is cylindrical instead of square, the diameter being about 8 inches.

These beams are sometimes made at home, but more frequently purchased, the price varying from R1 to R5 a pair. They are very durable, being made of hard wood, such as *maifak* or *bajarani*. A beam of *maifak* wood is said to last a century.

The warp is kept in a state of tension, by the beams being rolled round and then fixed in position, each by means of a rod (iv) which is pushed through one or other hole in the end of the beam till it touches the ground at an angle. The rods have to be removed when it is required to roll up the cloth or thread.

The main-posts play an important part in fulfilling the second and third objects of the loom. The beams, it will be remembered, were suspended only about half way up these posts. The tops of the posts are all cut into ledges, those on the front posts facing in one direction (*e.g.*, to the left), and those on the back posts in the other direction (to the right). On these ledges rests two bars, (v) the one supported by the front and rear posts on one side, and the other by those on the other side, and these two bars in turn support a cross-rod, (vi) which lies at right angles to them and about midway between the front and rear of the loom. When the rear posts are shorter than the front posts, the side bars are of course not horizontal, and so their upper edges are cut into deep notches like a very coarse saw-edge, that the cross-rod may rest upon them without slipping down. When the front and rear posts are of equal length, the side-bars are usually quite smooth.

The cross-rod is a thin but strong round rod of bamboo or wood, quite plain. Its length is slightly greater than the width of the loom. It is this cross-bar which forms the support for the reed and the healds.

While at use in the loom the reed requires to be enclosed in a frame for two reasons, first, to strengthen it and protect it from getting damaged, and, secondly, to add weight to it, so that the weft threads may be driven well home as they are shot.

(i) *Vernacular names*:—*Bikkaramar khuti* (Sibsagar and Tezpur), *dhoka khuti* (Mangaldai), *kukur* (Gauhati).
N. B.—It will be seen that the name a,plied to these posts in Sibsagar and Tezpur, is in Gauhati applied not to these, but to the four main posts. The name means " The Creator's posts."
(ii) *Vernacular names*:—*Sula merowa tolotha* (Tezpur), *sutar gari* (Goalpara), *ag tolata* (Golaghat), *narad* or *mijahari* (Cachar).
(iii) *Vernacular names*:—*Kapar merowa tolotha* (Tezpur), *kaporar gari* (Barpeta and Goalpara), *gurar tolata* (Golaghat), *ndrad* (South Sylhet), *narad* (Cachar).
(iv) *Vernacular names*:—*Kanmari* (Tezpur), *khilabari* (Barpeta and Goalpara), *khil* Goalpara), *khilamuri* (Goalpara), *kanai diya* (Sibsagar), *murakhuti* (Cachar).
(v) *Vernacular names*:—*Chhalimari* (Tezpur), *chalbari* (Gauhati and Cachar), *salibari* Maugald *salbari* (Goalpara), *bharbari* (Barpeta), *panjabari* (Goalpara), *jakhala* (Sibsagar).
(vi) *Vernacular names*:—*akowamari* (Tezpur), *chatibari* (Gauhati and Barpeta), *sakobari* (Mangaldai) *saldah-rabari* (Goalpara and Barpeta), *salbari* (Goalpara), *chhalimari* (Sibsagar).
N.B.—It will be seen that the name *sulbari* is applied in some parts of Goalpara to the side-bars and in others to the cross-rod.

The frame (vii) consists of two long flat wooden bars, each about 6 feet long, ⅛ inch broad, and 2¼ inches thick, and having a groove along one of the edges, and a hole near each end, passing breadthwise through it. The bottom bar is suspended horizontally with its grooved edge uppermost, from the top cross-rod by two strings (*naki jari*), one near either end. The top bar rests upon it with its grooved edge downwards, and the two are pinned together by two wooden pegs or pins (viii) passing through the holes at the two ends. The flat faces are, of course, vertical.

To insert the reed, the two pins are taken out, the upper bar lifted up, and the bottom edge of the reed set to rest in the groove in the lower bar; the upper bar is then again brought down, so that its groove fits on to the upper edge of the reed, and the two bars are again pinned together. The reed is thus supported with its length horizontal and its breadth vertical.

The strings supporting this frame are sometimes single, and pass direct to the upper bar. More usually, however, they are double and hang, not from the cross-rod above, but from rings, (*ghila* or *anguthi*), which are themselves suspended by strings from the cross-rod, sometimes direct and sometimes through the medium of other rings arranged like pulleys. In any case, when a double string is used, its ends are tied together, so that it forms an endless band crossing itself between the upper and lower bars of the frame which holds the reed, and thus forming two loops, one of which passes tightly round the lower bar, and the other passes at its bottom end round the upper bar and at its top end through the ring. (In Tezpur the arrangement is the same as here described, except that the figure of eight formed by the string is double, as the two ends of the string pass first upwards, then through the ring in opposite directions, and, lastly, downwards, being eventually tied together below the frame).

The arrangement for working the healds (ix) must be such that they can be pulled up and down alternately, the one shaft rising as the other falls. The device adopted enables this to be done with an alternate pressure of each foot, and is as follows :— From the upper cross-rod are suspended two (or, in the case of a very wide cloth, three) *nachani** (x) (the simplest form which is a straight flat piece of wood about 9 inches long by 1 inch wide), by means of strings (*nachani jari*) passing through holes in their centres. The *nachani* thus hang with their flat side vertical and their length parallel to the warp. The front end of each *nachani* is connected by a separate string with the upper rod of one shaft of healds, and the back end is similarly connected with the other shaft of healds. These strings may be single or double, but in any case they run straight down from the *nachani* to the rod.

The centre of the lower rod of the first shaft of healds is connected by single strings (*ba tana jari*) with a bamboo rod about 1 yard long and 1 inch in diameter which lies on the ground with one end pointing towards the weaver's seat; the lower rod of the second shaft of healds is in like manner connected with another bamboo rod similarly situated. These two rods† form, as it were, treadles (xi). They lie with one end pointing towards the weaver's seat, and it is near these ends that the strings are attached. The other ends are sometimes separately and independently fastened to the ground by wooden pins (xii) [*nigani khuti* (Tezpur) and *garaka khuti* (Gauhati)] which must however be sufficiently loose to allow of the rods moving freely up and down. More usually the rods are not fastened to the ground at all, but are, instead, joined together by means of a thin bamboo rod (*kukar bari* in Goalpara) which passes through holes near their centres.

The weaver, by pressing one treadle with her foot, pulls down the shaft of healds attached to it. This in turn pulls down the front ends of the *nachani* and consequently raises the back ends, which draw up with them the other shaft of healds. The pressure of the other treadle pulls down the second shaft of healds and draws up the first.

It may be noted here that the healds are much shorter than the frame which holds the reed, hence the strings supporting the *nachani* all fall between the two strings supporting that frame.

Sometimes, to lend additional weight to the healds, two moderately thick rods are tied to the lower rod of each shaft, and in this case the treadles are connected with these two heavy rods and not with the healds themselves.

There are two distinct kinds of *nachani*. The most usual form of the first kind .

(vii) *Vernacular names: —Draupadi, dorpati* (Nowgong), *dahtoni* (Mangaldai, Barpeta and Gauhati), *sal* or *tani* (Goalpara.)

(viii) *Vernacular names :—Baluabari* or *begulabari* (Gauhati and Barpeta), *bahulabari, baulabari* or *boulabari* (Goalpara), *nakibari* (Barpeta).

* Also called *nachani* (Gauhati) and *natani* (Goalpara).

† *Vernacular names:—Garaka, garaka bari, jutiaish* (Cachar).

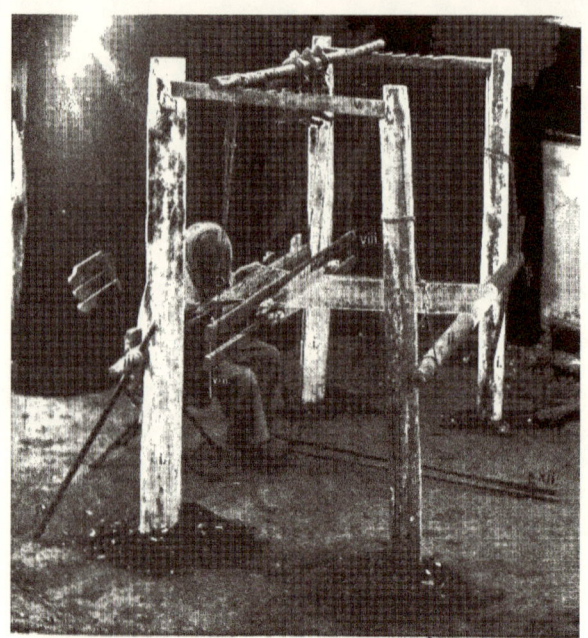

PLATE III.

THE LOOM (Side View).

Fig. 1.—4 Posts.
 „ ii.—Yarn beam.
 „ iii.—Cloth beam.
 „ iv.—2 Rods.
 „ v.—2 Bars.
 „ vi.—Cross rod.
 „ vii.—Frame enclosing the reed.

Fig. viii.—2 Wooden pegs.
 „ ix.—Shaft or healds.
 „ x.—3 *Nachanis*.
 „ xi.—Treadles.
 „ xii.—2 Wooden pins.

is a flat piece of wood (7 to 11 inches long by 1 inch wide) nearly straight, but having a circular projection from the centre of one side. Through a hole in this projecting disc is passed the string by which the *nachani* hangs from the upper cross-bar. A *nachani* of this kind can turn round through any angle, pivoting on the string which supports it. There are many varieties of this *nachani*, some are made of wood, some of bamboo, some of iron and some of brass. They are also fashioned to most quaint and graceful shapes, such for instance as a swan, but they all work on the same principle. They may be purchased for from 4 annas to a rupee per set. The second kind of *nachani* consists of two separate flat pieces of wood. The first of these (called *ghora* in Mangaldai and *bandari* in Tezpur) is quite straight, except that one end is shaped like a ring. The other piece is straight or only slightly curved, and is fastened by a wooden pin passing through its centre to the plain end of the first piece of wood, sufficiently loosely to allow of its pivoting through half a circle round this pin. This *nachani* is not suspended to the cross-bar by a string, but the cross-bar is itself passed through the hole in the first piece of wood which then hangs vertically from the bar, the other piece of wood is parallel to the warp but is not necessarily horizontal, as it is a vertical plane in which it revolves round the central pin. This second kind of *nachani* is reported only from the Darrang District (Tezpur and Mangaldai). The first kind appears to be used in all the plains districts of the Assam Valley.

. In Goalpara the *nachanis* are sometimes entirely dispensed with, and their place is taken by reels or discs of wood with grooved circumferences and holes through their centres. These discs (*ghila*) are about 2 inches in diameter and ⅓ inch thick. The required number of discs, two or three as the case may be, is threaded on a thin bamboo rod and this rod is supported horizontally by strings at either ends connecting it with the upper cross-bar. Round the grooved circle of each disc is passed a string one end of which is attached to one set of healds and the other end to the other set. The discs revolve freely round the central rod. Thus these discs serve the same purpose as the *nachani*. They are, however, suspended very much lower down (and so nearer the healds) than the *nachani* ever are.

9.—The Shuttle (xiii, Plate II).

Vernacular Names :—Mako or *maku* (Assam Valley), *nail* (Surma Valley).

The shuttle is a piece of wood about 19 inches long shaped very much like a light sculling boat, the ends being bevelled off and brought almost to a point. The width at the centre is about 1½ inch and the depth 1 inch. In the centre is a rectangular hollow (*khula*) measuring nearly four inches by 1¼ inch by ¾ inch In one of the ends walls of this hollow is a small hole, and in the other end wall, exactly opposite this hole, is a slit or notch. These are to receive the spool-pin, one end of which is inserted in the hole and the other dropped into the notch and there secured by a small peg ("*akali bari*) which is passed through a hole drilled across the notch from one side of the shuttle. This peg, which is called *thila* in Golaghat and *khili* or *phuti* in Goalpara, is made of bamboo, quill, bent cane or any other suitable material. In the centre of one of the side walls of the hollow is sometimes drilled a hole (*nakati phuta*) through which the thread may pass, but very often (*e. g.*, in Sibsagar and Goalpara) the thread is allowed to run freely over the side with no hole to guide it. In Sibsagar a shuttle which has a hole for the passage of the thread is called *charia mako*, one without is called *phalia mako*.

The best shuttles are made by carpenters of *nahor* wood and painted. In Goalpara, Mangaldai and Barpeta they cost 4 annas each, in Golaghat from 4 to 8 annas, in Gauhati from 8 annas to one rupee and in Sibsagar from one rupee to one rupee four annas. They are very durable.

The spool consists of a length of thread wound on a pin or hollow tube. Sometimes the thread is wound direct on to a very fine bamboo pin, which revolves in the shuttle when the thread is pulled ; but more usually it is wound round a small hollow tube of *ekra* or jungle reed, and this tube is slipped on to a bamboo or iron pin round which it freely revolves. In Goalpara a leaf of the *tal* tree rolled up is often substituted for the *ekra* tube. In South Sylhet the spool is made of a bamboo twig as large as the little finger.

The pin or tube on which the thread is wound is called *mahura kathi, bakuli bari, nai kathi* or *katha bari*; the pin round which the tube revolves (when a tube is used) is called *garbakhila, garabh khila* or *bukbari* (Gauhai), *gereli kathi* (Tezpur, Mangaldai and Goalpara), *sali* (Barpeta) or *sarisha bari* (Goalpara). The whole spool is called *mahura* (Assam Valley), *masura* (Goalpara), *nuli* (Goalpara and Cachar) and *náli* (South Sylhet).

10.—The Bhaunri (also called bhauri).

This is an instrument consisting of a figure-of-eight shaped piece of wood with a rod passing through its centre, at right angles to its face. The rod is about 20 inches long and about half an inch in diameter at either end, but it thickens out in the middle. The piece of wood is about a foot long and ¾ inch thick. It is shaped like a figure-of-eight except that at the centre there is a wide circle to admit of a square hole being cut in it to take the rod. The width of this circle and the loops at their widest part is 2¼ inches. It costs 4 annas and is very durable.

A *bhaunri* of the above description has been received from Golaghat, but it is not used for cotton. It is used only for winding muga silk off the cocoons in the following way :—The rod rests on two horizontal bars to which its ends are loosely bound. A woman sitting on one side of the instrument pulls out a thread from the cocoon and twists it round the rod, she then whirls round the figure-of-eight shaped piece of wood which makes the rod revolve and the thread is drawn off the cocoon which is now being held by a second woman sitting on the opposite side of the instrument.

The *bhaunri* is, however, included in the cotton weaver's outfit by Mr. Darrah and also in the report received from Gauhati. The description given by Mr. Darrah is very brief and might apply to the instrument described above : which, however, could not possibly be used in the way Mr. Darrah describes. In the Gauhati report no description is given.

There is a variety of the *bhaunri* used by the Miris of Golaghat for forming spools of cotton thread. In this the rod is much thinner and finely pointed at both ends and the place of the figure-of-eight shaped piece of wood is taken by a lump of clay. This is the only form of *bhaunri* used by the cotton weaver that I have seen.

11.—The Temple (xiv, Plate II).

Vernacular Names :—Putal (general), *putalbari* or *putalkata* (Goalpara), *phanik* (Habigunge).

This is an instrument used to keep the width of the cloth uniform throughout. There are two kinds used in Assam, the one for delicate fabrics and the other for those of coarser texture. The first kind (called in Gauhati *patiputal* or simply *putal*) is a flat stick, about half an inch wide, exactly equal in length to the width of the cloth on which it is to be used. At each end is a needle point, the needle being either stuck in or else tied on with thread. The second kind (called in Gauhati *tatiputal*), as described by Mr. Darrah, consists "of two rods of bamboo, crossed, each a little longer than the width of the warp. The free ends are furnished with little iron spikes which stick into the cloth. The other ends are united by a piece of string, which allows them to remain a couple of feet apart. Two loops of string, one on each side of the point where the rods cross, pass over the rods and the string which unites them. When these loops are pushed apart, the warp is stretched tight." The rods are generally round and about a quarter of an inch in diameter ; the points are, as a rule, simply needles affixed as described above.

The temple used in Habigunge is alluded to as "a bow of split bamboo." It is probably of the second kind.

Speaking generally of the weaving instruments used by the Assamese, those of bamboo are almost always made at home by the men of the household, with one exception, *viz.*, the reed. Those of wood or any other material are frequently home-made, but usually bought. It is very difficult to give an estimate of the total cost of these instruments ; in Nowgong it is stated at from Rs. 2-8 to Rs. 4, and in Barpeta at from Rs. 10 to Rs. 25. The former estimate is very low, but there is no doubt that for four or five rupees a family can set up a loom if they purchase only those instruments which cannot be home-made. The total cost of a single weaving outfit for a wealthy family is no doubt much larger than the highest estimate given in Barpeta, but the cheaper instruments are just as serviceable, though in some cases not so durable. But, for an ordinary working outfit, the durability of the instruments is so great in proportion to their original cost that the expenditure on plant forms an almost inappreciable item in the cost of the fabrics made.

The instruments described above are those used by the Assamese. The people of Goalpara use the same instruments, but do not follow exactly the same processes as those in vogue higher up the valley. The professional weavers in the Surma Valley have their own instruments, and use their own methods, though in some cases these are almost identical with those of the Assamese. A detailed account will be given only of the Assamese process of weaving, after which the main differences between it and the processes of the Goalpara people and the Tantis and Jugis of the Surma Valley will be pointed out. As regards the Goalpara process, however, the only radical peculiarity it exhibits lies in the warping ; the other peculiarities are quite unimportant and will be referred to in the description of the Assamese process.

The process of weaving in Assam Proper.

The process of weaving consists of three main stages, *viz.*, 1st, sizing and preparing the thread, 2nd, warping, and 3rd, weaving proper, *viz.*, shooting the weft. These main stages, however, all admit of further sub-division.

1st, Sizing and preparing the thread.

In the case of home-spun thread, when the process of spinning has been completed, the thread is left in the form of balls (called *sutalahi*, etc.), about the size and shape of a large onion and having a hole through the centre. One of these balls is taken up and a spindle (detached from the spinning-wheel) passed through the hole. The thread is then wound off the spindle on to a reel of the first kind (*latai*, etc., instrument No. 1) in the following way :— The loose end of the thread is tied to one of the rods in the framework of the reel. The lower end of the reel is then placed on a suitable raised support, and the handle turned rapidly round with the right hand. The spindle is meanwhile held in the left hand or placed in a small bamboo tube (*chunga*) fixed to the ground. The whole ball is thus wound off and other balls are similarly treated until the skein (*lecha, necha* or *kheo*) has attained the proper size, when it is taken off the reel and others formed in the same way.

This operation is called *sutalahi bhunga*, and is said to take ten minutes per skein in Barpeta.

The skeins are next all boiled together in an earthen pot (*charu*) with some rice or paddy. When the latter has been thoroughly boiled, both it and the thread are taken out of the water and the rice or paddy pounded in a paddy-husking machine (*dhenki*) until it is reduced to a glutinous paste or starch. The skeins are then smeared over with the whole of this paste, and in that state again boiled, after which they are taken out of the water and, one by one, slipped over a reel of the second kind (*cherekhi*, etc., instrument No. 2) which is similar in girth to the first reel, but much shorter, and so formed as to allow of the framework revolving round the central rod. From this reel the thread, while still wet, is wound off again on to the first reel, from which the skein is taken off, as soon as it is formed, and put on a bamboo rail (*dar*) in the sun to dry. The last part of this stage of the process is called *radiowa* (sunning) in Barpeta, and it is said to take one hour ; the remainder is called *mar diya* (general) or *suta sijowa* (Tezpur). This also takes one hour in Barpeta.

(*Varieties in this stage of the process* :—

(I) In Tezpur it appears that only one boiling takes place and that in plain water, but, after this boiling, the threads are mixed with the gum of boiled rice to strengthen them.

(II) In Mangaldai only one boiling of the threads is mentioned, after which they appear to be at once put in the sun to dry. The description is however brief. The object of the reeling after the boiling and before the drying is to straighten out the skeins which have become disordered during the starching and boiling, and so prevent the thread from matting together as it dries.)

In the case of ready-made thread, the skeins are taken as they come from the shop and straight away boiled and smeared with size. The process is otherwise the same as with home-spun thread, except that the skeins are much larger, and so require the second kind of reel to be much larger ; the *bor cherekhi* is therefore used.

In Golaghat the thread is boiled in water with half its weight of rice for an hour or more until the rice has reached the consistency of paste. The pot is then taken off the fire, and its contents left undisturbed till the next morning when the thread is taken off, reeled and put in the sun to dry.

Whether home-spun or ready-made thread be used, the skeins, when put in the sun to dry, are of the same size, *viz.*, that of the first kind of reel. As soon as they are thoroughly dry, they are taken down and divided into two equal sets, one for the warp (*dig, dighal suta* or *tana*) and one for the weft (*bani* or *putal suta*).

Of the skeins reserved for the warp one is taken up and slipped over a small reel of the second kind (*saru cherekhi*,) the rod of which is planted in the ground. The thread is then once more wound off, but this time on to a reel of the third kind (*ugha*, etc., instrument No. 3). The number of skeins rolled round each *ugha* depends on the size of the cloth, especially on its length, as will be explained hereafter.

This operation is called *ughalowa*, *ughowa* or *sutalowa*. In Barpeta it takes 15 minutes to wind 3 skeins on one *ugha*.

Of the skeins reserved for the weft, one is put on a small reel of the second kind which is planted in the ground. The thread is then formed into spools by being wound on to either a solid pin, or else a small tube of bamboo or ekra. When a solid pin is used, the thread is wound off the *cherekhi* on to the spindle of a spinning wheel, and the roll of cotton is slipped off the spindle on to the pin. When a hollow tube is used this is fixed on to the end of either a *bhaunri* or a spinning wheel and the thread wound on to it direct from the reel. This method of making the spools by means of the *bhaunri* is thus described by Mr. Darrah :—

"Sometimes the *bhaunri* is taken, and a small tube of bamboo or reed slipped on the thin end of the *bhaunri*. The end of the thread is attached to the tube, and, the *bhaunri* being twisted in the finger, the thread is wound round the tube. The figure-of-eight shaped piece of wood gives the necessary weight, and enables the twisting process to be carried on without much strain on the fingers. Women constantly prepare these spools for the shuttles while working the rice husker with one foot and nursing a child in the arms. When enough thread has been collected on the tube, it is slipped off the *bhaunri* and on to the needle of the shuttle."

But, as far as I can find, the *bhaunri* is very seldom used by the Assamese for cotton thread, and the only district that names it in the list of instruments used in weaving is Kamrup. I have, however, seen the Miris near Golaghat, who had in other respects adopted the methods of the Assamese, forming spools by means of a *bhaunri*. The *bhaunri* was laid with one end resting on a ledge, and the other end (holding the spool) supported on the finger of one hand. With the other hand the operator turned the rod round. Among the Miris, it is generally boys or girls who are engaged in making spools.

The *bhaunri* is, however, a very primitive instrument, and the process of forming spools by means of it is, at best, both tedious and slow. A far more rapid method, and one now almost universally employed, is to fix the tube on the spindle of a spinning wheel, and by turning the handle to wind the thread off the reel on to the tube. In Goalpara and Barpeta it is usual to take a long tube and to wind sufficient thread at equal intervals along its length. When the tube is full, it forms as many spools as there are rolls of thread, and these are broken off one by one as required for weaving. The whole tube with the rolls of thread upon it is called *takuri*.

At a house in Niohintagram, a village in the Goalpara sub-division, I was told that the winding of the thread on to these long tubes was done by the hand alone, neither the spinning wheel nor the *bhaunri* being used. There was a spinning wheel in the house, but it was old and out of order; the *bhaunri* was unknown. There are, however, few houses in which a spinning wheel in working order cannot be found. These spinning wheels are seldom used for spinning now-a-days, their sole use is for making spools. It is, therefore, quite exceptional for spools to be made by hand, and the process must be a very lengthy one. This method is, however, said to be used in South Sylhet. .

The spools of thread are made as large as the capacity of the shuttle will allow. The length of thread on each is therefore independent of the size of the cloth to be woven, and varies only with the fineness of the thread. The size of the cloth and the closeness of the texture are the elements which determine the number of spools required.

2nd, Warping (Plate IV).

The first step in the process of warping is to measure off on the reed a distance equal to the intended width of the cloth. Reeds vary in length, and the one selected is usually as nearly as possible of the same length as the cloth to be woven; if the reed be longer than required, the distance is marked off in the middle, i. e., an equal length is left at either end. The number of teeth in the space marked off is counted and the reed laid aside for the present.

A stout post, about a yard long and half an inch in diameter, is now driven (upright) into the ground, and from this post a distance is marked off on the ground equal to the intended length of the cloth (or rather about 9 inches more, as will be explained here-

PLATE IV.
WARPING.

A.—⎤
B.—⎥ 4 Posts.
C.—⎥
E.—⎦

D.—Short stick.
K.—*Karhani.*
⎣.—6 Small reels.

after). The measurement is made by means of a flat stick *kathi*, three feet in length. The distance being marked off, another post exactly like the first is driven in the ground at the far end. Between these posts and in a line with them two thinner posts (or more usually two flat sticks) of the same length are similarly planted—the one about one foot from one end post, and the other about two feet from the other end post. Midway between this last end post and the post two feet from it, a fifth is driven in in the same way; this is only about a foot in length and is nearly always flat.

These five posts being in one straight line may be called by the letters A, B, C, D, and E according to their position along that line. A and E will be the two stout end posts, B and C the two thinner posts or sticks, and D the short stick.

These posts are distinguished by the following names :—

A and E—*bati karha khuti* (Gauhati and Goalpara), *tantar khuti* (Tezpur) or *bar khuti* (Mangaldai).

B and C—*Saru bati karha khuti* (Goalpara), or *khuti cheri* (Gauhati).

D—*Bachani bari* (Goalpara), *bachani khuti* (Tezpur), *bachani chiri* (Tezpur), *ujand cheri* (Gauhati), *ujana khuti* (Mangaldai), *khutani chiri* (Barpeta).

The names are an indication of the nature of the posts. The word *khuti* means a peg or small post, as distinguished from *khuta*, which strictly means a large stout post (*e. g.*, the posts of the loom), *cheri* or *chiri* means a flat stick, as distinguished from *guri*, which means a round stick or rod. In future flat sticks will be called simply sticks, and round sticks will be called rods. *Bari* is a word of more general import.

Small reels (filled with sized thread) to the required number are now taken and planted close together in the ground, in a straight line with one another and with the end post A, this line being at right angles to the line of posts (A E). The reels are all on the same side of the line of posts, and the nearest reel is at a convenient distance from post A.

The number of small reels used depends partly on the width of the cloth to be woven and partly on the caprice of the weaver. In the upper districts of the Assam Valley the number of reels is always even, and varies from 4 to 12. The number most usually employed is 6 or 8, 4 being used only for weaving very narrow cloths, and 12 for very wide cloths. The choice between 6 and 8 depends on the weaver's fancy. The number of reels depending chiefly on the width of the cloth, the quantity of thread on each reel depends mainly on its length.

The weaver now takes up a *karhani*, and drawing out the loose ends of thread from the reels inserts them one by one through successive compartments in the *karhani*, and ties them in a bunch on the other side. Advancing with the *karhani* in her right hand, the weaver loops the knotted end of the threads over post A, so that an equal number falls on either side. She then walks up and down the line of posts, always on the same side, and lays the threads round and round the posts, each complete layer of threads forming a figure of eight, the centre (or intersection) of which lies between post A and B.

There is thus an intersection between each successive *set of threads*, the number in a set being equal to that of the small reels used. But for weaving an intersection (*mor*) is required between *each successive thread* of the warp. To make this, a second operator sits facing post D and on the opposite side to that traversed by the first weaver. When two complete layers of thread have been put round the posts, the second operator picks up the top thread of those farthest from her (outside threads) on the front of her first finger, pulls it towards her and picks up the top inside thread on the back of her finger, pushes it from her and picks up the next highest outside thread as she did the first, and so on until she has picked up all the threads on her finger—the outside threads on the front and the inside threads on the back. She then lifts up the threads by raising her finger, slips them over the top of the short post D, and presses them down close together to the bottom of the post. This post now passes through the space occupied a moment before by the woman's finger. It will be seen that the order of the threads has thus been changed at this point. Before, there came first one set of threads all on one side of the post, and then one set of threads all on the other and so on, but now the first thread of the first set is followed by the first thread of the second set, then comes the second thread of the first set and so on; and between each successive thread are now two intersections, one on each side of the post D, *i. e.*, one between C and D and one between D and E.

The operations of forming these intersections is called *bachha*.

The time taken to make these intersections is much less than that required for laying the threads even once completely round the posts. The first woman therefore goes on laying the threads while the second makes the intersections. As soon as the next two layers of thread are ready the second woman treats them exactly as she did the first, and so on until the required number of threads has been laid. The threads are then broken off from the reels and the ends knotted in pairs round post A. (In Tezpur they are said to be knotted as at the commencement, *i.e.*, all in a bunch.)

The reason why two layers are usually treated at one time by the second woman is that, if a greater number were taken, it would be very difficult to pick out the threads in their proper order, while if only one were taken, it would involve more work.

The number of times the threads have to be laid round the posts is calculated from the number of teeth in the space marked off on the reed. The number of pairs of threads (*kani*) in the warp is equal to number of these teeth (only one end tooth being counted). Now each complete layer of threads contains as many pairs as there are reels. Hence the number of teeth in the space marked off on the reed divided by the number of small reels used gives the number of layers of threads required. These layers are sometimes counted by the first operator herself, but the counting is more usually done by a third operator sitting near post A.

When the requisite number of layers is complete, one or two extra layers are put round the posts in order that a selvage [*aothi* or *doar* (Goalpara)] may be formed at each edge of the cloth. The way in which this is done will be explained later on.

The laying of the warp is called *bati karha* (general), *bati kara* (Goalpara) and *tena deowa* (Cachar).

(*Variations in the process* :—

In Barpeta the reels (*ugha*) are placed in the ground first and after them the posts. The order in which the posts are driven in is rather different from usual ; A is put in first, then B, then E, then D, then C. Here, too, as also in Goalpara, it is immaterial whether the number of reels be even or odd. The most usual number is 5 or 6. If 5 be used, the threads are placed over the posts in such a way that three fall on one side and two on the other. When the laying of the warp is finished, they are knotted together in two bunches, one of two threads and one of three, the latter being put over the end post in such a way that the side with the one in excess at the beginning has only one of these three, the other side taking two.)

The warp having been laid, it is necessary to prepare it for the loom. The first thing is to apply the reed. For this purpose posts C, D, and E, with the threads still round them are taken out of the ground, and E replaced by a long rod (about 1½ inch in diameter),[*] and C and D by long sticks about 1 inch wide. Rod E is now held horizontally and the threads opened out along it to the intended width of the cloth. This rod and sticks C and D are all slightly longer than this width.

The reed is now placed with its face vertical against rod E and tied to it at either end. The warp threads are then drawn through the intervals between the teeth in the marked off portion of the reed, one pair (*viz.*, one upper and its corresponding lower thread) through each interval. To pass the threads through the reed a woman sits down facing the reed, inserts the spindle of a spinning wheel or a hook specially made for the purpose (instrument No. 6), successively through each interval between the teeth, picking up each time one loop of the warp threads and drawing it through. Having thus drawn through a convenient number of such loops and threaded them on the spindle or hook, she slips them on to a thin rod (called *sala* in Tezpur and *sati* in Mangaldai), and continues the process till all the threads have been drawn through and threaded on the rod. This operation is called *rasbharowa* (Barpeta) or *rasbindha* (Tezpur). It takes three or four hours in Barpeta. The reed is now untied and rod E, to which it was bound, removed. Thus the new rod on which the threads have been arranged has really taken the place of rod E, the only difference being that it is behind the reed. This new rod may, therefore, henceforward be called rod E[1].

At this stage there are still three intersections in the warp, *viz.*, one between the reed and stick D, one between sticks D and C, and one between posts A and B.

Stick D is now pulled towards the reed and turned on edge so as to throw the

---

[* *Vernacular names*:— *Dangibari* or *dangi* (Tezpur, Mangaldai and Barpeta), *jilathi* (Barpeta), *jilathi* or *julothi* (Gau hati) and *taldhara* (Sibsagar).

N. B.—This rod and that inserted later on in place of A are subsequently removed and often eventually tied to the bottom rod of the healds to give them weight. When so used, they retain their original name, but the name *dangibari* or *dangi* is more usually applied to them when used for the first purpose, and the name *jilothi* or *taldhara* when used for the second purpose. These two rods are rather thicker than the average.]

intersection through the reed. In the gap between the intersection (now behind the reed) and the reed another flat stick exactly similar to stick D is inserted, and stick D removed. This new stick may therefore henceforth be called stick D¹. This stick is now turned on edge and another thin rod similar to that at E inserted in the gap thus formed between D and the intersection. This rod may be called rod x.

The weaver now brings forward the yarn beam (*sutar gari*, etc., ii, Plate II) and places it with the grooved face uppermost, on the ground close to rod E¹ and parallel to it. She then inserts rods E¹ and x in the groove of this bar, and ties them to the bar at either end. The intersection between rods E¹ and x is thus lost to view. There remains therefore only one intersection in the warp between *each succes-sive thread, viz.*, that between sticks C and D¹, and this is the main intersection (*mul mor*) on either side of which the healds are subsequently formed. The intersection between A and B is, it will be remembered, between each *set of threads*, and is there-fore of no use for forming the healds.

The first woman then raises the yarn beam slightly while the second woman drives two pegs into the ground in front of it, one at each end.

These pegs are about 2 feet long, 2 inches broad and ½ inch thick, and are called *kurmura khuti* in Tezpur, *saru khuti* in Mangaldai, and *batola khuti* in Gauhati.

The second woman now goes to the other end of the warp, takes out posts A and B and replaces A by a long stout rod (*dangibari*, etc.) and post B by a long stick (*chiri*). She then opens out the threads to the full width of the intended cloth along rod A, and, holding this rod horizontally at a short distance from the ground, pulls the warp tight, the bar at the other end resting against the pegs just driven in.

The first woman now passes the reed along the warp with great care for the threads often break, and have to be at once mended. To prevent breakages as much as possible, the woman continually brushes the threads in front of the reed with a special kind of brush (instrument No. 7) to smooth them and remove all adhering foreign substances.

The moving of the reed along the warp is called *tant chalowa* in Darrang and *ras chalowa* in Barpeta.

Having thus passed the reed a couple of feet or so along the warp, the first woman returns to the yarn beam, and turns it round wrapping up the threads around it, after which she fixes it so as not to revolve by pushing a stick through one of the holes in its end, until it reaches the ground at an angle. The second operator, meanwhile, moves up towards the first as required, keeping the threads taut the whole time. Throughout this process stick D¹ is kept close in front of the wrapped up portion of the threads.

The reed is thus passed on and on along the warp, the second intersection being thrown back through it as the first had been, and the threads are from time to time wrapped up round the yarn beam.

This operation (called *tant merowa*) and the last between them take an hour in Barpeta.

When the distance between rod A (in the second woman's hands) and the yarn beam is half a yard or two feet, the rod is lowered towards the ground and fixed in position, as the bar had been, by means of two more pegs, the warp now lying horizontally and at tension between the rod and the bar.

(*Variations in the process*:—

(i) In the districts of Darrang and Kamrup it is usual to remove all the posts as soon as the warp has been laid, and to roll up the threads carefully round posts A and B. The roll is then placed on the ground, where it remains until the reed has been applied and made to pass over sticks D and E, and the yarn beam has been attached. The threads are then unrolled, and posts A and B replaced respectively by a rod and a stick. Lastly the threads are opened out along the rod at A. The rest of the process is the same.

(ii) In Mangaldai and Barpeta not only are all the posts at once removed, but they are also all at once replaced by sticks or rods, as the case may be, and the warp is opened out to its full width and stretched to its full length between the two end rods (by means of pegs) for the purpose of applying the reed. It remains in this position (with the modification noted below) till the reed has been passed along the warp as far as required, after which the pegs holding rod A are removed, the yarn beam attached at the other end and the thread rolled round it. The pegs just removed are then driven in again to support rod A in its new position.

(iii) Another slight variation should be noted in Barpeta, *viz.*, when the reed is to be applied, it is tied, not to rod E itself but to the pegs supporting it. In either case, however, this rod must be lifted up from the pegs to allow the reed to pass beyond them.

(iv) In Mangaldai marks are made on the warp threads at every yard after the reed has been passed along, and before the threads are rolled up round the heavy bar. The distances are measured by the *kathi.*

It may be here remarked that, whether the warp be stretched tight or laid in a roll on the ground while the reed is being applied, it is, when only a short length of cloth is being woven, always wrapped up round the yarn beam at one time and not in short lengths as described in the text. But the latter method is the more usual as it has been explained elsewhere that, in the case of short cloths, it is usual to weave more than one in one piece.)

The warp is now ready for the formation of the healds, two shafts of which are always used in the Assamese loom. A shaft of healds consists of two sets of running loops, all the loops of one set being attached to a rod at the top and all the loops of the other set being attached to a rod below. Each loop of one set interlocks with the corresponding loop of the other set and the two loops enclose between them a single thread of the warp. The number of loops in each set of healds is equal to the number of pairs of threads in the warp. All the upper threads of these pairs (*kani*) are held by one shaft of healds and all the lower threads by the other. The loops of the healds are called *ba*, and, in Goalpara, also *bowa.*

Before commencing to form the healds, the weaver takes every precaution to see that the main intersection is in proper order, *i.e.*, that there is actually an intersection between each warp thread and that next to it. She first pushes two thin rods (*phulakia*) across the warp, one close to stick C and the other close to stick D[1], passing them very carefully above and below alternate threads of the warp, so that those threads which run under one rod may run over the other. Unless the positions of the rod and stick on either side of the intersection correspond, the stick is taken out and reinserted in the position occupied by the rod which is then removed. The weaver next presses stick B close to rod A to make sure that none of the threads overlap. If they do so, this can be detected and rectified at once as the intersection between A and B is between sets of threads and not single threads.

Having taken these preliminary precautions, the woman sits down close to rod A, facing the warp, and pulls stick C and the reed together close up to stick B. Then, drawing stick D[1] towards her till it is at a convenient distance, she turns it up on edge, and so forms a gap between the upper and lower threads between stick D[1] and the intersection.

The woman next plants in the ground to her right a reel of the second kind containing a skein of thick brown thread (called *ba bati*) specially prepared for the healds. Tying the end of this thread to a piece of bamboo, she passes it through the gap just formed between the threads. The threads of the warp, therefore, now pass alternately above and below the brown thread. The weaver then takes up a hollow bamboo tube about 1 foot long and 1½ to 2 inches in diameter, (called *bachunga* or *batolachunga* in Assam Proper and *bahati* in Cachar). Placing a long thin bamboo rod[*] along the top of this tube, she holds them both above the warp so that the tube just touches the threads and is at right angles to them. The left-hand end of the tube is held level with the left edge of the warp, and the right hand end of the long rod about level with the right hand end of the tube. The end of the brown thread is now unfastened from the piece of bamboo and tied in a slip-knot to the rod above the tube, at a point opposite the left edge of the tube. The weaver dips her thumb and forefinger in between the first and second upper warp threads (counting from the left), picks up a loop of the brown thread and brings it to the top between the same two warp threads, the brown thread playing out from the revolving wheel as she pulls. Holding this thread loosely between the thumb and forefinger the weaver draws it up along the near side of the tube, passes it between the tube and the rod above it, and then twists it twice completely round this rod. She then lets go the thread which runs down on the far side of the tube between the same two warp threads.

Thus one loop is formed picking up the first thread of the warp. Another is then made in precisely the same way picking up the second thread, the woman dipping her finger and thumb in between the second and third threads of the warp, and so on until the tube is almost entirely covered with loops. At this point a long thin rod (*sali* or

---

* [*Vernacular names:*— *bali, basali*, or *batcla sali* (general), *sirkathi* or *sorkathi* (Goalpara), *chhibkathi* (Sibsagar), *malsi* (Habigunge) and *phulukia* (Mangaldai).]

PLATE V.

THE PROCESS OF FORMING HEALDS.

nakisali) is placed inside the hollow of the tube, projecting mainly to the left, and the loops already formed are slipped off the tube on to the rod, and the tube moved on to the right. The process is repeated till a loop has been formed round every one of the upper warp threads. The brown thread is then broken off and fastened to the rod above the tube, by being twice or thrice hitched round it. The bamboo tube and the rod inside it are then removed, and the upper set of loops of the first shaft of healds is complete.

Stick D¹, which has all this time been edgewise, is now turned flat and stick C is turned on edge. Thus a gap between the upper and the lower threads of the warp is formed between stick C (behind the reed) and the intersection. This gap is on the near side of the intersection, the former opening having been on the far side. Thus the threads which were the lower threads at the point where the first set of loops was formed are the upper threads between the intersection and stick C.

The brown thread on the *cherekhi* is again tied to the piece of bamboo and passed through the warp as before but between the reed and the intersection. A second set of loops suspended from an upper rod is formed in exactly the same way as the first, the woman dipping her finger and thumb in close to the reed and between it and the bamboo tube.

Stick C is now turned flat.

Thus the upper halves of both shafts of healds have been formed. To form the lower halves the whole warp is turned over and again fixed tight. The loops are now seen hanging from the lower threads at each point. To form the second sets of loops, the first sets must be made to hang from upper threads. This can only be done by throwing the intersection through each set of loops in succession, for those threads that are the lower threads on one side of the intersection are the upper threads on the other side. The set of loops first made hangs from the lower threads between the intersection and stick D¹. To pass the intersection through this set, the weaver pushes stick D¹ to some distance from her, and stick C and the reed together close up to the intersection. She then turns stick C on edge and thus throws the intersection away from her. This may have to be repeated once or twice owing to the set of loops last made being in front of the reed. But eventually the intersection is thrown through the set of loops first made. Thus these loops now hang from the upper threads, but the rod at the bottom to which they are connected is still, of course, entirely below the warp, and thus the loops look as if they encircled both lower and upper threads, though in reality they do not.

Stick C is kept on edge close to the reed, and there is thus an opening between the upper and lower threads between it and the intersection. The end of the brown thread on the *cherekhi* is again tied to a piece of bamboo, and passed through the set of loops hanging from upper threads, and also between the upper and lower warp threads. A third set of loops is then formed in exactly the same way as the first two. Each loop now formed picks up both the upper thread and also the loop formerly made round it, *i. e.*, the old loop and the new interlock, and hold the thread between them.

One shaft of healds is thus complete.

Stick C is now turned flat and D¹ drawn up to the intersection and then turned edgewise. The intersection is thus driven towards the woman until it eventually passes through both the complete shaft of healds and the second set of loops. These loops are now seen hanging from the upper threads between the intersection and the complete shaft of healds. Stick D¹ is kept on edge close to this complete shaft, and the fourth set of loops is formed exactly as the third had been, but interlocking with the second set. Both shafts of healds are now complete except for one detail, *viz.*, the top and bottom rods of each shaft are tied together at their ends by string, so that the strain during work may be on that string instead of on the loops and the warp itself.

In the case of the first and fourth sets of loops the intersection lies between the reed and the place where the loops are formed. In forming these sets the woman, instead of dipping her finger in between the threads at a point beyond the intersection. more usually dips it in at a point between the intersection and the reed, following the thread which she wants to pick up in the loop, and which at this point is a lower thread, past the intersection (where it becomes an upper thread) till she reaches the brown thread.

The formation of the healds is called *batola, babocha* or *babhara*, but the last term is not used in the Assam Valley.

Variations in the process: —

(i) In the districts of Darrang and Kamrup the reed is passed along the warp beyond stick C, that is, a stick O is inserted behind the reed and stick C removed. This does not affect the method of forming the healds, but it is more convenient to have stick O between the reed and the intersection when it becomes necessary to turn this stick on edge.

(ii) In Tezpur for forming the loops of healds a solid piece of wood is sometimes used instead of the hollow bamboo tube. This stick, called *baphali*, is about 8 inches long, 2 inches broad and ½ inch thick. It has a groove in which the *nakisali* can be tied.

(iii) The formation of the healds is a very lengthy process. In Barpeta it takes four or five hours to form one set of loops on a warp 4½ feet wide. When speed is an object, two women work simultaneously, first at the two upper sets of loops, and afterwards at the two lower sets. From the description of the process given above it is clear that the two upper sets can be formed simultaneously, but the two lower sets cannot. For, after reversing the warp and before forming the lower sets of loops, it is necessary to bring the sets already made to the top, which can only be done by throwing the intersection through them. But there is only one intersection available for forming the healds, and so both sets of loops cannot be brought to the top at the same time, for one set cannot be made to pass the other. (This is obvious, for, originally, the two sets of loops lie on opposite sides of the intersection, and, if one be brought past this intersection, its loops then go over the upper warp threads at that point and its rod lies under the lower warp threads. It is, also, clearly impossible for both sets of loops to be made to cross each other at the point of intersection itself).

If, therefore, the two lower sets of loops are to be formed simultaneously, a second intersection is required. The intersection between A and B is of no use as it is not between every successive thread, and so the third intersection, *viz.*, that originally between posts D and E must be brought into use. This necessitates a modification in the process described in the text, as follows :—

When the loops have all been drawn through the reed and threaded on the thin rod (E¹), a long flat stick is inserted between the upper and lower threads between the reed and this thin rod. This is an additional stick and may be called stick X. The reed is then passed on as described in the text, but only rod E¹ (and not two rods is inserted in the groove of the heavy bar. Stick X is kept at a slight distance from the bar while the threads are being wrapped up, and so the intersection between D¹ & X remains in that portion of the warp which is not wound up.

The warp having been fixed in position the two upper sets of loops are formed simultaneously. The one is formed by the first woman between stick D¹ and the main intersection. The other is formed by a second woman between stick X and the intersection now brought into use. This woman sits at the other end of the warp (the yarn beam end) facing the first woman. The reel of thread used by her is fixed to *her* right, *i.e.*, on the opposite side of the warp to the reel used by the first woman. The warp is then reversed and the main intersection thrown through the first set of loops and the second intersection through the other set of loops. Thus both these sets of loops are brought to the top, the one no wlying between the main intersection and the reed, and the other between the other intersection and stick D¹. The last two sets of loops can, therefore, be formed simultaneously at these two points. They are accordingly so formed by the two women seated as before.

NOTE.—In this case it is rod X which is left in when the warp is carried to the loom, both C and D¹ being removed. The removal of rod D¹, which is the only rod between the two intersections, causes both these intersections to vanish. and so, when weaving is commenced, there is no intersection visible in the warp. The process of weaving is not affected thereby, but the warp is, at the commencement of weaving proper, in the same condition as it would be after the first weft thread had been shot, had the healds been formed by means of a single intersection.

3rd.—Weaving proper.

The healds having been formed, the warp is ready for the loom where the weft is to be shot. Stick C, being no longer required, is now removed, and the intersection can pass freely from B to D¹. The pegs are pulled out of the ground, and rod A and stick B are replaced by two thin rods which are both inserted into the groove of the cloth-beam. The intersection between A & B is thus lost to view. Thus there remains only one stick, D¹, between the upper and lower warp threads, and only one intersection visible between these threads. This stick is required to keep the warp threads in position, while the weft is being shot, and throughout that operation it is kept close to the yarn-beam. The intersection can, therefore, pass freely from end to end of the warp.

The whole warp is now carried bodily to the loom (instrument No. 8), the cloth-beam is suspended by loops of string from the two front posts, the reed is enclosed in its frame and the yarn beam suspended by loops of string to the two rear posts, the warp meanwhile being unrolled sufficiently to allow of this.

In some cases, instead of being suspended by loops of string, the cloth-beam is fastened to the posts themselves, the ends being inserted in holes in these posts. In cases where there are two shorter posts in addition to the two front main posts, the cloth beam is placed on ledges cut at the tops of these shorter posts so as to rest between them and the mainposts.

The yarn-beam is now turned round till the warp is fairly taut, and fixed by a rod through the hole at its end. The top rods of the healds are connected with the *nachani*, the strings from the front ends of the *nachani* being tied to the rod of the front shaft, and those from the back ends to those of the back shaft. The lower rod of one shaft of healds is then tied by a string to the one treadle, and that of the other shaft to the other treadle. In some places, *e.g*, Mangaldai, the lower rod of the healds is not connected directly with the treadle, but two bars are tied on to this rod to give weight to the healds, and these bars are connected with the treadle. In this case the two rods (*dangibari*, etc.,) originally put in place of pegs A and E during the warping process and subsequently replaced by thin rods, are tied to one shaft of healds, and two similar rods to the other shaft.

The warp now lies horizontally between the two beams at a height of from one to three feet from the ground, and is ready for the weft to be shot. Before weaving is commenced, however, it is usual, with the coarser kinds of fabrics, to brush the warp repeatedly with a brush (instrument No. 7) dipped in a sizing made of rice-paste (*kachu*) and the leaves of certain plants. In Barpeta a sizing called *tahan* made of flour or boiled rice is applied while the weaving is in progress. This sizing should be washed off as soon as the cloth is woven or the fabric would be ruined by it. With finer cloths this second sizing is never done.

The weaver takes her seat in front of the cloth-beam, facing the loom. Within easy reach lies the shuttle with a full spool of thread ; a supply of more spools is kept on the ground beside her either in a cane-basket (*mahura karani*), or more usually in an earthen pot containing a little water to keep the spools damp. This pot is called *mahura kharahi* (Tezpur), *mahura thowa malei* (Gauhati), *mohura thowa* or *salai* (Goalpara), and *guti ghara* (Mangaldai). A yard stick (*kathi*) is also generally at hand for making any necessary measurements; and, hanging from the cross-rod above, is a little cane-basket containing spare lengths of threads to repair breakages, and sometimes also sample patterns for ornamentations (*phul*) in the weaving.

Thus equipped the weaver commences work. Pressing one treadle with her foot, she raises one shaft of healds and lowers the other, thus making a gap between the upper and lower threads of the warp, and throwing the intersection against the cloth-beam. Through this gap she throws the shuttle with its spool of thread, say, from left to right, holding the loose end of thread on the left of the warp. This end is never fastened or woven in, it is simply cut off when the cloth is finished. A thread has thus been shot between the upper and lower threads of the warp, and in front of the intersection. The weaver now pulls the reed towards her and drives home this thread. She then presses the other treadle, thus making a fresh gap between the warp threads, but the position of these threads has been interchanged, *i.e.*, those which were originally above are now below and *vice versâ*. There are, therefore, now two fresh intersections between them, and as the threads are kept at tension by the healds, these intersections lie at their two extremities, *viz.*, one against the first thread of the weft and one against stick C. Another thread of the weft is then shot and driven home with the reed, and the shuttle having been thrown from right to left. Thus the intersection at the weaver's end is woven in. A second pressure of the first treadle again reverses the position of the threads and brings the remaining intersection from the far end and throws it against the weft thread just shot. The position now is, therefore, exactly the same as when the weaving was commenced. Another weft is shot from left to right and the weaving is continued, the same process being repeated again and again.

When about one inch of cloth has been woven, the temple (*putal*, etc., instrument No. 1) is adjusted, the two needle-points being stuck into the two edges of the cloth. When the cloth is very wide two temples at a slight interval from one another are used at one time. The temple or temples are moved on as the weaving proceeds.

When an *ohali* of cloth has been woven, *i.e.*, when the woven cloth is so long that the weaver cannot conveniently reach the gap beyond, the pegs are removed from the beams, the cloth wound round the cloth-beam and the pegs again adjusted. The weaving then proceeds as before.

When, eventually, all the warp has been wound off the yarn-beam, and it is required to wind the cloth still further round the cloth-beam, the rod at the far end of the warp is taken out of the groove in the yarn-beam, and connected with this beam by two loops of string, one at either end. These loops are, of course, of such a length as to keep the warp at tension between the rod they support and the cloth-beam, when the cloth has been wound round it. The weaving then proceeds, until finally the distance between the healds and the rod at the end of the warp is about eight inches. The weaving must now stop, for the reed and the healds can be worked no longer. The remnant of the warp *dahi-kata* cannot be utilised; it is accordingly cut off the cloth, a length of one or two inches only being left to form a fringe (*dahi*).

The actual weaving or shooting of the weft is called *boa* or *tant boa* in Assam.

The time taken in this stage of the process has not been reported from any district, and it is very difficult to calculate the aggregate time taken in weaving a particular cloth owing to the way in which the work is carried on. In Golaghat it is said to be the practice to finish the laying of the warp in one day, to form the healds the next day and to spend the third day in arranging the warp in the loom; after which the weaving proceeds very slowly in the weaver's leisure hours, the work often being left untouched for days together. It is, however, calculated that a *gamcha* would take 2 days to finish, a *churia* five yards long, 7 to 12 days, and a *khania, cheleng* or *pit kapor* 10 to 15 days. But these figures are mere approximations, as in another part of the report the time taken to weave a *churia* 5 yards long is stated as five days, and in a third place as a week or so if the weaver be engaged on nothing but this work.

In the Darrang district the weaving of an ordinary cloth (a rather vague expression) is said to take from 2 to 7 days when imported thread is used, and from 5 to 20 days when raw cotton is used. The latter estimate includes of course the time taken in spinning. The manufacture of a *dhuti* from raw cotton is said to take eight days.

In Nowgong the following estimates are given for the time taken in weaving different cloths; the estimate does not include the time taken in spinning the thread:—

A *borkapor* containing 1¼ seer of thread takes 12 days; in another part of the report this is given as eight days.

A *khania* containing half seer of thread takes 15 days.

A *churia*, containing 6 chattacks of thread, takes four days; and

A *cheleng*, with ordinary decorations, containing 6 chattacks of thread, takes six days.

The corresponding estimate in Barpeta is as follows :—

Borkapor	from raw cotton (2 seers)	.	.	.	.	2 months.
	„ thread (1 seer)	.	.	.	.	25 days.
Khania	„ raw cotton (2 seers)	.	.	.	.	25 „
	„ thread (1 seer)	.	.	.	.	12 „
Churia	„ raw cotton (3 seers)	.	.	.	.	1 month.
	„ thread (½ seer)	.	.	.	.	20 days.
Gamcha	„ raw cotton (¼ seer)	.	.	.	.	6 „
	„ thread (1/16 seer)	.	.	.	.	3 „

There is evidently a mistake in the figures for the *churia*.

The enormous difference in the figures from the different places shows that the estimates are of little value.

Concerning the time taken in weaving, there is a curious superstition among the Assamese which is thus described by the Sub-Deputy Collector of Golaghat :—" When a woman conceives without menstruation and gives birth to a child, the child is called *gora*, and the superstition is that such a child would be struck by a thunder-bolt and die unless a cloth woven in the course of a single day be given it to wear immediately after birth. Accordingly, when such a child is born, its mother will call in seven or eight women of the neighbourhood to help her and will commence and finish in a single day a little sheet of cloth to be given to the child to protect it from a premature and unnatural death. Except under these peculiar circumstances no woman would ever try to finish a cloth in a single day." I myself heard a reference made to this superstition while watching the process of weaving near Golaghat.

There are a few points connected with the Assamese process of weaving that call for further explanation.

The Selvage.

The selvage, an invariable accompaniment of Assamese cloths, is a line or stripe of extra thickness running along each edge of the cloth. Its primary object is to withstand the drag of the weft as this is shot through the warp. It does not, therefore, require to be so wide or strong as in machine-made fabrics. It is formed entirely in the warp in one of two ways. The more usual way is to utilise the ordinary warp threads, but to weave one, two or three of these at either edge double (or even treble) instead of single. In this case the process of warping is modified as follows: First, in the actual laying of the warp, several additional threads have to be laid round the pegs in excess of those required for the body of the cloth. Next, in applying the reed, two loops (or three as the case may be) are drawn together through the interstices at either extremity of the marked off portion of the reed. Lastly, the first and last few loops of both shafts of healds are made to enclose two (or three) warp threads instead of one. Thus if the selvage consists of three double warp threads at each edge, six additional layers of thread must be put round the posts; two loops must be drawn together through each of the first and last three interstices in the reed; and, in the forming of the healds, the brown thread must be drawn up first between the second and third threads, next between the fourth and fifth, then between the 6th and 7th, and subsequently between each successive thread until the other selvage is reached, when the order must be similar to that of the commencement.

The second method of forming the selvage is to use a single thread of extra thickness instead of weaving the ordinary thread double or treble. This must be provided for when the warp is laid.

The uses of the Intersections.

The warp, when laid, contains three intersections. Of these the first is between successive *sets of threads*, the number of threads in a set being equal to the number of reels employed in warping; and the other two are between successive *threads*. The first intersection is of use chiefly when the warp is being laid and the purpose it serves is to keep the threads in position till the second and third intersections have been made. This intersection prevents the threads of one set from mixing up with those of another set, and so all the threads retain their original relative positions with fair accuracy, and any displacement can be readily detected and rectified. When the number of threads in each set is very large, as is often the case in Assam, it is necessary, before the healds are made, to test the accuracy with which the main intersection has been made, and accordingly this intersection is brought into use again at that stage. The second and third intersections, *viz.*, those between each successive thread, are required only for the formation of the healds. When both sets of loops on each side are formed together, both these intersections are utilised. When the sets of loops are formed independently, only one of these two intersections is required. But as the warp forms an endless band, it is impossible to form one intersection of this nature without forming two, unless either the thread be cut or else each pair of threads be separately removed from the end post, reversed and then put back, which would be a very long process. Hence two such intersections are invariably formed. It has been shown how the second intersection is put out of sight when not required for use. It will be explained in the Goalpara process how the first is similarly got rid of at a very early stage in the process.

The making of the thread for the healds.

The thread used for the healds requires to be stout and strong, and it is desirable also, that it should be of a different colour from the warp threads to prevent mistakes occurring when the healds are being formed. This thread is made as follows:—

Three (or more) skeins or balls of ordinary thread are taken and the thread from each wound simultaneously round the upper part of an instrument called *katara* which is simply a cross made of bamboo, the body being about 6 feet long and the arms 1 foot each. This instrument is then struck upright in the ground and the ends of all the threads are tied together on the spindle of a spinning whorl which has its ends shaped like a crochet needle. This whorl is then rolled smartly along the thigh and shot into

x

space. It comes into position hanging by the threads from the cross-bar of the cross, and continues revolving for a very long time. The threads supporting it are thus twisted together, and, when this twisting has gone on sufficiently, the operator takes hold of the whorl and rolls up the twisted portion of the threads around the spindle, fastening it again round the crochet-needle-end. She then unwinds another length of thread from the upper portion of the cross and once more shoots the whorl from off her thigh as she did before. This process is repeated till the required length of twist-ed string has been made, when the ends of the threads are knotted together.

The string so formed is then steeped for a long time in the juice of the plum, supari or other tree. This steeping serves the double purpose of dyeing the string and gumming the strands together so that they may not easily get untwisted.

In Goalpara the cross-like instrument is not used. The threads are wound into balls and held up together in one hand as high as the arm can reach, the other hand being used for shooting the whorl. The balls of thread lie on the ground throughout the process.

The whorl is simply a round disc of wood (2 inches in diameter and ¼ inch in thickness) or of tortoiseshell, with a hole at the centre through which the spindle is so fixed as to project 10 or 11 inches on one side and only about 1 inch on the other. This instrument is called *takura* in Barpeta and *tákura* in Goalpara.

The motion of this instrument while revolving is very peculiar, the disc describing a comparatively large circle, while the top of the spindle describes a comparatively small one. This motion and the rapidity with which it is performed give rise to an expression very common in Goalpara, viz., *Takurar nichina nache* (She dances like a a spinning whorl), which is perhaps the most complimentary remark that can be made of a dancing girl. The simile describes very accurately one of those strange wriggling motions performed in an Indian dance, considered so graceful in the East yet appearing so graceless to the uninitiated European.

Size of cloths woven and system of measurement employed.

The length of the cloth to be woven is measured off on the ground, and its width upon the reed. The warping posts are nearly always set up in the court yard of a house and so the length of the cloth woven in one piece seldom, if ever, exceeds 10 yards. The width is regulated by the size of the reed, and so by that of the loom, and rarely exceeds 2¼ yards. But a single length of cloth is often cut up into several pieces to form several cloths, and in the same way two narrow pieces of cloth are often sewn together to form a single cloth of greater width. In Tezpur as many as 5 cloths may be woven in one piece. This does not affect the process of weaving, but as each cloth must have its fringe, it is necessary to leave a short length of warp unwoven between each cloth, which, when cut through in the middle, will form a fringe on one end of both cloths. These additional lengths of warp must be allowed for when the warping pegs are fixed, and the places where the warp is to remain unwoven must be marked as soon as the reed has been applied.

The system of measurement adopted by the Assamese is very interesting. They use two tables, the one purely numerical and the other a table of weights and measures.

The first table may be stated as follows :—

One pair of warp threads	=	1 *kani*.
2 to 12 *kani*	=	1 *karhani*.
20 *karhani*	=	1 *biha* or *siya*.

A pair of warp threads, one upper and one lower, is called a *kani*. As many *kanis* as there are reels used in warping form one *karhani* and 20 such *karhanis* form a *biha* (Golaghat) or *siya* (Goalpara). The word *biha* means in Assamese a score and *siya* a hundred. The application of these two terms is obvious, but not so that of the word *kani* which means an egg.

This set of measures is used to facilitate the calculation of how many times the threads must be laid round the posts to form the warp. Thus by walking once up and down the line of posts the weaver lays one *karhani* of threads, by walking 20 times she lays one *biha* or *siya*. The total width of the warp is generally a whole number of *biha* or *siya*. Thus in Golaghat two *biha* are generally taken for a *gamcha* and 6, 8 or 10 *biha* for other cloths. It has been mentioned in the description of the reed that the number of teeth in that instrument is marked off in hundreds, this should be modified however. In Goalpara the number of reels most usually employed being 5, a *siya* is generally equal to a hundred pairs of threads, and so the markings of the reed are at intervals of exactly one hundred teeth, but in Upper Assam a *biha* usually contains 120 threads, the number of reels employed being 6, and so the markings on the reed are ordinarily at intervals of 120 teeth.

It has already been stated that the length of the cloth is measured off in yards; but this is not the case with the width, which is usually marked upon the reed in *biha* or *siya*. In other words, the length is strictly measured, whereas the width is rather counted.

It will be seen that this table of measurements is purely numerical and does not in any way show the total quantity of thread required, as the amount of the thread in each *biha* or *siya* varies directly with the length of the warp. Two cloths of similar texture and of equal width will contain the same number of *biha* or *siya*, whether their length be equal or unequal.

To determine the quantity of thread required for any cloth a second set of measurements is used, which may be stated, in tabular form, as follows:—

Homespun thread.

8 *Sutalahi* = 1 *neoha*—about 2 tolas.
1 to 8 *neoha* = 1 *ugha.*
2 to 10 *ugha* = quantity of thread required for the warp.

Ready-made thread (*Tezpur*).

⅓rd chattack = 1 *lecha.*
3 to 5 *lecha* = 1 *ugha.*
6 to 10 *uga* = quantity of thread required for the warp.

The thread composing any cloth consists of two entirely distinct parts, *viz.*, that for the warp and that for the weft. The former is equal to the latter and is, therefore, half the total amount required for the cloth.

When homespun thread is used the unit in this set of measurements is the *sutalahi*, *i.e.*, the amount of thread spun at one time on the spindle of the spinning-wheel. In Barpeta three of these *sutalahi* make a skein or *neoha*; and three skeins or, in the case of a very short cloth, only one skein forms an *ugha*, *i.e.*, the amount of thread wound on to each reel of the third kind before warping is commenced. The number of such reels used depends on the width of the cloth. Thus for a very narrow cloth two *ugha* suffice, whereas a very wide one may require 10 or even 12. In Barpeta the number most usually employed is 5 or 6, in Upper Assam 6 or 8; in Goalpara 5; in Tezpur it appears to be never less than 6 nor more than 10.

The following measurements are given in Barpeta:—A *gamcha* or napkin requires 4 skeins of thread, 2 for the warp and 2 for the weft. For the warp two *ugha* are used, each equal to one skein. A *barkapor* (large wrapper) requires 60 skeins; for the weft 30 skeins; and for the warp 10 *ugha*, each equal to 3 skeins.

The above measurements are very rough owing to the unit being a variable quantity, but this is no serious defect as there generally remains some unused thread on the reels after warping is complete. The essential thing is to have sufficient thread on each reel, as that left over can be utilised again.

When ready-made thread is used, the unit of measurement is the skein (*lecha or neoha*).

These two tables of measurement are intimately connected with one another, and are both used together. The first is purely numerical, but by means of it the exact measure of the cloth is represented. The second, while showing the quantity of thread required, is much less accurate and can show that quantity at best but roughly.

The Goalpara process of weaving.

The Goalpara process resembles the Assamese process, but it has several very important points of difference. It will be sufficient here to note what those points are.

Several minor variations peculiar to Goalpara have already been mentioned in the description of the Assamese process. The main peculiarity, however, in the Goalpara process consists in the method of laying the warp. For laying the warp, the number of reels used is more often odd than even, the usual number being five. These reels (say 5) are first placed in a line in the ground and then the 5 posts (similar to those used in Upper Assam) are planted at right angles to them. The ends of the threads from each reel being passed through the *karhani*, two ends are twisted together, then the other three ends, and lastly the double and triple twisted ends are themselves twisted together.

The *karhani* is then brought forward and the ends of the thread looped over post A, so that two fall on one side and three on the other. The threads are then laid round the posts, not in a figure of eight (*i.e.*, two intersecting loops) as in the Assamese process, but in three loops, the intersections being between posts A and B and posts B and C. Thus there are at the outset two intersections between each set of threads instead of only one. Two intersections are then made between each successive thread at the post D and the threads pressed down over this post as in the Assamese process. There are now altogether four intersections, one between each post and that next to it. The warp having been laid to the full width and allowance made for the selvages, the threads are broken off and fastened round post A as they were at the outset with this exception that the double and triple twisted ends are not themselves twisted together, and the extra thread now passes on the opposite side of the post to that which had the extra thread at the beginning.

The warp having been laid, posts C, D and E are taken out of the ground and, of these, C and D are replaced by long sticks, and these sticks and post E with the threads round them are laid flat on the ground.

The weaver then sits down by post E, and takes up the reed, which she holds horizontally between her left arm and her side. She then slips a number of threads off the right hand end of post E, arranges them on the first finger of her left hand, and works them about till the nearest intersection to this end comes close against the back of her forefinger. The threads are thus wrapped tightly round this finger and are then arranged in proper order and spread out to the width required. The weaver then holds her finger with the threads on it behind the reed at the end of the part marked off, and with her right hand inserts a sharp and long wooden needle through the first interval in the reed, and with it picks the first loop of thread off her forefinger and draws it through the reed. She then draws the second loop through the second interval, and so on till all the loops have been picked off her finger and drawn through the reed. These loops, which are now threaded on the bamboo needle, are next slipped off this needle on to a thin round rod. Another lot of threads is then taken off post E and treated like the first, and so on until all the warp-threads have been brought through the reed and arranged on the thin rod behind it.

The reed is then pushed slightly forward and a stick (D¹) inserted between the threads, between it and the intersection which is now behind the reed. The stick at D is now removed and the reed is passed on beyond the next intersection. Another stick X is then inserted between the intersection and the reed.

The yarn beam is now brought forward, rod E inserted in the groove but not fastened, and the threads rolled up round the beam, the intersection between D¹ and E being rolled up with the warp-threads and lost to sight.

Posts A and B are now taken out of the ground and A replaced by a long rod. B is removed, and so the intersections on each side of it go out. These intersections are those between each set of threads.

There is, therefore, at this stage only one intersection visible in the warp, *viz.*, that between sticks D¹ and X. It is on either side of this that the healds are formed.

The beam and the rod at A having been fixed horizontally by means of pegs, and the warp having been stretched tight between them, the weaver sits at post A facing the warp, and forms the first set of loops for the healds between stick X and the intersection. This set of loops having been formed, stick D¹ is brought up against the intersection and turned on edge, so as to throw the intersection through the set of loops just formed. The threads picked up by this set of loops are, in this new position, the bottom threads.

Another long stick (Y) is now inserted between this set of loops and the intersection; and the second set of loops is made between this stick (Y) and the intersection. The first two sets of loops have thus been formed on opposite sides of the intersection, for the first was made on the side nearest the weaver and the second on the side farthest from her. They are now, however, on the same side and the second set is nearer to the weaver than the first set. The first set in its present position encircles lower threads, and the second set upper threads.

The warp is now reversed and again fixed in position. The first set of loops now hangs from upper threads and the second set from lower threads.

The third set of loops is next formed to interlock with the first set. Stick X is then brought up against the intersection and turned on edge, and so the intersection is thrown through the second set of loops, which is thus made to hang from upper threads. The fourth set of loops is then made to interlock with the second set, *i.e.*, between rod X and the intersection.

Sticks X and Y are then removed and the intersection can pass freely from C to D^1. It is accordingly brought past the reed and close up to C. A thin rod (C^1) is then inserted between the intersection and the reed, and stick C removed. Rod C^1 is now drawn close up to rod A and both are inserted in the groove of the cloth beam. The warp is now ready for the loom and is carried there and fixed in position. Rod D^1 remains in its place between the warp threads while the weft is being shot. When weaving is commenced, no intersection at all is visible in the warp, that between D^1 and B having been rolled up with the threads round the yarn-beam at one end of the warp, and that between A and C^1 having been put into the groove of the cloth-beam at the other end. The weaving commences from this latter end.

The way in which the loops for the healds are formed in Goalpara differs slightly from that in Upper Assam. A loop of brown thread having been brought above the warp (as in Assam) the thread is drawn up the inside of the tube; this portion is then held firmly against the tube with the left thumb, while the right hand portion is passed between the tube and the rod above it, twisted once completely round that rod, and then once completely round the tube in the opposite direction. The loose loop of brown thread is then thrown carelessly on the top of the tube. The thread thus forms a figure of eight round the tube and the rod, and when the thread is pulled up between the next pair of warp-threads another loop is formed around the tube before the second figure of eight is begun. It is this other loop that picks up the threads of the warp, the bottom loop of the figure of eight does not pick up any warp-thread. It will thus be seen that by this process two loops are formed round the tube for every one loop round the upper rod, exactly the reverse of the Assamese process, in which two loops are formed round the rod for every loop round the tube.

A variation of the Goalpara process is that the warp is often fixed to the loom-posts before the healds are made, and the healds are made when the warp is on the loom instead of when it is stretched close to the ground.

It will be seen that, in the Goalpara process, only one intersection is used for forming the healds. It is therefore impossible to form the first two sets of loops and also the second two sets simultaneously. But owing to the positions of these sets when being formed, it is the third and fourth sets which can be formed simultaneously and the first and second which cannot.

The Surma Valley process of weaving.

In the Surma Valley weaving by the ordinary loom is practised by two classes of professional weavers. The processes employed by these two classes differ slightly from one another, and both differ considerably from that followed in Assam Proper.

The Jugi loom and the weaving processes employed by the Jugis in Cachar appear to be very similar to, if not identical with, those of Assam, but the description received from Cachar both of the loom and of the processes used is very brief, and it is impossible from it to detect any points of difference. It is, however, clear that the processes employed are those of Assam rather than those of Bengal.

The total cost of the loom and other instruments is said not to exceed ₨5 even if bought.

The following is a short but concise description of weaving as practised by the Jugis in South Sylhet. It is almost word for word as received from the Sub-divisional Officer.

When the forepart of the spindle of the spinning wheel is full, the threads are transferred by twisting them round an instrument called *nathu*. (This has been described along with the instruments used in the Assam Valley). The rod having been taken out of the handle of the spinning wheel, the end of the *nathu* is inserted into the hole vacated and is turned by the hand so that all the threads from the spindle come round it. The threads are then taken off the reel and kept in rolls. Thus many rolls are formed and made ready for weaving (the process is not described).

Two posts (*khuti*) are driven into the ground the distance between them being equal to the length of the cloth to be woven. Between these posts and at intervals of about half a yard or two feet, strong split bamboos (*har*) are posted, and a roll of thread as mentioned above is again put on the reel (*nathu*). The operator takes the reel in her hand and walks from one post to the other laying the threads alternately outside and inside each successive split bamboo. The process is repeated until the threads attain the width required for the cloth.

This is the first day's work. The second day is spent by the weaver in a process called *fai, i.e.*, in examining the warp to see if it has been properly laid, and correcting any errors that may have occurred.

On the third day the warp is sized to strengthen it, dried and cleaned with a brush made of the roots of sugar cane tied to a bamboo handle. The sizing used is a gummy liquid prepared by steeping unboiled rice in water for some time and then reducing it to a powder and boiling it.

On the fourth day each thread of the warp is separately passed through the reed and the healds are formed. The threads are passed through the reed by means of a bamboo needle finely pointed at one end and having an eye at the other. " A piece of nut tree split and flat " called a *kalfat* is used for forming the healds.

The warp is thus made ready for the loom, and, in the meantime, the spools are formed, the thread being wound by hand.

" Thus," writes the Sub-divisional Officer, " on the fifth day a cloth is ready for weaving. I had one weaver weave his cloth in my presence and found him to weave 3 cubits of cloth, two cubits wide in six hours : the work including all the various arrangements of the warp in the loom (*taighar*) and actual weaving. This cloth will fetch only two annas."

The sizing is thus described :—" Unboiled rice is kept in water for some time, then powdered and boiled, and thus a gummy substance is prepared with which the warp is profusely sprinkled."

The loom appears to be of much the same nature as that in Assam, the warp being supported at one end (that nearest the weaver) by a round beam (*narad*) of polished wood, on which the cloth is wound as it is woven, this beam is mounted on two posts. The other end of the warp is supported by a piece of flat bamboo (*kharki*) tied to two posts. The height of the warp from the ground is not stated, but there is, beneath it, a hole in the ground about a cubit deep, and in this hole the weaver stretches his feet as he is weaving.

The loom and other instruments are all home-made.

The description of the Tantis' weaving received from Habigunge is as follows :— The thread is steeped in water and while still wet is wound on a *natai* (a reel of the first kind). On this it is allowed to dry and then the skein is taken off the reel and put in a starch made out of *khai*, a preparation of unhusked rice fried. The skein is next taken out of the starch and wound on to a large reel of the same nature as the first, and there allowed to dry. When thoroughly dry the thread is ready for laying the warp.

The warp is laid as in South Sylhet and then the pegs are all taken out of the ground, and the warp rolled up round them. The loops at one end of the warp are then cut and " each thread is made to pass through the threads of the *ba*, and then through each tooth of the comb " (reed) " and each end of thread is tied to a small rod which is fitted into a beam " (the cloth-beam). The other end of the warp is also cut and each thread tied similarly to another rod which is fitted into another beam (the yarn-beam). The posts are then replaced by flat sticks, and the whole warp wrapped round the yarn-beam, only 4 or 5 feet being left between the beams.

The weaver then sits down opposite the cloth-beam which is rather more than a foot above the ground, and, stretching his legs in a hole in the ground, about a foot deep, under the loom, he presses one treadle with his right foot and causes a shed in the warp. He then throws the shuttle through the shed from right to left and presses the thread home with the reed. He then presses the other treadle with his left foot, and throws the shuttle through the shed from left to right, and so on.

The sizing is thus described : " The starch is put on the thread by a brush to make the thread stronger before it is passed through the loom." This is not very clear.

When attaching the warp to the loom two men are required " for passing the thread through the reed and the *bas* " and four men to twist the warp round the beam.

The arrangement on the loom differs considerably from that in Assam. The cloth beam is supported on two posts called *biswakarma*, about a foot long, and 7 or 8 feet apart. It has holes at both ends to hold the rods that fix it. It is not clear whether the short posts on which it rests are two of the main loom posts or additional to them. The yarn-beam (also called *narad*) is hung up with ropes. The reed is suspended from poles above, it is not stated how many such poles there are, and no mention is made of any batten. The healds are connected with the treadles as in Assam, but there is no mention of their being supported from above. Further reference will be made to the healds hereafter.

In a warp 50 cubits long 25 bamboo sticks called *juya* are used by the Tantis. How many of these lie between the beams in the loom is not stated. In the Jugi process there are, at the time of weaving, between the two sets of warp threads, three rods of nutwood called *guli* and eight bamboo sticks called *chior*, like the *juya* of the Tantis.

The ends of the rods are tied with ropes to the poles that support the reed. In the Assamese process there are no such rods and only one stick. The necessity and use of all these rods and sticks is not clear, as the length of warp between the beams is only five feet.

The Jugi process in Habigunge differs from that of the Tantis in the fact that there is no yarn-beam, that end of the warp being tied to a rod which is in turn tied to a big piece of bamboo or wood. The healds in the Jugi loom, too, consist of only one *ba*, the working of which is not explained.

The time taken by the Tantis in preparing 40 yards of fine cloth is three months.

Of the instruments used by the Jugis, the *narad* and reed are bought from carpenters, the price of the former being R1 to R1-4, and of the latter R3-8 to R5; the shuttle is made by carpenters and blacksmiths and sold for from 4 to 8 annas; the brush is bought from people who live close to the hills and costs R1-8 to R1-12.

Of the Tantis' instruments the *narad* costs R2 to R2-8, but lasts twice as long as that of the Jugis, the comb R1-8 to R2 and the shuttle 8 annas to 12 annas. The other instruments are all home-made.

The chief differences between either the Tanti or Jugi process and that employed in Assam are as follows:—In the first place only one kind of reel appears to be used, instead of three, that reel does not revolve on its central rod. There are, however, two sizes of this reel. Secondly, the *karhani* is not used at all, but the reel is substituted for it. Thus the threads for the warp are laid round the posts, not in sets, but singly: and all the intersections are made as the threads are laid down. The number of posts used, too, is not fixed as in Assam, but varies with the length of the warp, the inside posts being at regular intervals of about a cubit in South Sylhet and about a yard in Habigunge. Thirdly, the method of applying of the reed is quite different from that used in Assam; here it is applied from the cloth-beam and not the yarn-beam end; and fourthly, there are several peculiarities in the arrangement of the warp and its accompaniments on the loom.

Many of these differences are due to the fact that in Assam only comparatively short cloths are woven in one piece, whereas in the Surma Valley long pieces are woven.

As regards the healds, the reports received from Habigunge and South Sylhet are both exceedingly vague, and so it is impossible to say whether they are similar to those used in Assam and formed in a similar way or not. In Habigunge they are thus described: "The Tantis use two *ba* instead of one as the Jugis do, one above and the other under the loom. The *ba* is made of strong thread doubled and tied to a small round rod made of split bamboo and alternate threads of the warp are passed through them, a similar one is placed under and in the same way. These two rods (called *malsi*) are tied to two pieces of bamboo with ropes. When one of the bamboos is pressed by the foot the one row of alternate threads goes down, while the other row (of alternate threads) comes up, thus making a gap for the shuttle to pass between." But from the description of the way in which the warp is prepared it would appear as if the healds were formed first and afterwards the warp threads inserted through them; for to quote the words of the report:—"Each thread is made to pass through the threads of the *ba* and then through each tooth of the comb," *i. e.*, the reed. It would be almost impossible to form the healds as they are formed in Assam unless the reed had been first applied.

The report from South Sylhet is still more difficult to understand. The heald (*ba*) is here described as "an instrument made of bamboo needles placed so close to one another as would admit one thread only." I wrote for a specimen of this instrument and an explanation of its use. The instrument was not procurable in the market, but the following further information respecting it was sent to me: "The warp-threads are entered into the *ba* outside the loom. Then two pieces of split nut trees (both together are called *kalfat*) are placed widthwise above the warp at a distance of about half a cubit from each other. Two of the four strong threads are twisted in opposite directions round one of the split nut tree pieces whose function it is to attach the alternate warp to it in such a way that if this piece is raised up the alternate warps will rise along with it. In the same way the remaining warps are attached to the other piece. The twistings of the strong threads are loose so that the nut tree pieces can be moved forward at pleasure." The arrangement in the loom has not been explained, but the above description would imply that the healds are worked not by treadles from below, but by some other method from above.

It would appear that in South Sylhet two instruments of a similar nature and both answering the description of the reed are employed in weaving. The one is called *lachh* and is described as "a kind of comb made of strong and small bamboo slices, arranged at such a distance as would admit only one thread." The other, called *atiyar* "is an instrument made of two flat pieces of wood, about 3 cubits long, and joined by very small bamboo needles so close to one another that the space between two needles is such as would admit only one thread. It is pendant by means of ropes with the beam of the house or anything over it. Its function is to keep the woofs as close to each other as possible in the course of weaving by means of the shuttle." The Sub Deputy Collector thus distinguishes between these two instruments. "The *atiyar* and *lachh*, though they resemble each other greatly in form, have quite different uses. The *lachh* is the same as the *ras*. It is used both outside and inside the loom, whereas the *atiyar* is used only inside the loom. The business of the *lachh* is to keep the warp threads straight and prevent them from coming in contact with one another, whereas the business of the *atiyar* is to keep the woof threads as close as possible when the texture is in the course of being woven." In Assam the reed performs both the functions here described, and so it is probable that in South Sylhet, also, only one instrument is used instead of two, especially as no mention is made of a second instrument in the description of the preparation of the warp. Possibly the *atiyar* may be the batten or case to hold the reed. In any case the three terms *ba*, *lachh* and *atiyar* appear to have been confounded and their meanings misunderstood.

The description of the Surma Valley processes of weaving given above is incomplete, but this has been unavoidable owing to the brevity of the descriptions received. I have had no opportunity of seeing the processes gone through, nor even of examining any of the instruments, as these were not procurable in time. The methods deserve a more complete examination as they differ widely from those of Assam and, at the same time, do not appear to be identical with those of Bengal.

A full and interesting account of Bengal weaving has been given by Mr. Taylor in his "Descriptive and Historical Account of the Cotton Manufactures of Dacca in Bengal," published in 1851. It is, however, too lengthy to reproduce here. A comparison between it and the various processes employed in Assam would be most interesting and instructive. It will be sufficient here to notice the chief points of difference. In the first place, the thread is received from the spinster wound on small pieces of reed, or made up into skeins. In this state it is steeped in water before being reeled. If the thread be on a reed when received, a piece of stick is inserted through the hollow of the reed and fixed horizontally in the cleft end of a bamboo held upright by the toes, while the reel is made to revolve with its end in a smooth cocoanut shell on the ground. When the thread is received in skeins it is put round a small wheel made of fine bamboo splints and thread. This is mounted on a stick round which it can revolve and the thread wound off it as before.

The thread is then divided into two parts, one for the warp and one for the weft. The warp-thread is steeped for three days in water which is changed twice daily. On the fourth day it is rinsed and put on a small wheel which is mounted on a stick; it is then reeled again into skeins of proper size. These skeins are tightly squeezed between two sticks and then left on the sticks to dry in the sun. When dry they are untwisted and put into water mixed with fine charcoal powder, lamp black or soot scraped from the surface of an earth cooking vessel. They are kept in this mixture for two days, then rinsed in clear water, wrung out and hung on sticks in the shade to dry. Each skein is again reeled and once more steeped in water for the night. Next day it is taken out, opened up and spread on a flat board and there smoothed with the hand and then rubbed over with a paste or size made of rice from which the husk has been removed by heated sand and a small quantity of fine lime mixed with water. After sizing the skeins are wound on large reels and exposed to the sun to dry. The thread is again reeled and sorted preparatory to warping. It is generally divided into three shades of thickness, *viz.*, the finest for the right hand side, the next finest for the left hand side, and the coarsest for the centre of the warp.

The yarn for the weft is not prepared till two days previous to its being required for use. Enough for one day's work is steeped for 24 hours in water, then rinsed and wound on large reels. It is then lightly sized with the same sizing as is used for the warp; after which it is transferred from small reels to large ones and put in the shade to dry. The yarn for the weft is prepared daily until the cloth is finished.

For laying the warp two parallel rows of rods are used, each having a post at either end. The rows are about 4 feet apart and equal in length (approximately) to half the length of the cloth. The rods between the end posts in each row are situated in pairs, the two rods of each pair being close together. The weaver holds a small revolving reel of warp thread in each hand, passes the ends, which are apparently joined together, over one of the end posts, and then walks along between the two rows laying the threads about the rods. He then turns round, carrying the threads round the posts at this end, and walks back laying the threads, in a similar way, along the second row till he reaches the other post at the end from which he started. He then turns round and retraces his steps, laying the threads in a similar way backwards along the second row of posts, round the end posts and back along the first row to the post he started from, and so on till the warp has attained the required width. At the bottom end of the handle of the reel is a glass ring through which the threads run off the reel.

To apply the reed, the warp is rolled in a bundle and suspended from the roof with one end hanging down to within a foot or two of the ground. The reed is suspended by two cords from the bundle and rods, so that it hangs slightly above the loose end of the warp with its sides parallel to the roll above. Two workmen sit down, one on each side of the warp. The first cuts a portion of the loops at the lower end of the warp and passes an iron wire or sley hook through the first division of the reed. The second workman twists the two outermost threads on the end of this hook and the first then draws them with the hook through the reed. The other pairs of threads are similarly drawn through successive divisions of the reed. The ends are knotted together in bundles of five or six on a small bamboo rod passed through the loops so formed.

It may be mentioned here that the finest reed used in Dacca contains 70 dents to the inch, over four times as many as the ordinary reed in Assam.

The reed having been applied, the warp is wrapped round it and unrolled from the other end; in this end is now inserted a thin rod which is put in the groove of the yarn-beam and there fastened with string. The beam is then hung in two loops of string attached to two posts (not the loom posts). The outer warp threads are then opened out to the width of the cloth, and the threads between them arranged and brushed with the frayed and softened end of a small piece of cane to make them smooth and parallel. A portion of the length having been thus treated, it is carefully rolled up round the yarn-beam and the process repeated till the whole is ready.

A portion of the warp is again unfolded and fixed tight as in the loom. The healds are then formed as in Assam, except that an oval piece of wood, about 8 inches long, is used in place of a bamboo tube and the thread for the healds is brought up round the oval piece of wood and passed once round the top rod, so that neither loop of the figure of eight is double. The canes on which the loops are crossed are fastened by string to four small bamboo rods, the two upper ones being attached, when placed in the loom, by strings to the upper bar; and the two lower ones to the treadles.

The warp is then attached to the loom as in the Assamese process, but great care is taken in the adjustment of the distances between the rings through which the strings of the reed pass, as these distances determine the range of motion of the slay, and this range regulates the force applied to the weft in weaving. The proper adjustment of these distances is considered by the weavers as one of the nicest operations connected with the loom. The treadles of the healds are contained in a pit beneath the loom, as in the Surma Valley and in some parts of Assam. The shuttle has spear-shaped iron points. The temple is formed of two rods each armed at one end with a brass hook or pin which is inserted in the edge of the cloth.

In weaving proper the weaver uses his left foot only to work the treadles, keeping his right foot bent under him. He sits on a mat or board placed on the ground. The Dacca weaver being endowered with a fine sensibility of touch and a nice perception of weight, possesses unrivalled skill in throwing the shuttle and driving home the weft with the reed. To lessen friction on the warp threads the shuttle, reed and slay are all oiled, and, to keep the threads moist, they are from time to time smeared with mustard oil, the brush used for this purpose being made of a tuft of fibres of the *nul* plant (*Arundo karka*). Each length of woven cloth is sprinkled with lime water to preserve it from insects before being rolled round the cloth-beam. The weavers are very careful in selecting a time of day for weaving, when the moisture of the atmosphere is most favourable for the work. The most suitable time of year is from the middle of May to the middle of August. Midday is too hot and dry for good weaving. In

I

very hot and dry weather shallow vessels of water are placed under the warp, so that the evaporation from the water may keep the threads moist. The rapidity and quality of the work vary greatly with different individuals.

It will be seen that the instruments and methods employed in Dacca are even cruder than those of Assam. There is not the same variety of reels, the *karhani* is not used. The threads are laid round the posts in pairs only instead of in sets. The method of applying the reed appears more primitive and the healds are more simple, each double loop being single in both its parts. It will be noticed that the reed is applied to the warp from the end subsequently attached to the cloth-beam and not from the yarn-beam end. The same is the case among the Tantis in Habigunge. It is, therefore, not passed along the warp before weaving as in Assam. The same object is attained by the careful arrangement and brushing of the warp from the other end. The temple used is of the same nature as that employed in Assam for the coarser kinds of cloth.

In spite of all this, there is no comparison in quality and fineness of texture between the outturn of the Assam looms and those of Dacca. The reason of this is partly that the reed used in Dacca is a much finer instrument than any found in Assam, but more especially that far greater attention is paid to details by the. Dacca weavers and much more labour and care are devoted to the work. This is most marked at every stage. The prepration of the threads both for the warp and for the weft is much more thorough in Dacca than in Assam, the sorting of the warp threads is quite unknown in Assam, and the steeping and sizing is there done by a much more rough and ready process. The threads in the warp are far more carefully arranged and smoothed in Dacca, and more attention is paid to the adjustment of the strings of the reed and to the manipulation of the reed and shuttle. The warp when in the loom is more carefully preserved and great pains are taken to keep it at the required moisture. Lastly, the cloth when woven is sprinkled with lime water to preserve it from insects. No wonder, then, that the cloths produced in Dacca far excel those of Assam in quality and workmanship. To weave a cloth as the Dacca people weave it involves an enormous amount of labour and the most careful application; it is the work of a professional class of artizans, the only means they have of earning a livelihood. The cloths are sold; the quality of the work therefore must be such as will suit the taste of the purchaser and allow the workman to hold his own against the competition of his fellow-weavers. To weave a cloth after the fashion of the Assamese is a pleasure rather than a duty. The work is done leisurely as suits the workman (or rather woman). This work is not a profession but rather a household duty. The cloths are used by the weaver herself or by her relatives, the standard of work, therefore, is fixed by the weaver; there is no competition and no one's taste to consult except the weaver's own and that of her family.

In Assam, the weaving having been finished and the size washed off, the cloth is ready for wear. In Dacca the cloths, before being sold, are subjected to a most thorough bleaching. No such process appears to be employed in Assam, even for the finest fabrics. Not a word of it is mentioned in any district report, and I have found no trace of it from personal enquiry.

PROCESS OF MANUFACTURE IN THE HILLS.

Simple as are the methods employed by the people of the plains, those of the hillsmen are even simpler and more rudimentary. The process of the plains is a distinct stage in advance of that of the hills. The former has reached the stage of machinery, the latter has not. In the plains the chief instruments used for ginning, for spinning and for weaving are all machines in the strict sense of the term, *e.g.*, the gin, the spinning wheel, the reels, the *karhani*, the loom, the shuttle. In the hills there are, strictly speaking, no machines, ginning is done by means of a plain rod, spinning by the spinning whorl. For weaving there are no reels,—the thread is wound in balls,—no *karhani* and no loom properly so called—the warp is laid round a simple arrangement of rods suspended in the air, and to effect this the ball or balls of thread are passed round the rods; the shuttle is nothing but a rod round which the thread for the weft is wound.

The Naga process is perhaps the best illustration of the methods of the hillsmen, for there the thread is usually homespun, so all the stages of the process are peculiar to the hills. The details of the weaving stage are seen best in the account of the Garo and Miri processes which are described at greater length. The Nora and Turung process of weaving is very distinctive, as it differs widely from the usual processes employed in either the plains or the hills.

The following accounts embody all available information concerning the process of manufacture among the various hill tribes. The arrangement of this section has been made uniform as far as possible with that of Part IV.

Manipuri Process.

Cleaning.—The process is the same as that in the Assam Valley. The cotton gin, called *kuptreng*, is that used by the Assamese.

Spinning.—The instruments used and the process employed are practically the same as those of the Assam Valley. The following are the Manipuri names of the different instruments used, with a description of any that differ from those of Assam :—

1. *Huitri.*—The bow-string.
2. *Lashing kapol.*—A cylindrical basket 3 or 4 feet deep ; the mouth is 1 foot 6 inches in diameter and the bottom 1 foot. It is used simply to prevent the cotton from flying away while being scutched.
3. *Langom.*—A rod, 4 inches long and $\frac{1}{3}$rd inch in diameter, used in rolling cotton into rolls called *maithap* (the *panji* of Assam).
4. *Tareng.*—The spinning wheel. Its different parts are called :—

   Tareng mayol.—The wheel itself.
   Wayenjei.—The two uprights.
   Tarengyot.—The spindle.
   Shimai.—The two uprights to which the spindle is fastened by means of two strings (called *tareng mana*) twisted into the form of a rope.

   The rolls of thread spun on this machine are called *langdum*.

Weaving.—The following instruments are used in Manipur for weaving apart from the loom. No descriptions have been given, so it is not known what they are :—

1. *Langchak mayol.*
2. *Tayot.*
3. *Langthok tareng.*
4. *Phihon kairak.*—This is also reported from Cachar, where it is said to be the same as the *mayaghara.*

Like the Garos and Miris, the Manipuris use two looms ; the first is similar to the Assamese loom, the second is of the description known as *beng* throughout the Assam Valley.

The following account is taken from the report received from Silchar :—

" The ordinary Manipuri loom used in making the finer cloths is broadly identical with the Jugis' loom, and both of these, again, appear to be broadly identical with that used in Assam ; the difference being in matters of minor detail only. .. The loom is almost always homemade. The Manipuri process of setting up the apparatus is, however, different and rather easier. They make a bamboo frame like a child's cot (about 4 feet 6 inches by 3 feet) called *youngkham* with four whole bamboo posts with two bars on both sides at the top, across and on which is placed another bar in a middle portion, from which hangs the *bu* (*nachai*), the two *narad* (*phikonoba*) being driven through holes made through the bamboo posts and retained in position by means of bamboo pegs. This is very convenient, and the whole thing may be removed to any place at pleasure. "

Then follows a description, in the vernacular of the Jugis' loom ; this need not be reproduced here, as it has already been explained that it corresponds very closely with that of the Assamese loom which has been described at some length. A model of this kind of loom from Manipur was exhibited at the Calcutta Exhibition, and is now in the Indian Museum.

The following is a list of the Manipuri names of this loom and its parts from Manipur. The words in inverted commas are the descriptions received from Manipur :—

1. *Pangayom.*—The loom itself (Manipur).

   Pangaiong (Cachar).

2. *Konaba* (Manipur).

   Konoba or *Phikonoba* (Cachar). The yarn-beam and cloth-beam " wooden rollers 7 feet long and 2 inches in diameter."

3. *Nachai.*—" Bamboo sticks six feet long and $\frac{1}{4}$ inch in diameter : eight of these are required for the loom." They appear to correspond to the Assamese *guri.*

4. *Singmit.*—"Bamboo sticks mu^ch thinner than the above, length the same,—eight are required for the loom." They probably correspond to the Assamese *chiri.*

5. *Samjet,* the reed; " comb made of bamboo and reed through which threads go in according to the width of the cloth required to be woven."
   Called in Cachar.—*Phigisumjet*;
   " " Hailakandi, *Samset.*

6. *Hanglakchai.*—Not described.

7. *Singkap.*—The temple; "a bamboo split, two ends of which are pointed. The length is according to the width of the cloth."
   Called in Hailakandi *Singap.*

8. *Shuna wupak.*—Not described.

9. *Shuna.*—Not described.

In Hailakandi the *nachoi* and *sona* together form the shaft of healds, the *sona* are the loops of threads, and the *nachoi* is the rod to which they are attached.

In Cachar the complete shaft of healds is called *nachoi,* the loops themselves *shuna.*

10. *Tamang.*—Not described.

11. *Nayongkhok.*—Not described.

12. *Khunet.*—Not described. " Two of these are wanted for a loom."

In Cachar the treadles are called *khongnet thawri,* so possibly the *khunet* of Manipur are the treadles.

13. *Pangandem.*—Not described, but evidently the same as *pangantem* of Cachar and *pangalthem* of Hailakandi, both of which mean the shuttle.

The tube of the spool is called *langcha* in Cachar and Hailakandi.

14. *Khoiru sadu.*—Not described.

15. *Kochi.*—Not described; probably the brush for smoothing the warp.

16. *Yongkham.*—" An oblong frame made of wood on which the above fittings are applied.

This corresponds to the *youngkham* of Cachar which is, however, said to be made of bamboo.

Besides these parts of the loom the following are reported from Cachar.

17. *Nart thawri.*—The string connecting the upper rods of the shafts of healds with the *nachani* above.

18. *Nart wak.*—The top cross bar from which the *nachani* are suspended.

These two may or may not be identical with some of those not described, *viz.,* 6, 8, 10, 11, or 14.

The process of weaving by this loom is the same as that in Assam.

The second kind of loom used by the Manipuris appears to be practically identical with that of the Nagas or that of the Bhutias described below. No detailed description of it has, however, been received from any district. The names of the different parts, as received from Manipur, are given below. None of them have been explained, but most of them can be identified from the description of similar instruments received from Hailakandi:—

(1) *Maitaiyom.* The loom itself.

(2) *Yetpu. Japu* in Hailakandi; a roller of bamboo or wood 1½ inch in diameter and feet in length. Two of these are used in the loom, one at either end of the warp. They are the upper and lower bars of the loom.

(3) *Utong. Uttong* in Hailakandi.—Pieces of bamboo placed between the warp, 2½ inches in diameter and 3 feet in length. Two are used in the loom.

(4) *Nayetchai.*—
(5) *Shunachai.*— These together probably form the shaft of healds. In Hailakandi each shaft of healds consists of a *nachai* and a *sona,* the *nachai* being the rod and the *sona* the threads forming the loops. The way in which these loops are formed has not been explained. The rod is about ½ inch in diameter.

(6) *Phisatem*.—This is probably the *tem* of Hailakandi which is a piece of wood or supari tree about 3 inches wide and 5 feet long, both edges being bevelled and well polished. "It is used for pressing home the woof thread to make the cloth thick."

(7) *Shanam*.—This is not described and cannot be identified. Only one is used in the loom.

(8) *Pangandem. Pangalthem* in Hailakandi.—An illustration of this is given. It appears to be oval or elliptical in shape with two rods projecting one from either end. The oval or central part contains a hollow with a hole at either end in which is placed the pin which carries the spool. The spool consists of a thin tube covered with a roll of cotton thread. The tube is called *langcha*.

(9) *Khoiru sadu*.—Not described, only one is used.

(10) *Khongkhang*.—Not described, only one is used.

Besides these the following instruments are reported from Hailakandi.

(11) *Singap*.—The temple. "A piece of bamboo having two pieces of iron like two pins at the two ends. Its length is equal to the breadth of the cloth. It is used to keep the breadth of the cloth even."

(12) *Samsel*.—The reed. It consists of two bamboo pieces parallel to one another and joined by very fine bamboo bars. It is used to keep the warp threads equi-distant when the nature of the cloth requires it. "It is used in preparing *gamcha* (towels) and nets only. Its use is to make the cloth thin. Thick cloth cannot be made by using it" (Hailakandi).

The process of weaving by this loom is similar to that of the Bhutias (page 77).

The loom and other instruments used in weaving by the Manipuris are all homemade or locally purchased. They cost about ten rupees and last a good many years; sometimes they are handed down from one generation to another.

Naga process.

The following description of the processes used by the Angami Nagas has been received from the Deputy Commissioner of the Naga Hills.

"Spinning raw cotton (*Tsaze anj*).

The cotton having been cleaned and bowed is rolled out light into rolls about the thickness of the middle finger and about four times as long, it is then ready for spinning. This operation is performed with the instrument sketched on the margin* which is locally called *themu*. It is made of bamboo with a small stone disc to give it weight and help it to revolve, and is about eight inches in length. The operator sits on a low stool, which brings her thigh to a height of about four inches from the ground. The *themu* is then laid against the thigh, the thick end being placed on something on which it will revolve freely. The end of one of the cotton rolls is then applied to the point of the *themu* which is then made to revolve rapidly by the right hand being rapidly drawn across it; as it revolves it engages the roll of cotton and as the operator raises her left containing the cotton roll, a thread is formed which is wound on to the *themu*. When the *themu* is full of thread, the cocoon is slipped off over the thin end and put aside. The next process is to wind the threads two at a time from the cocoon in balls (*lodzi*). The double threads on these balls are then twisted together (*kegye*) so as to form one hard thread. The thread is then made up into skeins and sized and dyed, if necessary. It is then again wound off into balls and is ready for the process of weaving." The Deputy Commissioner adds: "Spinning thread is the occupation of spare hours amongst the women, and it is quite impossible to give any estimate of the time taken in manufacture. The spinning wheel is practically unknown in this district except among the Kukis, and the primitive method of spinning thread on the naked thigh is that universally practised. Ready-made thread, if used, is, if necessary, re-twisted (*kegye*) sized and dyed and when wound into balls is ready for weaving."

Weaving.

"The process of weaving a cloth may be divided into two parts.

[* The sketch is not reproduced.]

" (1) The setting up of the threads on the various sticks comprising the loom. This is known as *kive rhe* amongst the Angamis and is a laborious process. Without having a loom in front of me I cannot possibly describe it.

" (2) The actual weaving, *kive do*. This process also it is almost impossible to describe without having a· loom to demonstrate on. It is that described in paragraph 40, page 47, of the 'Industries of Assam' (*i.e.*, the first-half of Mr. Darrah's description of the Bhutia process reproduced later on).

" In setting up the cloth (*kive rhe*) an assistant to handle the two balls of thread is usually employed, but this is not absolutely necessary. This process takes about half a day. No assistant is employed when the process of weaving is actually going on. A plain cloth with no inserted pattern would take a good weaver about two days of six hours each to make."

" The loom is home-made by the male members of the family. I can say nothing as to the durability of the various parts with ordinary wear and tear, if carefully kept they might last a lifetime."

The above description applies to the process employed by the Angami Naga tribe. " The methods of manufacture employed by the other tribes inhabiting this district," says the Deputy Commissioner, " are practically identical with those used by the Angamis. It is only amongst the Angamis that ready-made imported thread is used to any extent. Amongst the other tribes raw cotton is worked up into yarn in the manner described."

The following account has been received from the Sub-Divisional Officer of Mo-kokchong, a Sub-Division of the Naga Hills District.

Instruments used.

" There is only one kind of loom employed in the manufacture of cotton fabrics. It consists of the following parts :—

" (a) *Anen.*—A pair of rods about 2¼ feet long and one inch in diameter made chiefly of *nahor*.

"(b) *Alum.*—A piece of polished wood made chiefly of *nahor*, 2¼ feet long and 2¼ inches wide, flat along one edge and sharp along the other.

" (c) *Suksen.*—The shuttle, usually a small bamboo rod about a foot in length, on which the rolls of thread are wound up for weaving like a knitting needle.

" (d) *Anet.*—The Assamese *ba*.

" (e) *Anetdong.*—A piece of bamboo rod about 2¾ feet long on which loops are made connecting the *anet* with the threads of the lower warp.

" (f) *Imlung.*—A piece of bamboo rod the same size and similar to the *anet-dong*, but placed 6 inches above it. This rod is used to make a gap to allow the shuttle to pass between the threads of the upper and lower warp.

"(g) *Mong-mung*—A thick bamboo rod at the furthest extremity of the loom used to catch hold of the warp.

"(h) *Aphi.*—A net-work string, 3 to 3½ inches wide, the ends of which pass behind the back of the weaver and are fastened to the two extremities of the *anen*, thus making the whole warp tight.

"(i) *Juiang.*—A piece of polished bamboo about 2¾ feet long placed about 6 inches above the *anetdong* and on which the strings are wound.

" All the above instruments are made at home, well-to-do people buying or getting poorer people to make for them. The cost of the Naga loom is about rupee one only, and with ordinary wear and tear lasts five years."

Methods employed.

" The first process in the manufacture is the cleaning of the cotton, Naga name *semang*, which is done by means of a flat stone and a small rod about 6 inches long. The stone is placed on the ground and a small handful of raw cotton is placed on it. The rod is then rolled over the cotton with slight pressure in such a manner that the seeds at once separate from the fibre. A lot of the villages have now taken to use the Assamese *neothani* as they find it a much quicker process.

"The next process is scutching, Naga name *akar*, which is done by means of a bow-string. The bow is a piece of bamboo about 3 feet long and the string is of cane cut very fine. The cotton is then placed on the ground in a heap, and the fibres are separated by pulling and letting go the string. The cotton is now made into rolls called *maiti*. These are then taken and spun, which is done by means of an instrument called *bang*. This is a spindle about a foot long which passes through the centre of a circular flat stone about 2 inches in diameter resembling a small wheel and adjusted to the end of the spindle and united with the *maiti* (? *maiti*), so that one end seizes the roll and the other the spindle. The operator then takes up the roll of cotton and applies it with her left hand to the spindle and rolls the spindle round on her thigh with her right. The motion thus imparted to the spindle causes it to make a thread similar in size to the one already on the spindle. As soon as the thread has obtained the required number of turns, it is wound up round the spindle and the process is continued. The rolls of thread are now sized after having been boiled in rice water.

"The next process is the transfer to the warp which is prepared by two pieces of string of the required length of the cloth being fixed to the *mong-mung* and the *anen*. The different pieces of the loom are now fixed in their respective places. The operator then seats herself on a wooden seat about 3 inches high and finds the warp in front of her sloping up at an angle of about 60 degrees from the ground, and straps the *aphi* round her. She then takes two balls of thread in her hand and with the help of another woman passes the thread round and round between the *anen* and *mong-mung*, one ball of thread passing through the *anet* (*d*), over the *anetdong* (*e*) and round the *juiang* (*i*), the other passing below *anetdong* (*e*) and round the *juiang* (*i*); and this process is continued until the required width of the cloth to be made has been obtained. The two pieces of string which were first put on the warp are now taken off, and the operation of weaving commences by the operator sitting back, and thus making the warp taut. She now takes up the *anet* with her left hand and pushes the *anetdong* up towards the *juiang*. This makes the threads which do not pass through the loops of the *anet* tight and loosens the others. In doing this a space is formed between the threads of the warp, and, the *anetdong* and *juiang* being let go, the *alum* (*b*) is passed through, the flat edge being applied; it is then turned over, and when perpendicular the *suksen* (*c*) is shot through, leaving a thread the width of the warp between, and the *alum* is then pressed down, the sharp edge being applied this time. When the shuttle is passed from the right to the left the thread is below the threads which pass through *anet* and when passed from left to right, above. The operation is continued till the cloth is made.

"A skilful woman is considered to have accomplished a good day's work if she has woven a piece of cloth about 2 feet in length by 18 inches in width. The ordinary Naga cloths which are about 6 feet by 4½ feet take about three days to make."

From the above it is impossible to determine whether the Angami process and that of the Nagas of Mokokchong are identical or not. The description of the Mokokchong process is rather defective in parts. The exact course of the warp threads around the rods is not clear, and it is not stated how the healds are formed, or when. The *imlung* would appear not to be brought into use until the warp is laid. Its position appears to be identical with that of the *juiang*. If this be so, there are only three rods used in warping besides that on which the healds are formed. The threads passing through the loops of the healds are said to pass over this rod (the *anetdong*), in which case the healds could be worked by pulling downwards, but as the alternate threads (those passing clear by the loops) pass below this stick, it would appear impossible to pull the former threads through the latter by means of this rod.

The description is, however, sufficiently clear to show that the Mokokchong process of warping, while agreeing in principle with both the Garo and the Miri methods, differs in essential points from either. From the Garo method it differs in the fact that two balls of thread, and two supporting ropes are used instead of only one; and from the Miri process it differs in the fact that the threads pass round one of the intermediate rods (the *juiang*). Doubtless there are other points of difference.

In Volume XLIV of the Journal of the Asiatic Society of Bengal will be found an illustration of a Naga loom with the weaver at work. This drawing by Lieutenant R. G. Woodthorpe, R. E., accompanies a very interesting article by Captain J. Butler, B. S. C., entitled "Rough Notes on the Angami Nagas and their language." It shows the upper bar of the loom supported by two strings from the eaves of the house, and the lower bar apparently behind a heavy log (Asiatic Journal, Volume XLIV; plate XXI, fig. i.)

Process of the Kukis, Lalungs, Syntengs and Mikirs.

These tribes are the only inhabitants of the Khasia and Jaintia Hills who practise weaving to any extent.

The following is a list of the instruments used in that district, with the prices noted against all those that can be had to purchase. No detailed description of the process has been received.

1. *Ka tylliat.*—Cotton gin, price 8 annas. It is very similar to that used by the Assamese but perhaps even rougher. The foot-board is merely a stout piece of split bamboo.

2. *Ka ryntieh.*—Bow for scutching. The handle is of stout bamboo about 4½ feet long, the string of cane.

3. *Ka shirkha.*—Spinning wheel, price 8 annas. This is very similar to the Assamese machine. The wheel itself is made up of two frames connected with cane-work. A frame consists of three pieces of wood with holes through the centres, by which they are threaded on to the axle, and so form six spokes. The ends of the six spokes on one side are connected with the ends of those on the other by a double band of cane which passes diagonally across from the first spoke on one side to the first on the other side, then back to the second spoke on the first side, and so on backwards and forwards till the whole circumference has been completed. The spindle, about 13 inches long, is made of iron and is thickest towards the centre. At the blunt end is a bamboo ball, and about an inch from it is a second piece of bamboo shaped like a long glass bead. The spindle is not supported directly on the smaller uprights, but rests in two loops of cane which pass through holes in these uprights and project on the far side of the wheel, parallel to the cord. Inside these loops of cane are two small V-shaped pieces of iron, the ends of which face in the opposite direction to those of the bamboo loops. The spindle rests on the lower arms of these pieces of iron and a binding of string lashes the iron to the bamboo. The cord is kept in position by a vertical rod standing midway between the two small uprights. The small stand and the large stand are connected together by two parallel pieces of bamboo.

4. *Ka tainti.*—A horizontal bar at one end of the warp round which the woven cloth is rolled. This is a square wooden bar about 3 feet 8 inches long, and gradually increasing in width from 1¼ inch at one end to almost 2 inches at the other. Near the thick end are two holes through opposite faces of the bar, and beyond that the wood is cut to form a neck. The object of the holes is not clear.

5. *Ka khlieh tat.*—The opposite bar. This is 3 feet long, more or less round, and much thinner than the other bar. It is slightly curved, and is cut away to form a neck on the convex side at either end and on the concave side at the centre.

6. *Ka sharoh.*—The shuttle. This consists of a hollow bamboo tube about 16 inches long, open at one end only. From this end there are six splits in the tube extending for about 11 inches, which cause the mouth of the tube to contract and prevent the contents from falling out. The closed end is pared off almost to a point. Inside this tube is a plain rod of bamboo, nearly 9 inches long. This too is hollow and open at one end only, but it is not split. The closed end is rather thicker than the rest of the stick.

7. *Ka wait*—(*i.e.* sword or slice). A hard piece of polished wood for pushing together the threads of the weft. Price 4 annas. It is shaped like the blade of a pen-knife, the sharp edge measures 2 feet 10 inches, the width of the blade is nearly 2¼ inches and the breadth across the back is half inch.

8. *Ka snat.*—The reed, used in place of *ka wait* for pushing together the threads of the weft. Price 6 annas. This reed is exactly like the Assamese instrument but much shorter (only 19 inches) and much coarser, containing only 160 dents to the foot. It is enclosed in a case consisting of two pieces of whole bamboo about 1 foot 10 inches long and 1 inch in diameter which contain slits into which the sides of the reed fit. These two pieces of bamboo are tied together at either end by cane.

9. *Ka lane.*—(pr. lânay). The brush, I cannot say what it is made of, but it is of triangular shape with a short handle. The width at the bottom is 8¼ inches, and the total length, inclusive of the handle, 10¼ inches. It is very substantially made.

10. *Ka kla*—for winding thread. Very like the Assamese *ugha* in shape, but its use appears to be different. The central rod is about 1 foot 10 inches long and pointed at one end. The framework consists of 4 thin bamboo slips running through 2 discs of wood about 2¼ inches in diameter and 11 inches apart. The upper disc is in two semi-circular pieces (perhaps this is not intentional). The two discs have holes at their

centres through which the rod passes loosely, so that the framework is able to revolve. The four rods are bound together at either end, but do not meet.

11. *Ka lakhawin*—for winding thread. The use of this is not explained, but it appears to be a form of the *bhaunri*. It consists of a piece of wood shaped like a solid X, with a rod passing through its centre at right angles to its face. The rod is about 11 inches long and is thinner at one end than the other. On trial I find that the hollow stick inside the shuttle fits on to this thin end. The piece of wood is 6½ inches long and ¾ inch thick. Its width at the end is 3½ inches and at the centre 1½ inch.

A complete set of instruments has been received, from the Sub-Divisional Officer of Jowai. Besides the above instruments it includes (1) a hollow bamboo tube rather more than 1 inch in diameter, connected at either end to a rod by strings about 5 inches long; the tube is of the same length as the sword-stick and the rod about 4 inches longer; (2) a round bamboo about ¾ inch in diameter and about 3 feet long; (3) a thin rod of the same length as that attached to the tube above mentioned; (4) three thinner rods of the same length as the sword-stick; (5) two pieces of split bamboo 2 feet 4 inches long, flat on one side and rounded on the other, with a point at one end, the width across the flat side is ¾ inch, and the greatest thickness ⅓ inch; and (6) a pair of bamboo sticks about 2 feet 8 inches long, about ¼ inch thick at the back, and coming to an edge at the front which is notched like a saw edge at the centre, leaving 4½ inches (more or less) plain at either end. The names of these instruments and their use have not been stated. It is clear, however, that the loom is of the description known as *beng*.

The instruments are all home-made, generally by the weavers themselves. They are said to last for from 5 to 10 years.

A model Mikir loom with a piece of half-woven cloth upon it has been received from Tezpur. The arrangement of the warp is very similar to that in a Garo loom, which is described in some detail below, but it is not identical with it. One important point of difference is in the healds, of which there are two shafts, if they can be called by that name. The first, *vis.*, that next the weaver, consists of a series of loops hanging from a single rod, which pick up every alternate thread of the warp. This corresponds to that in the Garo loom. The second consists of a series of loops hanging from one rod but connected in some way with two other rods, one above the warp and the other between the upper and lower threads. It is very difficult to determine the exact arrangement of these loops as the thread has got disordered; but the loops pick up the same threads of the warp as are picked up by the first series, hence their use is not clear.

Another important point of difference is that the reed is used.

The several parts of the loom are as follows :—

(1) *Theneng.*—Two bamboos about 3 feet long and 1 inch in diameter round one of which the warp passes at the lower end. The other is placed alongside the first but above the warp.

(2). *Thehu.*—A strap which passes round the weaver's waist and to the ends of which these two bamboos are fastened. It is a band made of cane with a piece of wood fastened to each end. Its total length is about 2¼ feet and its width at the centre 2 inches.

(3) A stout bamboo round which the warp passes at the upper end.

(4) *Thelang pong.*—A hollow bamboo tube 16 inches long and 1¾ inch in diameter. This is kept between the upper and lower portions of the warp, *i.e.*, between that on which weaving is taking place and that which is for the time being out of use.

(5) *Ingthee.*—The reed, very similar to that from the Khasia and Jaintia Hills.

(6) *Harpi.*—The sword-stick, like that from the Khasia and Jaintia Hills but much smaller.

(7) *Pangday.*—Two hollow bamboos about 2 feet long and 1 inch in diameter, sliced off to a point at one end. These are placed between the upper and lower sets of the threads on which weaving is taking place one on each side of the healds farthest from the weaver. There is no intersection of the threads between them, *i.e.*, both pass under the same set of threads and over the same set.

(8) *Hee.*—The healds.

(9) *Owek.*—Thin rods. Besides those of the healds there are two such rods, one is at the point where weaving commences, and round this the threads are looped, alternate loops being in opposite directions; the other is between the two sets of the threads on which weaving is taking place. It is higher up than the upper *pangday* and there is an intersection of the threads between them.

κ

These form the whole of the loom itself. The shuttle is like that from the Khasia and Jantia Hills but smaller and the open end is not split. Two very crude designs are carved or rather scratched upon it. The rod inside is a piece of jungle reed more than a foot long. The shuttle is called *thelangpong* which would seem to be a general term for a bamboo tube. The temple is a flat piece of bamboo with a sharp point cut at both ends.

The half-woven cloth on this loom is less than 7 inches wide. There are five shavings of bamboo nearly half an inch wide woven in between the warp threads just before the cloth itself begins. The distance between the upper and lower bars is nearly 5 feet so the cloth when completed would be about 3 yards in length. The Mikirs cannot weave cloths more than half a yard wide, and therefore have to sew two or more such pieces together to form a cloth of ordinary width. The process of weaving is said to be the same as that of the Bhutias.

The following account has been received from Nowgong :— " The Mikir process of weaving is of a primitive character, and they can weave only a few varieties of cloth. The cotton is first dried and then cleaned by an instrument called *michang krei* similar to the *neothani* of the Assamese. The next step is scutching which is done by a bowstring called *licho*. The third step is to make the cotton into *panji*, the *panji kathi* of the Assamese is called *barlim* by the Mikirs. The Mikirs make the thread in the same way as the Assamese make *eri, muga* or rhea thread, *i.e.*, by an instrument called *takuri*. The *jatar* is also used but rarely, for the Mikirs believe that their household god is offended by the sound of the *jatar*. From the *takuri* the thread is transferred to a bamboo rod called *hanlam* instead of to a *hatlatai*. A *hanlam*-full of thread, corresponding to a skein (*lecha*) of the Assamese, weighs about one-fourth seer. The thread is sized in the same way as by the Assamese, being boiled in rice water. The rice powder (*chapling*) is first sprinkled on the skein of thread, and then it is boiled. The Mikir loom, *patherang*, is very simple and the cloth woven cannot usually be more than 4 cubits long and 1 cubit wide.

Kachari process.

The Kacharis of the Assam Valley follow the method of the plains and use the same instruments. In Cachar they use a *beng* loom similar to that of the Manpuris. The Kachari names for the different parts of their loom are given below with their Manipuri equivalents as used in Hailakandi :—

Cachar.	Manipuri.
1. Baran.	Japu.
2. Sugur.*	Sangap.
3. Rash.	Samset.
4. Kanshi.	Naohai.
5. Kantakri.	Pangalthem.
6. Samkar;	Tem.
7. Kongfong.	Uttong.

*This differs from the Manipuri *sangap* in being made of two cross sticks instead of one straight one. One end of each is fastened together by string, the fore ends being armed with iron points which are stuck into the edges of the cloth, (*cf*, the Assamese *putai*).

Garo process.

The processes employed and the instruments used by the Garos in cleaning and spinning are the same as those of the Assamese. For weaving they use the *beng* loom, and follow a process peculiar to themselves.

LIST OF INSTRUMENTS EMPLOYED.

I.—In Tura (Garo Hills District).

1. *Girgitha.*—The gin.
Parts.—Jachok, the upright stand. *Ahmelenga*, the rollers. *Jak*, the handle.
2. *Gettdhul.*—The bow.
3. *Chalangha.*—The spinning-wheel.
Parts.—Jachok, the uprights supporting the wheel itself. *Chalangha bukma* (*bukma*-belly) the basket wheel. *Jak*, the handle. *Jachik*, three uprights, half an inch apart, fixed in the stand at the spindle end. The central upright has a hole in it

through which the cord passes. *Takwa*, the spindle, fastened to the uprights by cane.

4. *Banagangon.*—The loom. It is like the loom used in the North-West Provinces and Oudh, only rougher in make. Its parts are :—

(i) *Banagaugon.*—Uprights, two in number.

(ii) *Banawaling.*—A horizontal bar, the ends of which are attached to the two uprights.

(iii) *Abom.*—A smooth bamboo which lies close to the weaver's waist, and round which the strands of thread are passed.

(iv) *Warichek.*—A piece of stick with teeth upon which the strands rest at the further extremity.

(v) *Brak.*—A smooth flat piece of wood which is used to beat down the cross threads in weaving.

The *Girgitha* is bought from Bengalis, the other instruments are made by the Garos. The cost of the lot is about 13 annas and they last four or five years, except the *girgitha* which lasts only one year.

The names of the different stages of the process are :—

Khilgorowfla	Ginning.
Bathheel	Scutching or bowing.
Khildingrikha	Spinning.
Banadokha	Weaving.

II.—In the Goalpara District.

1. *Kerkha.*—The gin.

2. *Chiri.*—The bow.

3. *Charangha.*—The spinning-wheel.

Parts.—As in the Garo Hills but *shilingshee*—the spindle when made of iron.

4. *Shing-o-dokha.*—The loom.

Parts.—(i) *Kasunra.*—A stout hollow bamboo about seven feet long—the ultimate support of the whole arrangement.

(ii) *Begandee.*—A smaller hollow bamboo about two inches in diameter and about 1¼ yard long, round which the warp passed at the upper end of the loom.

(iii) *Mekepra.*—A bamboo rod about half an inch in diameter and one and one-fourth yard long round which the warp passes at the lower end of the loom.

(iv) *Thashee.*—Three small bamboo rods about ¾ yard long and ¼ inch in diameter, lying between the upper and lower bars (3 and 4), round which the thread is passed during warping.

(v) *Sing-ki-mok.*—A strap passing round the weaver's back and fastened at each end to the lower bar (iii). It is about three inches wide in the centre and tapers to a point at each end, to which strings are attached. It is plaited out of string and is sufficiently long to pass round the weaver's back and touch the lower bar (iii) at either end.

5. *Chadatta.*—A wooden pin shaped like the figure 7, two of which are used to keep the lower bar (4, iii) in position during warping.

6. *Jagatu.*—A stout piece of coarse string (of jute or the like) used to keep the rods (4 iv) in position during the warping.

7. *Bree.*—The heddles or healds. These are described below.

8. *Wa-ma.*—A hollow bamboo tube about ¾ inch in diameter and 1 yard long. Its use is explained below.

9. *Meshel.*—A flat piece of tamul wood about ¾ yard long and 1¾ inch wide and very similar in shape to the blade of some pocket knives. One side is nearly flat, the other slightly rounded. The edges are both rather sharp, the one somewhat sharper than the other (but there is very little difference). In the centre it is about ½ inch thick. One end is pointed, the point being formed by one edge only being rounded off, sometimes the front edge and sometimes the back edge. This is used for pressing the weft threads home.

10. *Kolbo.*—A thin round piece of bamboo used instead of a shuttle. It is of the same size as the *thashee* (4 iv).

11. *Kente.*—The temple. A thin flat piece of bamboo about ⅛ inch wide equal in length to the width of the cloth being woven. It has a pin projecting from each end.

12. *Kulthap.*—A smaller instrument just like the *me-shel* (9) except that it is made of bamboo. It is about 1¼ foot long and ½ inch wide. It is used for picking out the threads when making a pattern on the cloth.

13. *Tokchanga.*—Three very thin and narrow strips of bamboo equal in length to the width of the cloth, or, rather, slightly longer. Their width is ⅛ inch or less. They are used to mark off the end of one cloth from the beginning of another.

Names of the different stages of the process :—

1. Bowing	*Chirisha.*
2. Forming rolls (*panji*) . . .	*Khilfanchi tola.*
3. Spinning	*Khildingrikha.*
4. Warping	*Bara shinga.*
5. Shooting the weft	*Bara dokha.*
N. B.—Raw cotton	*Khil.*
Cleaned cotton	*Khilap.*
A roll of cotton or *panji* . .	*Khilfanchi.*
Thread	*Khilding.*
Cloth	*Bara.*

The Deputy Commissioner of the Garo Hills says that the method of weaving employed by the Garos resembles that of the North-West Provinces and Oudh. Women and girls engage in the various processes, and there are, as a rule, three required in all. Small cloths take one day, large ones, two or three days to weave. No detailed description has been sent.

The following is an attempt to describe the process of weaving employed by the Garos living in the Goalpara sub-division.

The process consists of two stages only, *viz.*, warping and weaving.

Warping.—The weaver first lashes a long and stout bamboo (4 i) horizontally to a fence or some other suitable object, at a distance of about three feet from the ground. Round this bamboo two loops of string or cane are fastened, so as to slip freely along it. Another bamboo (4 ii) of smaller size is then suspended in these loops, which are so adjusted as to support it at either end. This bamboo is the bar round which the warp is to pass at the extremity furthest from the weaver. The bar at the other extremity (4 iii) is similar but much thinner. Holding this second bar parallel to the first, the weaver takes a thin rope (6) rather more than double the intended length of the cloth and passes it round both bars twice (so that it crosses itself above the bars) and then ties the ends together. The weaver now pulls the second rod away from the first until the string is taut, and then lowers it to the ground where a second operator fixes it in position by driving into the ground two nails or pegs, (5) one near either end. This is the only stage in the whole process where the services of a second person are required.

The bars having been thus fixed in position, the rope which takes the form of a cross above the bars and two parallel lines below, is pushed to the left hand end of the rods and adjusted so that the parallel portions are only 2 or 3 inches apart. Four thin rods (4 iv) are now taken and fixed by means of the rope between the upper and lower bars and parallel to them in the following way. The first is inserted in the loops of rope at a distance of about 6 inches from the lower bar so as to pass below the two parallel portions of the rope and above the two cross portions. The second is inserted about 8 inches higher up in the opposite way, *viz.*, so as to pass over the two parallel portions of the rope and under the two cross portions. The third is laid entirely over the rope at the same point as the second, to which it is tied by string at the left hand end. This rod is for forming the healds. The fourth is inserted about eight inches higher up in the same way as the first. It is between the third and fourth rods that the rope crosses itself. Thus on either side of each rod (excluding the third) the upper portions of the rope intersect with the lower portions and so the rods are held firmly in position, the crossing of the two upper portions of the rope giving additional stability to the whole. Like the upper and lower bars the intermediate rods project only slightly to the left of the rope, the main portion, about which the warp is laid, projecting to the right.

The loom, if such an arrangement of rods can be so called, is now complete and ready for the laying of the warp. For the sake of convenience the following notation will be adopted :—The upper bar will be called A ; the rod next to it (the 4th) B ;

the lower rod of the next two (the 2nd) C1; the upper rod (the 3rd) C2; the rod below these two (the 1st) D; and the lower bar E.

The thread for the warp (generally blue) is rolled into a ball, that for the healds (generally white) is wound on a card—the ordinary card on which darning thread is sold. The formation of the healds is part and parcel of the laying of the warp which is done as follows:— The ball of blue thread (for the warp) and the card of white thread (for the healds) are placed on the ground to the left of the rope, the former about equally distant from the extreme bars and the latter opposite rod C2. The free end of the blue thread is tied into a loop which is taken up on the left of the rope, passed over the rope and across to the extreme right, slipped on to the end of rod A and run back to the left close up against the rope. The end of the white thread is taken up and tied firmly to rod C1 at a point immediately to the right of the rope, i.e., in a corresponding position to the loop on the other rod.

The weaver who has up to this time been standing on the left of the rope, now walks round to the right and takes her seat opposite rods B and C so as to face the loom. Taking up the blue thread in a loop she passes this loop downwards to E, round it from top to bottom, thence upwards under all the rods to A, round it from bottom to top and back under B, past C to D over which the loop is slipped, the thread having been so manipulated that the first-half of the loop passes between C1 and C2 and under D, and the second-half back over D and under C1. (C1 lying immediately below C2, any thread passing under C1 must also of necessity pass under C2.) At this point there are four lines of thread crossing the rods C1 and C2, the first line running from E to A under all the rods, the second and third running only from A to D in the way above indicated, and the fourth running from A to E and thence over the rope to the ball of thread.

The white thread (for the healds) is now picked up in a loop which is passed over the 2nd and under the 3rd thread, slipped over the end of C2, brought back along this rod and thrown loosely to the left so as to lie on the portion of the warp already formed. The third line of warp thread is next twisted once completely round B and the whole pulled tight. Lastly, the fourth line of warp thread is picked up at a point above the warp between E and the ball, and looped round D so that the first-half of the loop passes over that rod and the second-half under it.

The cycle is now complete, for the thread runs from rod D to the ball in the same way as it did at the commencement of warping. The same operation is therefore repeated again and again until the warp has attained the required width.

The warp thread is then broken off and the end tied round D, the rod to which the other end had previously been attached. The thread for the healds is not broken off but the card containing the unused portion is picked up from the ground and passed over the rope, and on between the upper and lower warp threads to the other side of the warp where it is dropped on the ground. The thread is then hitched twice or thrice round the right end of rod C2 to keep it tight, and thus it remains during the whole process of weaving.

The warping is thus complete and the rope, which is no longer required, is untied and removed. There is now nothing to prevent either of the intermedate rods from moving along the warp, or the whole warp from moving bodily round the extreme bars.

Weaving.—From the point where the thread first passes round the lower bar (E), the formation of the warp consists of so many complete cycles each of which comprises, 1st, a pair of threads running the whole length from E to A and passing beneath all the rods; 2nd, a pair of threads (between the first two) running only from A to D and forming a loop round D; and 3rd, a pair of threads (to the right of the first pair) running only from E to D and forming a loop round D in the opposite direction to the loop formed by the second pair.

No weaving is done on the first pairs of threads which pass below all the rods so long as they remain in that position, and none is possible on the third pairs which have no healds. It is the second pairs of threads that are utilised for weaving. The threads of each of these pairs pass on opposite sides of both C1 and D: it is between these two rods that weaving is performed.

Before weaving is commenced it is necessary, therefore, to bring the portions of the threads between C1 and D within the weaver's reach, and also to bring the healds between these two rods. When at work the weaver sits with bar E in her lap—so rod D is now drawn down to bar E and laid upon it. The threads being looped round D in opposite directions, the whole warp moves round bodily as D is moved. When D reaches E the shorter loops of thread, *viz.,* those between D and E disappear, and the longer loops, *viz.,* those between A and D are lengthened out so as to form pairs of complete threads running the whole distance between the extreme bars. Rod C1 is then untied from C2, removed and replaced by a hollow bamboo tube of much greater diameter. This tube is not fastened to C2, which now remains between it and rod D.

The pegs that keep the lower rod (E) in position are now removed, and the weaver takes her seat on the ground (or a low stool) close to where the pegs had been, so as to face the loom. Placing the lower bar (E) on her lap, she passes a strap round her waist, and fastens the two ends to the corresponding ends of the two rods D and E, thus binding these rods firmly together.

The weaver, sitting upright, finds the warp at tension sloping upwards from her lap to the upper bar. To slacken it she has only to lean forward, and to tighten it again she has only to return to her original position.

To give her leverage, a peg or some such thing is fixed in the ground at a convenient distance in front of her against which she can press her foot as an oarsman uses the stretcher in a boat.

Weaving proper (i.e., the shooting of the weft) is now commenced. When weaving on this loom the Garos do not use a shuttle properly so called, nor yet a reed. The weft is wound round a thin bamboo rod just like the four central rods used in warping, and each shot is driven home by means of a sword-stick, viz., a flat piece of wood pointed at one end and bevelled at the edges. The cloths woven being small and coarse, there is no necessity for nicely regulating the distance between each thread in the warp.

When weaving is commenced there is an intersection of the upper and lower threads of the warp between rod D and the tube above it. Moving the healds up against this tube the weaver passes the sword-stick between the upper and lower warp threads at a point between the intersection and the healds. Then drawing the sword-stick towards her with both hands she drives the intersection against rod D on her lap. She then turns the sword-stick on edge, and through the gap so formed she throws the shuttle from left to right, meanwhile holding the loose end of the weft on the left of the warp.

Having laid the shuttle on the ground to her right the weaver turns the sword-stick flat, and with its blunter edge drives home the first shot of the weft.

Between this thread and the hollow tube there is no intersection of the warp threads. To form one the weaver leans forwards so as slightly to slacken the warp, pushes the tube upwards and away from the healds, takes hold of the rod round which the healds were formed, and, pulling it upwards, raises the healds. The lower threads of the warp are thus drawn up between those that were above them, and these latter in turn are, (if necessary), pushed down by the weaver who presses the warp gently on the part between the healds and the hollow tube.

There are now two intersections between the first shot of the weft and the tube above it. This tube is pulled down against the healds, which are still held in a raised position, and both tube and healds are drawn towards the weaver. Thus the nearer intersection is driven against the sword stick which is now taken out and replaced between the upper and lower threads on the far side of this intersection. This intersection is driven against the first woven thread in the same way as the first had been. The sword-stick is again placed edgewise and the shuttle-stick thrown through the opening from right to left, this thread being in turn driven home like the last. There still remains an intersection, so the weaver removes the sword-stick, carefully inserts it beyond this intersection, and passes it through the warp cutting a way through the upper and lower threads with the rounded portion of the edge. Having passed it through correctly she pulls the sword-stick towards her, and thus drives the intersection against the last woven thread. The sword-stick is now turned on edge and another weft thread shot from left to right and driven home as before, the whole process being repeated again and again. The healds, it will be seen, are brought into operation not after every shot of the weft but only after every pair.

Having woven so much cloth that she cannot conveniently reach farther the weaver unties the two ends of the strap and pulls the warp bodily round the extreme bars, rod D and the woven cloth thus passing underneath. When the end of the cloth already woven reaches the lower rod; the weaver places above it another bar exactly similar to E and binds the two bars together by readjusting the strap.

Then another length of cloth is woven in a similar way, and the cloth passed round below as before. This process is repeated until the end of the woven cloth, with rod D still in it, has passed up behind to the top of the loom, over bar A and down in front to B,— the rod round which some of the threads were twisted during warping,—it cannot pass that rod. The weaving accordingly proceeds until the distance between rod B and the last shot of the weft is too small to allow of the free working of the healds, when it must be stopped. There remains therefore a certain length of warp threads which cannot be utilised— this length is about one foot.

The cloth is taken off the loom as follows :— Rod C2 is first removed and the thread for the healds wound up on the card, for it can now run freely out through the opening between the upper and lower threads. (If a second set of healds be used for making ornamental designs upon the cloth, the string of this is next removed in like manner.) Another weft is shot from right to left and then the hollow tube is taken out and then rod B. After this the thread for the weft is broken off and the unused warp threads are cut through about an inch from the last shot of the weft. Lastly, rod D is taken out, the unused portions of the thread fall off and the cloth is left with a plain fringe at one end and a fringe of loops at the other.

In this description of the Garo process no mention has been made of the temple. This is exactly similar in make and use to the Assamese temple made of a single stick.

Two cloths are generally woven on the Garo loom. The cloths woven by the Garos usually measure from 3 to 4 feet in length; the distance between the extreme bars of the loom is generally 4 feet or rather less, and the length of the cloth woven is approximately double of this, but some allowance must be made for wastage. When two cloths are woven in one piece, they are divided off from one another by three or more flat slips of bamboo being woven in between them just like shots of the weft. After weaving is finished the cloths are cut apart between two of these bamboo slips and so a plain fringe is left at that end of each cloth.

The cloths woven by the Garos are very coarse; accordingly, instead of using coarser thread or twisting two or more strands of thread together, the Garos often wind two threads together on the same ball and also two on the shuttle. Thus each line of warp and weft consists of double instead of single threads.

The ornamentations on Garo cloths are very simple. In some cases they consist of nothing but lines of different colour running either lengthwise or crosswise. The former are made by introducing thread of the required colour into the warp, i. e., one or more cycles of the warp are laid with different coloured thread. The latter are made by using one or more extra shuttles containing thread of the required colour. The shuttle containing the main thread of the warp lies idle while one or other of the extra shuttles is being used, but the thread is not broken off. These plain lines, whichever way they run, involve no material change in the methods of weaving. They form a portion of the body of the cloth.

Sometimes, however, patterns are made upon the back ground, with different coloured thread. This thread does not form a portion of the body of the cloth, but might be removed without serious injury to the fabric. The simplest form of pattern is a broken line of colour (say white) running along the cloth. Such a line is formed by the introduction at the time of warping of an *additional* cycle of white thread. As explained above, each cycle gives a pair of upper threads (*viz.*, threads that pass over both extreme bars) and a pair of lower threads (*viz.*, threads that pass under both). To form a broken line the shuttle is passed not between the two threads of each upper pair but alternately over and under each pair. These broken lines are therefore always double and appear on both sides of the cloth. Any two such broken lines are usually separated by two single lines of warp thread of the ordinary colour.

The formation of these white lines involves a variation in the process of weaving, for the white threads must be capable of being pulled up and pushed down all together, but yet independently of the main threads. Hence a second set of healds is required to pull them up and a second tube to push them down. The loops of this set of healds are formed so as to pick up all the white threads (and no others) in pairs, instead of picking up alternate single threads. They are formed immediately above the main healds, i.e., between them and the first tube. The second tube is inserted close to the first exactly like it between the upper and lower main threads, but, unlike it, above *all* the white threads. These two tubes can be slipped over one another, so as to change places as required. When it is necessary to have all the white threads below the last shot of the weft and the tube next to it, the new tube is slipped over the old one so as to lie next the last shot of the weft. When the white thread is no longer required to pass under the tube next to the last shot of the weft, the new tube is slipped back over the old tube. The interchanging of the positions of these tubes has no effect upon the blue threads.

These broken lines appear to form the basis of all ornamental work in Garo weaving. Patterns are formed not by threads introduced between the shots of weft, as in the Assamese process, but merely by making the gaps in the broken lines of various sizes and recurring at different positions on the several lines. To effect this the weaver must be able to raise any one or more of these pairs of white threads independently of the rest. For this purpose a small flat stick pointed at one end is used. Picking out the threads the weaver carefully runs this stick above all the blue threads and under or over the white threads in the same order as the shuttle is required to pass between them, and lays it on the warp where it remains while the weft is shot. From time to time some of the threads are dropped off the stick and other (white) threads picked up upon it as the pattern requires. As may be imagined, the patterns so formed are very simple and the threads are usually picked up or dropped off in regular order from the right or left extreme rather than at the centre.

When done with for the time, the stick is of course removed.

If the body of the cloth be woven of double threads, so are the patterns, each line of threads in which is therefore quadruple instead of double.

The *beng* loom used by the Garos of Goalpara differs somewhat from that of the Garo Hills, *e.g.*, there is no *warichek*, and the top bar is suspended in loops from a bamboo instead of being fastened to two upright posts.

The Garo process of weaving is probably the simplest in Assam. No reed is used, and only one ball of thread; the implements are of the very simplest. The cloths produced are very rough, the threads running unevenly, and the texture, though comparatively close at the outer edges, becomes looser and looser towards the centre of the cloth.

It takes an hour to lay a warp of usual size, and an hour and a half, or rather less, to weave a foot of patterned cloth after warping is complete. Thus to weave two cloths (in one piece) each a yard long would take about ten hours—one for the warping and nine for the shooting of the weft. But the weaver can seldom keep at work for a full day, for the process is very tiring to the back. It is said, however, that with rapid work a woman can begin and finish in a single day a pair of plain cloths each a cubit wide and 3 to 4 feet long. Generally a pair of cloths either plain or coloured is finished in two days. The warping, if done leisurely, takes an hour and a half. The ordinary price of a cloth is eight annas, so a pair is worth one rupee; but the two cloths woven in one piece are not, as a rule, of exactly equal length.

The Miri process.

Cleaning and spinning.—It has been already mentioned that the Miris require two kinds of thread, one for their ordinary cloths and one for their *jin* cloth. The former kind is generally bought from the bazaar, but when spun by the Miris themselves, the ordinary Assamese methods are followed*, and the same instruments used. The thread required for the *jin* cloth must of necessity be much coarser and rougher than the coarsest imported thread available, and in consequence is always made at home. This coarse thread is called by the Miris *gabar-annoo* (*gabar* meaning the *jin* cloth and *annoo* thread). The process of spinning it is as follows :—

The cotton is first cleaned and scutched by the Assamese methods. It is then placed in a long heap and formed by the hand into a rough roll several yards long and of the same thickness as a *panji*. This roll is then smoothed and formed into proper shape by the woman rolling over it the same small tapering slip of bamboo as is used by the Miris for forming the smaller rolls. This slip is gradually passed along the rough roll as the smoothing proceeds. Thus several long rolls are formed.

These long rolls (*reboong*) are spun into thread by means of the Miri spindle (*papi*). This is like the *takura* of Goalpara but the disc which is of wood or tortoiseshell is about 3 inches in diameter, and the rod tapers to a fine point at the end. From one end of the prepared roll a thread about 1 foot long is twisted with the hand, and then tied to the spindle near the disc. The spindle is then placed in an inclined position with its thicker end resting on a concave surface (*e.g.*, a piece of a broken earthen pot) to keep it in position when whirled round, and held at the pointed end by the thumb and forefinger of the right hand. The woman then whirls the spindle rapidly round and holds the roll of cotton with her left hand near the spindle point. As the thread is drawn out, she extends her arm to its full length, and then twists the thread so formed round the spindle and repeats the process until the spindle is full. The thread is then transferred straight to the *yanke* which is a framework consisting of a small bamboo stick about 2 feet long with a cross piece about six inches long attached to each end. The skeins are next boiled in rice water and dried in the sun, after which the thread is ready for use.

Weaving.—Names of instruments employed—

(1) The loom *sumpa gegur* (Jorhat).

* There is a slight difference in the forming of the scutched thread into rolls. The small bamboo slip used by the Miris is about 1 foot long and tapers to one end ; it is called *pingkang*. This slip is held by the thick end and rolled with the open palm over the cotton which is placed upon a stool.

(2) Two uprights of bamboo, on which the end rod is supported about 2 feet from the ground. *Khunti* (North Lakhimpur, Jorhat).

(3) A round rod, generally a piece of whole bamboo, about 2 inches in diameter and about 3 feet in length, round which the upper end of the warp passes. *Pabu* (Jorhat), *paba* (North Lakhimpur).

(4) " A cornered stick generally of wood, 3 feet in length and 4 inches in girth, round which the warp passes at its lowest end." *Gegur* (Jorhat), *paba* (North Lakhimpur).

(5) A peg about 9 inches long struck in the ground to give leverage to the weaver's foot. *Siupude* (Jorhat).

(6) A rope tide at its two ends to the ends of the lower rod (No. 4) and passing round the weaver's waist. *Pogha* (North Lakhimpur).

Instead of this sometimes a leather strap is used, passing round the weaver's back and having its ends fastened to the *gegur* by ropes (Jorhat).

(7) A leather strap which is put between the weaver's back and to the rope which passes round it and supports the *gegur* (No. 4). It is 3 or 4 inches broad and about 18 inches long. *Gatak* (Jorhat).

(8) A round bamboo similar to the upper bar (3), lying between the upper and lower bars (3 and 4) about nine inches from the latter. *Nurbulung* (Jorhat).

(9) A round bamboo rod about ¼ inch in diameter and 3 feet long lying between the upper bar (3) and the *nurbulung* (8). *Ngelung* (Jorhat), *chikkau* (North Lakhimpur).

(10) The healds *tange* (Jorhat), *tauneh* (North Lakhimpur). These are described below.

(11) The balls of thread used for the warp, *annu alume* (Jorhat).

(12) A flat piece of hard and polished wood or *chewa* about 3 inches broad, 3 feet long and half an inch thick, sharp along the edges and at one end. The sharp end is round, thinner and rather narrower than the other end. This is used for driving the threads home as soon as they are shot. *Sumpa* (Jorhat), *sumpeh* or *beng* (North Lakhimpur).

(13) The temple, a single strip of bamboo of a length equal to the width of the cloth, and having sharp extremities. *Ubar* (Jorhat), *putal* (North Lakhimpur).

(14) A flat stick about 3 feet long and one inch wide used to separate a portion of the threads for the insertion between them of tufts of raw cotton in making a kind of blanket called the *mirijin, Japa* (Jorhat).

(15) The thin rod round which the healds are formed. *Chitika* (North Lakhimpur).

(16) A strip of wood of the same length as the *paba* (4) to which it is tightly bound with the cloth in between them. *Gugureh* (North Lakhimpur).

The above instruments are those used in Jorhat which have distinctive names either there or in North Lakhimpur. The following are additional instruments reported from North Lakhimpur only.

(17) A rope passing across the warp between the upper bar (3) and the *ngelung* (9), *Tankeb* (North Lakhimpur).

(18) Flat sticks like the Assamese *chiri* and used for a similar purpose ; two of these are required while weaving. *Orbi* (North Lakhimpur).

(19) A stool on which the woman sits. *Pira.*

The Miri process of weaving consists of two stages, warping and weaving. To form the warp the weaver takes two pieces of stout rope, each rather longer than the intended length of the cloth, and ties the two ends of each together, so that two separate loops or endless bands are formed. In one end of these she inserts a round bar (No. 3) which she fastens by cord to two upright posts nearly 3 feet apart, at a height of about 2 feet from the ground. In the other end of these loops she inserts a square rod (No. 4) and, sitting on the ground, places this bar horizontally on her lap and ties the two ends to those of a rope or strap which passes round her back. The position of the woman is such that the loops of rope are taut, and the ropes are arranged so that they are parallel to each other and lie as near as possible to the ends of either rod. The distance between the ropes is now rather more than the intended width of the cloth and the distance between the bars rather more than half the intended length. There is a peg driven in the ground against which the weaver can press her foot as she sits in order to get a leverage.

The weaver then takes up a rod (No. 8) just like the upper bar, and inserts it

L

between the two loops about nine inches from the lower bar, parallel to the upper and lower bars, in such a way that an intersection is formed between the two sides of each loop on either side of it, *viz.*, one between it and the lower bar and one between it and the upper bar. She then takes another rod (No. 9) similar to the last but very much thinner, and inserts it between the loops above the intersection. The side of the loops of rope now intersect each other once between the lower bar and the lower rod and once between the lower rod and the upper rod.· These loops of rope therefore hold the four rods firm and parallel to one another in a plane sloping gently up from the weaver's lap to the upper bar.

Starting from the weaver the bars and rods may be named according to their position in the loops of ropes; thus the lower bar will be A, the lower rod B, the upper rod C, and the upper bar D.

For the formation of the healds a thin rod (15) is laid above the warp over rod B to which it is loosely tied. To the end of this thin rod is fastened the brown thread for the healds. This brown thread is in the form of a ball which is brought from the end of the thin rod and thrown over the weaver's left shoulder on to the ground behind, where it lies while the warp is being laid.

The warp thread which has previously been rolled on two balls of equal size, is now laid round the bars and rods as described below. The weaver on the ground cannot conveniently reach farther than rod C, and so a second woman's services are required. The weaver passes the balls round rod B and bar A, and the second woman passes them round rod C and bar D, the balls being handed as required from one woman to the other just beyond rod B, *i.e.*, somewhere between rods B and C.

The ends of the threads on the two balls having been joined together, the knot is held over rod B, and the first ball passed upwards from that point under rod C to the top of bar D where the second woman holds it for the present. The second ball is then passed downwards from the knot above rod B, over bar A, round and back upwards under bar A, over the heald thread from left to right, under rod B, over C, and thence to the upper bar D, above which it is held by the second woman. As soon as the warp thread has been passed over the heald thread the first weaver takes hold of the latter at a point between her shoulder and the place where the warp thread crosses it, carries it between rod B and the thin rod above it and twists it round that rod, the continuation of the thread thus running from this thin rod over the weaver's shoulder as before. Thus the warp thread has been picked up in the first loop of the healds against this thin rod.

At this stage the balls are both being held against the top of the upper bar (D), the first ball to the left and the second close to it to the right. The first ball is now passed round the upper bar D and downwards under D, C and B and over the lower bar (A), round and back upwards under this bar (A) over B and C to the top of the upper bar, where it is held close to the right of the second ball. , The second ball is then passed round the upper bar (D) and downwards under D, C and B and over the lower bar (A) round and back upwards under A over the heald thread (which is then twisted round the thin rod as before) under B, over C to the top of the upper rod close to the right of the first ball.

The first ball is then passed downwards and upwards as before and after that the second ball, and so on till the warp has attained the right width, *i.e.*, till the space between the supporting ropes is full or nearly so. The balls are then carried downwards to the lower bar and the threads broken off the balls and left unfastened till the weaving has commenced. The heald thread is broken off and fastened round the thin rod, which is then untied from rod B. The supporting ropes are removed and the warp is ready for weaving.

It will be noticed that the course of the two outer threads is anomalous, but that the rest of the warp consists of sets of four threads, the arrangements of the several threads in each set being exactly similar. Commencing from the left the first set consists of the second, third, fourth and fifth threads whose position is as follows. The second thread passes over D and C, under B and A, and through a loop of the healds; the third thread passes under D, C and B and over A; the fourth passes over D and B and under C and A; the fifth passes under D, C and B and over A. The second and fourth threads are the upper threads of the warp, and it is between them that the weft is shot. The third and fifth threads are the lower threads of the warp, and on them no weaving takes place until they have been brought round to the top as described below. It will be noticed that the lower threads intersect the upper threads between A and B, and do not intersect each other. The upper threads intersect each other between rods B and C, and moreover the one thread passes through the healds and the other clear of them.

The weft is wound on a thin rod instead of a shuttle, and a flat stick is used to drive home each shot of the weft just as in the Garo process.

The weaving is commenced by inserting the flat stick, *sumpa*, between the threads of the warp just on the near side of rod B, and in exactly the same position relatively to the threads as that of this rod. It thus passes below those upper warp threads that run clear of the healds (*vis.*, Nos. 4, 8, 12, etc.), and above all the other threads. When properly inserted, the *sumpa* is turned on edge and the shuttle stick thrown across through the space so made from right to left. After this the *sumpa* is turned flat and the first shot of the weft driven home. The *sumpa* is then removed and rod B pushed slightly away from the weaver.

The weaver then takes hold of the healds by the thin rod (now detached from B), leans slightly forward to slacken the warp, and raises the healds, thus bringing to the top the threads that pass through the loops; at the same time she gently presses the warp to push down those threads which were previously at the top. There are now two intersections between the threads on which weaving is taking place, both between A and B. The *sumpa* is inserted in the gap between these two intersections, and turned on edge. The shuttle-stick is then thrown through from left to right on the near side of this stick, and this shot of the weft together with the intersection behind it driven home with the sharp edge of the flat stick. The *sumpa* is again removed and reinserted on the far side of the intersection, the intersection drawn towards the weaver and the stick turned on edge. Another weft is then shot from right to left, and the process repeated again and again.

When two or three wefts have been shot, the loose ends of the warp thread are passed round below the lower bar and woven in with the next shot of the weft.

When about an inch of cloth has been woven, the temple is affixed to keep the width of the cloth uniform throughout.

When about a foot of the cloth is woven, the strap round the weaver's waist is untied and the lower bar (A) taken out of the warp. The intersection between the lower and upper sets of threads, which has remained between this lower bar and the first end of the woven cloth, is thus allowed to go out. A bamboo rod about ½ an inch in diameter and of the same length as the bar removed is now inserted between the threads just below the upper bar D and through the same opening, *i.e.*, between the upper and lower sets of warp threads. This rod is brought down the whole length of the warp to the other end, and the woven cloth is passed round it till the thread last shot is directly above it. Another bar similar to this last, or, instead, the bar that has just been removed, is now placed above the warp on the top of the new lower bar. These two bars are then tied tightly together with the ends of the strap which is now readjusted round the weaver's back. The end of the cloth is thus held tight between these two bars.

The position of the upper threads relatively to one another has not been altered by this removal and readjustment of the lower bar. The weaving is therefore continued exactly as before and the cloth rolled round from time to time as occasion requires. Each time the cloth is rolled down, the strap has to be untied and subsequently retied. The object of tying the cloth up tightly between the two rods is to prevent the whole warp being pushed round the bars when the weft threads are driven home. At the commencement of weaving the same purpose was served by the intersection between the upper and lower threads.

At the end of the warp there remains a short length of thread which cannot be woven. The way in which the weaving is finished off is the same as in the Garo process.

Wide cloths and cloths of fine texture cannot be woven by this method. Only coarse cloths from one to two feet wide are woven. The process is a slow one, a cloth 18 inches wide and 8 feet long will take about 16 hours to finish.

The method of introducing ornamentations into the weaving has not been explained, but the following is an account of the process of manufacture of a special kind of cloth by the Miri loom.

The Miri *jin* cloth is a warm rug consisting of tufts of raw cotton with a backing of ordinary cotton cloth. It is made as follows. The warp having been prepared as described above, an inch or two of plain cloth is woven in the ordinary way.

Those threads which pass over rod B and clear of the healds (with the exception of 8 or 10 at either edge) are now formed into pairs by means of a flat stick about 8 feet long and 1 inch wide which is passed over two successive threads, under the next two, and so on to the other edge. This stick (*yapa*) is inserted from right to left and on the far side of rod B, but after insertion it is drawn towards the weaver to the near side of that rod. It is then turned edgewise and a tuft of clean cotton which has not been boiled is inserted in the gap so formed, under the first two pairs of threads passing over the stick just inserted. The right end of this tuft comes out on the right of the first pair of these threads and the left end comes up between the second and third pair. Another tuft is similarly inserted; under the second and third pairs of these uppermost threads, so that its ends project, one between the first and second pairs, and one between the third and fourth pairs. Another tuft is similarly inserted under the third and fourth pairs and so on to the end of the uppermost threads. Thus, omitting the two end pairs, there is a portion of two tufts of cotton under each pair of uppermost threads, and the ends of two tufts come up from opposite sides between each successive pair.

The tufts having all been thus inserted they are next driven home with the *sumpa* as if they were a shot of the weft. The *yapa* having been turned flat and pushed away from the weaver, two threads of the weft are shot exactly as if the cloth were a plain one. The *yapa* is then again pulled towards the weaver and turned on edge ; tufts are inserted as before and the same operation is repeated till the cloth is finished.

The process is most tedious. In North Lakhimpur a piece of *jin* cloth, 6 or 7 cubits long, takes nearly a month to weave ; in Jorhat a strip, 2 feet wide and six feet long, is said to take a full month, the workman doing six or eight hours' work a day ; in Golaghat a sheet consisting of two strips, each 5 cubits by 1¼ cubit, is said to take three months if the weaver spend seven or eight hours a day on the work, and no less than a year if she do her ordinary household duties as well.

The cloth thus produced is too narrow for a blanket, so two or more are often sown together by the edges, which, it will be remembered, are plain and contain no tufts of raw cotton.

The process of weaving by the *beng* loom described above is that in vogue among the Miris of Jorhat and Golaghat. From Sadiya no detailed description has been received. The report from the North Lakhimpur sub-division contains a mere sketch of the processes employed by the Miris of those parts. It seems to be identical with that used in Jorhat except in a few points of detail. In North Lakhimpur the upper bar (D) is said to be 3 feet longer than the intended width of the cloth, *i.e.*, about double the length of that used in Jorhat ; the woman sits upon a stool or piece of wood and, instead of resting one foot against a peg, she rests both feet against a thick wooden or bamboo stick supported by the peg. The arrangement of the warp about the bars and rods is said to be similar to that for weaving the common *izarbund*, with this difference, that in the latter case three rods only are used and in the former a much larger number. A rough illustration is given of the arrangement of rods in the loom for making a Miri *jin* cloth. It agrees with the description received from Jorhat, with the exception that between the upper bar and rod C a rope is shown as passing completely round the warp (breadthwise) ; and an additional flat stick is shown between the *sumpeh* (wooden stick for driving home the weft) and the woven cloth. The object of this additional stick is not clear, and it is impossible to say if the other sticks are arranged in exactly the same way as those in Jorhat, for the illustration does not show the order in which they pass over and under the threads, and no explanatory description is given.

Like the Garos, the Miris use the Assamese loom and the Assamese process of weaving in addition to their own, and the former are fast driving out the latter ; in fact at the present day it is practically only for making the *jin* or *jim* cloth that the Miris of the plains use the *beng* at all. The Miri names for the different instruments used in their own process of weaving are fast becoming forgotten ; it is only the older generation that knows these names, the Assamese terms being now most generally used.

From Sibsagar it is reported that the looms used in the district are all nearly alike, but the Miris sometimes work the looms without the *tolotha* (the cloth, and yarn beams). This may or may not be a reference to the *beng* loom.

The following description of Miri weaving is quoted from Mr. Darrah's " Note on Cotton." It differs materially from that given above, but its accuracy appears doubtful. " The method adopted by the Miris is somewhat similar to that in vogue amongst the Bhutias. The thread having been rolled up into a number of balls, the warp is made with them thus : Two women stand opposite one another, each having fixed in front of her a horizontal rod supported on two uprights. One end of a ball of thread is made fast to the end of one of these rods ; and the woman who tied the knot then flings the ball to her friend who passes it round the rod at her feet and flings it back. This is continued till a sufficient amount of thread has been wound round the two rods. The threads on one of these rods are then firmly tied and the warp rolled up around it. The rod with the warp around it is then fixed to a post and a woman takes her seat with the other rod in her lap. To the ends of this rod is now attached a strap of deer skin, which passes behind the weaver's back, and is just long enough to enable her to tighten the warp by leaning back and to loosen it by leaning forward. The weaving process is just the same as that of the Bhutias. The resulting cloths are long and narrow, and are stitched together by the sides to make a broad piece, exactly as is done by the Bhutias."

Regarding the processes followed in Sadiya the following information has been kindly supplied by the Assistant Political Agent.

"*Spinning.*—The cleaning, scutching and spinning is done in a similar manner to that described in paragraphs 19, 20, 21 and 22, pages 36 and 37 of Mr. Darrah's notes in "Some Industries of Assam;" the local Miris and Assamese both using the same implements as therein described, *viz.*, *neothani* for cleaning the cotton, *dhuna* for beating it, and the *jatar* for spinning the same.

"*Weaving.*—The loom used here by the local Assamese is the same as the one described in Mr. Darrah's work; and that in use by the Miris is similar to the loom in use, among the Bhutias, and described at page 47 of the same work.

"The Miris use two looms, one called Abor loom, the other *távta*, and with these looms they manufacture the warm rugs known locally as *puri* and the other clothes they wear.

"These looms have only one *dang*, and instead of the Assamese *ras* a piece of hard polished wood in the shape of a sword is used ;to push the threads of the woof home.

"They have no shuttle either ; its place being taken by a piece of thin rounded bamboo upon which some thread is wound.

"I have seen both looms in use amongst the Miris at work, and went carefully through Mr. Darrah's notes with the same being worked before me and can therefore conscientiously state that I have nothing new to acquaint you with regarding the local methods in use here for spinning and weaving."

Bhutia Weaving.

The processes employed by the Bhutias have not been seen by me and no report has been received concerning them. The following extract is taken from Mr. Darrah's "Note on Cotton."

"The Bhutia system of weaving involves a much simpler apparatus " (*viz.*, than the Assamese loom). "It is probably the simplest form of weaving known. The warp consists of an endless band of threads about 8 inches to 1½ feet wide. When woven each strip is about 12 or 14 feet long. The warp is formed by winding thread continuously round a pair of sticks placed as far from each other as half the intended length of the piece of cloth. The warp having been made, two pieces of wood, usually small boughs of trees with a fork at the free extremities, are fixed upright in the ground, and a rod having been passed through the band of threads forming the warp the former is placed in the fork of these uprights. These forks are about 4 feet from the ground. At the side furthest from the operator two wooden hooks are stuck in the ground as far apart as the uprights are and about 2½ feet from them. Another rod, which has been passed through the middle of the warp, is placed in the hooks, and the operator (always a woman) takes her seat on the opposite side of the uprights. The warp is then caught and tied up in a split bamboo, to the ends of which are fastened a leather strap, which passes across the back of the weaver. At this stage the warp passes over 3 rods, the one on the uprights, the one at the hooks near the ground, and the inner piece of the split bamboo. The operator sits on the ground, and leans back when she wishes to make the threads taut, and forward when she desires that they should be loose. A rod of bamboo, longer than the width of the warp, is then taken and a series of loops formed connecting it with every alternate thread. This corresponds to the *ba* of the Assamese. Next a stick, about 1½ inch thick, is passed carefully across the threads of the warp above the *ba* just made, in such a way that each thread that passed through a loop goes under the stick, and every other thread goes over it. This may be called rod No. 1. Higher up still, that is, nearer the rod over the uprights, a thin stick is inserted in such a manner that all the threads form loops around it before passing on. This may be called rod No. 2. The place of the Assamese *ras* is properly not taken by any part of the Bhutia loom. But the threads of the woof are pushed together by a hard piece of polished wood, about 2½ feet long and 2¼ inches in width, broad along one edge and sharp along the other. The shuttle is simply a joint of bamboo in which the spindle carrying the thread of the woof lies loose. Another joint of bamboo, filled with water, is always beside the weaver that she may keep the spindle moist.

The actual process of weaving is as follows: The operator seating herself, finds the warp in front of her, sloping up at an angle of about 60° with the ground to the rod that passes over the uprights. The strap passes across her back, and the split bamboo to which it is attached lies across her 'lap. Taking up the *ba* with her left hand, she pushes rod No. 1 up towards rod No. 2, holding the former between the finger and thumb of her right hand and pushing the latter downwards with the other fingers. This latter operation has the effect of tightening the threads which do not pass through the loops of the *ba* and loosening the others.

The *ba* being raised in the left hand, a space is formed between the threads of the warp; the two rods (1 and 2) being let go, the bamboo with the spindle is shot across by the right hand. The hard piece of polished wood is then taken up, and the thread that has just gone across is pressed down with it, the sharp edge being of course applied. The *ba* is then let go, and the shuttle taken up, while with the right hand rod No. 1 is brought down to and pressed close to the *ba*, the operator at the same time leaning back. This has the effect of making a gap between alternate threads of the warp between the operator and the *ba*, this gap being as wide as rod No. 1 is thick. At this point all the threads which pass through the threads of the *ba* are below, and all the others above, and when the shuttle is shot across from the left it leaves a thread above all those of the warp under which the previous woof had passed, and below all those above which the previous woof had passed. This second woof is then pressed into its place by the hard piece of polished wood already referred to. Then the *ba* is again raised and the operation continued. As soon as an appreciable amount of cloth is made, a piece of bamboo, just as long as the cloth is wide, with a sharp nail at each end, is fastened by its two extremities to the selvages to keep the cloth of proper width throughout.

From experiment it would seem that in a day of eight hours an industrious woman could do about 2 feet in length if the warp were 16½ inches wide, and about 4 feet in length if the piece were 7½ inches wide. That is, a woman would take approximately three and-a-half days to do a square yard."

This account is supplemented in some points by that of Colonel Dalton (then Lieutenant) published in 1849, which is as follows: " In weaving the women are seated on the ground. The web passes round three rollers of wood forming a triangle. One of these is attached by a leathern belt to the woman, one supported on two posts in front of her, and the third pinned to the ground farther off. The woman by her position keeps the web stretched to the necessary tightness. The shuttle is a small bamboo containing a roller for the thread. This she passes through the inclined web before her, working upwards and passing the woven parts round below, until the whole piece completed thus comes round."

The arrangement of the warp threads is in some respects remarkably similar to that in the Garo process, but there are very radical points of difference. It appears, from Mr. Darrah's description, that the warping consists of three stages instead of only one, viz., 1st the winding of thread round the end bars ; 2nd, the forming of the healds ; and 3rd, the insertion of the rods between the end bars. If this be so, the process must be extremely lengthy and also very difficult to perform. It may be remarked, however, that this description is incomplete. The way in which the end rods are placed when the warp is laid and that in which the healds are formed are not described nor is it explained in what way the rods are inserted. Mr. Darrah's description of the actual weaving is equally sketchy, no mention is made of the warp being passed round the rods as the cloth is woven, a most essential portion of the process. It is quite possible, therefore, that the description may be inaccurate, and it is not improbable that the warping consists of only one stage instead of three. It is clear, however, that the Bhutia process has one distinct advantage over that of the Garos in the fact that the bottom portion of the warp which is for the time being not required for weaving is stretched between the rod passing under the hooks and that on the weaver's lap, and is thus kept quite distinct and well away from the threads on which the weaving is being done, the latter passing upwards to the rod on the posts and thence downwards to the rod held by the hooks.

The names of the different parts of the Bhutia loom are not given by Mr. Darrah or Lieutenant Dalton.

Other Tribes.

Of the numerous tribes that live in Assam many use none but the methods of the plains, e. g., the Rabhas, Koches and several other tribes found in Goalpara.

There is, however, a great variety of tribes living in Lakhimpur, some of which are noted for skill in weaving and some again for ignorance of the art. The Singphos, according to Hannay, use two looms, the one like that of the Assamese and Burmese and the other like that of the Manipuris, Shans and other tribes on the North-East Frontier. A very brief description of the latter is given in Hannay's " Sketch of the Singphos" (1847) but it is so sketchy as to be hardly worth quoting. No information about the methods of these tribes has been received from Dibrugarh, for in the report from that place it is stated that only one variety of loom is to be found in the district, which is obviously incorrect.

There remains, however, to be described the loom of the Noras and Turungs and the methods of weaving used by these people. These are entirely distinct from any described above, and on this account are of peculiar interest. The Noras and Turungs appear to be of Shan descent and it is therefore to be regretted that the processes of the Shans of Lakhimpur have not been described, as a comparison might be instructive.

An interesting account of the process of the Noras and Turungs has been received from Jorhat and is given below in a somewhat condensed form.

Nora and Turung Weaving.

"The Noras, Turungs and Singblos are said to use the same form of loom which is however called by different names in the language of each tribe. The loom described below is used by the Noras and Turungs living in this sub-division. As in the Miri loom only narrow cloths from 1 to 2 feet wide can be conveniently made in this loom." The Noras and Turungs use imported thread, they seldom spin themselves, and when they do they follow the methods of the Assamese.

The following is a list of the principal instruments used in weaving by the Nora and Turung process.

1. Reels like those of the third kind in Assam. Several are required.

Nora   *Tamhang.*
Turung *Tamfang.*

2. Posts for warping—about two feet high. Four in number.

Nora   *Lakhuk.*

3. The reed. " It is exactly similar to the Assamese *ras* but much shorter."

Nora   *Phum.*
Turung   ,,

4. The frame to hold the reed. This consists of two round pieces of whole bamboo or other material of the length of the reed and about an inch in diameter, each having a groove cut along its length. Into these two grooves the top and bottom of the reed are fitted. The two round bars are then tied together by string at either end and the framework so formed serves the same purpose as the Assamese *dropadi*, but is much smaller and is not suspended. It appears to be the same as that received from the Khasia and Jaintia Hills.

Nora   *Phekphum.*
Turung   ,,

5. A hook exactly similar to the Assamese *hakota* (*viz.*, a flat instrument of brass, iron, buffalo horn, etc., shaped like a bill-hook and about 7 inches long) ; but differing from it in the fact that it has a string about 2 feet long attached to the straight end. This hook is used for pulling the end loops of the warp thread through the reed, these loops being slipped off the hook on to the string attached as occasion requires.

Nora   *Khahok.*
Turung   ,,

6. A framework peculiar to this kind of loom and thus described : " It consists of a round bar of wood, about two inches in diameter and 3 or 4 feet in length. Two oblong openings, about six inches apart, are made in each of its ends, so that in each opening may be fitted a flat bar of wood about 1¼ inch broad and 2 feet long. The openings are made with the longer sides along the length of the bar in such a way that the flat bars may be in a line." (' In the same plane' would express the meaning more clearly). " The round bar is fixed by nails or pins at the middle of the flat ones which are inserted in the openings at right angles to it. The ends of the two

flat bars on each end of the round one are connected by similar flat pieces of wood of equal length. The flat bars thus connected form the sides of an oblong at each end of the round bar. The warp is rolled on the portion of the round bar intervening between the oblong frameworks.

"When used, this instrument is held erect with one end of each of the frameworks on the ground and the round bar horizontal, and serves the purpose of the simpler *agtolotha*, (yarn beam) "of the Assamese used for rolling the warp."

Nora *Chareg*.
Turung *Chirag*.

7. Two bamboo uprights 3 or 4 feet high, and stuck in the ground about 3 or 4 feet apart.

These form part of the loom, and are used for supporting the *charag* (No. 6), while the healds are being formed and during the operation of weaving proper.

Nora *Chaoki*.
Turung „

8. A cross bar resting on the tops of the two uprights (*chaoki*) about one inch in diameter.

This cross bar forms the support for the *nachani*.

Nora *Mai-at-et*.
Turung „

9. A flat piece of wood or split bamboo with a round opening at the middle. It is similar to the Assamese *nachani*, but much longer, being 1½ to 2 feet long.

Two are used to make the healds. They revolve freely round the cross bar(No.7) which passes through the holes at the centre.

Nora *at-et*.
Turung „

10. The healds. The nature of these and the way in which they are formed are described below. Only one set of loops is used for plain weaving.

Nora *Khao*.
Turung „

11. The thin rod to which the healds are fastened; this with the loops of thread completes the shaft or set of healds.

Nora *Mai kat khao*.⎱ These names are however said to be vague.
Turung *Mai jip khao*.⎰

12. The hollow bamboo tube used for forming the loops of the healds. This is exactly the same as the Assamese *ba-chunga*.

Nora *Mak-kep-khao*.

13. The treadle. A piece of whole bamboo 1½ to 2 inches in diameter and about 3 feet long, placed below the warp, one end being attached by a string to the *at-et* (No. 9) and the other facing towards the weaver. Only one is used for plain weaving.

Nora *Mai-jep-kho*⎱ These names are very vague, being applied
Turung *Mai-tik-huk*⎰ also to other rods. The proper Nora and
Turung names for this instrument are not known. The Assamese word, *garaha*, is generally used by these tribes.

14. A bamboo rod about 2½ feet long and ½ an inch in diameter. This is placed crosswise above the warp near the healds, on the far side from the weaver. It lies above both upper and lower sets of warp threads, and is connected by a string attached to its centre to the treadle below. Its use will be explained in the description of weaving.

Nora *Mai-tik hok*.
Turung „

15. A bamboo rod of the same size as No. 14 inserted in the warp in place of one of the end warping pegs. This rod is subsequently attached to the central bar of the *charag* (No. 6) which serves the purpose of a yarn-beam.

Nora *Mai-kat-charag*

16. A rod of the same size as No. 14, but having "at each end two teeth about half an inch long, opposite each other. This rod is substituted for the other end warping peg and remains at the end of the warp at which weaving commences. On the top of this rod and above the upper threads of the warp is placed another rod with or

without teeth, and the two are bound together at each end so as to hold the warp firmly between them during the process of weaving."

Nora *Chapan.*
Turung „

17. A leather strap which passes round the weaver's back ; the ends are tied to the end rod of the warp (*chapan*) and the rod above it and bind these two rods tightly together with the warp between them. It is exactly similar to the *gatak* of the Miris.

Nora *chai-tai-lang.*
Turung „

18. A piece of whole bamboo about 2 inches in diameter and 2¼ feet in length inserted at the far end of the warp when the process of weaving proper is commenced.

Nora *Makhuk.*
Turung *Konghuk.*

19. A flat bamboo stick rather longer than the warp is wide and one inch in width, exactly similar to the Assamese *chiri.* It is used for passing the intersection through the reed, being introduced between the upper and lower sets of warp threads and turned edgewise.

Nora *Chetep.*

20. The shuttle. This consists of a flat piece of wood about two feet long, sharp and straight along one edge and about 1¾ inch thick at the middle of the other edge, which narrows down towards either end. In the wide central part of this broad edge is an oblong groove, or rather hollow, but 2¼ inches long and nearly 1½ inch wide at the centre. At each end of the hollow is a small hole to contain the pin which carries the spool. The ends of the shuttle are round and sharp.

The spool consists of a hollow tube of reed or bamboo with thread rolled on it. This tube is called *lut*, and is carried on a bamboo pin, the ends of which are fitted into the holes above mentioned, and round which it can freely revolve. The thread runs out of the hollow through an eye in one side of the shuttle. The spool is similar to the Assamese *mahura*, but longer. The thread is wound on it by the spinning wheel or simply by hand.

Nora *Tau.*
Turung „

21. The temple. This is made of bamboo and is exactly similar to the Assamese *putal* and is used in the same way, the only difference being that the Assamese *putal* rests above and the Nora or Turung *kung kai* below the cloth.

Nora *Kung kai.*
Turung „

The loom, for which there appears to be no special name, may be said to consist of the *charag* (No. 6) with the two uprights supporting it (No. 7), the cross bar above those uprights (No. 8) the *at-et* (No. 9) with the strings attached to either end, the treadle (No. 13) and the leather strap (No. 17) by which the rods at the near end of the warp are fastened to the weaver. It will be remembered that the reed and its framework are not supported in any way, except by the warp itself. This kind of loom is called by the Assamese the *sam* loom.

Process of weaving.

The warp.—Several Assamese *ugha* (No. 1) with a quantity of thread rolled on each, are struck upright in the ground. Four bamboo pegs (No. 2) each about 2 feet long are similarly posted in one line. These pegs have no separate names and are indicated below by the numerals. Peg No. 1 is nearest to the *ugha* and at a convenient distance from them: the line of *ugha* being at an angle to the line of pegs. The distance between the two end pegs, Nos. I and IV, is equal to the intended length of the cloth or practically a little more, allowance being made for the length of that portion at the end of the warp which has to be left unwoven.

" The free ends of the thread on the *ugha* being united by a knot and then made into a loop are put round peg No. IV. If there be an even number of *ugha*, an equal number of threads is put on each side of the peg. The loops of the thread are put round the peg in such a way that an intersection of the threads is formed between that peg and peg No. III. Let the sides of the pegs next the operator be considered as inside and those farthest from her as the outside, supposing she stands facing the pegs with the *ugha* to her right. All the threads are then carried together from pegs Nos. III and IV, inside peg No. II, outside peg No. I, and then inside it and again outside peg No. II. The operator then walks to pegs Nos. III and IV with the threads in her right hand and passes them outside peg No. III, inside No. IV, and then outside the same and again inside No. III.

The operation is repeated by the weaver, who walks to and fro with the threads in her hand and draws them from the *ugha* as she moves along. The threads are not actually caught by the hand. A piece of round and smooth stick, generally a porcupine quill, is held across the forefinger and the middle finger and the loop of the threads is inserted from the back of the hand between the fingers and caught against the quill; when the operator walks along, the fingers are held erect, the back of the hand being towards the *ugha* and the quill at right angles to the fingers." No *karhani* is used.

" When the warp has attained the required width the threads are left on the *ugha*, not broken off. It will be seen that the threads form two cross-sections, one between pegs Nos. I and II, and the other between III and IV, there being no intersection between Nos. II and III."*

Applying the reed. – The next stage of the process is the application of the reed (No. 3). Two women are required to pass the loops of the warp through the reed. This is held upright on the ground against peg No. I, so that its teeth are at right angles to it. One woman sits in a line with the pegs facing peg No. I and holding the reed against it. Another woman sits on her left facing the same peg. The first woman inserts the hooked end of the *khahok* (No. 5) between the teeth of the reed, and the loops are put on the hook by the second woman, while the first woman goes on drawing back the same through the apertures one by one from the lower to the upper end of the reed, so that one loop goes through each opening between the teeth. Usually the first loop is passed through one aperture single, then two loops together through the second aperture (for the selvage) and the rest, one by one. When several loops have come through and are held against the handle or flat portion of the *khahok*, they are, from time to time, slipped on to the string attached to its end. All the loops having been drawn through, the threads are broken off from the *ugha* and the ends being united together in a knot, are put round peg No. IV in the same manner as the other ends were put round the same peg at the commencement of the preparation of the warp.

The string is then replaced by a thin bamboo rod. It will be seen that there is no intersection of the two sets of warp threads between this rod and peg No. I. Another bamboo rod (No. 5), about 2½ feet long and about ¼ an inch in diameter, is inserted between the two sets of warp threads in the same position relatively to the threads as peg No. I, but on the opposite side of the reed, i.e., behind the reed. This rod replaces peg No. I and the thin rod which are now removed. It may therefore be called rod I.

The reed is then moved on towards peg No. II till the intersection between that peg and rod I comes behind it. Another rod, similar to rod I, is introduced behind the reed in place of peg No. II, in front, which is then removed. This may be called rod II. During this process, the two sets of thread on each side of the peg are, if necessary, held apart, by introducing a thin bamboo stick (No. 19) and turning it on edge.

Rods I and II are now held horizontal, and the reed is moved on towards peg No. III. A portion of the warp behind the reed is then rolled on the *charag* (No. 6) and the reed is moved next to peg No. III. The rolling is done thus :—The *charag* is held erect, that is, with the round bar horizontal and the oblong frameworks standing upright on the ground. The woman holding the *charag* in this position in front of her, faces the warp. Another rod (V) similar to rod I, is inserted in the space occupied by rod I, and this new rod is kept close to rod II ; the end of the warp with rod I in its loops is brought over the central bar of the *charag* (which is horizontal) and carried below, after which the ends of the rods are placed against the inner bars of the framework and on the side farthest from the woman holding the *charag*, that is, just at the place where they meet the horizontal bar at right angles. The *charag* is then turned round and the warp rolled up.

After a portion of the warp has been rolled up on the *charag*, pegs Nos. II and IV are replaced by similar rods which are then held horizontal by one of the operators, the other holding the *charag* erect with a portion of the warp rolled on it.

The warp, with its attachments, is now carried bodily to the uprights (No. 7) and the *charag* placed with its central bar horizontal and its oblong frames resting against the uprights. The warp is then stretched out and fixed tight by rod IV, at the

* Cf, ' the warp,' p. 81.

other end, being laid behind two pegs, which are one foot high, two feet apart, and four feet distant from the uprights.

Making the healds.—The warp is now ready for the formation of the healds. The weaver sits down opposite rod IV facing the uprights. There is an intersection of the warp threads between rods IV and III, then comes the reed, then rod II, then the second intersection, then rod V, and lastly the roll of warp on the *charag*. The healds which consist of only one set of loops, are formed in exactly the same way as in the Assamese process, except that the thread for the healds is made to form only a single figure of eight round the hollow tube and the rod above. This set of loops picks up every alternate thread of the warp. The thread for forming these loops is passed between rod II and the reed through the gap occupied by rod II.

When the loops have all been formed, the thread is broken off the *cherekhi* and its end tied to the thin rod above the tube and this tube is replaced by the rod inside it. These two rods are held close together and their ends are connected by strings to the near ends of two *at-et* (No. 9) which revolve freely on the cross bar (No. 8) on the top of the uprights (No. 7). The loops are thus held up by the two rods and support the upper threads of the warp, *viz.*, those which pass over rod II, which is now removed. The far ends of the *at-et* are connected by strings to the treadle (No. 15).

In the space between the two sets of the warp threads occupied by rod V is introduced a piece of a whole bamboo (No. 18) about two inches in diameter and of the same length as the rod which is now removed. Above the threads (both upper and lower) of the warp between this bamboo (No. 18) and the healds and parallel to them, is placed a bamboo rod (No. 14,) the middle of which is connected to the treadle by a string which passes vertically through the warp, between the threads. This rod remains close to the healds. Rod IV in the loop of the warp is replaced by a similar bamboo or wooden rod (No. 16) which has at each end of it two teeth about half an inch long opposite each other. Another rod with or without teeth is placed on the top of this, and the end of the warp is tightly secured between the two rods, the ends of which are now tied together with the strings attached to a leather strap (No. 17) which has been passed round the back of the operator. On the top of the horizontal bar of the *charag* and below the threads of the warp is inserted a bamboo strip to keep the threads tight and straight. When the warp is extra long, bamboo strips are put lengthwise on the top of the bar in the rolls of the warp at the time of its being rolled on the *charag* with a view to keep each complete circle of the thread tight and separate.

Weaving is generally done inside the house, in which case two posts of the house conveniently situated are utilised for the uprights, a bar being tied to them horizontally to serve the purpose of the cross bar.

Weaving. - The weaving is started by inserting a small strip, generally a thatching straw, in place of rods II and III which are then removed ; that is, the straw is inserted below the threads in the loops of the healds. It will be remembered that there was an intersection of the threads between rod II and the bamboo in place of rod V (No. 13). The latter is now moved a little towards the healds, and this intersection comes next to the straw. A second straw is inserted in the gap between this intersection and the reed, and is pushed home by the reed. After this, the weaving of the threads is commenced. The object of weaving the two straws at the commencement is to keep the edges of the warp tight previous to the introduction of the temple, which is inserted like the Assamese *putal* only below the cloth instead of above it.

The treadle is depressed either by the woman's foot or by a loop attached to it and passing round her big toe. The trendle being depressed, the ends of the two *at-et* farthest from the weaver are lowered and the near ends raised, by which the shaft of healds is brought up, while, at the same time, the rod (above the warp) connected with the treadle is pulled down and depresses the threads over the bamboo (No. 13) at the far end of the warp. When the treadle is left alone, this bamboo holds up to the surface the threads which pass over it.

When an inch or two of the cloth is woven, the temple is attached. The woven cloth is, from time to time, rolled up on rod IV and at the same time the thread at the other end unrolled, the *charag* being turned round for this purpose and then replaced against the uprights. The leather strap has, of course, to be untied and tied again to the extremities of the end rods every time the cloth is rolled up.

A woman can weave about two feet of cloth in six hours.

The above is a description of plain weaving by the Nora and Turung process, as nearly as possible in the words of the report received from Jorhat. The weak point in this description is that the way in which the threads are passed round the end pegs at the time of warping is not explained. It is clear that, if they were passed round in the same way as in the Assamese process, it would be impossible to pass the reed beyond the first intersection as described, for this intersection would be between the sets of thread and not between every successive thread. Suppose there are two *ugha*, then at peg No. IV the thread off one *ugha* (a) would be the bottom thread (No. 1), and that off the other *ugha* (b) the second(No.,2). The same order would be maintained till peg No. I was reached. Then the two threads would be looped round that peg and carried back above the first two threads, *i.e.*, the thread off (a) would become the third thread (No. 3) and that off (b) the fourth (No. 4.) The first loop is passed through the first dent in the reed and the second through the second dent. Therefore, on the opposite side of the reed from peg No. 1 the order of the threads would have been changed, *viz.*, the lowest thread would be No. 1, the next No. 3, then No. 2 and lastly No. 4 ; in other words, the lowest two threads must be those off the same *ugha* instead of those off different *ugha*. Thus threads Nos. 2 and 3 cross each other, and so the intersection cannot pass through the reed, as the teeth prevent it. Moreover, with an intersection between sets of threads and not between successive threads, the formation of healds for plain weaving is practically impossible, and so is the weaving itself. There is only one way that suggests itself in which this difficulty might be avoided. It is that the threads be passed singly round post No. 1, *i.e.*, that the lowest thread, or that off *ugha* (a) be passed round and made to intersect itself before the second thread [that off *ugha* (b)] be passed round. This would be a very easy process, seeing that no *karhani* is used, the threads merely running round a stick or quill in the weaver's hand.

At the commencement of warping the threads were said to be so looped round peg No. IV as to form an intersection between them, between that peg and peg No. III. It is not stated what kind of intersection this is, but there is little doubt that it is one between each thread and not one between the two halves of the first set of threads. If this be so, it is probable that the threads are passed singly round post No. IV as well as round post No. I, in which case both intersections would be of the same nature, *viz.*, between successive threads.

Fancy weaving.

Interesting as is this method of plain weaving by reason of its uniqueness, far more interesting and equally unique is the method of fancy weaving, employed by the Noras and Turungs of Jorhat. This method is used for weaving the cloth out of which bags are made. It is thus described,

The loom and other instruments used for preparing cloth for making bags are, with a few exceptions, exactly similar to those described above ; the warp is also prepared in the same manner, the only difference being in the manufacture of the healds, the thread for which must be much stronger than that required for plain weaving.

Before the formation of the healds begins rods II, III and V are removed, and both the intersections between the threads of the warp vanish.

In place of the one chain of loops used in weaving ordinary cloth on the Nora loom as described above, two chains of loops, each chain containing two sets, are used for preparing the cloth for bags, and the threads of the warp go into these loops in single and double pairs.

Let all the threads (both upper and lower) of the warp be divided into pairs and each pair indicated by the numerals, pair No. 1 being on the extreme left edge of the warp. A *cherekhi*, with a skein of strong brown thread upon it, is stuck in the ground on the right hand side of the weaver. The free end of this thread is tied by a noose to the end of a rod called *maitikhuk* similar to rods II and III, or actually one of them. The *maitikhuk* is then passed across below the warp from right to left, brought up on the left and laid on the warp with its left end level with the left edge of the warp, this string running down on the left side of the first pair of threads. In this position it is held by the left hand while the first shaft of healds is made upon it in the following way :—(i) a loop of the string is taken up on the near side (next the weaver) of the *maitikhuk* between pairs Nos. 1 and 2, and is slipped over it so that the continuation of the thread runs down on the far side of the *maitikhuk* but between the same . pairs of warp threads, *viz.*, the 1st and 2nd. (ii) Next a loop of the string is taken up on the far side of the *maitikhuk* between pairs Nos. 3 and 4, and slipped over it so that the continuation of thread now runs down on the near side. (iii) The string is taken up on the near side between pairs Nos. 5 and 6 and looped over the *maitikhuk*, so that the continuation runs down on the far side. (iv) The thread is taken up on the far side between pairs 6 and 7 and looped over the *maitikhuk*, so that the continuation runs down on the near side. The process is thus continued, the brown thread being picked up between the threads in the same order, stages (i) to (iv) being repeated again and again till the other end of the warp is reached.

Thus the brown thread has been made into the form of a series of loops hanging from the top of the *maitikhuk* alternately on the near and far sides. The loops on the near side form one set and those on the far side form another set. It will be seen that the—

1st	inside loop	catches	pair	No.	1	of the warp threads.	
2nd	,,	,,		Nos.	4 and 5	,,	,,
3rd	,,	,,		No.	7	,,	,,
4th	,,	,,		Nos.	10 ,, 11	,,	,,
5th	,,	,,		No.	13	,,	,,

and so forth, and that the —

1st	outside loop	catches	pair	Nos.	2 and 3	,,	,,
2nd	,,	,,		No.	6	,,	,,
3rd	,,	,,		Nos. 8	,, 9	,,	,,
4th	,,	,,		No.	12	,,	,,

and so forth.

When the first chain of loops has been finished, it is moved a little farther away from the woman and the second chain is manufactured between the first and the weaver in the same way as above, with this difference, that the threads of the warp go into the inside and outside loops alternately in double pairs, *i.e.*, the

1st	inside loop	catches	pairs	Nos.	1 and 2	of the warp threads.	
2nd	,,	,,	,,		5 ,, 6	,,	,,
3rd	,,	,,	,,		9 ,, 10	,,	,,

and so forth, and the—

1st	outside loop	catches	pair	Nos.	3 ,, 4	,,	,,
2nd	,,	,,	,,		7 ,, 8	,,	,,
3rd	,,	,,	,,		11 ,, 12	,,	,,

and so forth.

To weave the cloth for the purse.—Four *at-et* (*nachani*) and two treadles are required. They are of the same description as those used for plain weaving, and are supported in the same manner. The ends of the *maitikhuk* of the 2nd chain of loops (next the weaver) are connected by strings to the near ends of the two outer *at-et* (*i.e.*, those on the sides), the other ends of these two *at-et* being connected by strings to the furthest end of the right hand treadle. The near ends of the two inner *at-et* are similarly connected with the ends of the *maitikhuk* of the first chain of loops, the far ends of these *at-et* being connected with the end of the left hand treadle. The free ends of the treadles point towards the weaver.

Another rod, generally called by the Assamese name *gotamari*, similar to the *maitikhuk*, is introduced above the threads of the warp just below the *maitikhuk* in each chain of loops, and the middle of the *gotamari* in the 2nd chain is connected with the middle of the right hand treadle below by means of a string which passes vertically through the threads of the warp. The *gotamari* in the first chain is similarly connected with the left hand treadle.

The spool is also the same as that for weaving plain cloth, with this difference, that two threads are rolled together upon it, so that two are woven at one time. The rolling is done by winding the threads off two *nghu* at the same time.

The thread for the weft is generally dyed black.

It will be seen that, by the manufacture of the healds in the way described above, the threads of the warp are divided into four sets, the first and second sets going in double pairs alternately into the inside and outside loops of the 2nd chain (next the weaver), the third set in single and double pairs alternately into the inside loops of the first chain, and the fourth set—in double and single pairs alternately into the outside loops of the first chain. It is by raising and depressing those sets of the threads that the cloth for purses is woven. (This is rather confusing, but will be explained hereafter.)

When the right hand treadle is depressed, the inside and outside loops of the second chain hold up the threads in them, while at the same time the *gotamari* connected with that treadle depresses that portion of the warp which is below it and intervenes between the two sets of loops of that chain, the depression of the *gotamari* being also helped by the left hand. A space is, therefore, formed by the outside loops of the second chain, the double pairs in these loops being up and those in the inside loops down. Into this space a piece of whole bamboo about one inch in diameter and 1½ foot long, pointed at one end, called *pung kheng*, is introduced from the right hand side below the outside loops with a view to preserving the space. The treadle is then set free and the continuation of the space extends to the near side of the reed. The weft is then shot from right to left by the shuttle in the ordinary way and is first pushed by the shuttle (which is at once removed) and then driven home by the reed. The *pung kheng* is then taken out.

Next the left hand treadle is depressed, whereby the inside and outside loops of the first chain hold up the pairs of threads in them, while at the same time the *gotamari* just below the *mattikhuk* of this chain depresses that portion of the warp which is under it (*gotamari*) and which intervenes between the two sets of loops of that chain, and a space is consequently formed by the inside loops of the first chain, the alternate single and double pairs in these loops being up and those in the outside loops being down. The *pung kheng* is again introduced next the inside loops into this space and the treadle is set free. The continuation of this space similarly extends to the near side of the reed. The weft is then shot from left to right and pushed home as before. The *pung kheng* is then again taken out.

It will be seen that there is an intersection of the threads between the above mentioned two spaces into which the *pung kheng* was introduced. On the first occasion (before the first throw of the shuttle), the *pung kheng* was inserted on the near side of the intersection and, on the second occasion, on the far side.

The right hand treadle is again depressed and the inside loops of the second chain raise up the double pairs in them, by which a space is formed between these pairs, and those in the outside loops of the same chain. The shuttle is then shot across again from right to left and pushed home in the same way, the *pung kheng* not being brought into use this time. Thus the third thread of the weft is shot.

Next the left hand treadle is again depressed, when a space is formed on the far side of the first chain of loops, by the outside loops of that chain holding up the alternate double and single pairs. This space is permanently maintained by introducing the *mathuk* and keeping it in the warp next the *charag*. Into this space the fourth thread of the weft is shot.

"The weaving proceeds in the same way, the order of rotation in which the threads are shot being observed throughout.

" By the manufacture of the healds in the above way, a cloth containing angled ribs is made as will be seen in the purse sent separately.

" There is another process of manufacturing the healds by which beautiful diamond figures of different colours are raised in the cloth, but unfortunately nobody in this subdivision knows how to do it. There is only one woman in the Nora village who knows how to weave cloth of this description, but her eye sight has almost failed and she could not show me the process properly."

The above description is precisely that received from Jorhat with nothing but a few purely formal alterations made for the sake of brevity. A few observations are required to elucidate it.

(i) The first point to notice is the nature of the healds and the way in which they work.

The loops formed about each rod consist of two sets, one on the near side and one on the far side of that rod. The warp threads that pass through any of the loops formed on one side pass clear of all those on the other side.

The depression of the treadle causes the rod attached to it to rise and pull up with it the loops on either side. The near set of loops raises those warp threads that pass through any of these loops, and the far set of loops raises the remaining warp threads. At the same time, the *gotamari* which lies immediately below the upper rod and which is, in consequence, between the two sets of loops, is pulled down by the treadle and presses down all the warp threads. Thus the threads passing through the inside loops run from the near end of the warp, first slightly upwards to the near loops, then abruptly downwards to the *gotamari*, and thence slightly upwards to the far end of the warp. The remaining warp threads (*viz.*, those passing clear of the near loops and through the far loops) run from the near end of the warp, first slightly downwards to the *gotamari*, thence abruptly upwards to the far loops, and thence slightly downwards to the far end of the warp.

Hence it is clear that between the two sets of threads two gaps are formed, one on the near side and one on the far side of the *gotamari*, the upper threads in the former (those passing through the near loops) being the lower threads in the latter and *vice versâ*. So long as the treadle remains depressed, the downward pressure of the *gotamari* and the upward tension of the loops on either side prevent either of these gaps from extending beyond the *gotamari*.

Now, in weaving, the shuttle is always of necessity thrown through a gap on the near side of the reed. The *gotamari* corresponding to both series of loops are, however, both on the far side of the reed. Hence, so long as the treadle remains depressed, the gap on the near side of the *gotamari* can be made use of for weaving, whereas that on the far side cannot. When it is required to use the latter gap, it is necessary, first, to insert a rod in the gag (*i.e.*, on the far side of the *gotamari*), and secondly, to set free the treadle. The treadle being set free removes the pressure and the tension from the threads, and the far gap, preserved by the rod just inserted, extends from end to end of the warp. This gap is therefore now available for the shooting of the weft.

This explanation, being general, applies equally to either chain of loops.[*]

It would appear, therefore, that the insertion of the *pung kheng* and the setting free of the treadle before the second throw of the shuttle as mentioned in the description of the process given above were superfluous, seeing that it is through a near gap that the shuttle is then thrown. On the other hand, before the shooting of the fourth thread, the setting free of the treadle is necessary, as this thread is shot through a far gap, but this is not mentioned in the description. The insertion of the *makhuk* at this stage answers the same purpose as the intersection of the *pung kheng*.

(ii) The second point to notice is the relative position of the warp threads to one another during the process of weaving. In plain weaving on any loom the warp is always divided into two sets of threads, the threads of one set alternating with those of the other, and one set being raised whenever the other is depressed, and *vice versâ*, *i.e.*, the 1st, 3rd, 5th...threads always form one set, and rise when the remaining threads (the 2nd, 4th...) fall, and fall when the latter rise. Thus an intersection of every warp thread with those on either side of it occurs between each shot of the weft. In fancy weaving, such as that now described, this is not the case.

The reference, therefore, in the description, to the intersection between the first and second shots of the weft is rather misleading. There is, of course, an intersection of the warp between each shot of the weft, but in no case is this intersection between every successive warp thread, as some of those threads which pass over any one shot of the weft pass also over the next and some pass under it.

So, too, the classification of the warp threads into the four sets mentioned in the above description is rather confusing. To explain the nature of the weaving and the pattern formed upon the cloth, it is necessary to follow the course of each successive pair of warp threads, from the near to the far end of the warp, especially with regard to its position relative to each chain of loops.

It will be found that the first twelve pairs of threads of the warp form one cycle, the order repeating itself from the 13th, and also that the twelve pairs of threads of each cycle are divided into four groups as shewn in Plate VI (page 88.)

(a) Pairs Nos. 1, 5 and 10 pass through three of the near loops of both chains.

(b) Pairs Nos. 2, 6 and 9 pass through near loops of the second chain and far loops of the first.

(c) Pairs Nos. 3, 8 and 12 pass through far loops of both chain.

(d) Pairs Nos. 4, 7 and 11 pass through far loops of the second chain and near loops of the first.

Now, the first shot of the weft lies under those warp threads that pass through the far loops of the second chain, *viz.*, sets (c) and (d); the second shot under those that pass through the near loops of the first chain, *viz.*, sets (a) and (d); the third shot under those that pass through the near loops of the second chain, *viz.*, sets (a) and (b), and the fourth under those that pass through the far loops of the first chain, *viz.*, sets (b) and (c). The fifth shot passes like the first; the sixth like the second, and so on. Therefore each pair of warp threads passes alternately over and under two consecutive shots of the weft, but no two pairs of different groups pass over the same two consecutive shots. Each shot of the weft is a double thread, so the warp appears on each side of the cloth in small domino shaped patches, six abreast but overlapping, so that the top half of each is on a level with the bottom half of the next. The weft

---

[*]NOTE.—It would be inaccurate to call the chain of loops attached to one rod a shaft of healds, for, by the two methods of working it explained above, it really serves the purpose of two shafts of healds, and the cloth woven by this process is an example of a "four shaft twill." That name is therefore avoided.

appears in a similar form. Hence parallel ribs are formed upon the cloth, running diagonally upwards across the first six pairs of warp threads, then diagonally downwards across the second six, and so on, the whole appearing as zigzags running across the cloth. The exact nature of the pattern is shown in the accompanying diagram in which the black represents exposed portions of the warp and the white exposed portions of the weft.

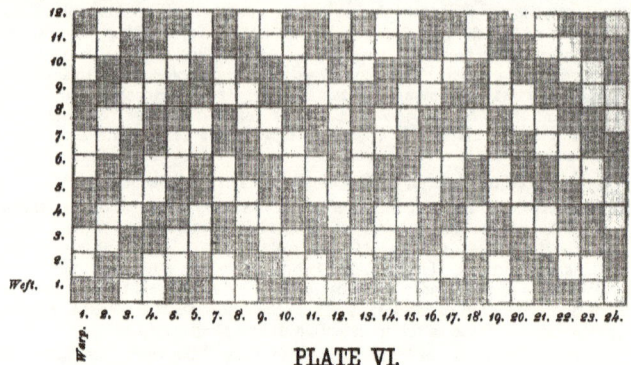

PLATE VI.

Diagram Illustrating the weave In the Nora cloth for making bags.

GENERAL SUMMARY.

It is impossible to draw a comparison between the methods of weaving practised by the various hilltribesmen of Assam owing to the meagreness of the information regarding most of them. From the above accounts, however, it will be seen that there is a very large variety in the instruments used and the processes of work. In fact, there are no two tribes whose methods appear to be exactly identical.

To compare the *beng* loom with the ordinary four-poster would be of little profit. It is sufficient to notice that the former is not suited for the production of fine fabrics even of small size. The method of working it causes a considerable strain upon the warp, and the constant jerks occasioned by the weaver leaning back would be sufficient to break any but the most substantial threads. The texture of the cloth produced upon this loom must necessarily be uneven and irregular. When no reed is used there is a tendency for the weaving to be closer at the edges than at the centre of the cloth, and when a reed is used there is no means of supporting it, so its whole weight is borne by the warp itself, except when it is being held by the weaver. Moreover the constant motion of the warp during the process of weaving is liable to displace the threads around the upper bar, even if they are securely fastened at the lower end, and so to cause unevenness in the tautness of the threads upon which weaving is taking place. The numerous devices to rectify this error are all but partial remedies. Thus, it is clear that the best fabrics produced upon the *beng* loom are coarse and rough.

Comparing the fabrics made on these two looms the Political Agent of Manipur says :—" The cloths made in loom No. 2 " (the *beng*) "are more durable than those of No. 1. The cloths made in the latter loom are thin, fine and less durable."

Among the products of the *beng* loom, perhaps the best fabrics are those of the Nagas, the worst those of the Mikirs. The former are carefully woven and excellent of their kind, the latter are of the roughest possible description. The difference is most marked. The Mikir cloths are quite outclassed by those of the Nagas, which compare not unfavourably with many woven in the plains upon the four-poster loom.

As in weaving cloth, so in spinning thread and cleaning cotton, the instruments and methods peculiar to the hills are so different from those used in the plains that a comparison is very difficult to draw. It is, however, interesting to note the striking resemblance between the instruments and methods of the hill tribesmen of Assam and those of the skilled workmen of Dacca. In cleaning, the men of Dacca use no gin, but manipulate the cotton on a board with an iron rod by a process almost identical with that of the Nagas of Mokokchang. In spinning, they use no spinning-wheel, but only a whorl even more primitive than that of the Nagas and the Miris. But the thread spun by these tribesmen is rough and uneven and suited only for the coarsest cloths, while that spun by the men of Dacca is the finest the world has yet produced. This difference in the quality and fineness of the thread is due almost entirely to the attention paid by the Dacca workmen to minute details, and the infinity of care and patience bestowed by them upon the work. In Dacca, after being bowed, the cotton "is lapped round a thick wooden roller; and on the removal of the latter instrument it is pressed between two flat boards. It is next rolled round a piece of lacquered reed of the size of a quill, and lastly, is enveloped in the smooth and soft skin of the *cuchia* fish, which serves as a cover to preserve it from dust and from being soiled whilst it is held in the hand during the process of spinning." The whorl, when not in use, is kept in a small flat work-basket, and when being used it rests upon a piece of shell embodied in clay. The spinster, while at work, applies chalk powder to her fingers from time to time.

No wonder that the thread spun in Dacca is far superior to any produced in Assam. But there are other causes that should not be lost sight of, *e.g.*, the natural dexterity of the Dacca workmen and the fact that these workmen are professional spinsters who earn their living by this work and have to satisfy the tastes of those who buy.

It may be noted here that the *nurakata* process, by which the finest thread in Assam is spun, appears even simpler than the ordinary methods of the plains. If a loose mass of cotton will give a finer thread than the same cotton made into rolls, what, it may be asked, is the use of forming those rolls ? No explanation has been furnished, but it may perhaps be merely to save time and trouble in the final stage of spinning. It may be, too, that the fineness of the *nurakata* thread is due chiefly to the skill of the workman and the careful preparation of the cotton.

That the machines used in the plains are superior to the crude instruments of the hill tribesmen admits of no doubt, and the former are fast driving out the latter. The *beng* loom has already, among many tribes, made way for the four-poster. The Kacharis and many other tribesmen settled in the plains have abandoned it entirely ; the Miris use it rarely except for the manufacture of their *jin* cloth ; the Garos, Manipuris and many others use both looms. But in the hills the *beng* still fairly holds its own. Not so the spinning whorl; the Nagas, it is true, still use this instrument and no other, and the Mikirs prefer it from religious scruples, but the Miris use it only for their coarsest thread, and the Garos have abandoned it entirely. The stone and roller for ginning have almost completely gone out of use, for it is only among the Nagas of Mokokchang that they are reported as being used at the present day.

PART IV.

The Fabrics themselves.

The cotton fabrics of Assam fall naturally into three main classes, *viz.* (1st) those of the Assamese, (2nd) those of the professional weavers of the Surma Valley, and (3rd) those of the hill tribes. These three classes differ widely from one another, and each will be separately dealt with. By far the least interesting cloths are those of the Surma Valley, which are practically identical with' some woven by the Tantis and Jugis of Eastern Bengal. The cloths of the Assamese and hill tribesmen are, however, of great interest. It is not the quality of the fabrics that distinguishes them from imported goods, but rather the peculiarity of the ornamentations upon them. These ornamentations form perhaps the most characteristic feature of the cotton fabrics of Assam, and so it is thought advisable to give some account of them before entering upon a detailed description of the cloths themselves.

Ornamentations.

The ornamentations on the cotton fabrics made within the Province can be grouped under two heads, *viz.*, 1st, those added to the woven cloth ; 2ndly, those made in the course of weaving. The second group is by far the more important.

1. Ornamentations added to the woven cloth.

The first instance of this variety of ornamentation is dyeing. It is not proposed here to discuss the methods of dyeing practised in Assam. The subject of dyes and dyeing was treated at some length last year by Mr. Duncan, and all available information will be found in Mr. Duncan's monograph. It may be stated briefly that dyeing among the people of Assam is an art of the past, at one time universally known, but now being rapidly forgotten. The most usual practice, however, was to dye not cloth but thread, and it is the dyeing of thread that has now been almost entirely discontinued; for the cheap imports of cotton thread in great variety of shade and thickness have crushed the local industry. It is improbable that this industry will revive, but not altogether impossible. A reaction appears already to have set in, in some places, against the coloured threads imported from Europe. In Lakhimpur the Assamese complain that the anilines and other dyes used by the foreigners injure the thread, and that the colours are fleeting. The vegetable dyes used in the Province are superior in both respects. But the people of this district appear never to have looked upon foreign coloured thread with such favour as those lower down the valley, so this reaction is hardly likely to extend.

The dyeing of woven cloth, however, has fairly held its ground. The people of the plains are far less fond of coloured clothing than their neighbours in the hills. The dyeing of woven cloth appears therefore always to have been confined to the hillsmen and more barbarous tribes, and among these people it is largely practised even at the present day. The Manipuris, the Nagas, the Mikirs and the Noras and Turungs of Jorhat still dye their own cloths. A specimen of cloth dyed by the Noras has been sent from Jorhat; the shade is a darkish blue; the colouring is very uneven, but is said to be very lasting [cf. Appendix (ii)].

Varieties of dyeing such as "knot dyeing—the tie-and-dye work for which Baran in the Kotah state is famed—appear unknown to the people of Assam, but Lieutenant Wilcox in 1828 noticed an example of this tie-and-dye work on some cloths of Thibetan manufacture worn by the Mishnees.

Stamping or printing of cloth also is little practised, though not absolutely unknown. Mr. Duncan, in his monograph on "Dyes and Dyeing," quotes from the report received from Sylhet: "There are three Mahomedans from Gorakpur in the town of Sylhet who carry on the business of printing cloths. But both the cloths and the dyes with which they are printed are imported articles." It is unfortunate that no account of the process has been given, but in all probability that there is nothing peculiar about it. The only example of printing by the people of this Province that has come to notice is to be found on a Manipuri cloth in the Indian Museum (No. 13 of the detailed list). This cloth is of white muslin, quite plain but for a design in pink which has evidently been stamped or printed on it. Time has not allowed of farther enquiries being made, but there is no reason to doubt that the cloth is from Manipur and woven and stamped by a Manipuri.

Another method of decorating woven cloth largely followed in Assam is by means of embroidery—chiefly in muga silk or gold and silver wire. The patterns formed in the body of the cloth will be discussed hereafter as they are produced at the time of weaving; but some cloths have embroidered borders sown on to them. The nature of these borders will be seen in the description of the *papidiya kapor* and *kareipi ban kara kapor*. Those of silk are probably formed in the same way as patterns in the body of the cloth. In former days the gold and silver wire (*guna*) used for embroidery was made within the Province by a class of workmen called *Gunakatia;* the process of manufacture was a trade secret, and no information concerning it has been procured. This is all the more regrettable as the class of *Gunakatia* is rapidly becoming extinct, and such men as still retain the name depend no longer on their professional occupation for a livelihood, but have taken to agriculture or other more profitable employments, and are fast losing or have already entirely lost their knowledge of the art for which they were once so famous. At the present day the gold and silver wire used for embroidery is imported from the West. This wire is far inferior in both quality and appearance to that of the *Gunakatia*. The latter was of pure material, never tarnished and was very lasting; the former is a mere imitation, and after passing once or twice through the washerman's hands it tarnishes and gets distorted with the result that the embroidery is ruined. It should be noticed here, however, that the embroidered borders are usually cut off before the cloth is sent to the wash, and again sewn on when it returns. But gold and silver wire and foil are used in the body of the cloth, as well as in the loose borders. As to the way in which this wire is used to form patterns on the cloth or on the borders, no information is available. Its use is known only to a few. There seems no reason, however, why it should not be treated in practically the same way as ordinary thread and an examination of the designs formed with it suggests that this is actually the case.

The use of gold thread is far more popular than that of silver, the colour of the former is much more attractive to the Assamese and the use of either is practically confined to those who can afford the more expensive.

These detached borders are sown on to the cloth by means of the needle, the use of which is a most interesting feature of the industry in Assam. Buchanan in Montgomery Martin's " Eastern India " says that it would appear that before the invasion of India by the Mohamedans the art of sewing was not practised there. However true this may be of India itself, it does not hold good as regards Assam, where the needle has been used from time immemorial. This fact has been established by one of those pithy and clever sayings so common among the Assamese, as will be seen from the following extract from a letter received from Babu Rajani Kanta Bordolai, Sub-Deputy Collector of Barpeta :—" Before the introduction of modern European needles, the Assamese used, all over the Province, brass needles manufactured by Benias or the goldsmiths. Every Assamese family was supplied with these articles by the Benias in exchange for rice and other eatables. They were almost similar to the modern article, but more lasting and flexible. For sewing *kanthas* and other coarse cloths big needless were used, and for sewing the sides of *mekhlas*, etc., small and fine needles were employed. For one *katha*, *i.e.*, half seer of rice, four needles could be got. There is a saying that—

" Dâkar bachan burâr kathâ
beji gandât châul kathâ."

which means that the dawk and the old men say that one *ganda, i.e.*, four needles can be got for one *katha, i.e.*, half a seer of rice, there being no monetary system of exchange then.

" I am sorry I could not procure an old needle. With the advent of the European article, the Benias have left off making these articles. However, I have got from an old Benia of 70 years of age two needles after the real Assamese pattern. They have been sent in a separate parcel."

The needles sent answer the above description, except perhaps as regards flexibility. They will be forwarded with the fabrics and weaving instruments collected to the Director of Land Records in Assam.

From Golaghat, too, it is reported that in days of old the Assamese used needles of their own, made of brass and iron, and resembling the modern article, except that they were larger and stouter.

The use of the needle in Assam is, and always has been, manifold. The clothing of the people includes several made-up garments—, coats for the men, petticoats for the women and bags for use on a journey. In the manufacture of all these the needle is used. A most interesting example is found in the making of patch-work cloths. In Golaghat used and worn cloths are cut up and the sounder portions sewn together to form a sort of rag coat worn generally by children. In Goalpara the Kacharis cut off the borders of their *gamcha* and sew them together into coats. These *Kachari* coats are true patch-work, and the effect of the many different coloured borders sewn together, with few or no white or even plain coloured patches visible is most startling.

But far the most important use of the needle is for the making of patterns on the cloth. It has been already mentioned that such patterns are usually formed at the time of weaving, but with the most expensive fabrics this is not always the case. In Golaghat it is said that patterns are worked by the needle upon *gutibulua kapor* and *karsipt ban kara kapor*. The Manipuris, too, are skilled in this kind of embroidery. In the border of their *fanek* they work with the needle most charming patterns in silks of brilliant colours.

There is one more way in which cloths are decorated after they are woven. This is by the attachment of different objects to the cloth. The Nagas, for instance, are very fond of fastening rows of cowrie shells upon the face of their cloths. Some tribes fasten brass plates and bosses in a similar way, others pieces of cut stone. In the Garo Hills a woman's waistcloth is often adorned with stone beads attached to the edges, and is sometimes worn in connection with a *senki* or waistband of stone and glass beads. This is tied round the waist as well as the waistcloth itself, and the combined effect is very pretty. An instance of the use of brass plates is found in the Garo *kadisil*, but the Garos are not the only people that use such plates.

In a similar way cloths are adorned with objects tied on to their fringes, but the subject of fringes will be treated later on.

3.—*Ornamentations made at the time of weaving.*

The next class of ornamentations comprises those made at the time of weaving. Of these the simplest are formed by using threads of different colours, thickness or material, no change in the process of weaving being required.

The dyeing of thread has been briefly referred to above, and no further remarks

N 2

are necessary. Here, however, it may be mentioned that the use of particoloured threads appear unknown in Assam, and so does the admixture of different materials to form one thread, unless a mixture of this sort is meant in the following passage extracted from the Mokokchang report :—" Red wool and dog's hair dyed red are mixed sometimes in the cotton fabrics by way of ornamentation. Red wool is mixed when weaving *sepiti* (the *mekhela* or petticoat worn by females) and dog's hair for the ornamental cloth called *subangiu*. The mixing is done by an instrument called the *jebsu* and is woven in with the thread in the ordinary manner."

This last sentence is not very clear; it may mean that a mixed thread is woven in, otherwise it is unintelligible. The *jebsu* is not explained. It is apparently not a whorl, as the name of that in Mokokchang is *bang*. It is probable therefore that the mixing of materials is in the cloth, not in the thread.

The subject of mixed fabrics has already been treated. The combination of threads of different materials in the warp or weft does not appear to be much used for the purpose of ornamentation, although the effect of such combination may be to produce a species of ornamentation. A strips of *muga* is, however, occasionally found as forming the background of more elaborate designs.

The process of weaving being unaltered, the use of threads of different colours or different thicknesses has the effect of producing lines or stripes along or across the cloth according as the mixture is made in the warp or in the weft.

In plain weaving the threads of the warp pass over or under those of the weft alternately with perfect regularity. Thus, when the weaving is fairly loose, only one-half of any thread, whether in warp or weft, is visible on either side of the cloth. A single thread of different colour from the rest forms therefore a broken line, and a pair of consecutive threads forms two such broken lines which, at a slight distance, look like one continuous line.

It is, therefore, almost invariably found that the different coloured threads introduced at one place in either warp or weft are of an even number, two or more. Two of such threads form a single line, and more than two together form a stripe which varies in width with the number of like threads composing it.

Independent cross lines and stripes are found usually at or near the ends of a cloth, but occasionally also at intermediate positions. These cross lines are often found in connection with an elaborate border at one end of a cloth, and form a part of such border. Sometimes a coloured stripe of this nature forms the background of a more elaborate design, such as will be described hereafter.

In the case of cloths woven on the four poster loom, stripes and lines of colour running lengthwise are much rarer than cross stripes and lines. The reason is obvious, for, to form a cross stripe, all that is required is to use two shuttles instead of one, the extra shuttle containing a spool of different coloured thread. When the first thread of the line or stripe is shot the main shuttle is merely left idle on the ground, and the additional shuttle brought into use. Similarly when the stripe is finished the additional shuttle is left idle on the ground and the main one picked up and again brought into play. There is no necessity even to break off the thread when the shuttle is laid aside, and this is not done except in cases when that shuttle will not be again required for some considerable length of cloth. But the formation of stripes running lengthwise is much more difficult, for the thread to form them has to be introduced at the time of warping. Now in the Assamese process warping necessitates the use of a number of reels (*ugha*) and a *karhani*, and so each variety of colour involves either the use of a separate set of *ugha* and a separate *karhani* or else the very tedious and difficult process of laying the additional threads in proper order round the posts by the hand alone. This latter process is comparatively simple if only one *kani* (pair) of threads be laid, and so it is not unusual to find a single coloured line at or near each edge of the cloth. It is said that in Sibsagar the only colour of thread used for such lines is red.

With the *beng* loom the introduction of different coloured threads at the time of warping is simpler. In the Garo process, for instance, all that is required is the use of a fresh ball of warp thread for each new colour. The number of successive warp threads of one colour is however not arbitrary, but depends on the cycle of the warp. Each colour must comprise one or more complete cycles, and at each change of colour the thread of one ball must be broken off and tied round the rod as if the warp were complete, and the end of the thread on the second ball must then be fastened on the rod as at the commencement of warping. Thus in cloths woven on the *beng* loom the introduction of lengthwise stripes is far more common than in those woven by the Assamese process.

The Surma Valley process admits of the formation of stripes in the warp as easily as in the weft, but as a matter of fact, they appear to be more usual in the latter.

By combinations of threads of different colours in either warp or weft many pleasing effects can be produced. The number is much greater when the combinations are in both. Two of the most interesting combinations are the *charkhana* of the Goalpara weavers and the checks of the Khamptis and other tribes in Upper Assam.

To produce the *charkhana* thin stripes of some dark colour (*e.g.*, red) are introduced at equal intervals in both warp and weft, the main colour of both being some light shade, such as yellow. The effect is a 'pattern of hollow squares of red on a background of yellow, which is most effective. The check is formed by both warp and weft being made up of stripes of different colours, which follow one another in regular succession, the order being often the same in both warp and weft.

Another curious combination of colours is produced by making the warp entirely of one colour and the weft entirely of another. A cloth received from Sylhet is of this nature, the colours being red and blue; the effect is that the cloth appears of a shade like purple, a cross between the two main colours.

It has been presumed throughout that the weaving is fairly open. In many cases, however, especially among the Hill Tribes, the weaving is very close, the effect of which is that the weft is hardly, if at all, visible. A noteworthy instance of this is found in the *fanek* of the Manipuris, in which the weft is often of some dark colour, such as red, while the warp is of many colours, some of which are light, but still the weft does not show through on either side of the cloth. The object, in such cases, of using coloured thread for the weft is not very obvious, but in the majority of cases, the colour is comparatively dark. It is possible that this dark colour, while not itself appearing, throws into prominence the lighter colours of the warp.

There is one arrangement of coloured stripes in the warp and weft which deserves special notice. In a Kuki cloth from North Cachar the body of the cloth was white, entirely white in both warp and weft, and the side borders were similarly entirely black. The result had been produced by laying a stripe of black on either edge of the warp, and by using, apparently, three shuttles simultaneously, two containing black thread and one containing white. One shuttle, containing black thread, would be thrown from left to right through none but the black threads on the left of the warp, and then thrown back from right to left through the same threads, so that the black thread on this shuttle would interloop with the white thread on the second shuttle. Similarly the third shuttle would be thrown through the black threads only on the right edge of the warp, and on the return throw this thread would be made to interloop with the white thread on the second or main shuttle, which in turn would pass through none but white threads. This much is evident from an examination of the cloth itself, but the details of the working have not been described.

A cloth from Manipur exhibits a further development of this system of ornamentation. In this, the body of the cloth is entirely white and the borders entirely black, but from the black border jut out simple designs in black extending into the body of the cloth. These designs are very indistinct and can be seen only if the cloth be held up to the light, as the warp is white and the weaving is very close.

The use of threads of different thicknesses instead of different colours is also not uncommon. The same effect may be produced by weaving together two or more threads of ordinary thickness. An example of this is exhibited in the selvage, the process of making which has already been described. Many other varieties of ornamentation are made in the same way, as for instance alternate ribs along the length of the cloth, and extending over the whole or any portion of its width.. These are made by passing two or more threads through one dent in the reed, and a single thread through the next, and so on. The ribs may be of the width corresponding to a single dent in the reed, as in the above example, or may be of the nature of raised stripes, each extending over two or more successive dents. The width of the plain weaving in between may vary in the same way.

Similarly, two threads may be wound together on the spool, so that each shot of the weft will consist of two threads instead of one, but this is not usual except in the case of the *beng* loom when the warp threads are often laid double, and then the object is not ornamentation, but the strengthening of the cloth.

In either of these cases the effect may be heightened by the double threads differing in colour from the single ones.

Numerous examples of stripes and lines of all the different kinds above described will be found in the *khaniya* and *cheleng* of Assam.

The next kind of ornamentation to be discussed is the fringe. With the exception of fabrics used for made-up garments, satchels and the like, and some of the very scanty garments of the hill tribes, nearly every cloth made in Assam possesses a fringe at one end or both.

At the time of actual weaving, whatever process be employed, the warp passes round a rod at either end, and at the far end of the warp a portion averaging about eight inches in length is left unwoven. Two portions of the warp, therefore, are always available for making fringes, *viz.*, that passing round the rod at one end and that left unwoven at the other. The former being very short, the fringe at one end of the cloth is of necessity very short, but that at the other end varies in length from one inch to six or even more according to the nature of the cloth and the fancy of the weaver When a short fringe is required at either end, the unwoven threads are cut off at the required distance from the last shot of the weft.

Fringes are of many different kinds, irrespective of their length. Some are quite plain, being merely the rough ends of the threads after the waste portion of the warp has been cut off. Some consist of loops just as they come off the rod at the near end of the warp. Sometimes these loops are cut so as to make the fringes at both ends of the cloth alike. More usually, however, the threads are formed into tassels by two or more being twisted together and knotted at the end. Sometimes the knots are dispensed with. An interesting point about these knots is that they are often used as distinctive marks, and persons frequently profess to be able to identify plain cloths which have no other distinguishing marks, solely by the nature of the knots on the tassels at either end. Whether they really can do so or not is open to doubt. The colours of these simple fringes correspond, of course, with those of the warp.

Sometimes more elaborate tassels are formed, *e.g.*, by tying a piece of tinsel or a bunch of different coloured threads on to the loose threads at the end of the cloth.[*] One very interesting kind of fringe or tassel is found in some Naga cloths, where the long ends of the warp threads are passed (several at a time) through blades of straw painted yellow.

The loose ends of the warp are not always formed into fringes; they are often cut off flush with the cloth; sometimes the loops of the thread are interlocked, and so the end of the cloth bound up; sometimes a piece of thick string is sewn along the end of the cloth. These devices are to be seen in many of the cloths of the Hill Tribes.

Fringes at the sides of a cloth are very rare, as they cannot be formed by ordinary weaving, but occasionally a number of threads much longer than the cloth is wide, are introduced between the shots of the weft as will be described hereafter, and the loose ends are left projecting from either side and forming fringes. A good example of such fringes can be seen in the *jymphong* or sleeveless coat of the Syntengs; which also has end fringes nearly a foot long.

There is one more variety of fringe, if it can be so called, which appears neither at the sides nor at the ends of the cloth, but in the cloth itself. It is produced by leaving a portion of the warp unwoven at the time of shooting the weft. The effect is a kind of fringe, the only difference between it and true fringe being that it has woven cloth at both ends of it. It has been called a "false fringe" in the description of many cloths given hereafter. These false fringes are very common in the cloths of both valleys. They are occasionally intended to serve a useful purpose, *viz.*, to mark off the ends of two cloths woven in one piece. The false fringe being cut through, two plain fringes result, one on either cloth. This is illustrated in a wrapper received from Sylhet. In Assam the term *agat chula diya* is applied to a cloth to indicate that it has a false fringe as just described.

Another variety of ornamentation is that produced by a different arrangement of the healds. One example of this is to be found in the cloth for Nora bags, a description of which has already been given. Another example is exhibited in the satchels made by the Khamptis of Lakhimpur, which are very similar to those of the Noras, but much more elegant and costly. The pattern upon them is quite different from that on the Nora bags, but is evidently produced in a similar manner. The effect is heightened by the use of threads of many different colours. It is unfortunate that no description of the process of weaving this cloth has been received.

This method of ornamentation is also known to the Manipuris, as can be inferred from some of their cloths in which zigzag ribs appear in the end borders. There is also another peculiar variety of texture found in some of the Manipuri cloths, *viz.*, the honeycomb. The exact way in which this is formed has not been explained, and is not obvious from an examination of the cloth itself.

---

[*] A tassel of this nature is called *ghughura* in Golaghat.

Another variety of ornamentation is that by which a fleece is formed on one side of the cloth. The method has already been fully explained in the description of the process of weaving the Miri *jin* cloth. A similar cloth, which however differs in essential points from this Miri *jin*, is the *pari* of the Kukis. A specimen of this cloth has been received from Silchar, but the process of manufacture has not been described. A somewhat similar device to this is the stuffing of cloth with cotton wool at the time of weaving to form a quilt (*c.f.* the *lashing fi*, Manipuri No. 86).

Numerous and important as are the modes of ornamentation detailed above, by far the most important, as it is the most interesting yet remains to be described. In this the ornamental design, though introduced at the time of weaving, is still entirely distinct from the body of the cloth itself, and might be removed without the fabric being seriously injured. Designs of this nature are formed by introducing between successive shots of the weft additional threads, the colour of which may be the same as that of the weft or different. These threads are not usually single, but several are inserted together, so that they may stand out in marked relief from the body of the cloth. Generally cotton is used, but frequently country silk, and more rarely pure silk or wool is used in place of cotton. These threads are not woven in with the same regularity as is the weft, *viz.*, alternately over one and under each set of alternate warp threads, but they are passed over and under these threads, upper and lower alike, in any order, the only thing governing that order being the nature of the design intended to be formed.

Designs of this nature are of many different kinds, among which the following may be mentioned as the most usual and most important.

First comes simple lines or stripes running across the whole width of the cloth. In these the additional threads are generally passed alternately over and under several warp threads in regular succession, *e.g.*, over one *kani* (or pair of upper and lower threads) and under the next; usually it is more than one *kani* over or under which they pass. A very favourite arrangement of this kind is a pair of such threads of the same colour close together (with one shot of the weft|between) the two threads running in the same way, but the one passing under those warp threads over which the other passes and *vice versâ*. The effect of this is a wavy or plaited line running across the cloth. Another favourite arrangement is of three such threads, the two outer threads being of one colour and the inner thread of another. Stripes of this nature are rarely made up of more than five lines of thread, and it is seldom that more than two consecutive lines are of the same colour. Such stripes are sometimes found by themselves, but are much more frequently used to finish or set off stripes containing patterns of more elaborate design, such as will be described below.

The next variety consists of small and independent designs. These are sometimes geometrical, such as diamonds, stars, triangles or crosses, sometimes artificial, *e.g.*, rosettes, but much more usually they represent some natural object, *e.g.*, a man, an animal, a bird, a fish, an insect, a butterfly, a flower, a tree, a fruit or leaf, a fan, a temple, but the variety is infinite, the whole range of nature being freely drawn upon. But these designs, while representing natural objects, are by no means true to nature. Indeed it is well nigh impossible in many cases to say what they are meant to represent. The difficulty is often intensified by the colouring used. Accuracy is sacrificed not only to symmetry, but also to variety of colouring and the exigencies of the occasion. Thus the trees depicted on Assamese cloths have an equal number of branches on each side and bear fruit in similar positions. If the fruit be red, it very often happens that the other leaves and the portion of the trunk on the same level are also red, the remainder being green. So, too, a brown elephant may be all white on the level of his tusks and all blue on a level with his eye. But oftentimes no attempt at accuracy is made, and a goat will be woven green simply because no other colour would harmonise as well, at least none of those in the weaver's basket.

Amid such inaccuracies it is rather surprising to find a close adherence to nature in points which to the Western mind might appear indecent. In one of the most handsome cloths I have seen in Assam, I found a representation of a deer which was realistic, but not beautiful.

These small and independent designs or *phul*, as they are called by the Assamese, are sometimes scattered over the body of the cloth apparently haphazard, but it is generally found on closer inspection that this arrangement is regulated by the way in which the cloth is worn, the exposed portions being more lavishly ornamented than the rest. At other times, however, these designs are arranged in rows between two stripes or lines of the nature above described, and in this way they are often made to form part of a wide border at one end of the cloth.

There is another variety of designs formed in this way, *viz.*, a patterned stripe running across the whole width of the cloth. This stripe is usually divided into square or rectangular portions, each portion consisting of a frame containing some geometrical design, varied occasionally by the introduction of rosettes or flowers to fill the blank spaces of the pattern. Sometimes these rectangles or squares are all of the same size and contain the same design repeated again and again from one side of the cloth to the other, but more usually two or three different designs are found in one border, one or more being rectangular and the others square; and these designs follow one another in regular succession across the entire width of the cloth. The frames are usually formed in the same way as the designs themselves. Sometimes instead of being enclosed in frames the different designs are divided off from one another by some simple figure. These figures exhibit great variety. One of the most common and at the same time one of the simplest and most effective consists of an elongated letter X having the upper and lower portions filled in with V's of graduated sizes, those in the lower half being of course inverted. These are formed by cross threads which appear on the face of the cloth where required to form a portion of the figure, but lie out of sight beneath the warp in the intervening, portions. The thickness of each parallel line in the figure is generally about equal to the interval between any two adjacent lines, and so two patterns of very similar nature are formed on the two sides of the cloth. Another good instance of these figures is the *gacha* (candlestick) which is even simpler and not less effective; it somewhat resembles the letter I, but not entirely.

It has been said that these designs are usually geometrical, but that they are sometimes varied by the introduction of rosettes in the blank spaces. When this is the case the rosettes are often formed independently of the geometrical design and in a slightly different way, being woven not into the upper and lower threads together as is the main design, but into only one of these sets of threads. The consequence is that these rosettes appear on only one side of the cloth, the under portion of the thread lying above the other set of main warp threads. At the same time portions of these threads are usually more or less visible from the reverse side of the cloth, owing to the fact already mentioned that these additional threads are usually not single, but in sets much thicker in the aggregate than the main threads of the cloth.

Sometimes these stripes, especially if narrow, are continuous throughout the width of the cloth and are not divided into squares and rectangles. In all such cases the designs are very simple. Sometimes they are purely geometrical consisting, for example, of a series of parallel, curved or angular lines like the symbols often used in maps to designate a chain of mountains; in some such cases there is an interval between each line, in others lines of different colours follow each other in immediate succession. Sometimes these stripes represent a natural object, such as a creeper, a rough approximation to a snake, or the like; sometimes they are hardly geometrical or natural, as in the case of a chain of loops, each loop enclosing a Maltese cross.

The ornamentations just described are formed, as already mentioned, by introducing additional threads between the shots of the weft. The way in which small independent designs are made is as follows :—Both treadles being set free, the upper and lower sets of warp threads come together. The weaver then takes up a small flat stick, and counting out the threads of the warp, passes the stick over and under these threads in exactly the same order as that required for the thread for the design. She then turns the flat stick on edge, and, in the gap so formed, inserts the additional thread, holding one end close to one side of the gap. She then presses this thread fairly close with the edge of the stick, which she turns flat for this purpose and then removes. Then, pressing the treadle, she shoots another weft in the ordinary way, and with the reed drives home this and the additional thread behind it. Both treadles are again set free, and the flat stick once more inserted between the warp threads in the required order, which may be the same as before or different according to the nature of the design being made. The long end of the extra thread is next passed through the gap in the reverse direction. It is then pressed close with the stick and the stick removed ; another weft is shot and this and the thread behind it are driven home with the reed. The process is repeated in this way till the design is complete.

Thus any number of designs may be formed at different positions on the cloth. When two or more designs are abreast or overlap, they are, unless very far apart, usually connected together and woven with one thread, *i. e.*, that portion of each pattern which lies between the same two shots of the weft is usually formed with the same piece of additional thread, this thread passing above the warp threads where it is intended to appear on the face of the cloth, and below all the other warp threads, including all those lying between the two designs.

The formation of lines or stripes of this nature extending across the whole width of the cloth is exactly the same in principle, being in fact only a modification of the process by which the several small independent designs are connected together and woven with one thread. It may be mentioned, however, that when these small designs are made independently of one another, which is frequently the case, the flat stick used is very short, whereas when a line or stripe is formed or when a number of such small designs are connected together and formed at one time a much longer stick has of necessity to be used.

In Tezpur two such sticks are mentioned. The first, called *bachani chiri* (counting stick), is described as a very fine and flat stick ⅛ inch broad, used for counting the threads when ornamentations are being formed. The second called *phulchari (phulcheri*), in Gauhati is described as a still finer stick fixed in the warp at the time of forming ornamentations.

The above description applies to the process employed with the four-poster loom. That employed with the *beng* loom, is practically the same. It has already been described under the Garo process of weaving and needs no further explanation.

The order in which the additional threads pass under and over the main warp threads depends largely on the nature of the pattern being formed. In any but the most simple patterns, it is very difficult, if not impossible, for the weaver to remember this order exactly. This difficulty is heightened by the fact that in most cases, if not universally, the cloth is woven face downwards, and so it is impossible at the time of weaving to detect an error as, in most patterns, especially in those representing natural objects, the wrong side of the cloth, which is all that is visible to the weaver, exhibits nothing but a confused mass of threads.

The consequence is that none but the most skilled and practised weavers can form any but the simplest design without having in front of them some pattern to guide them in their work. Barpeta seems to be an exception to the rule, for there the weavers are said to work out their designs from memory by dint of practice.

The patterns so used vary largely over the Province, or rather over the Assam Valley and the Hills, for in the Surma Valley their use is said to be unknown. They may be divided into three main classes.

(1) The simplest form of pattern consists of pieces cut off an old ornamented cloth. These old samples are largely used in the lower districts of the Assam Valley, *viz.*, Goalpara, Kamrup and Darrang. A selection of such patterns is usually kept in a basket suspended from the upper cross-bar of the loom.

(2) The most advanced form consists of drawings on paper, used only by the Manipuris. The Political Agent writes as follows:—"The Manipuri weavers do not use any pattern from which they copy the designs on the borders or in the body of their cloths." But later on in the report he says: "The Manipuris use a large variety of patterns, and while there is a falling off in the fineness of their work, their taste artistically seems to maintain its standard. The patterns are drawn out on paper by the operator as required." These two statements appear at first sight contradictory, but what is probably meant is that the same paper pattern is not used twice over and that the pattern is designed afresh for every cloth. If this be so, the variety of designs on Manipuri cloths is practically unlimited. In any case the Manipuris are far more advanced than any of the other weavers in Assam. All other kinds of patterns used in Assam are concrete representations of the woven cloth itself. To design such a pattern requires merely a knowledge of weaving and a certain power of imagination. But to be able to represent on paper a design in a woven cloth requires a considerable knowledge of drawing and the ability to realise from a picture the effect of the design when woven on the cloth itself. It would be very interesting to see some of these paper designs, but unfortunately none have been sent. The way in which they are used has not been described. It may be noted that the Dacca weavers for their *jamdanees* use paper patterns which they place below the warp at the time of weaving.

(3) The third and most common kind of pattern found in Assam is that called *chaneki*. These *chaneki* are universally used in Lakhimpur, Sibsagar and Nowgong to the exclusion of any other kind. In the districts of Darrang and Kamrup also they are to some extent employed. They exhibit great variety, and a full discussion of the subject of *chaneki* would be very lengthy. It is sufficient to describe the kinds most commonly used.

(i) The first class, which is becoming more and more popular nowadays, especially in Lakhimpur, comprises *chaneki* made of thread woven upon thin slips of bamboo.

The thread represents the warp and the bamboo slips the weft. Each slip passes over and under the threads in the same order as the additional threads at the time of weaving are required to pass over and under the warp threads of the actual cloth.

Twenty-two distinct varieties of this class of *chaneki* have been received from the Assistant Political Agent of Sadiya, who said that many more could be collected if required. The varieties all represent differences in the *chaneki* themselves and are independent of the designs upon them. Further varieties have been received from other districts, *vis.*, Sibsagar and Darrang.

The thread on these *chaneki* is sometimes white, sometimes coloured and sometimes of unboiled cotton like that used by the Miris for their *jin* cloth.

The slips are generally of bamboo, but sometimes of jungle grass, and occasionally both kinds are found in the same *chaneki*. When of bamboo the slips vary very much in size and shape. They are generally more or less round and very fine, but sometimes they are much more substantial and sometimes they are flat rather than round. In length these slips vary from four or five inches to three feet. The largest *chaneki* reported is three feet square, but none received are nearly so large as that.

Some *chaneki* of this nature contain only one design,—generally a border design,—some contain two or more up to as many as 15. When there is more than one design, each is divided from the next by a bit of plain weaving, which is generally very small containing not more than six shots of weft. Sometimes a portion of the thread is left unwoven, and so false fringes are formed in the middle or near the ends of the *chaneki*.

Sometimes the threads form a fringe at each end of the *chaneki* and in this case there is a short length of woven cloth between the last design and the fringe. But more usually both ends are strengthened by one or two thicker rods of bamboo or even by a stout whole bamboo, so that the *chaneki* may be suspended by the one, while the other by its weight keeps the whole in position. Occasionally a piece of stout string or rope is fastened on to the *chaneki* to form a handle by which it can be suspended. In some cases the rods or rollers are found at one end only.

In some *chaneki* the slips are not merely woven into a number of cotton threads forming the warp, but they are woven into a complete cloth background, in which both warp and weft are formed of thread. These patterns appear to represent the actual designs on the cloth more closely than any others, for the slips do actually take the place of additional threads.

Again some *chaneki* in which the weft is formed of bamboo slips contain small designs woven in coloured thread on the background formed by the main pattern. Small designs of this nature on the actual cloth have already been mentioned, and it is evidently for such cases that these *chaneki* are intended.

The *chaneki* of this class received from different districts exhibit many differences in matters of detail which have not been mentioned above, but enough has been said to show that there are many varieties among them.

(ii) Another class of *chaneki* consists of patterns in which both warp and weft are represented by bamboo slips. They are in reality small bamboo mats. These *chaneki* represent sometimes border patterns, sometimes individual designs, but very rarely pictures of natural objects. The slips representing the weft are usually all of equal width and disconnected. Those representing the warp, however, vary in width, the wide slips being split for the greater portion of their length into so many narrow portions. The narrow portions are of approximately equal width and represent single threads of the warp; they are much narrower than the slips representing the weft.

Very few *chaneki* of this class have been received, and all of them are very similar. In one or two instances, however, a single long slip is made to represent two shots of the weft, being passed through once and then doubled back and passed through again in the reverse direction, just like the thread in actual weaving.

(iii) There is a third class of *chaneki* quite distinct from the two just mentioned. These *chaneki* are made out of leaves. A portion of a large leaf is taken and in it parallel slits are cut at equal distances so as to follow the grain. The portion between two consecutive slits represents a single thread of the warp. To represent the weft, bamboo slips are threaded through the slits at right angles to them, so as to pass over and under the intervening portions in the same order as the additional thread would pass over and under the warp threads in the cloth itself.

The most usual material for these *chaneki* is the broad or outer portion of the betel leaf (*dhakua*). If the pattern be large, this is used in its entire thickness, but for small patterns it is pared down and made much thinner. Sometimes a dry plantain leaf is used and sometimes even a green plantain leaf, but a *chaneki* of this nature should be used while the leaf is fresh, as the withering of the leaf renders the design indistinct and leaves the slip so loose as to readily fall out. Of the specimens received some seem to be made out of other trees, *e.g.*, the date and cocoanut, but it is difficult to tell from the specimens themselves, and no descriptive account has been sent with them. None of the specimens contains more than one design, and all of these are individual designs, most of which represent natural objects.

These *chaneki* appear to be the oldest of all used in Assam, but they are now being driven out by those made of thread and bamboo slips. They are, however, still largely used throughout the districts of Lakhimpur and Sibsagar, and also to some extent by the weavers of the Borgaon, Balipara, Bisunath and Gohpur Mouzas in Darrang. The weavers of all parts of the Darrang district, however, use portions cut off old clothes in preference to any other patterns. In this district *chaneki* made of thread and bamboo slips are used in the Sadr sub-division by those weavers who do not use those made of betel leaf (*dhakua*).

Chaneki are made by the older women of the household. They are very durable and are handed down from one generation to the next. The patterns now worked out are as a rule merely copies of old ones with or without modifications.

There seem to be no Assamese names to distinguish the three kinds of *chaneki* but this word appears to be used in Darrang as signifying only those of the first kind, *viz.*, those made of thread and bamboo slips. In other places the word *chaneki* appears to be applied equally to all three kinds. Generally speaking, *chaneki* are named according to the design upon them. Thus the design of a tree is called *gach phul*, and the *chaneki* containing this design is called *gach phular chaneki*. When a *chaneki* contains several different designs it is named accordingly, but such names are probably not often used.

The word *phul* seems to be applied equally to individual designs and to portions of a border stripe, and in some cases its meaning is extended to cover ribs or coloured lines. The following list contains the names of some of the *phul* formed on the cloths and patterns received from different districts or named in the district reports. The list might be indefinitely extended, as even in the cloths and *chaneki* recieved there are very many designs of which the names have not been mentioned. It is, however, long enough to give a fairly good idea of the favourite objects depicted by the weavers of Assam. The names of *phul* representing natural objects explain themselves, but in many cases the design bears little or no resemblance to the object it is supposed to represent. In the case of geometrical designs the names are fanciful and often unintelligible. The *phul* are classified according to the districts from which they have been received or reported. No further classification has been attempted, as in many cases it is not known whether the designs are natural objects or purely geometrical.

List of Ornamentations on Assamese Cloths.

From Barpeta.

1. *Kotari debya.* Flower of *kotari debya* tree.
2. *Kachei.* A worm.
3. *Cholikhur.* A razor.
4. *Goloch.* A white flower with 5 lobes and a ball.
5. *Ajodhyar dama.* The drum of Oudh.
6. *Bartal.* Big cymbal used on occasions of *sankirtan.*
7. *Sarutal.* Small cymbal used by drummers called *dhulia.*
8. *Khutital.* Very small cymbal called *manjura*, used by singing parties.
9. *Makhimur.* A fly's head.
10. *Taraguti.* Seed of the taraguti plant.
11. *Juti.* A small white flower.
12. *Dimaru.* The fruit of the fig.
13. *Nagesvar.* The flower of the *nagesvar* tree.
14. *Bari bera.* A kind of grass which forms excellent fodder for horses.
15. *Ashtakadam.* Eight kadam flowers.
16. *Nutanatka.* A new silver coin.
17. *Boghaku.* The eye of the common paddy bird.
18. *Tagar.* A flower.
19. *Megdor.*
20. *Chandar merghar.* The circular house built by Chundo Sodagar to keep himself and his family safe from snake-bites, as *Mnlsa*, the Goddess of snakes, had cursed him.
21. *Mejmachia.* Table and chair.
22. *Bechiar tal.* Cymbals used in making nautch girls dance.

23. *Kathanda.* A white flower.
24. *Bolichanda.* Talc.
25. *Dalicha.* A carpet.
26. *Chikantemital.* Cymbal and *temi, i.e.,* a small case for holding limes.
27. *Bar dama.* A big drum.
28. *Saru dama.* A small drum.
29. *Athbichani.* Eight fans.
30. *Kekrisoi.* The carved roof of the *dola* used to carry the bridegroom on the occasion of a marriage ceremony.
31. *Bar kadam.* Large *kadam* flower.
32. *Saru kadam.* Small *kadam* flower.
33. *Bhanda.* The unyielding man of Padmapuran.
34. *Makoradant.* The teeth of a spider.
35. *Phular-dola.* A palkee made of flowers.
36. *Padma chaka* The ovary of the lotus.
37. *Bok phul.* The *bok* flower.
38. *Ahok phul.* A small yellow flower.
39. *Surja kanti.* The sun flower.
40. *Chandra kanti.* A kind of flower.
41. *Barjola.*
42. *Saru jola.*
43. *Bar mokaddama.* A big law suit (a stamp pattern).
44. *Saru mokaddama.* A petty law suit.
45. *Kapal chenga.* The fruit of a creeper.
46. *Tilokh.* The mark of sandal paste worn by *Boishnabs.*
47. *Betar jahi.* A forest of cane.
48. *Panch pahia late.* A creeper with five branches.
49. *Bar padma.* A large lotus.
50. *Satpahia padma.* A lotus with seven petals.
51. *Guna phutuki.* Spots made of silver lace (specimens received from Mangaldai and Tezpur).
52. *Poro chakua.* A pigeon's eye.
53. *Chip jari.* Fishing rod and line.
54. *Bhotgutia.* A mark of disease in the throat.
55. *Jatar chatni.* The framework of the spinning wheel.
56. *Achra jal.* Fishing net.
57. *Arsi.* A looking glass (specimen received from Jorhat).
58. *Garo chaka.* A kind of flower.
59. *Khat khutia.* Bedposts.
60. *Chob.* A finger ring.
61. *Thaka chob.* A cluster of rings.
62. *Rajimala.* A creeper.
63. *Chira sandah.** Fried rice or paddy.
64. *Hatighora.* Elephants and horses.
65. *Ghora manuh.* Horses and men.
66. *Dhanu kar.* Bows and arrows.

The following are additional examples of ornamentations, found on cloths made in Barpeta:—

67. *Lata.* A creeper.
68. *Bakul.* A kind of flower (specimens received from Mangaldai and Tezpur).
69. *Khonda chapa.*
70. *Saru khonda chapa.*
71. *Belpat.* The leaf of a bel tree.
72. *Salika thutia phul.* The beak of a mina.
73. *Chapa chakuli.*
74. *Baiha patia.* A pattern in the shape of an oar.
75. *Padmalata.*
76. *Dhekia patia.* A tiger (this word also means striped).
77. *Uthachapa.*
78. *Kadam.* A kind of tree.
79. *Karoni.*
80. *Bichani.* A fan.
81. *Chira phul.*
82. *Penpeli phul.*
83. *Galicha mukhpat.**
84. *Cherilata.**
85. *Parong.**
86. *Uttamureh pat.**
87. *Tiahjalia phul.**
88. *Soarnalata.** (A *muga* border.)
89. *Bichanipad.**
90. *Kesari.* A lion.
91. *Mora sharai.* A peacock.
92. *Hati.* An elephant.
93. *Gahari.* A hog.

94. *Charai.* A bird.
95. *Karapara.**
96. *Chain kara.**
97. *Ranga pari.** Red border at the sides.

From Tezpur.

1. *Loheri.*
2. *Angatha bakul.*
3. *Babari.** An edible plant (1 specimen from Tezpur and 6 from Jorhat).
4. *Nara padum.* A kind of flower.
5. *Barpadum.* A large lotus.
6. *Kharika chapa.* (Specimen from Sibsagar.)
7. *Bar chapa.**
8. *Parua gati.* Ants.
9. *Bhaonriya.*
10. *Kech.*
11. *Kekowa kech.*
12. *Hati gachh.* Elephants and trees.
13. *Mokaddama.* A law suit.
14. *Agnigar.*
15. *Japa.* A clothes basket.
16. *Pakhila.* A butterfly; (specimen from Golaghat).
17. *Thop tara.* A cluster of stars.
18. *Pitha.* A loaf.
19. *Agheretia.*
20. *Kep.* A two pronged instrument for raising bamboos.
21. *Charai khujia.* A bird's footprint.
22. *Pira khuria.*
23. *Changeri pahia.* The petals of a *changeri.*
24. *Indra malati.* A kind of flower.
25. *Butao.* Embroidered spot.

Also several varieties of creepers (*lata*) and *chakali** (*see* Golaghat).

From Mangaldai.

1. *Sipahi gati.** Soldiers.
2. *Pat bakul.* A kind of flower.
3. *Kakal chinga,**
4. *Lata bakul.**
5. *Hahini champa.*
6. *Pado.* (These, 2 to 6, are all flowers, etc.)
7. *Amjhukia.**
8. *Bichina pad.**
9. *Au khulia pad.**
10. *Maniraj.** (2 varieties.)
11. *Nichhaka pado.**
12. *Mokari khujia.**
13. *Chhoto charpati.**
14. *Bhatei pad ghoira.** (2 varieties.)
15. *Ghoira.**
16. *Kena pado.**
17. *Pukhuria pad.**
18. *Magar phul.**
19. *Hat phul.*"
20. *Pado chhakia.**
21. *Phumura gulia.**
22. *Bhutia phul.**
23. *Kar phul.**
24. *Chalangi bati.**

Most of these patterns (7—24) are of border designs or of designs found in borders. The names, in most cases, explain themselves :—

From Jorhat.

1. *Chapa.** (5 varieties, 2 of which are on one *chaneki.*)
2. *Dalit dhar utha chapa phul.**
3. *Athpahia chapa.**
4. *Tin pahia chapa phul.** (2 varieties.)
5. *Dhariya chapa.**
6. *Sat kali khora chhapa phul.**
7. *Saru khora bachani.**
8. *Bor khora bachani.* *
9. *Saru manuh.**
10. *Bar manuh.**
11. *Majalia manuh.**

12. *Bar pankata.**
13. *Gathi.**
14. *Saru gati.**
15. *Bar gati.**
16. *Keni khora.**
17. *Tini kali khora changari.*
18. *Bar changari phul.**
19. *Mojiu changari phul.**
20. *Bar pakhila.**
21. *Saru pakhila.** (2 varieties.)
22. *Datit dhar utha puni phul.**
23. *Bar phul.**
24. *Bura an phul.**—(2 varieties,)
25. *Gachha phul.**—(4 varieties.)
26. *Phula au phul.**
27. *Bar padum.**
28. *Saru padum.**
29. *Beli.**
30. *Gachh phul.**—(3 varieties from Jorhat and 1 from Golaghat.)

Nearly all these are individual designs, a large number of them representing trees or flowers. It has been thought unnecessary to translate the names, which explain themselves.

From Golaghat.

1. *Pan kata.**—A long and narrow border design.
2. *Lata phul.**—   Ditto in the shape of a creeper.
3. *Guti phul.**—A small spot of colour in the body of the cloth.
4. *Neul.**—A weasel.
5. *Saru guti.**—A very small spot of colour in the body of the cloth.
6. *Gacha.**—A figure for separating two portions of a border stripe; it represents a candlestick.
7. *Dol.**—A shrine.
8. *Ut.**—A camel.
9. *Pohu.**—A deer.
10. *Garia phul.**—Plain white ribs across the cloth.
11. *Kankai.**—A double broken line dividing off two divisions of a border stripe.
12. *Kheoni.**—A stripe of *muga*.
13. *Chapa.**—A rectangular geometrical design forming one length in a border stripe.
14. *Chakuli.**—A square geometrical design which is found in alternation with the *chapa* in a border stripe.
15. *Kali.**—Spots of colour interspersed in border-stripes.
16. *Daria.**—White ribs running lengthwise.

From Sibsagar.

1. *Dagar phul.**
2. *Gali phul.**
3. *Ghan champa.**
4. *Kharika champa.**
5. *Au phul.**
6. *Chakuli phul.**
7. *Chira champa.**
8. *Gachh phul.**

The exact nature of the ornamentations would be best understood from pictures of them, but the list will serve to show the objects most commonly depicted by Assamese weavers. It would be interesting to know which of these designs are found in every district of the Assam Valley and which are characteristic of particular localities, which are found on many fabrics and which, are confined to but a few. But there has been no time nor opportunity for enquiring fully into these points. In the description of the different fabrics many of these designs are mentioned, but the number of fabrics examined is not sufficient to allow of any general conclusions being drawn.

It will be seen that many of the designs in the list have several varieties, but these varieties though not identical, all bear a close resemblance to each other. The names of the designs are, in fact, with a few exceptions, specific. There are, however, several generic terms in common use among the weavers of Assam to represent the different kinds of ornamentations on the cloths they weave, and in many instances these terms give rise to the names of the cloths themselves. Thus a *paridiya kapor* is a cloth with *pari* or side borders; a *garidiya khania kapor* is a *khania* cloth with *gari* or stripes of a particular kind; similarly with the *gariali kapor*, the *seldiya kapor*, *muga butidiya cheleng, darioli cheleng, achu phular khania* and many others.

Designs marked * are those of which specimens have been received.

The extent to which different modes of ornamentations are used on the same cloth and the way in which the designs are grouped, will be seen in the detailed description of cloths, but there is one very characteristic feature of the cotton fabrics of Assam which should be noticed here. This is the end border or borders. Nearly every cloth made in the plains and a great number of those made in the hills have an end border of some description or other. These borders consist sometimes of nothing but a pair or two of plain ribs or coloured lines, such as are found at the end of a *bor kapor* or *khania*. Sometimes, on the other hand, the depth of the border extends to as much as three feet, as in the Kachari *gamcha*, in some of which the borders at the two ends cover between them three-quarters of the whole cloth. Between these two extremes there are numerous intermediate varieties. In the case of borders of a moderate width (up to perhaps six inches) such as are found on the cloths of Upper Assam, there is generally one main stripe, much wider and more elaborate than any other, which forms the centre of the border, the remainder of which consists of pairs of narrow and simple stripes and lines arranged in similar order on each side of this central stripe and so forming as it were a framework for it. The design on the central stripe is usually geometrical, the stripes on either side are either quite plain (*viz.,* formed by a variation of colour in the weft), or consist of a creeper or a row of rosettes or small natural objects. Between each stripe there are usually two or more lines of coloured thread, and sometimes also a narrow portion of plain cloth without any ornamentation whatever. In borders of greater depth the same principle is followed, but, in this case, instead of a single central stripe, there are usually several main stripes about which the narrower stripes and lines are grouped in more or less symmetrical order.

Side borders are much rarer than end borders, and are found in very few cloths. Good instances are to be seen in the *paridiya* of Assam and in the *patani* of the Rabhas. These borders (unless detached) involve much greater labour than end borders, and this is probably the reason why they are comparatively rare. In Assamese cloths when found they are usually at the extreme edges, and are, therefore, strictly speaking, borders; in the Rabha cloths, however, they occupy a more central or rather intermediate position, and are of the nature of stripes rather than borders.

The side borders in Assamese cloths are called *pari*; it is doubtful whether there is any corresponding term for the end borders, unless it be *anchol,* which seems to include not only the border itself, but also the fringe and the intervening portion of plain cloth. The word *anchu,* which means coloured thread, is often applied to coloured stripes at the end of cloths, and cloths having such stripes are called *anchu diya* or *anchuali.*

Regarding the colours used in the ornamentations of cloth, there is little to be said. It has been already mentioned that, in the plains, the thread used, whether white or coloured, is usually bought in the bazaar. The colours most often used are, therefore, those most usually found in the bazaar. It may be mentioned, however, that the Assamese are very fond of any shade of yellow, but especially of gold. Those who can afford it, therefore, use gold twist on their finer fabrics, and those who cannot, often use *muga* thread as the best substitute for it. There is a very marked difference in the nature of the colours used in different parts of the Province. In the Plains of Upper Assam, where the weavers are the Assamese, the characteristic feature of the colouring is delicacy. The fabrics themselves are white and the colours in the borders are such as *muga*, saffron, light green and rose. In Lower Assam, where the weavers are rather the more civilized hill tribesmen who have settled in the plains, delicacy of colouring is not a distinctive feature. These fabrics are often entirely coloured, and even those that are white are really a mass of colour, for the depth of the borders is out of all proportion to the length and breadth of the cloth; and the colours are much more powerful,—red, black and yellow and the darker shades of blue and green are those that find the greatest favour with the weavers. Light shades, it is true, are used as well, but only in connection with the deeper and brighter colours to add variety. In the hills the feature of the colouring is sombreness. The fabrics are sometimes entirely white, as with the Kukis, sometimes white with coloured stripes and sometimes coloured. The colours usually found are black and red-brown, with shades of dark blue that are difficult to distinguish from black; yellow and green also are sometimes used. The dyes are frequently home-made from vegetable matter, and possess none of the brilliancy of anilines and other chemical dyes of European manufacture.* Among the hill tribes, however, there are some notable exceptions to this rule, *e. g.,* the Singphos and the Manipuris, who indeed can scarcely be called hillsmen. The brilliant colours of the Singphos and the exquisite tints on many of the Manipuri cloths form a most marked contrast to the dull and sombre colours affected by the more barbarous tribes. In the Surma Valley very little colouring is used.

This variation of colouring is accompanied by a corresponding change in the texture of the fabrics. The cloths woven and worn in Upper Assam are of much finer texture than the corresponding cloths in the lower districts ; and, though some coarse cloths are found among them, yet these are generally devoid of colouring, (e. g. borkapor). In Lower Assam fine fabrics are comparatively rare, but such as are woven are tastefully decorated with slight borders of quiet shades like muga (e. g., the chadar of Barpeta). None of the cloths which exhibit a mass of brilliant colouring have any pretensions to fineness of texture, and the heavier the colouring the coarser the cloth. It is the same in the hills, where the dull and sombre colouring is well suited to the gross coarseness of the texture.

The artistic taste of the weavers varies considerably with the locality. In Part I of this monograph it has been mentioned what places and people are most skilled in weaving. But with more particular reference to artistic taste, it may be said that the people of Upper Assam are far superior to those living further west. The fabrics of Lakhimpur and Sibsagar have a peculiar charm, and include many real works of art such as would hold their own against even the best productions of Dacca. The weaving of fine and delicate cloths is, of necessity, confined to the rich, and it is impossible to compare them with the more common-place productions of the masses. In the same way it is useless to compare any of the cloths woven by the plainsmen with those of their neighbours in or from the hills. But many of the hill tribes are by no means backward in artistic taste. In Nowgong, for instance, the Lalungs are said to excel the Kochs and Kalitas, but their skill and taste are devoted chiefly to the weaving of eri cloth. The cotton cloths made by the Miris of Golaghat are by no means inartistic, and some of them in every way excel many of the productions of the Assamese themselves. Of the people residing beyond the plains, the Manipuris are true artists, and in the matter of art none of the other tribes can at all approach them.

Whether the artistic taste of the weavers in Assam is improving or deteriorating appears to be an open question, for the information received from different districts varies very considerably. In North Lakhimpur it is said that there is no artistic taste. In Sibsagar the chaneki of the past and present are the same ; in Barpeta, too, the artistic taste has remained unchanged. In Nowgong an improvement appears to be taking place. There are some common designs which are used for borders and ornamentations by all classes of people. Those who are specially skilled and experienced sometimes work out new designs, but nowadays women generally show their skill in the manufacture and ornamentation of muga and silk clothes. The designs of the present day are more numerous and show better artistic skill than those of ancient time. The lack of variety is probably due to the fact that the cloths most woven in Nowgong are those of the plainer and cheaper kinds. In Dibrugarh it is said that, while the art is deteriorating, the artistic taste of the Hipinis is improving, but the change is very slight. Here, too, the skill of the weavers is at present devoted chiefly to the ornamentation of silk cloths. In Kamrup and Golaghat the artistic taste is said to be steadily improving, while in both Tezpur and Mangaldai it is admittedly deteriorating. To draw any general conclusions for the Assam Valley from these reports would be impossible. In the Hills the taste of the weavers is stereotyped, and no improvement or decline is apparent. In the Surma Valley there is practically no display of art.

The influx of foreigners and foreign goods from Europe has had little effect on the artistic taste of the Assamese. Among all the cloths received from different districts, there is not a single one in which the ornamentations show any direct trace of Western influence. The fabrics imported are not imitations of Assamese cloths, but substitutes for them. There is therefore no fear for the present that such importations will injuriously affect the native taste. On the other hand, there is no hope that they will improve it, for most of the fabrics imported are comparatively plain, and such ornamentations as they contain are of the cheap and nasty kind with no pretence to beauty. Indirectly, however, there is no doubt that the imports from the West have a prejudicial effect on the home goods even in the matter of art. The cheapness of imported cloths renders weaving, even to supply the wants of the household, less and less profitable, and tends therefore to make the weavers less careful in their work. It is only the commoner cloths that are affected in this way. All classes

---

* In Mokokchang only homespun thread is used, and this is of three colours, viz., white, called angmorong, price R4 per seer ; black, called esaker, price R6 per seer ; and red, called sungong, price R 12 per seer.

of fabrics, especially the more expensive, are however affected by the substitution of cheap imported thread for the better but more expensive articles made at home. It is only ornamental work that is now referred to, and the native dyes and gold and silver wire were, without doubt, superior to their substitutes imported from the West. Thus, though the artistic taste of the workmen may be as good as ever, yet the designs worked out are less effective owing to inferiority of execution and material.

The general characteristics of the ornamentations on the cotton fabrics of Assam have been noted above, but they may be here briefly recapitulated, when it will be seen that they are characteristics not peculiar to Assam, but common to the whole of India. But if their characteristic features are not peculiar to Assam, the fabrics themselves are, and this peculiarity might itself be called one of their characteristics.

The first feature about the ornamentations is harmony, not only in the grouping of figures and designs, but also in the blending of colours. Even in the most highly-coloured patterns there is no harshness or discord. This applies equally to the products of the plains and to those of the hills.

The second feature is symmetry, not only in the grouping of designs, but in the figures themselves. Symmetry in the arrangement of the figures in a row or of the stripes in a border has a pleasing effect, but symmetry in the portraiture of natural objects produces the effect of artificiality. It may be repeated here that truthfulness is sacrificed, not only to symmetry, but also to variety of colouring no less than harmony. The number of shades at the weaver's disposal is very limited, so where colour is an object, the weaver's aim is to make the fullest use of the shades she has ; and even where an attempt is made to follow nature's colours, the nearest shade available has often to be rejected, because it will not harmonise with those next to it.

The third feature is the variation of the ornamentation according to the texture of the fabric. It has been shown already how the colouring is adapted to the texture ; in a similar way the extent and nature of the ornamental work vary with the texture. Deep borders and large designs are seldom found on cloths of delicate texture. Such cloths, even when profusely decorated, contain comparatively narrow borders and small designs, and the work in both borders and designs is lighter and more open than that on coarser cloths.

The fourth feature is the suitability of the ornamentation to the purpose for which the fabric is intended. Cloths intended for use rather than show are usually very plain, e.g., the waistcloths or lower garments of both men and women, the warm sheets for use on the body or on the bed, and the small cloths used as bathing towels. On the other hand, those cloths, whose primary object is adornment, are profusely decorated, e.g., the light sheet or shawls and scarves worn by both men and women on special occasions, and the *tangali* worn at theatrical performances. There are, however, exceptions to this rule, e.g., the Khampti bags, the Assamese hand-kerchiefs and the Kachari *gamcha*, all of which are intended primarily for use, but are very freely ornamented.

The fifth feature, and the last that will be noticed, is economy of design. It is only those portions of a cloth which are exposed to view at the time of use or wearing that are much ornamented. Thus the *khania* and other double sheets are quite plain for one half of their length, i.e., that half which is beneath, and even in the upper half the designs are much closer together, and often much more elaborate in those portions which are most exposed to view. In the same way, with bags which are made of two thickness of cloth, the inner part or lining is quite plain, and only the outer sides are decorated. This is found to be the case even where the lining and outer part of the bag are formed of a single length of cloth. So, too, the Kachari *gamcha* are often tied round the body with the whole of the borders at both ends hanging well in view ; at other times they are worn as *puggris*, and so arranged that the greater portion of the colouring is exposed.

The Cotton Fabrics of the Assamese.

The cotton fabrics of the Assamese comprise exactly such as are sufficient to satisfy the requirements of a civilized but primitive community. They consist almost entirely of articles of clothing, with a few towels and bed cloths and a variety of bags.

Nearly all the fabrics leave the loom ready for wear. The women of Upper Assam, it is true, wear a petticoat, but this is made simply by hemming the ends of two pieces of cloth and sewing them together at the sides. The men, too, wear a coat with sleeves and buttons, but its manufacture is very simple, as it is rather a shapeless garment. There are also two varieties of fancy coats, called *ghagri* and *jama*, reported from Golaghat, but these are worn only at theatrical performances and marriage ceremonies, so their use is very limited, and they are hardly worth consideration. The other made-up garments are all made of imported cloth, and should therefore scarcely find a place among the Cotton Fabrics of Assam. They have been included in the list below because, though not woven, they are made up within the Province; they are however a very unimportant class.

The bags are of a similar nature. Some are made of imported cloth, the rest consist of a single piece of cloth which requires no cutting into shape, but is merely doubled over and sewn together at the sides.

Of the other items in the list, there is only one that calls for notice, *viz.*, the mosquito curtain. This is remarkable as being made of cloth, not net. The specimen received is a clumsy article, and very small; the roof is formed of one piece and the four side walls of another which measures only 18½ feet.

There is nothing of the Assamese to correspond with the *than* of the Jugis; its nearest equivalent is the *charkhana*, which is intended rather for conversion into made-up garments than for use as a sheet. But this *charkhana* is reported only from Goalpara, the lowest district of the Brahmaputra valley, and though its size varies considerably, it never exceeds that of the *borkapor*, which is the longest cloth woven by the Assamese. Except the *charkhana*, all other fabrics are made for use as one particular garment (or the like).

The classification of the fabrics of the Assamese is very difficult, because, not only is the same name used in different districts to designate different garments, and similarly the same garment known by different names in different places, but further the one cloth is often put to many different uses. The fabrics have, however, as far as possible, been grouped according to the uses for which they are primarily intended. The groups are not entirely distinct from one another, and so some cloths of very similar nature have been unavoidably separated. Thus the *gamcha* is really a towel, but in Gauhati the name is used as an equivalent for *tiyani*, a kind of waistcloth; in Tezpur a variety called *gatlowa gamcha* is, as its name implies, a body sheet or shawl; and in Mangaldai the *phali*, a cloth just like *gamcha*, is used as a head dress.

The variety of fabrics made in the several districts will be seen from the following table which includes none but cloths made by the Assamese themselves, and only one of each distinct variety included in the detailed list given below :—

	Body sheets or shawls, double and single.	Waistcloths for men and women.	All other fabrics that leave the loom ready for wear.	Total of fabrics that leave the loom ready for wear.	Made-up garments, etc.	Grand Total.
Kamrup . . .	9	9	8	26	19	45
Sibsagar . . .	11	4	7	22	5	27
Darrang . . .	10	4	6	20	3	23
Nowgong . . .	7	3	3	13	5	18
Lakhimpur . . .	9	2	2	13	...	13
Goalpara . . .	3	3	6	12	4	16
Total ...	24	11	19	54	24	78

From this table it will be seen that by far the greatest variety of fabrics is made in Kamrup, both of those that leave the loom ready for wear and of those that are subsequently made up. The difference is most marked in the case of made-up garments, but this difference is more apparent than real, for the list received from Kamrup includes a great number of articles made of imported cloth, whereas no such articles have been reported from any other district except Goalpara, and consequently the variety of such garments in those districts is very small.

Of scarf-like fabrics, those made in Kamrup are equally divided among the three classes, but in all other districts, except Goalpara, the number of body sheets or shawls equals or exceeds that of the other two classes put together. The preponderance is most marked in Lakhimpur, where the number of body sheets produced is as large as in Kamrup, while the total of scarf-like fabrics is exactly half. The greatest variety of shawls seems to be found in Sibsagar. It is true that in the list several shawls from Golaghat are classed by themselves which might more strictly be grouped under more general heads, such as *khania* and *cheleng* ; but, at the same time, the varieties of *khania* and *cheleng* reported from this district are much more numerous than those from any other. The preponderance is therefore real. Here it may be noticed that in Upper Assam the people make but few cotton waistcloths ; those who cannot afford silk buy the *dhuti* imported from the West. In Central and Lower Assam the waistcloths for the masses are still as largely made at home as other fabrics. The reason is doubtless that the body sheets and shawls of Upper Assam do not really come into competition with foreign goods, owing to the character and excellence of their ornamentations, whereas in other parts of the Valley the superior fineness of imported shawls outweighs the very slight advantage which the ordinary home-made articles possess in the matter of ornamentation ; and even there it is found that the finer shawls are still made at home, whereas the manufacture of the finer waistcloths has almost ceased.

It has been said that the cotton fabrics of the Assamese are sufficient to supply the wants of the people. This must not be misunderstood ; the variety is ample, the quantity is totally inadequate. But the industry has been discussed already, it is now only the fabrics themselves that are under consideration. It may be interesting to note here which particular fabrics are reported as being made in the greatest numbers in the several districts. They are as follows :—

In Lakhimpur —The *khania* and *cheleng* (N. Lakhimpur).
In Sibsagar.—The *cheleng* and *gamcha* (Sadr) ; also the every-day dress of the people, *viz.*, the *khania, churia, mekhela*, and *riha* (Golaghat).*
In Nowgong.—The *borkapor, khania* and *gamcha*.
In Darrang.—The *borkapor, tinai churia, gamocha, gat lowa gamocha, khania, pit khania, chakathia, mekela, riha, tinhatia, murat bindha* and *cheleng* (Tezpur). The *dhuti, telach, mokcha, patavi* or *mekhela, aguran, bukbandha*, and *tinhatia* (Mangaldai). All these are said to be largely made and worn.
In Kamrup.—The *borkapor, mukcha, gamcha, telach*, and *churia*, which form the every-day dress of the people.
In Goalpara.— The *dhuti* and *patani*.

A comparison of these lists with the table given above will show that Darrang, while standing only third in point of variety, has every right to be called the centre of the cotton-weaving industry. Speaking broadly, the greatest variety of cotton fabrics is found in the centre of the Valley and the least at the two extremities, East and West.

There is one more point to be considered, *viz.*, the use of the fabrics as distributed among the different classes of the community. In the detailed list the use of each fabric has been explained as far as it is known, but in Barpeta the fabrics have been classified according to the people who use them, and the particulars given below, though applying only to the Barpeta sub-division, give an excellent idea of the wardrobe of an Assamese at the present day. In some places some of the garments are replaced by those of silk and many by those imported from abroad, but with these reservations the lists are very typical. †

Townspeople.

1. *Paridiya kopor.* A highly ornamented shawl.
2. *Gunar phular khania.* A shawl with gold and silver ornamentations.
3. *Khania.* A shawl with borders of *muga* or coloured thread.
4. *Chakathia.* Ditto ditto but smaller.
5. *Chadar.* Ditto ditto but woven single instead of double.
6. *Riha.* A narrow ornamented sheet worn by women round the breast.
7. *Churia.* A man's waistcloth, plain.
8. *Gamocha.* A bathing towel with simple borders.

Thus, among the townspeople, the home-made cotton fabrics used at the present day consist almost entirely of sheets and shawls. It is quite different with the country folk.

---

* This is as stated in the report from Golaghat. My personal experience, which however was very short, was that the *churia* at any rate was seldom made at home, and that the *mekhela* was very frequently of silk.
† It is very interesting to compare the costume of the present day with that of the days before the advent of British civilization, which is thus described from Barpeta :—
"The habits and tastes of the people were simple in those days. A *churia* (*i.e.*, waistcloth) a *buku-chola* (*i.e.*, short *chapkan*), a *khania* (*i.e.*, wrapper) and a *gamcha* (*i.e.*, towel), formed all the clothing of a gentleman of those days. The villagers on the other hand dressed themselves in a *tiyani kapor* (*i.e.*, short waistcloth), a *gamcha* and a *barkapor* (*i.e.*, double sheet). Ladies of high rank used to wear *mekhelas* and *rihas* made of *pat* or *muga*, and a *khania* made of cotton as an overcloth. Village women indulged in two or three simple pieces of cloth such as a *patani* (*i.e.*, waistcloth) and an *aguran* (*i.e.*, wrapper) or a *mekhela, riha* and *barkapor*, all made of cotton.
"The manufacture of cotton fabrics by the women of each household was enough to meet the wants of the nation."

Villagers.
WEALTHY MEN.

1. *Borkapor.* A large sheet worn on the body, double.
2. *Pachra.* A smaller ,, ,, ,, single.
3. *Chola.* A coat.
4. *Dhuti.* A large waistcloth.
5. *Panigamcha.* A smaller ditto.
6. *Bhatkhowa kapor.* A very small waistcloth worn at meal times and 'on pure occasions.'
7. *Gamocha.* A bathing towel.
8. *Mukmocha.* A smaller towel for drying the hands and face.
9. *Talpara.* A bed sheet.
10. *Garur kapor,* A pillow case.
11. *Mohori.* A mosquito curtain.

WEALTHY WOMEN.

1. *Barkapor.* A large body sheet worn double.
2. *Aguran.* A large body sheet worn single.
3. *Telach.* A shorter, but wider ditto.
4. *Mekhela.* A made-up petticoat.
5. *Patani.* A waistcloth.
6. *Bhatkhowa kapor.* A waistcloth of the same size used at meal times.
7. *Talpara.* A bed sheet.
8. *Garur kapor.* A pillow case.
9. *Mohori.* A mosquito curtain.

WEALTHY BOYS.

1. *Borkapor.* A double body sheet.
2. *Pachra.* A single ditto.
3. *Chola.* A coat.
4. *Panigamcha.* A waistcloth.
5. *Bhatkhowa mukcha.* A narrow waistcloth worn at meal times.
6. *Gamocha.* A bathing towel.

WEALTHY GIRLS.

1. *Aguran.* Single body sheet.
2. *Telach.* Ditto
3. *Mekhela.* A made-up petticoat.
4. *Patani.* A waistcloth.
5. *Bhatkhowa kapor.* Ditto used at meal times.

None of the fabrics worn by the wealthy village people appear to be ornamented. The women and girls seem rather badly off for towels.

MIDDLE CLASS MEN.

1. *Barkapor.* A double body sheet.
2. *Pachra.* A single ditto
3. *Gamocha.* A waistcloth.
4. *Panigamacha.* A short ditto.
5. *Bhatkhowa kapor.* A norrow waistcloth worn at at meal times.
6. *Mukcha.* A towel.

MIDDLE CLASS WOMEN.

1. *Aguran.* A single body sheet.
2. *Mekhela.* A made-up petticoat.
3. *Patani.* A waistcloth.
4. *Bhatkhowa kapor.* A smaller waistcloth worn at meal times.
5. *Murat lowa.* A head dress or veil.
6 *Kantha.* A blanket or bed sheet.

MIDDLE CLASS BOYS.

1. *Telach.* A single body cloth.
2. *Chola.* A coat.
3. *Mukcha.* A towel.

MIDDLE CLASS GIRLS.

1. *Aguran.* A large single body sheet.
2. *Telach.* A smaller ditto.
3. *Patani.* A waistcloth.

Among the fabrics used by the middle classes of the villagers only the *gamocha*, *panigamcha* and *mukcha* of the men appear to be ornamented.

COMMON MEN.

1. *Bar kapor.* A large double body sheet.
2. *Pachra.* A single body sheet.
3. *Panigamcha.* A waistcloth.
4. *Mukhmocha.* A towel.

COMMON WOMEN.

1. *Telach.* A single body sheet.
2. *Patani.* A waistcloth.
3. *Murat lowa.* A veil or head dress.

COMMON BOYS.

1. *Telach.* A single body sheet.
2. *Mukhmocha.* A towel.

COMMON GIRLS.

1. *Telach.* A single body sheet.
2. *Patani.* A waistcloth.

The fabrics used by the common villagers are all ornamented in some way or other.

The total absence of towels from the wardrobes of women and girls of all classes of villagers is remarkable. It will be noticed that it is only the wealthy boys who indulge in the luxury of a waistcloth.

In North Lakhimpur it appears that the *churia, chador, pagori* and *mona* are used solely by men, the *mekhela* solely by women and all other fabrics equally by both sexes.

Here, too, the garments worn specially at weddings are the *paridiya kapor, khaniya, phul bacha, paguri* and *gamocha.* There are no priests' robes, and the clothing worn by the Mohamedans is almost all imported.

There is little more to be said about the clothing worn on special occasions, or by special classes. The more expensive sheets and shawls are of course used only by the rich and even by them not on ordinary occasions. The *ghagri* and *tangali* are worn together in Golaghat at theatrical performances, and the *jama* or *jamachola* is a magnificent flowing robe worn by the bridegroom at a marriage ceremony.

The following list includes all the cotton fabrics reported from different parts of the Assam Valley, except such as are made exclusively by the hill tribesmen who have settled in the plains. Under each head all available information has been given, and descriptions of particular cloths have been given in all cases where specimens have been received or examined. One important point has been omitted from the detailed descriptions, viz., the weight of the cloth. The reason of this is that no weighing machine was available when the description of the cloths was being taken, and approximate weights would be worse than useless. Most of the fabrics described, however, are being sent to the Director of Land Records and Agriculture in Assam, and there may be some future opportunity of weighing these specimens.

In the general descriptions where the weight is given, this represents the amount of thread required to make the cloth and not the actual weight of the cloth itself. The weights are only approximate, and it is not known whether they include that of the thread used for ornamentations, or represent only the weight of thread used in the body of the cloth.

A.—Body Sheets or Shawls.

The cloths worn as body sheets or shawls form by far the most important and interesting class of cotton fabrics made by the Assamese. Many are used alike by men and women and comparatively few are confined in their use to one sex only. It will be convenient, therefore, to group them according to the form in which they are worn rather than according to the class of persons wearing them. Thus considered, they fall naturally into two main classes, viz., those worn double and those worn single. The former form the more important group and will be first described. It is on some of these shawls that the greatest artistic skill is displayed ; some, on the other hand, are entirely devoid of ornamentation.

1.—Bar kapor, Dangari kapor or Satkathia.

This cloth is found in every portion of the Assam Valley, except perhaps Goalpara. It is thus described by Mr. Darrah :—" A large, coarsely-woven, heavy but very durable cloth generally used by both sexes, much in the same way as a shawl is used in England. There are a large number of different kinds, and the names vary in different districts." As regards the names, the term *bar kapor* (big cloth) is applied to it in every district ; *dangari kapor* (which is pure Assamese meaning the same thing) is practically confined to the districts of Lakhimpur and Sibsagar; *satkathia* (which means 7 *kathi* long, a *kathi* being roughly a yard) is reported from Mangaldai alone.

The characteristics of this cloth are warmth, durability, plainness and coarseness. Is very thick and always worn double, serving the purpose of a wrapper or shawl for the villagers' daily wear in the winter. Its purpose is essentially comfort, not show. As a rule it is entirely plain, but in some places it has a coloured border at one or both ends ; these borders are never very elaborate. It is worn equally by men, women and boys, except in Mangaldai where women do not appear to use it. Its size varies from 15 × 2¼ feet for a boy (in Barpeta) to 27 × 4½ feet for a man (Golaghat) ; its price from 12 annas to 4 rupees ; and the amount of thread in it from ¼ to 1¼ seer. In Jorhat the size is stated as 9 feet × 4 to 5 feet. This evidently refers to the cloth as folded for wearing, the full length being 18 feet. The greatest width for a cloth of this kind is quoted in North Lakhimpur as 5¼ feet, but here the length is only 21 feet, so the cloth is really smaller than the largest size found in Golaghat.

In Barpeta the *bar kapor* is used by men of all classes among the villagers and also by the women and boys of the richer village families. The following sizes are quoted :—

(*a*) 18 × 4½ feet, containing one seer of thread; price R1-8; worn by wealthy village men.

(*b*) 16¼ feet × 4½ feet, containing one seer of thread; price R1-8; worn by other village men. That worn by men of the common class is said to have black or red borders.

(*c*) 16½ feet × 3¾ feet, containing ⅔rd seer of thread; price R1; worn by wealthy village women.

(*d*) 15 feet × 2½ feet, containing ½ seer of thread; price 12 annas; worn by wealthy village boys.

This cloth, in spite of its plainness, is very interesting on account of its practical nature. There is really no equivalent for it among imported fabrics, the nearest being the coarse Bombay sheets selling at 8 annas to R1-4, but these are always worn single. This is the only cloth of Assamese make that has been adopted by the Bangali coolies working on the tea gardens in Assam. Being reasonable in price and very warm and lasting, it is found by the coolies to be on the whole a profitable investment, and is used by them in the winter months as a wrapper during the day and as a sheet at night. In one garden in Golaghat in 1895 about 200 coolies bought *bar kapor* from the nearest Kaya's shop. These cloths had been manufactured in Nowgong and were sold retail in the garden at R1-8 each. They gave satisfaction and were expected to be in even greater demand last cold weather.

Detailed account of specimens received from different places.

No. (i). *From North Lakhimpur.*—A perfectly plain white cloth of very coarse imported thread, the only variation of any sort being two double lines of double threads near one end ; the fringe at this end is some 7 inches long ; that at the other, 2¼ inches in length, is just as it left the loom, *i. e.*, the loops of threads have not been cut. Size 17 feet × 4 feet 3 inches; price R3.

No. (ii). *From Dibrugarh.*—This cloth was made at Khowang by a Kachari. It is of coarse thread, apparently homespun, and is more closely woven than the last. It has a few double threads in the weft at either end, but is otherwise quite plain. The fringe at each end is about 3 inches long. This is a far superior cloth to that from North Lakhimpur. Size 18 feet × 4 feet 3 inches ; price R4.

No. (iii). *From Barpeta.*—This cloth is of finer texture than that from North Lakhimpur, but, like it, is made of white imported thread. At one end is a narrow border worked in blue on a background of red weft, the pattern, called *tiah jalia phul*, being such as to leave this background exposed in the form of diamonds all along the line. The other end has a plain cross stripe of red, rather over ¾ inch deep. The fringes are twisted together into tassels. Size 18 feet 8 inches × 4 feet; price R2-8.

2.—Pit kapor, Pit khanis, Tita karia.

This cloth is reported from Dibrugarh, Golaghat and Nowgong only. It is a variety of the *bor kapor*. The name *pit kapor* is used in all these places, but *tita karia* appears peculiar to Nowgong. The cloth is there described as the " same as *bor kapor*, but finer and considered warmer. It is so named because at the time of weaving the thread is always kept wet." Its size is 21 feet × 4 feet, the same as that of the *bor kapor;* its price is R2-8, plain. The description of this cloth received from Dibrugarh is rather vague, but it amounts to the same as that from Nowgong. It is that the *bor kapor* " is called *pit kapor* when woven by wetting the threads of woof and warp." The description received from Golaghat is as follows :—" This is the same as *khania kapor*, but very coarse, and there are no decorations in it of flowers, etc. This is for rough use only, commonly used by the lower class of people, both males and females. It measures 24 feet × 4 feet; price R2 to R4." This description would evidently apply to the *bor kapor* which is, however, listed as a different cloth and described as " A large sheet of cloth, a coarse wrapper, used by villagers during the winter; size 27 × 4½ feet; price R1-8 to R3." The intrinsic difference between the two cloths is, however, brought out in the description received from Nowgong and given above.

A cloth called *pit khania* is reported from Tezpur, where it is said to be the same as the *khania*, except for the fact that the warp is formed of boiled thread and the weft of raw thread. It has no ornamentations, except a line of red at one end. It is used at home by persons of both sexes. It is 18 to 21 feet long by 4 to 5 feet wide. Its price is 2 to 3 rupees. In constant use it lasts about 9 months.

The cloth thus described is evidently the same as the *pit kapor*, and its description is, therefore, placed here instead of under the head *khania*.

Specimen.—A cloth called *pit kapor* was shown to me at Golaghat. It was of plain white country cotton thread, measuring 19½ feet × 4½ feet with no ornamentations except a plain fringe at either end and a single line of red running across it at one end. It was said to be worth R2 or R2-8 and to be used by men in the cold weather.

3.—Gelap.

This is a coarsely woven but very durable shawl measuring 18 feet × 3¾ feet. It is made at Goalpara and worn by both sexes; price R2 to R3. It is said to be the Goalpara equivalent of the *bor kapor* (No. 1).

4.—Chakathia.

This is reported only from Tezpur, Mangaldai and Barpeta. In Mangaldai it is said to be the same as *satkathia* (or *bor kapor*), but smaller in size and used only by females. The name indicates its length, *viz.*, 6 *kathi* (or yards).

In Tezpur it is described as being the same as the *khania kapor*, but smaller in size, and having gold or silk ornamentations at one end only. Size 18 feet × 3½ feet. It is used twofold for every-day wear by both sexes and can be had for from R2 to R4; in constant use it lasts for about 9 months.

In Barpeta the *chakathia* appears to be used only by the townspeople. It is 15 feet long and 3 feet 9 inches wide; it contains ¾ seer of thread; price R1. It has the same ornamentations as the *khania* (No. 7).

5.—Dopati.

This is similar to the *chakathia* (No. 4), but rather lighter in texture. The borders are embroidered with *phul* of cotton thread. It is used by respectable women to cover their entire body and screen it from sight while they are going from one place to another; price R1-8.

This description received from Mangaldai, (the only place from which the cloth is reported), does not bring out the characteristic feature of a specimen received from the same place, *viz.*, that the cloth, though worn double, is really made up of two smaller cloths which are sown together side by side.

Specimen from Mangaldai.—This is a very wide but comparatively short cloth, being 6 feet 2 inches in width and 8 feet in length. It is made up of two cloths each 3 feet 1 inch wide joined together by a sort of knitting which is very neatly done. The body of the cloth is covered with rows of large white rosettes, the rows being about 6 inches apart, and the rosettes in one row opposite the vacant spaces in the next. The ends have each an inch deep border of brown-red thread with some blue. Along the outer and inner edges of these borders run three or four red-brown threads in the warp. Besides this there is a set of nine raised stripes in plain white running near the outer edge throughout the whole length of the cloth. The texture is medium fine. The price is not stated.

6.—Dolai kapor.

This is a cloth reported only from Golaghat. It is described as consisting of two separate sheets sewn together, one above the other, instead of being one long sheet doubled as is the case with the *khania*. It has borders at the ends only and not along the sides. It is used as a winter sheet.

This cloth is very possibly the same as the *dopati* (No. 5). The word *dolai*, as applied to the *paridiya kapor* (see No. 9, specimen iii) appears to have a definite meaning which hardly applies to this cloth, unless the fact of the two sheets being sewn together gives this cloth the name *dolai*.

7.—Khania.

This is, as Mr. Darrah describes it, "a highly ornamented shawl, worn double and generally 21 feet × 4 feet. Usually very finely woven and elaborately adorned along the borders with graceful designs of flowers and creepers. Sometimes the whole of the front sheet of the *khania* is tastefully decorated with flowery spots. The ornamentation is usually made either with silk or coloured thread or with a mixture of silk and gold or silver."

In size and shape and mode of wearing the *khania* is exactly similar to the *bor' kapor*, the essential points of difference between the two being that, whereas the former is, as a rule, coarse and plain and intended for warmth in the cold weather, the latter is finely woven, usually ornamented and intended for wear at all times of the year, some varieties being more especially suited by their ornamentations for use at festivals, weddings and on other occasions of ceremony. This cloth is worn alike by both sexes, but more usually by townsmen than by villagers. It is invariably folded, like the *bor kapor*, across the centre to form a double shawl of half the length of the cloth. The economy of ornamentation is very well marked in this cloth. The cloth being worn double, only one-half is exposed to view, the other half is invariably plain, the only form of decoration it ever contains, being a simple line running across the free end.

There is, however, always a fringe at each end of the *khania* so that the shawl when worn appears to have a fringe at one end and none at the other, for those at both ends come together when the cloth is doubled and, being equal in length, coincide with one another and appear to form a single fringe. The body of the cloth is always of white thread, and the most usual and characteristic borders are those of *muga* silk ; but coloured cotton thread and gold and silver wire are also often used, and therefore the varieties of *khania* are very numerous ; some of these varieties are described below.

The price of the *khania* varies enormously according to the fineness of the thread and the nature of the ornamentation. The cheapest quoted is R1-8 (Sibsagar) and the dearest R120 (Tezpur). There is, however, one peculiar point about the price of this cloth which is difficult to explain, *viz.*, that in North Lakhimpur, Sibsagar and Mangaldai where the dimensions of the *bor kapor* and the *khania* are said to be the same, the average price of the *khania* is given as less than that of the *bor kapor*. It may be taken for granted that the prices so shown are those of the plainest *khania*, but even then it would be natural to expect the *khania* to be more expensive than the *bor kapor* (which is essentially a plain cloth), owing to the superior fineness of its texture. In other places where such a comparison is possible this is seen to be the case.

The following are a few peculiarities of the descriptions received from different districts :—

In North Lakhimpur two sizes of the *khania* are mentioned, *viz.*, 18 feet × 4½ feet and 21 feet × 5½ feet, exactly the same as those of the *bor kapor*. It is not stated whether these are both full sizes or not, nor what particular purposes they serve. The description given, *viz.*, "with *phul* at one end," is rather vague. The specimen sent, however, is quite plain, except for a narrow border of red thread on a yellow background at one end and a simple line of red thread at the other. Thus when doubled for wear the cloth answers the description, having a border at one end of the upper or exposed half and being quite plain at the other. The cloth in fact appears to be an example of the *achu phular khania* described below.

In Golaghat the *khania* is said to be worn more usually by women than by men. In Nowgong the *khania* measures 18 feet × 4 feet and contains ½ seer of thread. In Tezpur the ornamentations are said to be either of silk or else of silver or gold thread. " In some instances gold ornamentations are made at one of the ends and at half the border and surface to make the cloth appear more gaudy for wear at weddings....... Ornamented *khanias* for wear at weddings can be had at R30 to R120."

In Gauhati the *khania* appears to be intended only for special wear, being worn by both sexes at ceremonies and festivals; highly ornamented ones are used as bridal robes. The price here varies from R2-8 to R10-0, so none are very expensive. In Mangaldai the only ornamentations used are of silk thread and of gold or silver wire.

In Barpeta the *khania* is included in the wardrobe of the townspeople only. It is ornamented with *chopa chakuli phul*, *batha pathia*, *dhekia pathia*, *kanda chapa*, *utha chapa*, and *padma lata*. The price is given as R2; size 21 feet by 4½ feet; weight of thread 1 seer.

The following are the principle varieties of *khania kapor*. It will be seen that the *khania* closely resembles the *cheleng* as regards varieties of ornamentation, the main difference between these two cloths being that the former is worn double and the latter single. The *khania* is also found in greater variety than the *cheleng*.

(*a*) Uka khania kapor.

This is a variety of *khania kapor* having no floral designs in the body of the cloth, but only borders of muga silk. So called in Golaghat.

Specimen seen at Golaghat.—A cloth 13 cubits long (the breadth has not been noted), of medium thick cotton thread, with a border of muga, about 3 inches wide at one end, and a line of red thread at the other. Otherwise quite plain. Commonly worn for ordinary wear by men and women. Worth R1-8 to R2. It was called simply a *khania*, but is evidently an example of the *uka khania* if the term *uka* be really applied to *khania*; but this appears doubtful as the word means uncoloured and without ornamentations, and is therefore inapplicable to any kind of *khania*.

(*b*) Muga phular khania.

A *khania* in which the end borders are made of muga thread. Price from R2 to R2-8 (Jorhat). From the description, which is rather vague, this would appear to be the same as the *uka khania* of Golaghat, and this is all the more probable seeing that no cloth called *uka khania* is reported from Jorhat, and the term *uka* is applied to the *cheleng* only when that cloth is entirely devoid of ornamentation, the term *phuldia*, or *phulam* being applied to *cheleng* with end borders.

Specimens from Mangaldai, Gauhati and Barpeta are described below. In Tezpur the price of an ordinary *khania kapor* with silk ornamentations is R3.

(*c*) Achu phular khania.

This is a *khania* in which the border is of coloured cotton yarn; price about R1-8 (Jorhat). A specimen, described below, has been received from North Lakhimpur.

(*d*) Gunakata khania, Gunar phular khania or Gunar khania.

The *Gunakata khania* is described in Jorhat as the same as the last two cloths, except that the borders are of gold (or rarely silver) thread instead of cotton or silk. Its price is 4 to 10 rupees.

This (*guna kata*) is the only variety of *khania* cloth reported from Dibrugarh. Its price is Rs. 10. It is worn by both men and women. Specimens from Jorhat and Dibrugarh are described below.

In Tezpur the price of a *khania kapor* with gold or silver ornamentations is from 4 to 6 rupees.

In Barpeta a cloth called *gunar phular khania* is included in the wardrobe of the townsmen of both sexes. It is described as a sheet with a fringe of gold or silver lace (probably a border, not a fringe, is meant) 21 feet by 4 feet, price Rs. 10. It is evidently a much finer and more carefully woven cloth than the ordinary *khania*, which is priced at Rs. 2 only. The difference is due in some measure to the price of the gold thread (Rs. 6), but partly also to the extra time required for the weaving of the *gunakata khania.* The latter takes three months to make out of raw cotton and one month in the actual weaving—the ordinary *khania* requires only 25 and 12 days respectively.

The following is the description of a cloth called *gunar khania* shown to me at Golaghat. A cloth like the *khania* described above but of much finer thread. It has at one end a border of gold thread about 2¼ inches deep and at the other 3 double lines of gold thread. Otherwise it is quite plain. It is worn chiefly by men but also by women at evening parties and marriages. Worth Rs. 2 to Rs. 2·8.

(*e*) **Pit khania** *the same as pit kapor, q. v.*

(*f*) **Garidiya khania kapor.**

A cloth of this name, brought to me at Golaghat, was of the following description :—

Length 18 feet, width 4 feet, made of rather fine thread—at one end is a border of gold thread, at the other a plain white *gari,* at both plain fringes ; the edges (*aothi*) are thicker than the body of the cloth. The border is 2 inches deep and made up as follows :— First a patterned stripe, than a wavy design called *lata phul* between two double lines of gold thread, next a second patterned stripe, followed by *lata phul* as before, then a slight interval and lastly a row of very simple figures (shaped <), an inch distant from the fringe. The *gari* at the other end consists of plain double threads in the weft alternating with single threads as follows, 4 double, 4 single, 34 double, 4 single, 4 double. This is about an inch distant from the fringe. Ribs (*thiya gari*) of double thread ⅓rd of an inch wide and ⅓rd of an inch apart run from one end of the cloth to the other.

This cloth is worn by both men and women, when not at work, for ordinary outdoor wear. The cost of a ribbed cloth like the above but without the borders of gold thread is Rs. 4 or 5—a cloth of the same description but without ribs would cost Rs. 3.

(*g*) **Dariali guna khania.**

Specimen seen at Golaghat.—This is a cloth very similar to the last, made of fine imported thread 19½ feet long (width not noted), having plain white stripes or ribs (*dariya*) running throughout its length. The upper half has a pretty border of gold thread about 2 inches deep at one end only, the bottom half is quite plain. There appears to be no selvage. This cloth is worn by women when paying visits. It is worth Rs. 2-8 or Rs. 3.

(*h*) **Buta banowa (or butadiya,) khania kapor.**

Specimen seen at Golaghat.—This is an ordinary white *khania* made of country thread. The bottom half has no ornamental designs. The top half has, at the fringed end, a two-inch border of gold thread, *viz.,* a single stripe in which the pattern is made up of rectangular designs. At the other end of the top half is a border stripe ⅜ inch deep. The body of the cloth (in the upper half) is dotted over with plain white flowers called *buta,* which are arranged in rows across the cloth, the number in each row being 26 at the fringed end and decreasing at intervals to 23 at the folded end. These *buta* vary considerably in shape and size but none are of any special interest.

The cloth described above was seen by me at Golaghat ; it is worth Rs. 3-8 to Rs. 4 and is worn by women only.

(*i*) **Guti bulua khania.**

This name is applied in Jorhat to a *khania* the upper half of which is adorned with flowery spots of either muga silk or gold twist. No detailed description of this cloth is given. It appears to be very similar to the *butadiya khania,* but it is not known if the *guti* is the same as the *buta* ; in any case the *buta* in the particular cloth shown to me were of white cotton thread.

In Golaghat a cloth called *guti bulua kapor* is described as a variety of the *khania* having *guti* or particular kinds of flowers woven into the body of the cloth, and end borders generally of muga. It is worn by women when going to *sabha* or other meetings.

(*j*) **Paridiya guna khania,** *a variety of paridiya kapor, q. v.*

(*k*) **Karsipi khania.**

This is evidently the same as the *karsipi bankara kapor, q. v.*

(*l*) **Nurakata sutar khania.**

This is a variety of *khania* made in Nowgong. Its essential features are that it is made from fine *nurakata* thread and is tastefully ornamented. Its price is R20 to R30. The *nurakata* thread has been described under the account of spinning.

Specimens.—Six *khania* have been received, one from each of the following places :—North Lakhimpur, Dibrugarh, Jorhat, Mangaldai, Gauhati and Barpeta. As regards measurements they agree with the general description given above and it is sufficient here to note the peculiarities of each. All are unornamented except for the end borders. The cloth from North Lakhimpur has a border at one end only, the pattern being of diamond-shaped designs worked in red on a background of yellow. The other end has a narrow stripe of red, only four red lines in the weft. The thread is imported and medium fine. Price R1-8. The cloth (*gunakata khania*) from Dibrugarh has a 3-inch border in gold thread at one end and the next end is quite plain except for 6 white raised stripes. The thread is fine home-spun. This cloth was made by an Assamese lady at Dibrugarh. Price R10. The cloth from Jorhat is also a *gunakata khania*, and has a 3-inch border at one end and a plain stripe at the other, both in gold thread. The border is less effective than that in the Dibrugarh cloth, and the plain stripe consists of only 4 lines of thread. There are no raised stripes. The thread is fine imported. Price R2-8 second hand; when new it would cost R5 or rather more.

The other three cloths have muga borders at one end only, that on the Barpeta cloth being 2 inches deep and called *Svarnalata*, that on the Mangaldai cloth 3 inches, and that in the Gauhati cloth 3½ inches. At the other end the Barpeta cloth has merely 2 lines of muga thread, the Mangaldai cloth one very narrow stripe of red, and the Gauhati cloth nothing but a white raised stripe. There are no other ornamentations except in the last named cloth which has a plain white stripe of extra thickness along each edge. The cloths differ slightly in their texture and in the nature of the fringes. The Gauhati cloth has a long false fringe at either end.

8.—Phul Bacha kapor.

This is described from North Lakhimpur as a very rich cloth used as a shawl or Benares cloth. Two varieties are mentioned, *viz.*, one with *muga buti* all over the body, and one with *guna* (gold or silver twist). There are two sizes of each cloth, *viz.*, one 18 feet by 4½ feet and one 21 feet by 5½ feet. The price of the *muga buti* variety is R4 and R5 and that of the *guna* variety R6 and R8 according to size.

From the dimensions and general description and also from a specimen received, it is evident that the cloth is merely a variety of the *khania*; in all probability it is the same as *guti bulua khania*. It is however shown separately from the *khania* in the list received from North Lakhimpur.

Specimen.—From North Lakhimpur.—This is a cloth of fine texture in all respects like a *khania*. It has a border of muga thread nearly 3½ inches deep at one end and a very narrow plain red stripe at the other. It measures 17½ feet by 3½ feet. The upper half is covered with rows of muga *phul* (oval-shaped rosettes) 2½ inches apart. The distance between the rows varies from 2 inches at the fringed end to 3 inches at the folded end. Price R2-8a.

9.—Paridiya kapor, Jor kapor.

This cloth is merely a variety of the *khania*, but it deserves to be listed by itself owing to its magnificence, and to the fact that it is shown separately in all the district reports. It is thus described by Mr. Darrah :—" An embroidered shawl, very finely made and most artistically ornamented. This article of clothing is made and worn only by the upper classes. It is the highest example of the art of weaving as known in Assam. A single *paridiya kapor* will cost from R40 to R200, according to the fineness of the materials used and the nature of the decoration employed. The ornamenting thread is usually gold or silver twist, sometimes both, and the design, though generally confined to the borders, spreads sometimes over the whole article. Flowers and birds are the commonest patterns, but those consist sometimes of nothing but graceful curves arranged symmetrically along the borders. Occasionally a *paridiya kapor* is made by attaching to a centre piece of very finely woven muslin-like material, border pieces ornamented by the few Mohamedans who still retain a knowledge of the art of weaving with gold and silver thread."

This cloth is reported from Dibrugarh, Jorhat, Golaghat, Nowgong, Gauhati and Barpeta, and a specimen so named has been received from North Lakhimpur. It is not made in the Goalpara District, and it is not included in either of the lists received from the Darrang District. It appears strange that it should be made in both sub-divisions of Kamrup and yet in neither of those of Darrang, but the lists received from the latter district are carefully drawn up and very comprehensive, so the fact, though strange, appears true. In Nowgong this cloth is rarely made at the present day; here and in Dibrugarh and Gauhati the description is the same as that given by Mr. Darrah. In Gauhati it is however further stated that this cloth is worn by both bride and bridegroom at weddings and generally by rich and respectable families at marriage festivals. The price varies with the ornamentations and the amount of gold thread used, ranging between R40 and R120. Its size is 20 feet by 4 feet.

In Barpeta the *paridiya kapor* is described as a large ornamented sheet measuring 21 feet by 4 feet, and sold for from R200 to R300. The cost of manufacture from raw cotton is said to be R17¾-7-6, *viz.,* cotton (2¼ seers) 0-7-6, lace R150 and six months labour R24; from imported thread R167-8-0, *viz.,* thread (1 seer) R1-8-0, lace R150 and 4 months' labour R16. This is the only cloth in the whole list of which the selling price exceeds the cost of manufacture, the labourer's wage being reckoned at 2 annas per day or R4 per month. The reason is that in this cloth the cost of labour is very small in proportion to that of the material, whereas in other cloths the reverse holds good. This cloth is worn in Barpeta by townspeople only. The nature of the ornamentations is not described.

In Jorhat there are two kinds of *paridiya* cloth, *viz.,* the cloth ordinarily known by that name and the *karsipi bankara kapor.* In Golaghat the latter is described as a separate cloth and, judging from the few specimens brought to me at Golaghat, it would seem that the two cloths are usually considered distinct, though undoubtedly they are of the same nature. The *karsipi* has peculiar features of its own and is quite as much a distinct cloth from the *paridiya* as the *paridiya* itself is from the *khania.* It is therefore described under a separate heading.

The description of the paridiya given in the Jorhat report is as follows :—

"*Paridiya* or *Jor kapor.* These are very fine and valuable shawls highly decorated. They are worn by women only. They are generally doubled by adding a plain sheet on the backside, and hence the name *jor kapor* (*jor* =pair). There are two varieties. One has the borders decorated with designs of gold or silver twist or both. The design is sometimes extended to the whole centre-piece, flowers, creepers and birds, squares and diamonds being the usual patterns. The borders are generally woven in one piece with the garments. The ornamentations on the centre piece are invariably woven with it. Price from Rs. 10 to Rs. 40. The other variety is called *karsipi bankara kapor.*" The size is not stated.

The fact of this cloth consisting of two separate pieces, the one sewn to the other, is remarkable and distinguishes it from the *khania kapor.* This peculiarity, however, appears to be purely local. None of the cloths called *paridiya* brought to me at Golaghat were of this nature. They all consisted, like the *khania,* of a single length, folded in the middle, the one half being plain.

Mr. Darrah's description covers both the *paridiya* and the *karsipi* but, in the range of prices, it is far too narrow. For while some of the *paridiya* of Barpeta cost as much as Rs. 300, the specimen received from North Lakhimpur is priced at Rs. 6 only, and it is certainly not worth more.

Specimens—No. (i).—From North Lahkimpur.—This is very similar to the *phul bacha kapor* from this place but differs from it in having a border at each end of the upper half and also along both edges. These side borders extend from one end border to the other and consist of strips (1¼ inch wide) sewn on to the cloth. The border of the fringed end is over 3¼ inches deep, the central and main stripe being nearly 2 inches deep. That at the folded end is about 1¼ inch in depth, and is much plainer. The *phul* in the body of the cloth are also more plentiful and, though nearly all alike, contain a few variations. At the fringed end of the bottom (or plain) half, is a very narrow stripe consisting of four muga threads. All the ornamentations are in muga silk. The upper and lower halves of this cloth are sewn together at each side. Price Rs. 6.

No. (ii).—Seen at Golaghat.— A cloth 19½ ft. long and 4¼ ft. wide with a selvage along each edge and a plain fringe at each end. It is folded double and the top and bottom halves are sown together at each side. The bottom half is quite plain except for a *gari,* made up of three double lines of muga in the weft, ¼ inch in width and about ¼ inch from the fringe. The upper half is highly ornamented.

The peculiar feature of this cloth consists in its side borders, which are woven on separate strips sewn on to the main cloth and detachable at pleasure. The one border extends from the fringed end to the fold and even slightly beyond. It is 2 inches wide, and consists of a stripe containing 42 rectangular designs, each 2⁹⁄₁₆ inches long, with a stripe (*kheoni*) of muga on either side. These rectangles are about

$\frac{1}{16}$ inch apart, and in the interval is a *kankoi* consisting of three dotted lines of muga thread. The other border is of a similar nature and the same width, but is shorter, as it does not reach the fold. It contains only 20 small rectangular designs, which are $2\frac{7}{16}$ inches long, the remainder of the stripe consisting of one long rectangular design. This portion of the cloth, it may be noted, is seldom exposed during wear.

The end borders are much bolder. One, about $\frac{3}{4}$ inch distant from the fringe, is $4\frac{3}{4}$ inches deep, and very ingeniously made up. The main portion is a stripe about 2 inches deep containing two different rectangular designs (each $2\frac{1}{4}$ inches long), which alternate with one another, but are divided off by three bars of muga thread. The two rectangular designs are similar, but not identical; there are eight of each and a portion of a 17th at the extreme end of the stripe. This main portion is set in a framework of narrow fancy stripes, all very simple in design. On the side nearest the fringe are three such stripes; the two outer ones are alike, and contain double lines which form zig-zags with spots in the angles, and the third, which lies between them, contains merely a series of parallel diagonal lines with a few curved lines at the far end for the sake of variety. On the other side these three stripes recur in the same order, but in this case each stripe is immediately succeeded by a row of solid squares.

The border at the other end of the cloth is only $1\frac{1}{2}$ inch in depth and less elaborate. It is one inch distant from the fold, and midway between the border and the fold occurs a row of 44 simple triangular rosettes woven in muga thread.

The body of the cloth is covered with small designs (*phul*) arranged in rows across the cloth. Between the end borders there are 36 such rows, which are comparatively wide apart at the folded end, but get nearer and nearer together as they approach the fringe, near which they close in very rapidly. Thus, of the 36 rows, only 16 fall in the half nearest the fold and 20 in that nearest the fringe; the distance between the 24th and 25th rows from the fold is $3\frac{1}{4}$ inches, between the 26th and 27th 2 inches, and between the 30th and 31st $1\frac{3}{4}$ inch, the succeeding rows being at more or less equal intervals, *viz.*, $1\frac{1}{4}$ inch. From the last row to the border is 2 inches.[*]

Not only do the rows get nearer together, but the number and nature of the designs in each row undergo a similar change. Thus, the first 16 rows are all alike, each containing 12 designs called *guti phul*. The following 10 rows, *i.e.*, the first half of the rows on the fringed end, also contain 12 designs apiece, and these designs are like those in the preceding rows with the following exceptions :—In the 17th row the 7th design from one end is a *gacha* (candlestick), instead of a *guti*; in the 20th the designs are alternately a man riding an elephant and a man on foot; in the 24th there are three new designs, *viz.*, a horse, a flower, and a mongoose, which are so arranged that every alternate design is a flower and the intermediate designs are alternately a horse and a mongoose. The next four rows (27th to 30th) contain each 23 small designs *saru guti phul*, and then follow five rows of still smaller designs or rosettes, 46 in a row; the last row of all contains similar rosettes much farther apart, there being only 19 in the row.

The economy of design is excellently illustrated in the arrangement and nature of the ornamentations on this cloth.

*No. (iii).—Seen at Golaghat.—*This cloth, which is even more handsome than the last, is $19\frac{1}{2}$ feet long and nearly $5\frac{1}{2}$ feet wide. It is made of imported thread, and its texture is very fine, like muslin. At each end is a plain fringe, but the cloth is doubled over at the middle and the two halves sewn together at either side. The lower half is quite plain, but the upper half is profusely decorated entirely with gold wire, which gives to the cloth an alternative name, *viz.*, *sonwali kapor* or the cloth of gold. The designs on the body of the cloth are not sewn in, but introduced at the time of weaving; had they been sewn in, the cloth would, it is said, have become a *dolai paridiya kapor*. The side borders are also woven into the cloth itself, and are not on detachable strips.

The main border at the fringed end is about 3 inches deep, but beyond this is a narrower border $\frac{3}{4}$ inch deep. The border at the folded end is $2\frac{1}{2}$ inches deep, and consists of two portions ; first, a row of elaborate trees laden with fruit, each in a rectangular frame, the successive frames being divided off by a bar made up of arrow heads or wide Vs, one above another. This row is 2 inches deep, and is set in a

---

[*] It is interesting to note that from the 26th row, when the rows begin to fall close together, the designs in one row are connected at the back of the cloth with the corresponding designs in the next, *i.e.*, one continuous thread is used in forming them. The pattern on the face of the cloth is of course unaltered thereby.

frame of two gold lines, each containing four threads. The second portion of this border is a continuous design in the form of a chain, each link of which has a spot in the centre. This chain is set in a similar framework, and is altogether ⅛ an inch in depth.

The side borders, nearly 2¼ inches wide, are both alike, being of the same pattern as the deeper border at the fringed end. They both extend over the whole length of the upper portion of the cloth, *viz.*, from the fringe to the fold.

The body of the cloth is profusely decorated with cross rows of flowers set in diamond frames. The arrangement is, however, not uniform over the whole cloth; there are two distinct patterns, the one extending over the half nearest the fringe, and the other, which is more open and far less elaborate, over the half nearest the fold. Each of these patterns is itself broken; the first at exactly ⅔rds its length (from the fringe), by a row of designs (*phul*), similar to the others, but much larger; the second at the ⅝th row from its junction with the first, by a discontinuity, *i.e.*, there are no *phul* at this point. These breaks are evidently intentional.

A further element of variety is found in the endings of the pattern along each side border. Looking from the fringe, the right hand side is that most exposed to view when the shawl is being worn, and here the edge of the pattern on the body of the cloth is most irregular—the framework is made to end in various ways, and the contents of the frame along the edge are similarly varied. The usual ending for the framework is a whole diamond, but many other arrangements are adopted, the most favourite perhaps being a pair of half diamonds or a large M. The designs in these frames are sometimes found alone, sometimes accompanied by rosettes, one, two, or even three in number, at times by a candlestick or butterfly. But in spite of these irregularities there is a general plan of arrangement pervading the whole. From the border at the fringed end to the break in the first pattern, the framework at the edge, whatever its shape, contains two rosettes in addition to a design (*phul*) like others in the row, but rather smaller. From this point to the break in the second pattern the frame contains a single *phul* uniform in size and shape with others in the row. Beyond this break the frame contains a full-sized *phul* and in addition a butterfly in each angle. There is only one exception to the uniformity of this arrangement, *viz.*, that in one of the first five rows of the second pattern the framework, which ends in a half diamond, contains in addition to the full-sized *phul* a rosette in the right hand bottom corner.

The left hand edge is much more uniform, the framework invariably ending in a half diamond or inverted V. The contents of these half diamond frames, however, vary along the edge, but on a definite principle. From the fringe to the break in the first pattern they consist of single designs like others in the row, but smaller. From this break to the end of the first pattern these smaller designs are accompanied by two rosettes. Thence to the break in the second pattern there is no such design, only a single rosette, after which the contents are like those in the right hand edge, *viz.*, a full-sized design with a butterfly in each angle of the frame.

This cloth, which cost Rs. 80 or Rs. 100 to make, exclusive of labour, is nearly 15 years old, and has been preserved with extreme care, the only damage suffered being one minute hole and a slight shrinkage of the gold wire at the folded end. Such cloths are worn among the upper classes, at marriage ceremonies, by the bridegroom or any of the ladies present.

*No. (iv).—Paridiya Guno Khania.   Seen at Golaghat.—*This cloth, though described as a *khania*, is evidently a *paridiya*. No cloth of this name is reported from any district, but there is little doubt that the name was correct, as it was given me by an Assamese gentleman who brought the cloth for my inspection. This goes to show that the name *paridiya kapor* is but an abbreviation of *paridiya khania kapor*, which means a *khania* cloth with side borders.

This particular cloth was made by an Assamese lady of good position in the Golaghat Sub-division. It is worth 25 or 30 rupees, and is worn only by ladies at assemblies.

This is a *khania*, 18 feet long (width not noted), made of imported thread. The lower half is quite plain. The upper half has borders woven on the cloth on all four sides, and is profusely decorated with flowers in the body. All the ornamentations are of gold thread. There is a plain fringe at either extreme end of the cloth.

The border at the fringed end of the upper half is composed of a central stripe of elaborate diamond pattern, set in a frame of two graceful and narrow cross stripes, one on either side. The border at the folded end is similar, but narrower and less elaborate. It is only ⅔rds the width of the first border, and consists of simpler oblong designs divided off from one another by triple bars. The lines on either side are also plainer than those at the fringed end. This border is about six inches from the fold.

Both side borders are of the same pattern, *viz.*, a stripe containing diamond-shaped designs with slightly ornamented edges. These borders are of the same width as that at the folded end, but rather plainer. They extend only up to this border, but two lines of gold thread which divide them off from the body of the cloth run right on to the fold.

The body of the upper half of the cloth is covered with rosettes, more or less oval in shape. These rosettes are all of the same size, and are arranged in rows across the cloth. These rows are much closer to one another at the fringed end than at the folded end, and the number of rosettes in each line varies in a similar manner. There are altogether 40 rows of these rosettes between the two end borders, and by folding the cloth again it is seen that 23 rows fall in the one half (that with the fringe), and 17 in the other. The 10th row from the fringed end differs from all the others, the rosettes in this row being not oblong, but uniform in shape like a flower of four petals. There are 17 such rosettes or flowers in this row. The number of rosettes in the other rows varies from 17 near the fringe to 12 near the fold.

10. Karsipi Bankara kapor; karsipi khania; karsapi.

This cloth is reported from three places only, *viz.*, Jorhat, Golaghat, and Now-gong. In Jorhat it is called a variety of the *paridiya*, in Golaghat it is described as a separate cloth, and in Nowgong the word *karsapi* is used as identical with *paridiya*.

The description received from Jorhat is as follows:—"The *karsipi bon kara kapor* is made by tacking most artistically embroidered border pieces on to a home or European made centre piece of fine quality, which is also very finely embroidered in various patterns. The ornamenting thread is gold or silver twist. This kind of garment is made only by a few old Mussalmans of the Jorhat town, and will probably disappear in the near future, as the younger generation is not learning how to work the embroidered decorations. The price of this kind of garment is from Rs. 50 to Rs. 150."

From Golaghat this cloth is described as follows :—

"The name means a cloth having embroidery of gold thread. Various kinds of flowers and natural objects are portrayed both in the border and in the body of the cloth. All this embroidery is made with the needle after the cloth comes woven from the loom. The cloth measures 24 feet by 4 feet. It varies in price from Rs. 50 to Rs. 200. It is worn by both sexes, but generally by females. Such cloths can generally be seen in the homes of respectable persons only."

From these two descriptions it appears that the characteristic features which distinguish this cloth from the *paridiya* are, first, that all four borders are embroidered strips sewn on to the cloth, and, secondly, that the designs on the body of the cloth are of gold or silver thread not woven into the cloth but worked by hand after the cloth has left the loom.

These characteristic features are both present in a specimen received from Jorhat and in a cloth seen by me at Golaghat and called *karsipi khania.*

Specimens—No. (i)—Karsipi bankara kapor.—From Jorhat—This is a handsome shawl of exceedingly fine texture. It has borders along both edges and at both ends of the upper half, all sewn on ; the lower half is absolutely plain, except for the fringe. The side borders are nearly 2 inches wide, one end border is 2½ inches deep and the other slightly deeper. These borders are of practically the same design in gold foil, with spots of red cotton thread. Besides the borders the cloth is ornamented with large leaves arranged in rows and covering the whole of the upper half. There are also spots worked in gold foil between the leaves. The upper and lower halves are two distinct cloths sewn together at the edges and the end without a fringe. The size of the double cloth, as worn, is 8 feet 4 inches by 4 feet 2 inches. Price Rs. 75.

There is, it will be seen, a remarkable similarity between this cloth and the *karsipi khania* of Golaghat, which is all the more interesting from the fact that this cloth is quite new and the other very many years old.

No. (*ii*) *Karpisi Khania.   Seen at Golaghat.*—This garment, which was said to be used only by bridegrooms at the wedding ceremony, consisted of two separate sheets, each measuring 9 ft. × 3¾ ft. sewn together at the edges. The lower cloth was a mill-made muslin cloth quite plain. The upper sheet was woven in Assam. The body of this sheet was covered with handsome flowers, there being 20 rows of these equi-distant from one another. These rows contained alternately six and seven flowers each, and between each flower was a spot. All these flowers were sewn with the needle (*bezire bowa*), and not woven. The cloth had also borders of silver foil at its ends and sides, all four being attached after the cloth left the loom. The side borders were 1¾ inch in width, the pattern being made up of handsome rectangular designs in silver foil relieved by five dots of coloured wool—red, claret, and violet. The end borders were alike, ½ an inch in width, and of nearly the same pattern as the side borders, with the exception that the edges of the framework were more ornamental.

This particular cloth was very old, but similar cloths are still made. The value when new, was Rs. 35 to Rs. 40.

11.—Sing pahu bacha kapor.

This is a cloth which used to be worn only by the Raja and other members of the Royal Family, and by them only on occasions of festivals, etc. Now-a-days it is worn by ladies generally and by bridegrooms in the same way as the *paridiya kapor*, but it is in very few families that the cloth is found.

This is by far the most handsome cloth of any I have seen in Assam. It is not included in any of the district reports, but I was fortunate enough to have one lent to me by a descendant of the last reigning Ahom Raja, and was thus able to take a detailed description of it. It appears to be a variety of the *paridiya kapor*, but for many reasons it deserves a separate description.

This cloth is made of the very finest white home-spun cotton thread. It has a plain fringe at either end and a selvage along each edge. It measures about 21 ft. × 5 ft., but is folded double for wearing. The lower half is quite plain, except for a white *gari* near the fringe. The upper half is profusely decorated.

The body of the cloth is covered with figures arranged in rows across the cloth. There are 28 such rows, each containing 11 figures, but the arrangement of the figures in the second row is different from that in the first, and thenceforward these two rows follow one another in alternation to the other end of the cloth, the figures in any one row being opposite the intervals in the next. Besides these main figures there are stars or small rosettes indiscriminately scattered over the cloth so as to form a kind of irregular framework for them. The figures in the first row are a deer, a bird, and a shrine (*dol*) repeated in the above order from one side to the other; thus there are four deer, four birds and three *dols*. The second row contains the same 3 figures arranged in the same order, but in this case the first figure is a shrine (*dol*) and the eleventh is a new design, *viz.*, a solid diamond. (In the fourth and subsequent alternate rows, the place of the diamond is taken by a rosebud with stalk and leaves,—a very pretty design). The shrine is such only in name and might be taken for almost anything. The bird is a most ferocious creature, but very angular ; the deer is at once too life-like and utterly unreal : its general limp appearance forms a marked contrast to the martial bearing of the noble bird beside it. The general effect of the pattern on the body of the cloth is very striking and far from inartistic.

The borders of the cloth are very pretty. Those along the two sides and that across the folded end are equal in depth (1¾ inch) and alike in pattern. Each consists of a single stripe between two quadruple lines of golden thread. In the stripe irregular octaganals alternate with smaller diamonds, the vacant spaces being filled with floral designs like leaves. The border across the fringed end of the cloth is 2¾ inches deep and far more complex. It consists of a main stripe of elaborate pattern set in a framework of narrow stripes and rows of figures, the arrangement being as follows :—

(1) A row of stars or small rosettes.

(2) *Pankata.* A succession of graceful curves between two triple lines of golden thread.

(3) The main stripe, made up of three distinct designs, one square and two rectangular, repeated in regular sequence along the whole length of the stripe ; the last is incomplete. These designs are very similar to one another, the square one is called *chopa* and the others are two varieties of *chakuli*, but their distinctive

names could not be ascertained. Each design is separated from that next to it by a bar made up of inverted V's, one above another, like a chain of mountains in a map.

(4) *Pankata*, as above.

(5) A wide space containing a row of stars as above.

(6) *Pankata*, as above, about 2 inches from the fringe.

The characteristic feature of this stripe is symmetry without monotony.

This cloth is 40 or 50 years old, and was made by one of the Assamese *tantis* or professional weavers who flourished in the time of the Rajas. Its original cost was between Rs. 200 and 250 ; and it is now almost as good as new, having been preserved with extreme care by being wrapped in a plain cloth of equal size which appears to be an example of the *bagal* (No. 12).

12.—Bagal.

This cloth is never used for wearing, but is a wrapper for preserving valuable cloths or shawls of the nature just described and may, therefore, be appropriately classed with them.

In Golaghat the *bagal* is made of coarse home-woven cloth and is triangular in shape having a long cord fastened to one angle. The shawl to be protected, having been folded up, is placed upon this wrapper, the two corners of which are doubled over and then the third with the rope is brought down, and the whole secured by the rope being wrapped round and round and fastened. This wrapper costs 4 annas.

In some cases, instead of this wrapper, the shawl has a perfectly plain cloth made of exactly its own size. When not required for use the shawl is placed upon its plain counterpart and the two are wrapped up together as one cloth.

In Gauhati the *bagal* is described as a satchel or sort of bag made out of a piece of cloth 2 ft. square, in which clothes are kept. Its price is 4 annas.

The name *bagal* is also applied to a small bag (*mona*) carried under the arm.

The next class of fabrics to be described comprises those that are used as single body-sheets or shawls. These also form a very interesting group.

13.—Cheleng.

The *cheleng* is a sheet almost universally used in the Assam Valley, being found in every district and sub-division east of Barpeta, though it changes its character somewhat from East to West. It is a superior kind of shawl often intended for special wear, being made of fine thread carefully woven. The most usual size is 9 feet by 3 feet though this varies to some extent with the weaver and the place of manufacture ; the largest being 12 feet by 3¾ feet in N. Lakhimpur and the smallest 9 feet by 2½ feet (in Sibsagar) and 7¼ feet by 3 feet (in Jorhat). In Jorhat a *cheleng* measuring 7¼ feet by 3 feet takes ¼ seer of thread, and in Nowgong one measuring 9 × 5 feet takes 6 chattacks. The *cheleng* is almost invariably ornamented in some way or other, the most usual form being a border of *muga* thread at either end. The different kinds of ornamentations will be more fully described in discussing the different varieties of *chelengs*. The price, of course, varies with the fineness of the thread and the nature of the ornamentations, but ranges between 4 annas and Rs. 5.

In the Lakhimpur and Sibsagar districts the *cheleng* is worn by men, women and children alike, but in Golaghat generally by men and only at the time of paying visits or taking a stroll. In the Darrang district and the sadar Sub-Division of Kamrup it is worn by men alone, and, in the latter place, only on special occasions. In Mangaldai it is described as being used in the hot weather.

It is worn exactly like the *chaddar* or sheet of the Bengalis.

The following varieties of the *cheleng* are found :—

(a) Uka cheleng.

This variety is entirely plain, having no ornamentations whatever. Its price varies from 4 annas to 8 annas in Jorhat according to size and quality. The price of an imported cloth equivalent to it is about the same. In Nowgong a plain *cheleng* costs 12 annas, the size being 9 feet by 3 feet.

(b) Achu diya cheleng.

This also is quite plain, with the exception of a narrow border of coloured thread generally red at either end. The price of a *cheleng* of this nature in N. Lakhimpur is 8 annas when the size is 9 feet by 3 feet and 12 annas when 12 feet by 3¾ feet.

(c) Phuldiya cheleng; phulam cheleng.

This is plain in the body but has flowers of coloured cotton or silk thread at the ends. In N. Lakhimpur a cloth of this kind measuring 9 feet × 3 feet costs Rs. 1-4 and one measuring 12 feet × 3¾ feet costs Rs. 2. In Nowgong the smaller size costs R1-8, and in the Golaghat a *cheleng* measuring 12 feet by 3 feet, with borders of *muga* thread costs Rs. 2. In Tezpur the cost of a silk-bordered *cheleng* 9 feet by 4½ feet varies from Rs. 1 to Rs. 3. In Mangaldai the price is much lower, a *cheleng* measuring 9 feet by 4 feet with *phuls* in the borders costing only from eight to twelve. There is no doubt, however, that the cloths made here are much coarser than those made higher up the Valley.

(d) Guna kata cheleng.

This differs from the last only in the fact of the borders being made of gold or silver twist (*guna*) instead of thread. The price varies from 3 to 5 rupees.

(e) Paridiya cheleng.

This has coloured borders not only at both ends, but also along both sides. It is reported from Jorhat alone, but a specimen has been received from N. Lakhimpur. It must be distinguished from the *paridiya kapor* which is not a single but a double shawl.

(f) Garidiya cheleng.

This has stripes of silk, coloured thread, etc., running lengthwise only, or both lengthwise and crosswise, with or without ornamental borders. The price of ornamented *cheleng* (b to f) varies in Jorhat from 8 annas to Rs. 2.

(g) Dariali cheleng.

This is much like the last, but the lengthwise stripes are plain white (*dariya*) instead of being coloured.

The following is the description of a *dariali cheleng* brought to me at Golaghat. "Made of plain white imported thread very fine. Length 10½ feet × 3¾ feet. At each end is a border consisting of two triple rows of gold thread. Throughout the length of the cloth, at equal intervals, run *daria* or stripes formed of four white threads of several strands, the thread of the body of the cloth being single." There are no borders at the edges. The effect of the plain stripes crossing the golden coloured border is very pretty. The cloth is worn only by women. Its value is R1 to R1-4-0.

(h) Muga buti diya cheleng.

This is a *cheleng* with *buti* or spots of muga thread all over the body of the cloth. (The more usual name for such spots is *buta*.) The price of this cloth in North Lakhimpur is Rs. 2 for a small size (9 feet × 3 feet) and Rs. 2-8 for a large size (12 feet × 3¾ feet).

Specimens.—No. (i)—From North Lakhimpur. Paridiya cheleng.—This is a white cloth made of medium fine country thread, 8 feet 8 inches long × 3 feet 7 inches wide. It is quite plain except for a border design in muga thread about 2½ inches deep and 2 pairs of narrow muga stripes at each end and a ¼ inch *pari* at each side. The main part of the border design is about ¼ the entire depth, and consists of long rectangular designs. The first pair of stripes is about 3 inches off this border and the second rather more than 3 inches farther along. The *pari* is of red cotton thread and is not at the extreme edge of the cloth. The *muga* borders are very pretty. Beyond this border at either end is a 1½ inch false fringe, then about ¼ inch of cloth with a broken line of red running along it. The real fringe is very short, about ¼ inch. The price of this cloth is 8 annas.

No. (ii)—From Dibrugarh.—This is a *cheleng* made at *Khowang* by a Kachari weaver. It is very similar to the last, but is made of imported thread and has no red about it. The whole ornamentation consists of the end border designs in muga thread which are in this case altogether some 4 inches deep and close to the end of the cloth. There is no false fringe, but the real fringe is nearly two inches long, the threads, as is so often the case, being twisted together in pairs. The cloth is rather large; size 10 feet × 4 feet. Price Rs. 2-8.

No. (*iii*)—*From Gauhati.*—Similar to the last but even plainer, as the end borders are not an inch deep. The thread is country-made and very soft. The border consists of a single diamond-shaped design in muga thread, rather pretty. The size of the cloth is 7 feet 6 inches × 3 feet 7 inches. Price 15 annas.

14.—Seldiya kapor.

This cloth is thus described : " *Sel* (commonly pronounced hell) means *pari, i. e.*, border of various kinds of specimens of flowers, beasts or the like. Thus the name means a cloth with a *sel* or border. This is used both as *dhuti*, wearing cloth, and as *chaddar*, sheet, worn by females generally and by males at marriage ceremonies. The price varies from Rs. 4 to Rs. 10." This description, received from Golaghat, is so vague as to leave a doubt as to its exact nature. It is probably, however, a variety of *cheleng*, suited by its plainness for occasional use as a *dhuti* or man's waist cloth. The fact of its ever being used for this purpose shows that it is a single and not a double sheet.

15.—Garidiya kapor.

This is described as follows from Golaghat. " This is the same as *seldiya kapor*, but the borders are always of white thread, whilst those of *seldiya kapor* are always of coloured cotton or muga thread. The price of such cloths varies from Rs. 4 to Rs. 8. They are worn by males and females."

This description is too vague to allow of the exact nature of the cloth being determined. It is shown as a separate cloth from the *cheleng* in the Golaghat report, but there is a little doubt that it is in fact a variety of the *cheleng* very similar to the *garidiya cheleng* (No. 13i) ; the latter however is said to have coloured and not plain stripes. Owing to the vagueness of the description this cloth has been shown by itself.

16.—Pachra.

The *cheleng* is the single body sheet most prevalent in the Assam Valley. The *pachra* which is also an ordinary single body sheet or shawl is found only in Lower Assam, *viz.*, in the districts of Kamrup and Goalpara, and is worn only by men (and boys). The main distinction between this and the *cheleng* is that the latter is made of fine thread and tastefully decorated, whereas this is made of coarse thread, and the decorations, though often profuse, are far inferior in design and workmanship. This distinction is not peculiar to this cloth, but is found in most cases where a comparison is possible between the cotton fabrics of Upper and Lower Assam.

The *pachra* is described in Gauhati as a thickly woven single wrapper used by males for general wear in the villages.

It is thus discriminated from the *chaddar* or *cheleng* which is here used for special wear. It measures 9 feet × 3¼ feet. It has coloured patterns woven at either end, and is sometimes coloured red or yellow. It ranges in price from 12 annas to Rs. 1-8. This description applies also to the *pachra* of Goalpara. In Dhubri the *pachra* (or *chaddar*) varies in size according to the wearer, from 6 feet × 3 feet to 8¼ feet × 3¾ feet, and in price from 8 annas to Rs. 1-8. It is either plain or decorated, the ornamentations in the latter case consisting of embroidered ends, an inch to 2¼ inches deep, made of coloured thread woven into the cloth.

In Barpeta the *pachra* is used only by the villagers—men of all classes and boys of the richer class only. The sizes of the men's *pachra* are given as 9 feet × 3¾ feet, containing ½ seer of thread, for a wealthy villager ; 7¼ feet × 3¾ feet (⅔ seer) for one of the middle class, and 6¾ feet × 3 feet (₅⁄₁₆ seer) for the poorest. The selling price of each is quoted as the same, *viz.*, 8 annas, but the cost of manufacture differs considerably owing to the difference in size. The boy's *pachra* measures 6¾ feet × 1½ feet, contains ¼ seer of thread and costs 6 annas. No mention is made of any ornamentations except in the case of that used by the men of the middle class, which is said to have a black or red border.

Specimens.—*No.* (*i*)—*From Gauhati.*—This is a plain white cloth made of coarse imported thread loosely woven ; the only ornamentation of any kind being a half inch border near each end, and a false fringe beyond it. The border is very simple, consisting of red thread so woven as to leave a series of Maltese crosses in white with a rectangular setting of red, each rectangle being divided off from the next by bars of white and red. The size of the cloth is 8 feet 3 inches × 3 feet 3 inches. The price is not stated.

No. (ii)—From Gauhati.—This is a *garidiya pachra*. It is really a *chaddar* and was so labelled originally, but the word *chaddar* has been crossed out and *pachra* substituted. It is made of fine white thread. Its peculiarity is that it has cross stripes throughout its length. These stripes are not coloured, but formed by each shot of the weft being double instead of single. Besides this its only ornamentation consists of a border at each end about 1¾ inch deep. This is in red, blue and yellow, the main colour being red, and the design rectangular. The size of the cloth is 9 feet 3 inches ×2 feet 10 inches. The price is R1.

No. (iii)—From Barpeta.—This is a true *pachra*, very like the first (No. i), being made of coarsish thread and having no ornamentation, but a very narrow border near either end. One border is about ⅜ inch deep and consists of merely hollow diamonds of blue thread standing out in bold relief on a background of red, with blue edges. This design is called *cheri lata*. The other border is only about half as deep and consists of much smaller blue diamonds in relief on a background of red with no blue edges. The size of the cloth is 8 feet 8 inches × 3 feet 6 inches. Price 15 annas.

17.—Chaddar.

This is a cloth very similar to the *cheleng* and used for the same purpose. It is however worn exclusively by men. The name *chaddar* is a Bengali word. Cloths so called are reported from North Lakhimpur, but not from any other place in the Lakhimpur, Sibsagar and Nowgong districts. In Darrang and the sadr sub-division of Kamrup the name is used synonymously with *cheleng*, and in the district of Goalpara synonymously with *pachra*. It is therefore only in North Lakhimpur and the Barpeta sub-division of Kamrup that the *chaddar* appears to be a distinct cloth. The description of it will therefore be confined to these two places.

From North Lakhimpur two descriptions of *chaddar* are reported, the one plain and the other with *phul* or embroidery at the ends. Each is found in two sizes, *viz.*, the larger 12 feet × 3¾ feet and the smaller 9 feet × 3 feet. The price of the former is 12 annas for the small size and R1 for the large; that of the latter R1-4 for the small size and R1-12 for the large. The only distinction drawn between the *chaddar* and the *cheleng* is that the latter is described as a rich cloth, but the price of the plain *chaddar* is higher than that of the least ornamented *cheleng* given in the list, so that the description hardly appears to hold good. The plain *chaddar* would seem to correspond to the *uka cheleng* above described, and the ornamented *chaddar* to the *phul diya cheleng*, but there may be some radical distinction which causes them to be shown separately ; and which does not appear on the face of the report.

In Barpeta it is only the townspeople who are said to use the *chaddar*, which is described as a sheet used as a wrapper, 12 feet long × 4½ feet wide with ornamentations, *e.g., lata, chainkara, bakul, saru khonda chapa* and *belpat*. It costs R2-2-6 to make out of raw cotton and R1-11 out of bought thread ; it sells for R1, which sum would also purchase its equivalent among imported fabrics. It contains ¾ seer of thread. From this description it appears that the *chaddar* is at once the most highly decorated, the largest and most costly single sheet worn in Barpeta.

The following description of the *chaddar* is given by Mr. Darrah : "*Chaddars* or sheets.—These are almost invariably quite plain, except when made of the finer kinds of cotton yarn. In this case they are some times as fine as muslin, and only prepared by women of respectability for private use. These carefully woven fabrics are generally decorated with elaborately-worked patterns of flowers, fruits, and birds in coloured threads, sometimes of silk, sometimes of cotton. The embroidered ends are called *phuls* and almost every woman has her own particular pattern." This description of Mr. Darrah's would apply almost equally well to the *cheleng*, which is thus briefly described by him : "*Chelengs*—These are similar to the above (*viz., khaniya kapor*), but are usually only 3 feet × 10 feet in size. They are finely woven, and ornamented in much the same way as the *khaniya* but seldom to the same extent." The main distinction between a *cheleng* and a *khaniya*, which is not brought out in this description, is that the former is worn single whereas the latter is invariably worn double.

If there be any difference between the *cheleng* and the *chaddar*, it would appear to lie not in the quality of the cloth, nor yet in the extent to which it is decorated, but rather in its nature. As far as can be seen, the word *chaddar* is applied only to imported sheets of this nature and to sheets made in imitation of the Bengali or imported sheets. *

---

* The fact that the borders of *chaddar* are often of muga thread hardly supports this theory. Perhaps the true explanation is that *chaddar* are worn by men and boys only, while *cheleng* are worn by every one.

Sheets made by the Assamese, and after the fashion of the Assamese are called *cheleng* in Upper Assam and *pachra* in Lower Assam; the former are as a rule made of fine cloth and are often extensively and tastefully decorated, the latter are much coarser in texture, and their ornamentations while quite as extensive as those on the *cheleng* are far inferior in design, workmanship and material.

Specimens.—No. (i).—From North Lakhimpur.—This is a plain white cloth made of fine imported thread with no ornamentations except the end borders and the fringe. Both borders are of muga thread, about $2\frac{1}{4}$ inches deep. One is rather more elaborate than the other having spots of red cotton thread at the centre of the design in the main stripe which is about $\frac{3}{4}$ inch deep. The other has a main stripe about 1 inch deep, but with no red spots. There is nothing remarkable about this cloth, but the borders are very chaste, the size is 8 feet 4 inches × 2 feet 5 inches. Price 12 annas.

It is difficult to distinguish this from the *cheleng.*

No. (ii).—From Mangaldai.—This is a much more elaborate cloth than the last, but coarser. The main colour is blue, but the end borders have a background of yellow in the weft, which is however barely visible owing to the heavy pattern woven on to it. The body of the cloth is covered with flowers (*phul*) in yellow, white, red and blue. These are in lines and vary much in design, some being like rosettes, some being mere geometrical designs and some representing birds, animals and men. To name the birds or animals is quite out of the question. Were the cloth an old one, they might be taken for extinct species, but unfortunately the cloth is very new. These *phul* are arranged in lines, and as a rule all those in one line are alike except as regards colour, but sometimes even this is not the case. The variety is wonderful, as scarcely two rows are alike. The border at each end is about $2\frac{1}{4}$ inches deep, and consists of uninteresting red designs worked on a background of blue and yellow as mentioned above. These designs are rectangular and divided off by narrow bars of plain blue and yellow cloth, *i.e.*, the simple background with no pattern woven over it. The fringes are some 4 inches long, several threads being twisted together. Size 5 feet × 2 feet 2 inches, Price not stated.

N. B.—In Mangaldai the word *chaddar* is used as synonymous with *cheleng,* and so the general description of *chaddar* given above does not apply to cloths from this place.

No. (iii).—From Barpeta.—This is a cloth of very fine white thread, with no ornamentations except the borders at the sides and ends. The end-borders consist of alternate thin stripes of muga thread and double cotton threads (white). They are about an inch wide. The end-borders are similar, but there are besides the plain stripes a patterned stripe containing simple designs in muga thread and two false fringes each about $\frac{1}{4}$ inch deep. Counting all these the entire depth of each end border is about $2\frac{1}{4}$ inches. The fringes are formed into tassels by the threads being twisted together and knotted at the ends. This is rather a dainty cloth and very soft to the touch. I think the thread is homespun. Size 8 feet 10 inches × 3 feet 8 inches. Price R1-9.

The borders are called *chira sandah* and *parang.*

The single shawls above described are all worn by men alone or equally by both sexes. The following are worn exclusively by women and children.

18.—Riha.

The *Riha* is a kind of scarf common to all districts of the Assam Valley except Goalpara. In Lakhimpur, however, cotton *riha* are not made, the material used being muga silk. The following description from Jorhat will give an accurate idea of this cloth:

"Length up to $13\frac{1}{2}$ feet and breadth from 2 to 3 feet. Cotton *riha* are not worn by the Assamese women with the exception of those who are very poor and cannot afford to get silk ones. They are however used by the Miris, Deoris and other tribal communities. Such *riha* are generally made of pure cotton thread, or cotton and silk mixed, *i.e.*, one forming the warp and the other the woof. The ends of the *riha* have invariably an ornamented border about 2 inches deep, woven in one piece with the garment, and a fringe which consists of the unwoven portions of the warp, about 2 inches long, left for this purpose at the ends and twisted afterwards by hand. Sometimes the edges are also made of coloured yarn in which case they have of course to be provided for at the time of preparing the warp, by putting the required quantity of coloured thread on each edge. The price of this variety is from 6 annas to 12 annas.

" The Assamese women wear the *riha* by adjusting one end round the waist and bringing the other end over the left shoulder, then round the back and under the right armpit and again over the left shoulder, and then over the head, leaving the end of the cloth free over the breast."

The Miri women prefer more showy *riha* which will be described hereafter.

The above description applies to all the *riha* of Assam, except that, from Nowgong only, plain *riha*, without any flowers, are reported, their price being 1½ annas. In Tezpur the ornamentations are red or blue. In Barpeta the following designs are used on this cloth : *Batha pathia, Babari, Chainkara* and *Dhekia.* The size of *riha* does not vary very much ; the length ranges between 10 feet (in Nowgong) and 15 feet (in Tezpur), and the breadth between 1½ feet (in Nowgong) and 2¼ feet (in Sibsagar and Barpeta). The price never exceeds R1-4.

In Barpeta it is only the townswomen that wear the *riha*, the villagers wearing in its place the *aguran* or *telach* alone, or the *aguran* and *murat lowa* together. The *riha* is here described as a cloth to cover the breast. The size is 12 feet by 2¼ feet, containing ¼ seer of thread, and its price 12 annas.

Specimen.—From North Lakhimpur.—This is a truly typical *riha* for common wear, a plain white cloth of fairly fine country thread with no ornamentations except a stripe of red at each end broken with lines of yellow; these stripes are about 1½ inch deep. The fringes are made into tassels knotted at the end. Size 11 feet 9 inches by 1 foot 9 inches. Price 8 annas.

19.—Telach.

This cloth is reported from three sub-divisions only, *viz.*, Mangaldai, Gauhati and Barpeta. In Mangaldai it is said to be equivalent to the *cheleng* or *chaddar*; and in Gauhati to the *pachra* which is distinguished from the *cheleng* or *chaddar.* In both these places it is used by males only. In Barpeta, however, it appears to be a different cloth from the *cheleng*, the *chaddar* or the *pachra*, and is worn only by village women and children of both sexes. It is described as a cloth to wrap round the body. The following varieties are found :—

(a) A sheet 7½ feet long by 3 feet wide, containing ½ seer of thread, used by wealthy village women. No ornamentations are mentioned. It sells for 7 annas.

(b) A sheet similar to the last but smaller, being 7½ feet by 2½ feet and containing ¼ seer of thread. It is worn by wealthy village girls and sells for 5 annas.

(c) Size 6 feet by 3 feet (¼ seer) worn by boys of the middle class. No ornamentations. Sells for 8 annas.

(d) Size 3¾ feet by 2¼ feet (⅛ seer), worn by girls of the middle class. No ornamentations ; sells 3 annas.

(e) Size 4½ feet by 1 foot (this is probably a misprint for 3 feet) with a red or black fringe called *kara pari*, price 5 annas, worn by women of the commoner class. It contains ₁⁄₁₆ seer of thread.

(f) Size 3¾ feet by 2½ feet (⅛ seer), with ' pigeon eyes ' border made of red and black cotton, price 3 annas, worn by common village boys.

(g) Size 3 feet by 2¼ feet (₁⁄₁₆ seer), with *makhimuria* or *salika thuthia phul*, price 2 annas, worn by girls of the common class.

It will be noticed here that it is the commonest classes of people who are fondest of ornamental designs. It appears strange at first sight that while the wealthy and poorest village women both own a *telach*, those of the middle class do not. The explanation of this is that three different cloths are worn by village women as covering for their breast and head, *viz.*, *telach, aguran* and *murat lowa.* Women of each class have two of these, *viz.*, the wealthy an *aguran* and a *telach*, the middle class an *aguran* and a *murat lowa*, and the poorer class a *telach* and a *murat lowa.*

Among the village boys the *telach* forms the upper clothing of all except those of the wealthier families, who wear a double sheet (*bor kapor*) instead. All but the poorest have also a coat (*chola*).

The *telach* is worn by all the village girls, but whereas it forms the sole article of clothing of this nature among the poorest classes, it is supplemented by an *aguran* in the case of those more favourably circumstanced.

Specimen.—No. (i).—From Mangaldai.—This is large heavy cloth made of imported thread, not fine, but closely woven. It is white and perfectly plain except for the fringes and a *gari* at each end in place of a border; this *gari* is made by a few white threads being shot double instead of single in the weft. Size 12 feet 9 inches by 3 feet 10¼ inches. Price R1-4,

No. (ii).—From Mangadai.—This is a cloth of finer texture with ornamentations at each end in red, blue, yellow and green, consisting of a one-inch border of rectangular design with a row of men on horseback holding a fan in one hand and a staff in the other; on the other side of the border there is also a row of half-rosettes with a line of red thread beyond them. Size 9 feet by 2 feet 6 inches. Price not stated.

No. (iii).—From Mangaldai.—This cloth is very similar to the last, but of still finer texture. The ornamentations at the ends are more elaborate, the border being 1¾ inch deep, and the row of mounted horsemen being replaced by a much more varied design, 3 inches deep, comprising men on horseback under a pointed archway, alternating with a man on foot and a little bird on a big bird's back, with numerous rosettes scattered about. The colours used are red, blue, yellow, green and white. Size 9 feet by 3 feet. Price not stated.

No specimen of the *telach* has been received from Barpeta where alone it appears to be a distinct cloth.

20.—Aguran.

This cloth has already been referred to in the description of the *telach*. Like that cloth it is only reported from Mangaldai, Gauhati and Barpeta.

In Mangaldai it is described as a sheet 9 feet by 3 feet, worn by women and girls partly on the head as a veil, and partly round the waist. It costs from 8 annas to 14 annas, and lasts for a year or 18 months.

In Gauhati it is described as a wrapper 9 feet by 2 feet worn instead of the *riha* by those women and girls who wear the *patani*. There are two kinds, the one plain, costing from 8 annas to R1-8 and worn on ordinary occasions, the other ornamented with end borders of coloured thread, or silk or gold; these are for special wear and cost from R4 to R5. Both kinds have fringes at either end.

In Barpeta the *aguran* is described as a big sheet to wrap round the body. It appears to be used by the women and girls of the wealthier middle class villagers and by them alone. No ornamentations are described. There are four sizes mentioned, *viz.*

(a) That worn by the wealthier women, measuring 9 feet by 2¼ feet and containing ¼ seer of thread; price 8 annas.

(b) That worn by women of the middle class, 9 feet by 2¼ feet (⅛ seer); price 8 annas.

(c) That worn by girls of the wealthier class, 6 feet by 1⅓ feet (⅙ seer); price 4 annas.

(d) That worn by girls of the middle class, 4¼ feet by 1¼ feet (1/12 seer); price 4 annas.

Specimens.—No. (i).—From Gauhati.—A cloth of very coarse imported thread loosely woven, quite plain except for a single border at each end worked in red with a few blue spots on a background of yellow weft. The yellow is hardly visible. The border at one end is an inch deep, that at the other rather more. Each has a very narrow stripe running alongside. Size 12 feet by 2 feet 6 inches; price R1.

No. (ii.)—From Gauhati.—Almost exactly like the last, but the end borders are even smaller, *viz.*, 1 inch and ¾ inch deep, and there is no additional narrow stripe. The texture and size are the same. The price is not noted.

21.—Gatlowa gamcha.

This cloth is reported from Tezpur alone, but specimens of a cloth bearing this name have been received from Gauhati and Barpeta. That from the former place is labelled *gatlowa* or *aguran* for special wear, that from the latter *gatlowa* or *riha*. In Tezpur it appears to be distinct cloth and is thus described: "This cloth is nothing but a small *riha* about 2½ yards long and 1 foot broad, used round the waist by girls about to attain puberty, in the mauzahs to the west of the Bhoroli. It has little ornamentation at either end, or none at all. It is sold for 6 annas to 8 annas and lasts for about six months.

Specimens.—No. (*i*).—*From Barpeta.*—This *gatlowa* or *riha* is a cloth of medium texture, made of imported thread. Size 11 feet 9 inches × 2 feet 9 inches. It is quite plain except at the two ends which have a heavy border about 3¾ inches deep worked in red with a little green on a background of yellow weft. There are some lines of green in place of the yellow at the outer and inner edges of this border. Beyond this border are 3 cross lines of red thread close to the fringe, the threads of which are twisted together to form tassels. The price of the cloth is R2, which is high on account of the borders. The name of the pattern in these borders is *ulta murch pat.*

No. (*ii*).—*From Gauhati.*—This *gatlowa* or *aguran* for special wear is a strong cloth of rather coarse white thread. It is much shorter than the ordinary *aguran.* It is plain except at the ends which have a two-inch border in blue on a red background, with red edges ; and also another narrow border about ¾ inch deep on a plain background. Each border has a row of red threads and a row of blue running along its outer and inner edges. Size 7 feet by 2 feet 6 inches. Price 14 annas.

22.—Uparani.

This cloth is a kind of sheet measuring 7 feet by 3 feet 6 inches used by women and girls over the *aguran,* but only by the richer classes for special wear. It always has fringes, and ornamentations of silk and gold thread. It costs from R4 to R5. It is reported only from Gauhati, and no specimen has been received.

23.—Bukbandha.

A cloth used in Mangaldai. Its name means " the breast binder." It is six feet long by 3 feet wide and is worn round the breast by women and girls alone. It costs 6 to 8 annas and lasts from 2 to 3 months. It is worn by women in addition to the *tinhalia* when attending festivals or other religious ceremonies.

24.—Pao kapor.

A coarsely woven sheet worn by the women and girls of the lower classes in Dibrugarh, to wrap round the upper half of their bodies. Price 8 annas.

Specimen.—From Dibrugarh.—This cloth was made by a Kachari weaver of Khowang. It is of plain white imported thread, of rather fine texture. Each end has a very pretty border worked in muga thread on a background of yellow-green. The border pattern is rectangular, with centre pieces of eight red diamonds so arranged as to form one large diamond, the middle of which is a ninth small diamond in blue, and at the centre of that is a tiny spot of muga thread. The diamonds are woven in with the main design, the muga threads of which run all across the cloth but do not appear on the face, where the coloured diamonds are—except at the central points. Hence the coloured threads on the back of the cloth are covered by the muga threads and are only visible between them. The fringes of this cloth also are very pretty, the white threads being knotted close to the edge of the cloth so as to hold a little tuft of red thread. The whole tassel, red and white, is only ¾ inch long. Size 12 feet 4 inches by 2 feet 4 inches. Price R1.

25.—Saru kapor.

A small sheet for the use of children. The price varies with the size from 4 annas to R1, (Dibrugarh).

This completes the list of shawls made by the Assamese. The next class of fabrics to be described consists of waistcloths for men and women. Those for the men have many different names, but these names are not used with exactly the same meanings in all districts and it is practically impossible to discriminate exactly one cloth from another. In the description of several of these cloths reference is made to the *gamcha,* which might perhaps have found a place among them, but the most general and primary use of that cloth is as a bathing towel, and so it has been described under the head of towels (*cf.* No. 43).

B.—Waist-cloths.

The following varieties of men's waist-cloths are found.

26.—Churia, Dhuti, Bhuni, or Accha.

This is the ordinary waist-cloth of the Assamese, corresponding exactly to that worn in Bengal. The Assamese name is *churia*, but the Bengali equivalent, *dhuti*, is often used, especially in Lower Assam. The term *bhuni* appears peculiar to Mangaldai, and *accha* to Goalpara, but in both these places the word *dhuti* is more generally applied to this cloth.

This cloth is usually made of plain white thread, homespun or imported, and is very little ornamented. It varies considerably in size, the largest quoted in the districts reports being 15 feet by 8 feet (in Barpeta), and the smallest 6 feet by 1¼ feet (in Dhubri). It is however, perhaps, only to the larger cloths that the name *churia* or *dhuti* is strictly applicable.

The texture of *churia* seems to vary considerably as will be seen from the following table which shows the size and weight of *churia* in a few different places :—

Golaghat	*churia*,	15	feet by	4½	feet,	contains ⅔	seer of	thread.			
Jorhat	„	10½	„	3	„	„	⅔	„	„	„	
Nowgong	„	10	„	2½	„	„	⅓	„	„	„	
Tezpur	*samarani*,,	15	„	5½	„	„	⅔	„	„	„	
Mangaldai	*dhuti*	12	„	4	„	„	⅓	„	„	„	
Barpeta	*churia*	15	„	8*	„	„	⅔	„	„	„	
„	*dhuti*	10½	„	3	„	„	⅓	„	„	„	

Thus the *churia* of Barpeta and the *samarani churia* of Tezpur are evidently much finer than the *dhuti* of Barpeta and Mangaldai, and the *churia* of other places. The explanation is probably that the finer waist cloths in the Upper Valley are of silk and those of Mangaldai of imported cloth. In Barpeta the fine *churia* is worn by townspeople and the coarse *dhuti* by villagers, as might have been expected.

The ornamentations on these cloths usually consist of a plain white or coloured stripe at each end. From North Lakhimpur two kinds are reported, one 12 feet by 3 feet plain with one or two *achu*, and the other 13½ feet by 3 feet with red thread at both ends. A *churia* received from this place, however, does not answer either of these descriptions. In Gauhati the *churia* is sometimes coloured black or red, and in Dhubri the *dhuti* sometimes blue.

The price of the *dhuti* or *churia* varies considerably over the Valley, but ranges between 4 annas and 4 rupees. In Dhubri it is 4 annas to 12 annas, in Jorhat 6 annas to 10 annas, in Nowgong 8 annas, in North Lakhimpur, Sibsagar and Goalpara 8 annas to 10 annas, in Gauhati 12 annas, in Mangaldai one rupee, and in Golaghat 1 rupee to 4 rupees. The last figure seems excessive.

In Barpeta the price of the *churia* is given as one rupee and that of the *dhuti* as 8 annas. The former is there worn only by the townspeople and measures 15 feet by 8* feet, the latter only by wealthy village men and measures 10½ feet by 3 feet. It is not clear if any distinction is here drawn between the two cloths, as both appear to be made at home, and no ornamentations are mentioned on either. There is however a difference in texture, which has been noted above.

In Mangaldai the same cloth is known by the names *dhuti, bhuni* and *pani gamcha* (*cf*. 27). In Tezpur there are two kinds of *churia*—(1) *Tiyani churia*, a small waist cloth measuring 12 feet by 2 feet without any ornamentation, used by men only at night or while bathing (*cf*. 28) ; (2) *Samarani churia* a large waist-cloth 15 feet by 5½ feet, equally plain but used for general wear. Price 12 annas. In Mangaldai and Tezpur *churia* are said to last for three months.

Specimens.—No. (i).—*Churia.—From North Lakhimpur.—*This cloth does not answer the description of a *churia*, but is more like a *gamcha*. It measures 7 feet by 1 foot 4 inches and is made of white thread, with a cross stripe of three red lines at each end. On both sides of the cloth the edges of the warp are made of muga silk to a width of ¼ inch. At one end is a short fringe, quite plain, at the other end a longer fringe in which the threads are rolled up together in sets. Price 6 annas.

---

* This may be a misprint.

No. (ii). Paridiya dhuti.—From Barpeta.—A white cloth, measuring 11 feet×
2½ feet, with a plain fringe about 1¼ inch long at either end. The only ornamentations are the side and end borders; the former are plain stripes of red ⅜ inch wide at the extreme edges; the latter consist of one stripe and a few lines of red. Price 9 annas.

No. (iii).—Garab-sutia dhuti.—From Mahgaldai.—This is not a cotton fabric, but a mixed fabric, the warp being of muga silk and the weft of cotton. It is quite plain except for two red stripes at each end, about 1½ inch apart and one about double the width of the other. These stripes are formed by using a shuttle containing several strands of red thread in place of the ordinary shuttle with a single strand of white. There is also a two-inch fringe at each end, the threads of which are twisted together in sets and knotted. The size is 12 feet by 2½ feet. Price R7.

27.—Panigamcha.

Cloths called *panigamcha* are reported from three places only, *viz.*, Jorhat Mangaldai and Barpeta, and in each place the cloth called by this name is different. In Jorhat the *panigamcha* is a bathing towel, a variety of the *gamcha* (No. 43), in Mangaldai it is the same as the *dhuti*, and in Barpeta it is a distinct cloth.

In Barpeta the following varieties of *panigamcha* are found :—

(I) Size 9 feet by 2 feet, white with no ornamentations. Price 5 annas. Amount of thread required ¼ seer. Worn by a wealthy village man, who usually possesses a *dhuti* and a *bhatkhowa kapor* as well.

(II) Size 6 feet by 2 feet 3 inches, white with *karapari*. Price 6 annas. Amount of thread—required ⅛ seer. Worn by a village man of the middle class; a shorter waist-cloth than the *gamcha* which he usually also owns.

(III) Size 9 feet by 2 feet, white with red or black fringe (probably border is meant). Price 5 annas. Amount of thread ¼ seer. Worn by a common village man, his sole waist-cloth.

(IV) Size 4½ feet by 4 feet 2 inches, white and plain. Price 4 annas; thread ₁⁄₁₂ seer. The larger waist-cloth worn by a wealthy village boy, the other being a *bhatkhowa mukcha.*

In Barpeta therefore the *panigamcha* is seen to be a coarse* waist-cloth smaller than the *dhuti*, but larger than any other kind with the exception, in one instance, of the *gamcha.* It is not used by townsmen at all and is worn only as a second waist-cloth by the adult villagers of the richer and middle classes. It is the chief waist-cloth of the wealthy village boys and the only garment of that nature owned by the commonest village men.

Concerning waist-cloths in general it is interesting to note that the townsmen use only one kind of home make ; of the villagers the wealthy men have three, the boys of the wealthy and men of the middle class families have two, the poorest men have only one and the children of all but the rich have none at all.

The description of the *panigamcha* of Jorhat will be found under the head *gamcha* (43).

Specimen.—From Barpeta.—A cloth measuring 9 feet by 2 feet 7 inches and very similar to the *paridiya dhuti* except as regards size. There is however a very thin stripe in addition to, and about ⅛ an inch distant from, the border stripe on each side; the end borders are also deeper and are accompanied by a false fringe. The side borders are called *rangapari*, (*ranga=*red). Price 13 annas.

28.—Tiyani.

A waist-cloth for ordinary wear varying in size from 7 ft. × 1½ft. to 10 ft. × 2ft. It is made of coarse thread and is sometimes coloured red, black or yellow, it occasionally has also small coloured patterns woven at both ends. It is called *tiyani*, because it is worn while bathing; it is also called *gomcha.* It is practically the same as the *tiyani churia* of Jorhat and the *panigamcha* of Barpeta.

If the weight and size are correctly stated the *panigamcha* of the wealthy village boy is much finer than that worn by any other class, which is difficult of explanation. The extraordinary shape of this garment, however, makes it probable that 4 feet 2 inches is a misprint. The true width is, in all probability, half a yard.

29.—Bhatkhowa kapor.

This is a small plain white waistcloth used in Barpeta by those villagers (men, women and girls) who can afford an extra cloth at the time of taking their meals and bathing. The following varieties are enumerated :—

(i) Size 6 ft. × 3¾ft. containing ⅓rd seer of thread and costing 8 annas ; worn by wealthy women.

(ii) Size 6 ft. × 2¼ft. containing ⅛th seer of thread and costing 5 annas ; worn by wealthy men.

(iii) Size 6 ft. × 1½ft. containing ⅛th seer of thread and costing 5 annas ; worn by middle class men.

(iv) Size 4½ ft. × 3ft. containing ⅛th seer of thread and costing 8 annas; worn by middle class women.

(v) Size 4½ ft. × 2¼ft. containing ⅛th seer of thread and costing 4 annas ; worn by wealthy girls.

No ornamentation or colouring is mentioned.

Specimen from Barpeta.—A cloth measuring 9 ft. 2 in. × 2 ft. 4 in. made of coarse red thread, with two green stripes along each side and a plain green border at each end. It is interesting to note that the side stripes appear of a dull green and the end borders of a bright green, although the thread used in both cases is of exactly the same shade. Price 14 annas.

This cloth hardly answers the description given in the report as regards either size or colour.

30.—Bhatkhowa mukcha.

A plain white waistcloth, measuring 4½ft. × 1½ft. used in Barpeta by wealthy village boys at meal times. Price 4 annas. It contains ⅛th seer of thread. It appears to be identical with the *bhatkhowa kapor*, except that its size is smaller than that of the smallest cloth of that name.

31.—Kakalbandha.

A towel or napkin used as a waistcloth in Gauhati "to serve the purpose of a belt." It varies in size from 9 ft. × 1 ft. to 7 ft. × ¾ft. It has fringes and wide coloured borders at both ends. It is generally made of coloured thread, red, black or yellow. It is worth 4 annas to R1-8.

This cloth is very similar to the *gamcha*, but rather larger as will be seen from the description of the specimens received.

Specimens.—No. (i). from Gauhati.—A yellow cloth, measuring 7½ ft. × 1 ft. 2in. with a fringe over 5 inches long and an elaborate border about 7 in. deep at each end. The threads of the fringes are twisted together in sets. The border consists of a main stripe 4½ in. deep, containing a diamond-shaped pattern ; a row of large diamond-shaped designs 1½ in. deep with small designs scattered about, and two narrow stripes. The colours in the whole border are red, purple, green and blue. Price 12 annas.

No. (ii) from Gauhati.—A red cloth, measuring 8 ft. × 1 ft. 4 in. having fringes and borders at both ends. The border at one end is 5 inches deep and consists of a main stripe 2¼ in. deep and 3 narrow stripes with intervals of plain cloth between. The colours are yellow, dark blue, green and greenish yellow. This border is really prettier than the more elaborate borders in specimen No. (i). The border at the other end is very similar but only 4½ in. deep.

32.—Tangali or Tamali.

This cloth is reported from Tezpur, Nowgong, Golaghat and Jorhat. The description received from Tezpur is as follows:—"*Tangalis* are belts used by males only, size 4 yards by 6 inches, having the two ends embroidered with ornaments of silk, red cotton thread or gold wire. The last kind is also ornamented on the surface and the borders, and is used with wedding garments by males. The price of ordinary ones is 8 annas each, while that for those with gold ornamentations is from R5 to R10. It is not always used and therefore lasts for many years."

In Golaghat the *tamali* or *tangali* is thus described :—"This is a long but very narrow cloth with profuse decorations at both ends, consisting of very deep borders (from 6 to 10 inches deep). The cloth is 20 ft. long and 1½ ft. wide, and is used by men in Golaghat as a belt to tie round the waist at theatricals (*bhaona*) when the *ghagri* (No. 57) is worn. It is so adjusted that the ends hang down in front, the whole of the elaborate borders being thus exposed to view, and adding to the beauty of the *ghagri*."

Another variety called *tangali gamoha* is said to be of the same nature, but measuring only 9 ft. × 9 in. A typical border is reproduced in the report. It consists of a main stripe set in a framework of two creepers, one on either side. The main stripe is made up of diamond-shaped designs (called *phul*), the × shaped space between each diamond being divided up into a number of small squares by cross lines very close together; this filligree work is called *gaoha*. Each of the creepers forming the framework runs between two lines of coloured thread.

In Jorhat the *tangali* is a variety of *gamoha* worn by men when engaged in playing the *khol* or *mridang* (two kinds of drums) at any ceremony. It is 3 to 4 ft. long and about 1 ft. wide, with floral designs on the body and elaborate borders at the ends, made of either coloured cotton thread or gold or silver twist. It is tied round the waist, so that its ends hang down in front. In former days the bridegroom used to wear a *tangali* at the wedding, but this custom has gone out of fashion (the *tangali* here is very short).

In Nowgong the *tangali* is used at *bhaona* by Assamese and Mikirs. It measures 10ft. × 6in. and costs 8 annas.

Specimen from Jorhat.—A white cloth measuring nearly 5ft. × 10 inches, with end borders 9 inches deep and gay tassels formed by bunches of red, blue and yellow cotton thread and silver tinsel being tied on to the ends of the fringes, the threads of which are twisted together in sets. In one end border the background is all of yellow weft, and the deepest stripe is about 1¾ in. deep. The colour of the designs is red interspersed with a few spots in blue. The other border consists of two parts; the one, 3½ inches deep, containing two stripes on a yellow background, and the other containing four on a plain white background. In both parts the colour of the designs is entirely red.

33.—Jangali.

A cloth which is not reported from any district, but is thus described by Mr. Darrah—" A kind of waistband with fringes at both ends, worn by men in the Brahmaputra Valley." I made several enquiries about this cloth, but could find no one who knew of it. I was told in Golaghat that the Mikirs wore a waistband or belt with a name like this. The word may be a misprint for *tangali* (No. 32), but probably it is not so, as *jang* is the Assamese for a thigh.

The Assamese women use two varieties of cotton waistcloths (the *patani* and the *pachrangi*), and a true petticoat (*mekhela*). The two former are difficult to distinguish; the latter should properly be included in made-up garments, but it is put here for comparison with the *patani*, and the making-up is so simple that the garment hardly deserves the title of made-up.

34.—Mekhela or Mekhla.

The following description from Jorhat gives a very good idea of an Assamese petticoat (*mekhela*) : " This is made by sewing together the edges of two equally long pieces of home or European made cloth, the ends of which are left open and terminate in a hem about an inch broad. This is a sort of petticoat in the form of an elongated sack open at both ends. Its length is about 4 ft. and the circumference about 5 ft. It is worn only by the female sex and its size varies of course with the size of the woman. It is worn by adjusting it either above the breast or round the waist. The women of the labouring or cultivating class generally put it on above the breast, which means raising the lower end of it up to the calves so as to leave the legs more free for walking or working and to protect the cloth from mud and water. The Assamese *mekhela* is invariably plain and made of home-made thread or European yarn of natural colour without any ornamentations. A piece of cloth 10 ft. long and 2 ft. broad is sufficient to make a *mekhela* 5 ft. long and 4 ft. in circumference, and requires about half seer of thread. The price of such a *mekhela* is from 6 to 10 annas. This kind of plain *mekhela* does not, however, find much favour with the Miri women who appear to be fond of coloured raiments." If a piece of cloth 10 ft. long be used, as mentioned above, it is necessary to cut it into two equal halves and then to sew these together at the sides, not ends, the ends being hemmed. When adjusted round the waist the petticoat reaches to the ankles. The method of adjustment is by pulling it tight round the body and then tucking in the loose end. In Mangaldai it is said to be worn from breast to ankle.

Like the waistcloths of the men the petticoats of the women are little ornamented, and never contain any design except an occasional border at the bottom, which is, however, extremely rare. In Gauhati *mekhela* are sometimes coloured black, but the most usual colour everywhere is white.

Cotton *mekhela* are not made at Sibsagar at the present day, nor are they reported from Dibrugarh. In Golaghat they are used only by Miris and the lowest classes of the Assamese. They are found in all other districts of the Brahmaputra Valley except Goalpara.

The usual size is 9 ft. × 3 ft., but in North Lakhimpur a larger size also is worn, *viz.* 10½ ft. × 3¾ ft. The price varies from 4 annas to R2-8.

In Barpeta the *mekhela* is worn only by the villagers and, among them, only by the rich and the grown up woman of the middle class. The *mekhela* worn by women measures 6 ft. × 3 ft. 9 in., and contains ¼ to ½ seer of thread, it is worth eight annas; a-girl's size measures 4½ × 2½ ft., contains ½ seer of thread, and costs 4 annas.

Specimens.—No. (i) from North Lakhimpur.—This is a perfectly plain white *mekhela* woven of country thread. It is made up of two pieces of cloth, each 3 ft. 10 in. × 2 ft. 7 in., sewn together at the sides and having a broad hem (*patuli*) at top and bottom, so that the petticoat is about 8 ft. 7 in. long and 5 ft. in circumference. Its price is 6 annas.

No. (ii) from Gauhati.—This also is perfectly plain, but it is made of much coarser thread, imported. It is 3 ft. long and 5 ft. 4 in. in circumference. Price not stated. It is made just like the last. This is for ordinary wear.

No. (iii) from Gauhati.—This is a red and white check, all the warp consisting of 6 red and 6 white threads alternately, and the weft in the body of the cloth being of red and white threads alternating in the same way. But at each end, *i.e.*, at the top and at the bottom of the garment as worn when made up, there is a border about 1 ft. deep consisting of stripes of yellow (6)*, red (5) and blue † (1), varying in width from ¾ in. to 1¼ in. each. There is a further element of variety introduced in the shape of lines of red, white, yellow and blue running either between the stripes or along the centre of them. The extreme end of the weft is of white thread for about 1 in. The cloth is made like the last two, but the hems are only slightly over ½ in. deep. The size is 3 ft. 9in. long and 6 ft. 6 in. in circumference. The thread is medium fine, and imported. Price R1-2. This cloth is for special wear. It is said to be also sometimes called *patani.*

No. (iv) from Gauhati.—This is a large and elaborate *mekhela* used, for bridal wear, by the Kacharis and other lower classes. It is said to be also called *patani.* The thread is medium coarse. The body of the cloth is red, but there is a border about 10½ inches deep at top and bottom. This consists of 6 patterned stripes, each about ¾ inch deep; the pattern is very simple and made of yellow thread woven in between the shots of red weft.* Between each of the first five stripes there is a stripe of plain red, besides some red, white and blue lines. Between the 5th and 6th patterned stripe there are three rows of some imaginary animals like stags with humped backs. Rosettes are interspersed between the animals and the two are alternately yellow and white. These rows are woven on a stripe of yellow, 3 inches deep, which forms the background.

The cloth is 4 ft. 6 in. in length and 7 ft. in circumference. Price R2-8-0. The hems are ½ in. wide.

No. (v) from Barpeta.—Plain white, but with a border nearly 4 in. deep at one end only, the bottom end as worn. In this border there is a background of red weft for about 2½ in., the rest being plain white. The design itself is in blue thread woven upon this background with dark blue threads of several strands, so that it

---

* At one end there are only 5.
† At one end this stripe is green.

stands out in bold relief. This design is of more than usual interest, the portion on the red background being the main part, and that on the white merely additional to give it a finish; it is called *galicha mukhpat*. The size of this cloth is 3 ft. 3 in. in length and 5 ft. 6 in. in circumference. The hems are very narrow, *viz.*, about ¼ in. Price 14 annas.

35.—Patani.

This is a waistcloth or simple sheet used by some women in the districts of Kamrup and Goalpara in place of the *mekhela* or true petticoat. It is worn in very much the same way as the *mekhela*, being wrapped once round the body and tucked in at the side.

In Goalpara the *patani* is the only form of home-woven lower garment used by the women. It is used also as a body sheet or shawl. Its size is 7½ ft. × 3 ft. and its price varies from 8 annas for a plain cloth to R4 for one highly decorated. The more elaborate *patani*, however, are made by the Rabhas and Meches and will be described under the fabrics of the hill tribes.

In Gauhati the *patani* is used in places only; its size is 7 ft. × 3½ ft. and its price is 8 to 10 annas for a plain cloth and R1-8-0 to R2-8-0 for a fancy one, the ornamentations in the latter consisting of deep end borders and side stripes of coloured thread. The plain *patani* are worn on ordinary occasions, the fancy ones being reserved for special wear.

In Barpeta the *patani* is used by all classes of women and girls among the villagers, the townswomen do not wear it. The following varieties are enumerated:

(i) Size 6 ft. × 3¾ ft. containing ⅓ seer of thread, worn by wealthy women. Price 8 annas.

(ii) Size 5½ ft. × 3¾ ft. containing ¼ seer of thread, worn by middle class women. Price 8 annas.

(iii) Size 4½ ft. × 3 ft. containing ⅓ seer of thread and having red and black borders called *karapari*, worn by common women. Price 6 annas.

(iv) Size 4½ ft. × 2½ feet containing ⅓ seer of thread, worn by wealthy girls. Price 4 annas.

(v) Size 3¾ ft. × 1½ feet containing ₁/₁₀ seer of thread, worn by middle-class girls. Price 3 annas.

(vi) Size 3 ft. × 2½ ft., containing ₁/₁₀ seer of thread, and having a red and black border; worn by common girls. Price 2 annas.

As regards lower garments generally, the village women of Barpeta are much better off than the men. All women but the very poorest have three such garments, and so has the wealthy girl; the remaining women and girls have one lower garment a piece. It is not possible from the report to say whether the use of the *patani* and *mekhela* by those who possess both is indiscriminate or not; and it is very difficult to tell the exact difference between the *patani* and *bhatkhowa kapor*, but, in all probability, the two cloths are really the same, the latter name being restricted to such as are set apart for use at meal times.

The name *patani* is sometimes incorrectly applied to the true petticoat or *mekhela*.

Specimens.—No. (i) from Gauhati.—This is a plain cloth made of coarse white imported thread with no ornamentation except a border at each end composed of 6 red lines running crosswise and separated from each other by white lines, the whole being less than an inch in depth. The fringes are quite plain and loose, the threads not being rolled together to form a tassel. The cloth is 6 in. long and 2 ft. 6 in. wide. Price not stated.

No. (ii) from Barpeta.—This is a plain white cloth 7 ft. 3 in. long and 3 ft. wide. It has no ornamentations except a plain cross stripe at each end; one 1¾ in. deep and one 1½ inch deep, and a lengthwise stripe about 1½ inch wide at each side. The end stripes are red, but the monotony is broken by four or five double lines of yellow running through them. The side stripes are entirely red and at the extreme edges of the cloth; they are called *gariapari*. The price of the cloth is R1-4.

The length of this *patani* is greater than that of any mentioned in the report.

36.—Pachrangi.

This is a waistcloth reported from Gauhati and Goalpara as a separate cloth from the *patani*. The size of the two is however the same and so is the description, with this exception that the *pachrangi* is invariably coloured, being frequently striped and elaborately decorated with handsome borders. The price is accordingly comparatively high, *viz.*, from R2·4 to R4 in Gauhati and from R4 to R5 in Goalpara. There is nothing whatever in the reports to show the difference between an ornamented *patani* and a *pachrangi*. I made personal enquiries into this matter in Goalpara and was informed by several persons who ought to know that the name *pachrangi* was never applied to cotton cloths at all, but only to *endi* cloths similar in size and shape to the cotton *patani*. This is probably the true interpretation, but the strict use of the terms does not appear to be always adhered to (*cf.*, Rabha fabrics).

C.—Head Dresses.

The next class of fabrics is that comprising head dresses for men and women, a very small and not a very interesting class.

37.—Paguri.

This is a plain cloth of rather fine texture, the usual width of which is 1 foot and the length from 15 up to 38 ft. The largest size is from Tezpur, *viz.*, 45 ft. × 1½ ft. The *paguri* is sometimes coloured red or yellow in Gauhati. It is said to be no longer made in Mangaldai. It varies in price from annas 8 to R 2, chiefly according to size.

Paguri are not commonly worn by the Assamese now-a-days, and probably they never were much worn, to judge from the following quotation from a translation of Mahammed Cazim's "Description of the Kingdom of Assam in the Alemgeer Namah" written in the 17th century :—

" As they " (the Assamese) " are destitute of the mental garb of manly qualities, they are also deficient in the dress of their bodies; they tie a cloth round their heads, and another upon their loins and throw a sheet round their shoulders ; but it is not customary in that country to wear turbans, robes, drawers or shoes." Mahammed Cazim was rather hard on the Assamese, but his description holds good to the present day in most respects. Many of the Assamese have, however, lately developed a great fondness for shoes, especially in Nowgong.

*Specimens.—No. (i) from North Lakhimpur.—*A very long and narrow strip of cloth of exceedingly fine texture. Size 27½ ft. × 9 in. It is perfectly plain except for a short fringe, a narrow yellow stripe and four pairs of double woven threads at one end only. Price 6 annas.

*No. (ii) from Mangaldai.—*This cloth is a marked contrast to the last, being of coarsish thread, closely woven and very heavy for its size. It has no ornamentations except at the two ends, one of which has 3 blue and 2 yellow stripes, and the other 2 yellow and 1 blue stripes, all narrow. The fringe threads are loosely twisted together. Size 7¼ ft. × 1 ft. 3 in. Price not stated.

38.—Murat bandha.

This is probably the cloth referred to by Mahammed Cazim in the passage quoted above. It is reported from Tezpur only where it is described as being almost the same as the *tangali* (No. 32) but without any ornamentations. The *tangali* in Tezpur is 12 ft. × 6 in, in size. The *murat bandha* is worn round the head by males of the labouring class instead of a turban. Its price is 8 annas and it lasts about a year.

39.—Murat lowa.

This is a small cloth worn on the head as a veil by women of the middle and poorer classes of villagers in Barpeta. The size used by a woman of the middle class is 4¼ ft. × 2¼ ft. containing ¼ seer of thread, price 4 annas ; that worn by the poorer women is 3 ft. × 1½ ft. (⅒ seer) ; price 2 annas. The latter is ornamented with the *karapari*.

An interesting comparison might be drawn between this head dress and that of some of the continental peasant women of Europe.

*Specimen from Barpeta.—*This is a cloth of fine texture but roughly woven. Size 5 ft. 8 in. × 2 ft. 6 in. It has at each end a border of red on a background of yellow striped with blue. There is also a double line of blue near the fringe at one end and a double line of blue with yellow in the centre near that at the other. The edges of the cloth have 3 narrow stripes of blue, and the body of the cloth is covered with rows of small blue, red and yellow rosettes, all of nearly the same design. The pattern of the end borders is called *chira sandah*. This cloth is called a *murat lowa* or *telnoh*, and is said to be used as a head cloth by big women and a sheet or body cloth by girls. It is not mentioned how a little woman wears it. The price is only 4 annas.

40.—Tinhatia.

This is a cloth about 4½ ft. long and 2 ff. broad, worn as a veil by women in Tezpur and Mangaldai. Its name denotes its length (3 cubits). In Mangaldai it is used daily by women and lasts for from two to three months. Its price is 6 to 8 annas. It is here used also at festivals and on other special occasions in connection with the *bukbandha* (No. 23). In Tezpur it appears to be worn only by the women of Boncholi mouzah. It has no ornamentations.

41.—Dohatia.

A cloth similar to the *gomcha* but rather larger, used by women over the head as a veil. Price 4 to 8 annas. (Dhubri.)

The name of this cloth would indicate its length as being 2 cubits, but from the description it would appear to be longer.

42.—Phali.

This is a cloth reported from Goalpara only, where it is described as a head dress for men 6 ft. long and 1½ ft. wide, costing from R1 to R1-4. This cloth is said to be used by the Garos and Rabhas only, and is probably the same thing as the Kachari *gamcha*.

From Mangaldai, however, five specimens of *phali* have been sent, and these are described below. The purpose for which used and the people who make them are not stated. They are therefore entered in the list of Assamese cloths.

Specimens.—No. (i) from Mangaldai.—This is a plain white cloth 7 ft. 10in. × 2 ft. 1in., with no ornamenations except at the ends, one of which has a triple border altogether about 2 in. deep and the other a border 1½ in. deep. These borders are woven of cotton thread, red, blue and yellow at one end and red and blue at the other. The fringes are twisted and knotted. Price not stated.

No. (ii) from Mangaldai.—This is very similar to the last, but the end ornamentations are much more elaborate. At one end is a seven-inch border of red, blue, yellow and green cotton thread, consisting of two parts, the design in one being geometrical and the other containing a succession of three curious animals (camels) of different colours and sizes, with a man standing on the top and holding a large fan in each hand. At the other end the border is of almost the same pattern but much smaller, being altogether only 4½ in. deep ; the colours are the same. This cloth measures 7 ft. 6 in. × 2 ft. 6 in. Price not stated. The border design is called *bichanipad.*

No. (iii) from Mangaldai.—This is a blue cloth 8 ft. 6 in. × 2 ft. The border at each end is of cotton thread red, salmon, green and white, and consists of a central design with a row of pointed arch-shaped *phul* along each edge which runs between two thin stripes each made up of two yellow and one green shot of the weft. The border at one end is 4 in. deep, that at the other 2½ in. Price not stated.

No. (iv) from Mangaldai.—This also is a blue cloth size 7 ft. 6 in. × 2 ft. . in. The borders at each end are very elaborate and extensive, and, in addition to these, there is a plain red stripe running along each side of the cloth, one being 1 in. wide and the other ¾ in. wide. The end borders are of equal size, *viz.*, altogether 15 in. deep. Each consists of one main stripe between two minor stripes, and three rows of natural figures. The main stripe, which is 4 in. deep, is made up of octagonal designs. The minor stripes are alike and contain a simple forked pattern. Of the three rows, one is a series of men standing on horseback and other little animals ; the second is a series of two animals, a small one standing on the back of a large one, and the third a series of men standing on elephants. In all three rows there are diamonds besides the main figures ; each row is divided from the next by a triple line of two colours, red and white, red and yellow, or salmon and yellow. The colours of the main borders are yellow, white and salmon, those of the three rows of figures, yellow, red and white. Price not stated.

No. (v) from Mangaldai.—This is a bright red cloth size 6 ft. 3 in. × 1 ft. 9 in. The ornamentations cover more than two-thirds of the cloth, being nearly 2 ft. 3 in. deep at each end. They consist of rows of natural figures, deep stripes of geometrical design, and numerous thin fancy stripes and lines of coloured thread. The natural figures form a complete zoölogical collection, so great is their variety in shape and colour,—elephants, camels, men, dogs, stags, goats and others which defy accurate classification. There are also little designs like shrubs, and we have in one row a blue goat nibbling at a white shrub, a white goat at a succulent green shrub, and a green goat at a dark blue shrub; it may be the same goat changing colour with the shrub it eats. At one end of the cloth the colours are blue, green, yellow and white, at the other end the same with the addition of an orange. At this end there is also a new design apparently representing a thatched shed or open cow-house seen from one end. To attempt to give a detailed description of the whole border at either end would be mere waste of time. The effect is most striking.

The ends of this cloth are hemmed, and have tassels affixed. These tassels are of twisted white thread 3 in. long with bunches of orange, blue and yellow cotton at the ends. Price not stated.

This completes the list of those cotton fabrics which are used by the Assamese primarily as articles of dress. There remains a miscellaneous class of scarf-like fabrics which are used for various purposes, e.g., as bathing towels, handkerchiefs or bedsheets. But it is impossible to draw a strict line between garments proper and cloths such as these. Thus the bathing towel is almost invariably used also to tie round the waist if long enough for that purpose, and a cloth that is worn as a double sheet or wrapper by day is often used as a blanket by night.

D.—MISCELLANEOUS SCARF-LIKE FABRICS.

43.—Gamcha.

The most important cloth of the miscellaneous class is the *gamcha*, the nature and use of which are so varied that it might find a place in any of the classes of scarf-like fabrics. Its primary use is, as its name implies, a bathing towel or body wiper (*ga*—body and *mocha*—to wipe). As such it is used by men and boys, but its uses are very varied; sometimes it is used as a light sheet thrown over the shoulder like a *chadar*; sometimes it is tied round the waist as a belt or even as a waistcloth; sometimes it is worn on the head as a *puggry* and occasionally it is used like a handkerchief to carry *tamul* and other little luxuries.

Many varieties of *gamcha* and cloths of similar nature have already been described (e.g., Nos. 21,27,28,31,32,41,42). There remains the *gamcha* proper, which is of no special interest, and it will be sufficient to give a very general description and point out a few peculiarities of different districts; for the *gamcha* is found in every portion of the Brahmaputra valley.

The *gamcha* is a long but narrow cloth usually made of coarse thread and varying in length from 3 ft. to 7½ ft. and in breadth from 9 in. to 2 ft. The shape is not always the same, for the longer ones are often narrower than many of those much shorter. The *gamcha* is sometimes white and sometimes coloured, sometimes plain and sometimes highly ornamented at the ends. The *gamcha* of the Assamese, however, are not nearly so elaborate as those of the Kacharis and other hill tribes which will be described hereafter. The price varies from one anna to one rupee or slightly more.

In North Lakhimpur two varieties of *gamcha* are mentioned, one plain (called *uka*), and one ornamented with floral borders (called *phulam*). Both are the same in size, viz., 7½ ft. × 1½ feet, and used for the same purposes, viz., as bathing towels or for carrying *tamul*.

In Jorhat there are three varieties of *gamcha*, viz., the *panigamcha*, the *gamcha* proper and the *tangali*. The *panigamcha* is here used as a towel and is therefore distinct from the cloths of that name described above (No. 27). "They are made of coarse thread, either homespun or imported, and are either plain or with edges of coloured yarn and ornamentations at the ends. Price between 2 and 6 annas." The *gamcha* proper are superior in quality and far more elaborately ornamented. "They are used as a part of dress by the male sex, i.e., as a *paguri* or covering for the head or as a scarf, in which case it is worn loosely round the neck or shoulders. Some are made entirely of coloured European yarn, sometimes with stripes of coloured yarn or with beautiful ornamentations at the ends as well as in the whole cloth. The price of this class varies from 6 annas to R1." From these descriptions it will be seen that the *panigamcha* is used as a towel in Jorhat and the *gamcha* proper as an article of dress,—the reverse of the usual order.

In Tezpur the *gamcha* usually has stripes of red (*achu*) at both ends.

In Gauhati the *gamcha* is described as a waistcloth, the name being synonymous with *tiyani* (No. 28).

In Barpeta the *gamcha* is used by the townspeople and wealthy villagers as a bathing towel and by the men of the middle class of villagers as a waistcloth (larger than the *panigamcha*). That used by townspeople measures 6 ft. × 1¼ ft. and is ornamented with *kadam*, *karani*, *bakul*, *bichani*, lions, elephants, pigs, peacocks and other birds. It contains ¼ seer of thread and is sold for 4 annas. That used by the wealthy village man measures 7½ ft. × 9 in., contains ₁⁄₁₀ seer of thread, and costs 6 annas; that of his son measures 5½ ft. × 1½ ft. and contains ⅛ seer of thread, but is worth only 4 annas. The difference in shape is worthy of note. The *gamcha* used as a waistcloth by men of moderate means measures 9 ft. × 3 ft. and contains ⅜ seer of thread. It has coloured borders (*karapari*) and costs 8 annas.

In the Goalpara district the only *gamcha* of interest are those made by Kacharis.

Specimens-No. (i).—*Seen at Golaghat.*—This is a typical Assamese *gamcha* of its kind. It is made of white imported thread and measures 6 ft. × 1ft. 2 in. It has no ornamentations except the borders and fringes at its ends and a single line of red along each side, made by inserting a *kani* of red thread in the warp. The end borders are alike and of the following nature. Near the fringe is a plain particoloured stripe ¼ in. deep; this is followed by a false fringe (*agat chula diya*) about ⅜ in. long with an equal depth of plain white cloth beyond; then comes the main part of the border 1⅜ in. deep. The particoloured stripe is composed of different coloured threads as follows:—First, 3 white, then 3 yellow, then 2 red (shot double), then 3 yellow and 3 white, the whole forming a pretty and symmetrical stripe. The main part of the border consists of two thin stripes containing *pankata* and *gacha* designs in red with 5 green spots (*kali*) dotted on a background of yellow weft.

At one corner of each fringe is a small mark made by wrapping a leaf round the thread and squeezing out the juice. This shows that several cloths were woven in one piece; the stain being intended to mark the division of two cloths.

No. (ii).—*Gariali gamcha—Seen at Golaghat.*—This is about 1 ft. longer and 2 in. wider than the last. The border is 1¾ in. deep. The chief point of interest about this cloth is that it is ribbed lengthwise; the white ribs giving it its distinctive name.

No. (iii).—*From North Lakhimpur.*—This is a small cloth made of fine white thread. It has a border at one end over 1⅓ in. deep, and 3 plain red stripes at the other end, the central one being made up of 6 shots of the weft and the 2 outer ones of 2 apiece. At each side is a similar threefold line of red, about three times the width of that at the other end. Besides this there is a false fringe at each end in addition to the end fringe, and a line of red (2 threads) running along the narrow woven part between these two fringes; otherwise the cloth is quite plain. Size 5 ft. 9 in. × 1 ft. 5 in.

No. (iv).—*From North Lakhimpur.*—This is coarser than the last and has no side borders and no false fringes. The only ornamentations are a border 1½ in. deep at one end and 3 plain red stripes at the other, the central stripe consisting of 4 red shots of the weft and the outer ones of three each. Size 5 feet 10 in. × 1 ft. 1 inch.

No. (v).—*From North Lakhimpur.*—This is very much like No. iii but has no side borders; the ends are however more elaborately decorated, one having a border over 2¼ in. deep and the other one over 2¼ in. These borders are of red thread on a background of yellow. The false fringes are also longer and the red stripe between the false and true fringes consists of 6 shots of the weft. The size of this cloth is 5 ft. 9 in. × 1 ft. 4 in.

These 3 cloths (Nos. iii, iv and v) together cost 10 annas.

No. (vi).—*From Dibrugarh.*—This cloth is also of fine texture and has a border at each end and two red stripes along each side. At one end the border, which is of red thread on a very faintly-coloured background, is 1⅓ in. deep and the design is very pretty but admits of no description. The border at the other end is 1 in. deep and much simpler. Besides this there are two false fringes at each end and 3 lines of red at one end and 2 at the other. The true fringes are less than ¼ in. long. The size of this cloth is about 6 ft. × 1 ft. 3 in. Price 8 annas.

*No. (vii).— From Dibrugarh.—*This cloth is rather coarser than the last, but still of fairly fine texture. It has a border 6 in. deep at one end, consisting of two rectangular patterns worked in red, blue, yellow, and green thread, the design probably representing a tree with wide spreading arms. The border at the other end is nearly 1¾ in. deep, the designs being also in red, blue, yellow and green, but very different from that at the other end. There is a false fringe at each end and beyond it is a double line of coloured thread; that at the main end is red and that at the other yellow. The true fringes are very short but differ in length at the two ends. The sides of this cloth have each one wide red stripe with two narrow red stripes on either side of it, size about 6 ft. 6 in. × 1 ft. 8 in. Price one rupee.

This cloth was made by an Assamese lady of Dibrugarh and is intended for use as a towel; the decorations, therefore, appear rather excessive.

*No. (viii).—From Jorhat.—*This is an Assamese ornamented *gamcha,* a nice little cloth, pretty and chaste. Each end has a border nearly 4 in. deep worked in red with a little green on a background of yellow. Then follow 4 lines of oval rosettes *(phul)* red and green, 6 to a line, those in the last line being smaller than the others. The fringes are twisted into tassels with bunches of red and green thread at the ends. The size of this cloth is 7 ft. × 12½ in., so in spite of the design and tassels at each end there is still left plenty of plain cloth for use as a towel.

*No. (ix).—From Mangaldai.—*This is a cloth of medium texture, 6 ft. 10 in. long and 1 ft. 7 in. broad. The borders at each end are of red thread on a background of yellow, one being 4 in. deep and the other 3¾ in. There are also false fringes and broken lines of red on yellow backgrounds.

*No. (x).—From Mangaldai.—*This cloth is very similar to the last, but about a foot longer, and the borders are specked with blue and have blue edges. Besides this the borders have lines of trees and arches along their inner edges and four stray *phul* of indescribable design appear quite capriciously upon the body of the cloth. There are two false fringes at either end with a red and blue line between them. Price not stated.

*No. (xi)—From Mangaldai.—*This *gamcha* differs from all the others in being red instead of white. Probably it is not used as a towel. The border at each end is altogether 6 inches deep and contains four stripes, one 3 inches deep, two ½ inch deep and one ¼ inch deep. The main stripe consists of a central design with edges of forked pattern. The colour of the central design is blue with touches of yellow. The edges are of yellow, blue and white. The narrower stripes are of red, blue and yellow. The fringe threads are twisted together and knotted so as to form tassels. The size of this cloth is 5 feet 8 inches × 1 foot 6 inches; its price is not stated.

44.—Mukhmocha.

This is a towel used by the villagers in Barpeta. It is shorter than the *gamcha* and seems to be generally coarser in texture. That used by the wealthier men is 4½ feet long and 1½ foot wide and contains ₁₆/₁ seer of thread; its price is 8 annas; that of the common men measures 4½ feet × 1 foot (½ seer) and has a red or black border; price 2 annas; that of the common boys measures 4½ feet × 9 inches (₁₆/₁ seer), and is ornamented with *chiraphul* (little conical spots) and *penpeliphul.* Price 2 annas. Thus it will be seen that the length is always the same, but the width differs in each case.

The *mukhmocha* is the only towel used by the common classes (men and boys) of Barpeta; the wealthier villagers have also a *gamcha,* but judging from the size and weight, in their case the *gamcha* is the coarse towel and the *mukhmocha* the fine towel which might be expected from the names; for *gamcha* or *gamocha* means a body-wiper, *i. e.,* a bathing towel and *mukhmocha* means a face wiper, *i. e.,* a towel for drying the hands and face.

45.—Mukhcha or gatoka.

This also is a towel found in Mangaldai, Gauhati and Barpeta. The word *mukhcha* is possibly a corruption of *mukhmocha;* the word *gatoka* which is used in Mangaldai as equivalent to *mukhcha* means practically the same as *gamocha (toka=to wipe dry).*

In Mangaldai this cloth is used by both sexes; its size is 4 feet × 1 foot, and its price is 2 annas. Its ends are embroidered with *phul* or flowers. It is said to last two to three months.

In Gauhati it varies in size from 3 to 6 feet in length and 1 to 1½ feet width, and in price from 3 to 6 annas. It is generally used as a bathing towel. The cultivators however, sometimes tie it round the head or waist when they go out to work. It is generally plain but has coloured patterns woven at both ends and is sometimes made of coloured thread, red, black or yellow.

In Barpeta it is used as a towel for drying the hands and face by villagers of the middle class, both men and boys. That used by the men is 4½ feet × 9 inches in size and contains ₁⁄₁₆ seer of thread; it is decorated with *karapari*; its price is 2 annas. That used by the boys is larger, being 4½ feet long and 1 foot 2 inches in width, but contains only ₁⁄₈ seer of thread. Its price is the same, *viz.*, 2 annas; no ornamentations are named. This is the only towel used by men and boys of this class. The difference of texture estimated by weight and size is very marked, and leaves doubts as to the correctness of the figures.

It is difficult to discriminate between these three cloths, the *gamcha*, the *mukhmocha* and the *mukhcha*. The last two are probably the same and differ from the *gamcha* only in being of rougher make and woven from coarser thread.

Specimen.—From Barpeta.—A white cloth of medium texture measuring 6 feet × 1 foot 8 inches and perfectly plain except for a few stripes and lines of blue. Along each side runs a single narrow stripe *kalapari*, and each end has a broader stripe (lying between two lines) and also two independent lines. The fringes are short and plain. Price three annas.

46.—Chulchata or murata.

A towel, 3 feet long and 1 foot wide, used, to dry the hair after bathing, by women only. Occasionally, however, when engaged on outdoor work, women wear it tied round their heads to keep their hair clean from dust and dirt. Its price is 3 or 4 annas. It is reported only from Gauhati.

47.—Urmal.

This is a handkerchief, the use of which, however, is not for blowing the nose, but for holding betel-nut, etc., tied up in the corner. It is sometimes carried in the pocket, but more usually tucked into the *churia*.

Assamese handkerchiefs are more often of silk than of cotton, and the latter kind is reported only from Golaghat. They differ considerably in size, shape and colour according to the taste of the weaver; they are usually highly decorated and are often made entirely of coloured thread.

Specimens.—All seen at Golaghat.—No. (i). A red cotton handkerchief 22 inches long and 30 inches wide made of imported thread. Both ends of the cloth have tassels and borders and the body is covered with flowers arranged in rows. There are, altogether, eight such rows, six between the two end borders and one beyond each. The flowers in any row are all alike in shape. Only two shapes are found, and these alternate with one another in the rows except that those in the two rows beyond the borders are all alike. The number of flowers in a row are alternately six and five throughout. The colours of the flowers are yellow, white and orange, the arrangement being as follows:—First row (beyond the fringe at one end), all the spots are yellow; second row, 1 orange, 2 yellow and 2 white; third row, 1 white, 2 orange and 3 yellow; fourth row, like the second; fifth row, alternately white and yellow (3 of each); sixth row, 3 yellow and 2 white; seventh row, alternately yellow and white (3 of each); eighth row (beyond the fringe at the other end), 2 orange, 2 yellow and 1 white. The arrangement of the different coloured spots differs in every row except the second and fourth which are alike.

The loose threads (*dahi*) at the end are made into tassels (*ghugura*) by bunches of thread being tied on. The colour of the tassels so formed is alternately green and white.

The border at each end is made of Bengali thread, the colour of the weft being yellow. It consists of a central stripe between two rows of small and simple flowers. The main stripe consists of large designs each made up of seven small diamonds, six arranged in a circle and one in the centre. These rosettes are divided off from one another by narrower geometrical designs.

No. (ii). A cotton handkerchief made by a Dom woman and used at marriage ceremonies by both men and women, but generally men, size 24 inches × 14 inches. Colour red with white stripes.

At one end is a plain fringe only, at the other there is also a false fringe which is separated from the true fringe by only 5 shots of weft.

The body of the cloth is red, but is divided into seven panels by white stripes running lengthwise as follows:—At the extreme edge of the cloth on each side are 6 white warp threads, then 8 red, then 12 white; then 8 red and then 6 white. Thus 3 white stripes are formed close together, and these are followed by an inch and a half of plain red cloth, beyond which is another set of three white stripes, similar to the last. Thus there are four sets of three white stripes, two at the extreme side edges and two at distances of 1½ inch from them. Between these last two sets are four single stripes, each consisting of six white warp threads. Thus the cloth is divided into seven panels which are utilised for the arrangement of the flowers.

Starting from the end with the false fringe there comes first ¼ inch of plain red cloth, then a white border, ¼ inch deep. The design of this border is a succession of circles touching each other and each having a plain square cross in the centre. On either side of this design run two white weft threads not far apart.

At one inch distance from this narrow border comes the first row of flowers. There are ten such rows, each containing seven flowers, viz., one in each panel. All the flowers in any one line are alike in size and shape, but vary in colour. The flowers in the first row are large symmetrical figures probably meant to vaguely represent a tree with the branches weighed down by ripe fruit at their ends and birds sitting upon them—the flowers and birds are, however, not exactly life like, being shaped like diamonds—the figure might represent almost anything, but it is by no means ungraceful. The colours of the figures in this line are yellow (2), green (2), blue (1), and white (2). The flowers in the second row, which is 2 inches from the first, consist of small rosettes each made up of seven triangles—six arranged in a circle and one placed in the centre. The colours are white (2), yellow (3), green (1), and blue (1). The flowers of the third row are still smaller and more simple than the last, being plain ovals with a square cross in the centre. The colours are yellow (2), white (3), and green (2). The flowers of the fourth row are like those of the second, but the colours are green (2), white (2), blue (2) and yellow (1). The flowers of the fifth row consist of three Vs with 3 cornered spots in the angles; the two outer Vs are inverted, the central one being erect. The colours of these flowers are white (3), yellow (1), blue (2), and green (1). These five rows cover one-half of the cloth. The other half also contains 5 rows, but the distribution of these rows is different from that of those in the first half. The sixth row is like the fifth and the colours are the same, but arranged in different order. The seventh row is like the second, but the colours are white (4), blue (2), and green (1). The eight row contains new flowers consisting of a single V with double arms and a triangular spot in the centre. All are white except one of the end ones which is blue. The ninth row is like the eighth, but the V-shaped designs are upside down and the colours are green (2), white (3), yellow (1), and blue (1). The last row contains a new design, viz., a diamond with the sides double and a square cross in the centre; the colours are white (3), green (2), blue (1), and yellow (1). The arrangement of the colours in no two of these rows is the same.

Beyond the last row is an elaborate border. First comes a white chain-like pattern of diamonds with Xs between them, running all across the cloth and bordered by two white lines on each side. Then comes about the same depth of plain cloth, and lastly, beyond that, comes a row of seven camels,—blue (2), yellow (2), green (2), and white (1), the colours being arranged symmetrically, blue on the outsides and so on, the white being in the central panel. On each side of this row of camels are two white lines not far apart.

All the ornamentations on this cloth are woven in the cloth and made of cotton thread. The effect is very striking.

No. (iii).—This handkerchief does not, strictly speaking, come under the head of cotton fabrics as it is made of muga silk; it is included here because the ornamentations, which are very profuse, are all made of coloured cotton thread.

The handkerchief is 2 feet 7½ inches long and 14 inches wide. The edges are woven with double threads (jor) to form a selvage. The colour is the natural colour of the silk.

The two ends are alike, each having orange, pink, blue and green tassels. Then comes an inch of plain cloth beyond which is the end border 2½ inches deep. This is a diamond patterned stripe woven in red on a background of yellow cotton weft. At the centre of the diamonds are blue and green spots in the shape of a short thick cross. This main stripe has a narrow frame on either side.

Between the two end borders are twelve rows of rosettes, the alternate rows being alike. The first row consists of two different rosettes alternating with one another (4 of each) ; the one is of the favourite seven-diamond-spotted circular pattern and the other an elaborate oval made up of lines, dots and bars. The second row contains only seven rosettes, all alike and similar to that last described, but almost circular in shape.

The rosettes are of red, dark green, light green and orange, the colours being distributed without any regularity. The price of this handkerchief is Re. 1.

48.—Khuti kapor.

This is a square handkerchief with borders on two parallel sides. It is sometimes worn by children as a head dress, the borders being well exposed to view.

It is reported only from Golaghat.

49.—Tamol Bandha.

This is a kind of handkerchief 3 feet long by 1 foot wide, used in Gauhati by women to hold betel-nut when travelling or on their way to outdoor work. Its price is 2 annas to 4 annas. Another variety is described from the same place. This is 5 feet by 1 foot, generally made of coloured thread and having no ornamentations. The price is 12 annas to Re. 1-4.

50.—Hachoti.

This is a small cloth used for holding *tamul-pan* (betel-nut, etc.) It is described, from Golaghat only, as a *gamoha* with a pocket in one side. It is generally of muga silk, but occasionally of cotton.

51.—Charkhana.

The *charkhana* is made only in the Goalpara district and stands quite alone among the cotton fabrics of the Assamese; it is used, not as a cloth or garment, but as a piece of cloth to be cut up and made into coats, waistcoats, shirts and pantaloons, It varies greatly in size and workmanship and therefore also in price. The average size is that of a large single body sheet or wrapper. The texture is usually coarse and the weaving often indifferent. As might be expected, it contains no elaborate ornamentations, but the *charkhana* is not a plain cloth and the pattern on it gives it its distinctive name. This pattern is a sort of check made up of hollow squares formed by introducing thin lines of a second colour at regular intervals in the warp and weft, the only variation being broad stripes of the second colour in the weft near the ends of the cloth. The main colour is usually light and the second colour deep.

I saw several *charkhana* in course of manufacture in Goalpara. The width of one was 500 threads (about 2½ feet) and the length a little over 7 feet. The body of the cloth was yellow, and the lines red. On each edge of the warp were 9 pairs of red threads, then 2 yellow, then 2 red and then 12 yellow. The arrangement of the rest of the warp was uniform, the following cycle of threads being repeated again and again, *viz.*, 2 pairs red, 1 yellow, 2 red, 12 yellow.

The weft had yellow, then red, then yellow threads next the fringe, then a *phak* or false fringe, beyond which yellow and red alternated as in the warp. There was a cross stripe of red one inch deep near the end.

Tilak phul were dotted over the cloth with no regularity, but just as it suited the weaver's fancy. These were woven in with scraps of loose thread as already described, two shots of the weft being laid between each length of the extra thread. The designs were very rough and very simple. The weaver was a young girl, not very skilful at the work.

52.—T lpara or Talatpara.

This is a bed-sheet, made in the four lower districts of Assam. It is quite plain and varies in size from 4½ feet by 3 feet (the smallest size in Dhubri) to 9 feet by 4½ feet (Tezpur) and in price from 6 annas (Barpeta) to 14 annas (Dhubri).

In Barpeta it is included in the wardrobe of men and women of the richer village classes, the size in each case being 6 feet by 3 feet, and the weight of thread ¼ seer.

Specimen.—From Mangaldai.—This is a plain white bed-sheet, 5 feet 8 inches by 3 feet 6 inches, made of coarse cloth closely woven. It has no ornamentations except a red stripe of 4 threads in the weft at each end. There is, properly speaking, no fringe —only the rough ends of the thread.

53.—Anai.

This also is a bed-sheet made of loosely-woven cloth, size 7½ feet by 3½ feet, price Re. 1. The name appears peculiar to Goalpara. It seems to be the same as the *Talpura* (No. 52).

54.—Chadari.

This is a cloth made in Goalpara and used at night instead of a quilt. It is made up of two narrow strips 2½ to 3 feet wide and 18 feet long. These two are sewn together side by side and the cloth so formed is used double, the size of the double cloth being therefore 9 feet by 2½ to 3 feet.

This concludes the list of cotton fabrics properly so called. It remains to describe only those articles and garments that are made up out of cotton fabrics, the majority of which have no special interest as regards Assam.

E.—MADE GARMENTS.

55.—Chola.

This is an ordinary short coat with sleeves, made of plain white cloth with no decorations. It has no peculiar features and so requires no detailed description Such coats are worn generally by the lower classes of men and boys. Muga silk coats of the same description are often worn instead. In Barpeta the only classes who wear the *chola* are said to be the boys of the middle and wealthier classes and the men of the wealthier classes among the villagers.

The cloth from which this coat is made measures 6 feet by 2½ feet and contains ⅛ seer of thread for a man and 4½ feet by 1½ feet (⅟₁₆ seer) for a boy in Barpeta ; the price being respectively 5 annas and 3 annas. In Tezpur the cloth, called *chola kapor*, measures 9 feet by 3 feet, and costs 10 annas. In Gauhati it is called *cholar kapor* and measures 6 feet by 2 feet. Its price is 6 annas to 8 annas.

The above description refers only to the ordinary *chola*. The following varieties of *chola* are also found.

(a) Baku chola.

This is a kind of waistcoat with short sleeves and fastened in front with cords instead of buttons. There are two kinds in Gauhati, the one for general wear made of coarse cloth and the other for special wear made of fine cotton or sometimes silks and brocades.

In Golaghat it is a jacket often having floral designs woven in. It costs from Re. 1 to Rs. 3.

This coat is worn only by men and boys.

(b) Enga chola.

This is a long coat with sleeves which hangs to the ankle. It is used for special wear by men only, generally priests or old gentlemen of the orthodox class. Nowadays it is made of imported cotton cloth. It costs Rs. 2 to Rs. 3 (Gauhati).

(c) Heloi chola.

This is a long coat made of pieces of old and torn cloth patched together. It is used by the commonest people during the winter, especially by cultivators when at work in the field. It may be called a patchwork or rag coat (Golaghat).

(d) Jama chola or Jama.

This is a long flowing gown worn by bridegrooms at weddings. It is made of fine cloth, nowadays of imported cloth. It has long sleeves and reaches to the heels. Its price in Gauhati is Rs. 3 to Rs. 5. In Golaghat it contains magnificent borders at the bottom, and also designs of flowers, etc., in the body.

In Gauhati a cloth called *jama kapor* is described as "a thin but fine cloth made to prepare bridal gowns used by bridegrooms ; size 18 feet by 3 feet; price 12 annas to Re. 1." If this be the cloth from which the *jama chola* is made, it would seem that tailors' charges were high in Assam as elsewhere.

56.—Phutuye.

This is a kind of waistcoat made of coarse cloth for general wear, chiefly at outdoor work, by cultivators, fishermen and mahouts, cow-herds, buffalo-herds, etc. It costs from 6 annas to 8 annas in Gauhati, the only place from which it is reported.

57.—Ghagri.

"This is a frock generally made of a sheet of blue cloth sewn at one end." It is worn in Golaghat by the singers at theatrical performances (bhaona). The tamali is worn with it.

58.—Mirjay.

A kind of coat with long sleeves used by men and boys for special wear. It hangs down to the waist only and is tied in front by a string. Price Re. 1 to Re. 1-8 (Gauhati).

59.—Kurta.

A kind of coat worn by men and children. It reaches nearly to the knees. Price annas 8 to Re. 1-8 (Gauhati).

> 60. Kot (coat), price Re. 1-8 to Rs. 2-8.
> 61. Chapkan, a long coat, price Rs. 2-8 to Rs. 3.
> 62. Kamij, a shirt,   „   12 annas to Re. 1-8.
> 63. Paijama, loose trousers, „   Re. 1-4 to Rs. 2.
> 64. Thenga, pantaloons,   „   Re. 1-4 to Rs. 2.

These five are made of imported cloth and used by men and boys, generally by those working in Government and other offices, and living in towns. They are made to order by local tailors, but ready-made ones are also imported from Calcutta (Gauhati).

65.—Tupi.

A kind of cap covering both ears, used by men and children, sometimes made of coloured cloth. Price 2 annas to 6 annas (Gauhati).

66.—Jolonga.

A bag 18 inches square with a cord by which to hang it from the shoulder. It is used by men for carrying clothes, eatables, etc., when travelling. It is made of coarse cloth and costs from 2 annas to 6 annas in Gauhati, Re. 1 in Goalpara, and from 3 annas to 4 annas in Dhubri. In the last place the cloth from which jolonga are made is usually 3 feet by 1¼ foot, and is sometimes plain and sometimes decorated.

In Goalpara jolonga made of red, white or blue kharua cloth with white tape round the edges are on sale in the bazaar for 3 annas.

67.—Mona.

This is a bag smaller than the jolonga and generally used for carrying betel-nut, etc. It is made of coarse home-spun thread called ubhia suta. It costs 4 annas in Nowgong.

The following varieties of the mona are also found.

(a) Khampi mona.

This is the same as the ordinary mona. The peculiar name used in Mangaldai is evidently a corruption of Khampti mona; the bags made by the Khamptis being of a very superior nature. It costs from 4 to 5 annas, but its place is now being usurped, it is said, by the Bhutia mona which, however, is not described.

Specimen.—From Mangaldai.—This is a bag made of a single piece of cloth about 6 feet 6 inches long and 7¼ inches wide. It is made in a very ingenious way. The ends having been hemmed, about 14 inches of the cloth is doubled over at each end, and the upper and lower parts are sewn together at one side only, the one along the right side and the other along the left. The whole cloth as it now stands is next folded exactly in the middle, so that the two double ends lie one over the other. These two double ends are then drawn outwards till their unsewn edges come together at the middle, the sewn edges being on the outside. The unsewn edges of the two ends are then sewn together, the upper edge of one end to the upper edge of the other, and so on. The result is a bag about 15 inches wide and 13¼ inches deep, with a wide belt-like strap by which it can be hung over the shoulder.

The cloth is roughly woven of very coarse white thread, and is quite plain except that a few of the threads consist of two strands, one red and one white.

This however is probably accidental, as in no case does the red strand continue along the whole length of the thread.

This is a very coarse, but serviceable bag. Price not stated.

(b) Buphalia mona.

This is a double bag, 6 feet long by 1¼ foot wide. It is made by sewing two bags, about two feet apart from one another, one at either end of a piece of cloth. This centre piece of cloth is thrown over the shoulder, and so the bag is carried. It is used for carrying clothes, rice and other eatables on a journey. It is sometimes made of coloured cloth. Its value is 6 annas to 10 annas (Gauhati).

(c) Jal mona.

This is a cylindrical net bag 9 inches long by 3 to 4 inches in diameter. It has two cords at each end, one of which is so arranged that by pulling it the mouth of the bag is closed. It is used by workmen and labourers for keeping rupees and pice, being worn by them tied round the waist. It costs one to two pice only (Gauhati).

In Goalpara there is, for sale in the bazaar, a mona similar to this, but open at one end only. One kind made of red or white jin cloth is sold for five pice, and another of Mirzapur cloth (printed in colours) for 4 pice. They are made locally out of imported cloth.

68.—Jalia or Dalmona.

This is described from Goalpara as a small jolonga netted. No further particulars are given. This is probably entered in the list by mistake, as it would seem to be an ordinary net bag and not a cotton fabric.

69.—Batua.

This is a small but very useful bag, made out of home woven cloth. It is used for carrying, on a long journey, betelnut, tobacco and opium and also money. Its price in Golaghat is 12 annas. In Gauhati it is described as a money-bag, having three or four compartments or pockets; its mouth is shut up with loop cords provided for the purpose. It is used for the same purpose as in Golaghat. It measures 4 inches × 6 inches and is sometimes made of coloured cloth. Its value is 6 to 8 annas.

70.—Thunupak.

This is a purse or very small bag (4 inches by 3 inches) used for keeping money. It is sometimes made of coloured cloth. Its value is 1 or 2 pice only (Gauhati).

71.—Arkapor.

This is a large curtain with brass or horn rings used as a temporary screen or purdah under a shamiana or to partition off a room. It is always made of coloured cloth. Its size is given in Gauhati as 24 feet × 4 feet, and its value as 5 to 7 rupees. In Golaghat it is 60 feet × 6 feet and costs from 5 to 10 rupees.

N.B.—If this be a single piece of cloth, it is by far longest in the Brahmaputra Valley, but probably it is not.

In Nowgong the cloth is generally striped by using varieties of coloured thread (achu). It is, however, more usually made of eri cloth or coloured cotton cloth brought from the bazaar. Its price is given as R8 without floral designs. Size various.

72.—Garu kani or Garu kapor.

A cloth woven for making pillows; cost 4 annas plain in Nowgong. In Gauhati this cloth is woven of coarse thread, sometimes coloured red, black and yellow. Size 3 feet × 2¼ feet. Price 4 annas. In Barpeta homemade cloth for pillows is used apparently only by the wealthier village men and women. It costs 2 annas, and measures 2¼ feet × 1½ foot.

The embroidered end of a round pillow is called garu chak or tala.

73.—Garu Gilip.

This is a pillow case. Size 3 feet × 2 feet. Price 4 annas.

74.—Kantha.

This is a kind of cotton blanket, size 6 feet × 4½ feet, used by women of the middle class of villagers in Barpeta to throw over the body at night. The price is not stated but it is said to cost R 2-10-3 when made from raw cotton and R 1-10 when made from bought thread. The amount of thread required is ¾ seer.

75.—Lep.

A quilt made in Goalpara. Size 9 feet × 4½ feet. Price R 4 to 5.

76.—Rezai.

Rezai are made in the Goalpara bazaar of various sizes, an average size being 9 feet × 4½ feet. Price R 2-8 to R8. They are used as warm shawls during the day and as bed quilts at night. The stuffing consists of raw cotton cleaned by the Dhunias, a few of whom come down from Arrah to Goalpara just for the cold weather, going back home about February. These Dhunias charge 2 to 3 annas a seer for bowing the cotton. The cases are made of imported cloth, and are stuffed and sewn by tailors in the bazaar.

77.—Athua or Mohari.

These are mosquito curtains. They are made in most parts of the Assam Valley of home-made thread, specially woven. They are sometimes white and sometimes coloured, *e. g.*, green. The thread is usually coarse, and the cloth loosely woven. The size of mosquito curtains in Tezpur is 7½ feet × 4½ feet × 4½ feet, and the cloth from which they are made is 36 feet × 4½ feet. They cost R2 and last about two years. In Sibsagar the curtains cost from R1-8 to R4, and in Golaghat from 12 annas to R1. In Gauhati the cloth for making a mosquito curtain measures 24 feet × 4 feet, and costs from R1 to R4. In Barpeta the mosquito curtain appears to be used by men and women of the richer villagers alone, that for a man costs R 1, that for a woman R1-4, a rather unexpected difference. Both are of the same size and texture, the cloth from which they are made being 24 feet × 3 feet and containing 1 seer of thread. In Nowgong the special cloth for mosquito curtains is now very rarely made. Price R2.

The name *athua* is used in Tezpur and higher up the valley, *mohari* being used in Mangaldai and Kamrup.

Specimen from Mangaldai.—This mosquito curtain is made of coarse but very loosely woven cloth. There are two distinct pieces of cloth; one, to form the roof, measures 5 feet 9 inches × 3 feet 6 inches, the other, to form the sides, being 18 feet 6 inches × 3 feet 9 inches. This latter piece is sewn together at the two ends, and then one side is sewn to the four sides of the roof. A rope is also laid along this seam and sewn there, a loop being left at each corner, passing through the cloth to the top and being there tied in a knot close to the corner. These loops are used to hang up the curtain. The size of this curtain is 5 feet 9 inches × 3 feet 9 inches × 3 feet 6 inches.

78.—Simul cotton cloths.

A list of the cotton fabrics of the Assam Valley would be incomplete without a reference to the cloths made of *simula tula* or cotton of the *simul* tree (Bombax heptaphyllum). The following is a report from the London Society of Arts on some Assam cotton cloth of this nature : "Two large pieces of cloth made from the down of the Simul or tree cotton, Bombax heptaphyllum, from Gauhati in Assam, the place of manufacture.

"On examining the cloth it appears that the fine soft down of the Bombax has been spun into a light wove slightly twisted cord or roving, and that this is made into cloth by interweaving it with warp and sort of common thin cotton thread, much in the manner of carpeting. It composes a loose cloth, incapable probably of being washed without injury, but considerably warm, very elastic and light.

"From the shortness of the staple and the great elasticity of the fibre, it is not at all probable that it could be spun by the machinery now in use for cotton spinning, but the combination which it exhibits of fineness of fibre with great elasticity will, no doubt, make it rank high as a non-conductor of heat and therefore fit it for making wadding and for stuffing mats and perhaps mattresses. When carded with wool, it might probably form the basis of fabrics of great warmth, lightness and silky softness."

This report is dated 1836, and the down of the simul tree appears to have made little headway since as a material for weaving cloths. Its use, however, for this purpose, has not been entirely abandoned, as will be seen from the following extract from the Mangaldai report. "Sometimes *simalu tula*, the cotton of the simul tree, is used as a substitute for cotton. A kind of fabric called *tolpara* is prepared of which the breadth is made of *simalu tula* and the length of cotton. Some people of Bonmajha in mouzah Dipila still use this fabric. The cotton of the *simalu* is divested of the seed and husk and scutched and then used." A specimen *tolpara* has been received from Mangaldai. It is a small plain cloth measuring 2 feet 8 inches × 2 feet 2 inches, with a fringe twisted into tassels at either end. The warp is of ordinary cotton and the weft mainly of simul thread, but this is strengthened by some weft threads of ordinary cotton. Its price is R1. The use to which this cloth is put is not stated, but from its name it would appear to be used as a bed sheet. This particular specimen, however, would be very small for this purpose.

Besides the above fabrics cotton tape is made in the Brahmaputra Valley, but no particulars have been received. There is also a curious garment worn by the Sings or Sikhs of Nowgong, *viz.*, a pair of cotton knickerbockers in appearance much resembling à well tied *dhuti*.

THE COTTON FABRICS OF THE SURMA VALLEY.

Concerning the cotton fabrics made by the Tantis and Jugis of the Surma Valley but little information is available. The descriptions contained in the district reports are very brief, and only ten specimens have been received, six from Sylhet and four from South Sylhet. It is therefore impossible to make any general observations regarding the fabrics of this valley. The six cloths sent by the Deputy Commissioner of Sylhet, together with four others made by the Hill Tribesmen of the district, had been collected from the several sub-divisions and "form a model collection of all good textures made in this district." These six cloths together with the four from South Sylhet make an excellent group and lead to the belief that, had further enquiry been practicable, much of interest might have been elicited in spite of the forlorn condition of the industry in this valley.

The most marked feature about these fabrics is the strong contrast they exhibit with those of the Assamese. There are none of the elaborately ornamented shawls which occupy such an important position among the fabrics of the Brahmaputra Valley. On the other hand, there are excellent examples of long sheets of cloth intended not for use as they leave the loom, but to be cut into pieces and made up, *e. g.*, the *than* or *gilap* and the cloth for mosquito curtains. The contrast between the mosquito curtain received from South Sylhet and that received from Mangaldai is perhaps the most striking of all. Among the fabrics from Sylhet the *chadar* and *rumal* are excellent examples of fine and careful weaving, and the *sari* and *dusuti* are scarcely less interesting on account of the peculiarity of their colouring.

1.—Gilap or than.

This is reported from Silchar, Sonamgunge and Maulvi Bazaar (South Sylhet.) In the first two places it appears to correspond more or less to the *bor kapor* (No. 1 of Assam), but in the third, though used for the same purpose, it is a long piece of cloth which is cut into lengths as required.

In Silchar the *than or gilap* is "a species of thick, large and durable cloth used in the cold weather as a sheet or wrapper. These are of different sizes to suit the young and old and are made up of two pieces stitched together sideways. They are invariably of white thread and quite plain, and are sold, according to size and quality, at prices varying from 8 annas to 3 rupees. The usual man's size is 9 feet × 4 feet 6 inches, but sometimes it is made 18 feet × 4 feet 6 inches or 5 feet and is worn double."

In Sonamgunge "the only article that is now produced by a few families of weavers, and that is worth mention, is what is called in Bengali *gilap*. These *gilaps* are used as winter cloths, a pair being 6 yards long and 4½ feet broad. The price of a pair is Rs. 2 or 3. The only places which produce the cloth are village Budharail in Paraganah Athusgaon, and Dohalia. The cloth produced at Budharail is without any coloured borders, but that produced at Dohalia is striped with threads of red colour. These *gilaps* are still prized as there is nothing like them among the imported cloths and as they are considered cheap."

In South Sylhet a *than* or *gilap* is described as a double wearing sheet, one pair lasting for two or three years. The colour is white and the size 36 feet × 2¼ feet.

From this it would seem that the *than* or *gilap* is a long sheet cut into lengths as required. This is probably the case in Silchar and Sonamgunge also. "A *gilap* costs R1-12, whereas a similar sheet of European manufacture will cost R1-8, the durability in both cases being the same."

A specimen *gilaph* has been received from Maulvi Bazaar. A perfectly plain cloth made of coarse white thread and measuring 34 feet × 2 feet 8 inches. It has a selvage at each side and a few double threads at each end, with fringes, that at one end being looped. It is more closely woven and not quite so coarse as the *dhuti* No. 4 from this place. Price R4-12.

A cloth described as a wrapper has been sent by the Deputy Commissioner of Sylhet. It measures 36 feet by 2 feet 2¼ inches, and is of medium texture. It is not plain white but duster-patterned, comprising squares of blue on a background of white, this pattern being formed by the warp and weft each containing alternately ten white and two blue threads. At one edge is a stripe of blue ⅜ inch deep and at the other edge is a stripe of white. Near each end is a blue stripe ⅝ inch deep, and between that and the fringe, a line of blue (two shots of the weft). The fringes are rather over ¼ inch long, one being in loops. At the centre of the cloth are two. cross stripes of blue like those at either end, 1½ inch apart. This shows clearly that the cloth is cut in two between these stripes and thus forms two pieces each 18 feet × 2 feet 2½ inches. These two pieces are probably sewn together to form a double body sheet or wrapper 18 feet × 4 feet 5 inches.

There is no doubt that this cloth is a *than* or *gilap*, though it is merely called a wrapper. Respecting this cloth the Deputy Commissioner writes that it " is a sample from the Sonamgunge sub-division. It is supposed that the cloth is an imitation of the sheets that are manufactured by the weavers of the neighbouring districts of Mymensingh and Tipperah. Although the exhibit comes from Sonamgunge, there is reason to believe that the weavers of other places of the district can turn out such articles, so that it may be accepted as a sample representative of the whole district."

The price of the cloths from Sylhet has been given in a lump sum, so individual prices cannot be given.

2.—Dusuti.

This is also a body sheet or wrapper very similar to the last. A specimen from Sylhet is a strong cloth of medium texture measuring 18 feet × 2 feet 2 inches. The warp is red and the weft green, the resulting colour being rather effective. The only ornamentations are three narrow red lines and a 1-inch false fringe at each end. The true fringes are very short, one being in loops. Besides this, at half the length of the cloth, are two more sets of red lines with two 1-inch and one ¼-inch false fringes between them, the intention of these being evidently to form two wrappers by cutting through the small false fringe. The two wrappers so formed would then be exactly alike, and each would be uniform at both ends. The weft in this cloth is alternately closely and openly woven, which gives the cloth a sort of striped appearance, the red showing more clearly where the weaving is loose, and the green where it is close. There is such irregularity in the succession of this open and close weaving that it is doubtful if it is intentional.

3.—Chadar.

This is described in South Sylhet as a single wearing sheet, 18 feet × 2¼ feet, colour white. It lasts about two years.

In Habigunge the Jugis make *uranichadar* 10½ feet long, and sell them at from R1-12 to R 2.

Two specimen *chadar* have been received from Sylhet. They are said to be peculiar to Laskarpur in the Habigunge Sub-division, as the weavers of nowhere else can make such cloths. Both are of exceedingly fine texture, loosely but very carefully woven.

The first, which measures 10 feet × 4 feet 2 inches, is quite plain except for a white border on each side and at each end, consisting of stripes and lines of thicker thread. There are also two very small false fringes at each end besides the true fringe which is ¼ inch long at one end and ⅛ inch at the other.

The second is smaller, measuring 7½ feet × 3 feet 2 inches. This has a ⅛ inch stripe of yellow, broken by a very narrow stripe of white, along each side at the extreme edge ; there are also lines of thick white thread. At the ends there two yellow stripes, two yellow lines and two white lines. The fringes are very short, and there are really no false fringes, though a very slight gap is left twice at each end in the weft ; this is noticeable only on close inspection.

Both these cloths have a small design like a trade mark woven in at one end—these designs are probably not meant as ornamentations, but only to show who made them.

4—Dhuti.

A waistcloth like that of the same name used in Bengal. From Silchar it is described as "similar in every detail to the Manipuri *fijong* or the Kachari *gainthuo.*" In Habigunge the Jugis make *dhuti* 15 feet long and sell them at R2·8 and R3. In Maulvi Bazaar the waistcloth is made of plain white thread and measures from 12 to 13¼ feet in length and 3 feet in width. A specimen received from this place, however, is smaller, being 11 feet 4 inches by 2 feet 6 inches. It is made of coarse thread loosely woven and is absolutely plain except for the selvage along each side, and three quadruple shots of weft at one end and two at the other. The fringes are very short, that at one end being in the form of loops just as it left the loom. The price of this cloth is 12 annas.

5.—Kachuta.

Small *dhuti* which the cultivators and other labouring classes put on when at work. They last from two to three months. Colour white. Size 9 feet × 2¼ feet (South Sylhet).

6.—Sari.

This is the chief cloth worn by a woman and is similar in every respect to that of Bengal. It has not been mentioned in the lists of any sub-division, but a specimen has been received from Sylhet. This is a most interesting cloth. It measures 10 feet by 2 feet 10 inches. The body of the cloth is formed of a red warp and a blue weft. On each side there are stripes and lines formed by white and blue thread in the warp. At one end there is a plain fringe only ⅜ inch long, and a stripe of yellow formed by four sets of four yellow threads in the weft with two blue threads between each set. The other end, however, is ornamented for a long distance, but very simply, *viz.*, merely by stripes of different colours. Starting from the end there comes first a fringe about 1 inch long ; then follows a piece of ordinary cloth 1 inch deep, with two yellow lines across it ; then a false fringe 3 inches long. Beyond this is 1¼ inch of plain cloth ; then a stripe of red, 1½ inch deep, with four yellow lines forming a border on either side ; then nearly 2¼ inches of plain cloth broken only by a red stripe through the middle. Then follows a length of 4 inches in which the weft is formed of threads in pairs alternately red and yellow. Beyond this is a stripe of plain cloth, then one of red with four yellow lines across it, and then another plain stripe ; these three vary in depth from 1 inch to 1¼ inch. The remainder of the decorated part consists of three red stripes, 1½ inch deep, at equal intervals with a broken band of yellow along each edge and a thin red and yellow stripe behind and before. The depth of these ornamentations is altogether 2¼ feet. The patterns on this cloth are formed simply by the use of different coloured threads in warp and weft, except the broken bands of yellow which are woven in in addition to the main weft.

The cloth is made of rather coarse thread closely woven and looks as it would wear well.

7.—Gamcha.

This is a towel like the *gamcha* of Assam, but plain white. In Silchar it is said to be similar in every detail to the Manipuri *iru khu-lei* and the Karachi *rihaha.* In Hailakandi its size is 6 feet × 1½ foot and its price to 2 to 4 annas; here it is used as a bath-towel for drying the body and as a sheet. In South Sylhet its size is given as 2¼ feet × 1½ foot, and it is used for drying the hands and face. A specimen received from Moulvi Bazaar, however, measures 7¼ feet × 1 foot 8 inches. It is made of coarse white thread loosely and roughly woven, and has a narrow stripe of red at one end and a deeper stripe with two lines of red at the other. The fringes are very short. The price, 6 annas, seems excessive.

8.—Rumal.

This is a handkerchief, a specimen of which has been received from Sylhet and like the *chadar* from that place, it was made at Laskarpur where it is a speciality of the local weavers. It is made of exceedingly fine thread very carefully woven. It is white with stripes and lines of black at the sides and ends. There are one false fringe and one true fringe at either end, each about ⅜ inch long. The size is nearly 20 inches square.

9.—Mosari.

This is a mosquito curtain. In South Sylhet the cloth is first made into a *than* and then sewn to form a curtain. It is said to last for two years. An excellent specimen has been received from South Sylhet, measuring about 6 feet × 4 feet × 4 feet 9 inches. The roof consists of two pieces, each 6 feet × 2 feet, and the sides of ten pieces, each 4 feet 9 inches × 2 feet, the long sides having three such pieces each and the short sides two. Round the line of juncture of the roof with the walls is sewn a tape of thick soft cotton. This tape is ¼ inch wide and consists of a number of cotton threads woven together by cross threads at considerable intervals. At each corner of the net, a loop of this tape is left. This is bound round close to the net and the edges of the tape sewn together so that the loop looks very much like a length of a circular lamp wick.

The material of which this net is made can hardly be called cloth, it is so loosely woven as to be really a net. Owing to the size of the meshes the practical use of this mosquito curtain is doubtful. The cloth or net is made of fine thread, the warp consisting of four blue and four white threads alternately, and the weft of blue alone. The only variation in the pattern occurs at the top ends of two of the panels, that help to form one of the long walls. In these panels, for nearly 3 inches at the extreme end, the loosely woven blue weft is replaced by closely woven white weft, beyond which is an inch stripe of thick black (or very dark blue) thread closely woven. This stripe is broken by three narrow particoloured stripes running through it, two of which are yellow, red and white, while the third, which lies between them, is yellow, red and yellow ; beyond this stripe are three white threads in the weft, and then the blue commences. There seems no particular object in this decoration, and it is probably merely the two end pieces cut off one long length of net or cloth out of which the curtain is made. The net is so elastic that the ends of the several panels are not in one line at the bottom of the curtain, though the panels appear to be of the same size—exact measurement is difficult. Owing apparently to the stretching of the net, an extra piece about 2 inches long and 2 feet wide has had to be joined on to the top of one of the panels at one end. Allowing for waste at the places where the different pieces are sewn together it would take a *than* of net 60 feet long × 2 feet wide to make a curtain of this size. The price of this particular curtain is only 14 annas, which appears very cheap. There is a marked difference between this curtain and the coarse specimen received from Mangaldai in Assam (No. 77) . The latter would be much hotter, but probably far more durable and more effective in keeping out mosquitoes, the purpose for which it is intended. The difference in the formation of these two curtains is noteworthy.

10—Jal.

This is a net, size 6 feet × 3 feet. Nets are made of several sizes ; price from R1 to R3 (South Sylhet). The purpose for which these nets are used is not stated.

COTTON FABRICS OF THE TRIBESMEN LIVING IN OR BORDERING ON ASSAM.

The third class of fabrics comprises those peculiar to the tribesmen of Assam. Some hill tribesmen who have settled in the plains weave fabrics exactly resembling those of the Assamese; these fabrics will not be described again and their number is very small, as it is often found that, when the ruder races abandon their national costume, they exchange it, not for more civilised garments woven by themselves, but for ready made cloths imported from the West.

Among the fabrics peculiar to the tribesmen, many are of the poorest possible description, coarse, plain, indifferently woven ; some, however, are of the very highest order, the sheets of the Nagas are unequalled for durability and careful weaving, the *fanek* of the Manipuris for the beauty of their embroidery, their puggeris for fineness of texture; some again, exhibit varieties of weaving unknown to the people of the plains ; the bags of the Noras and Turungs, the rugs of the Mikirs and Kukis, the honeycombed towels of the Manipuris have no equivalents among the fabrics of the Assamese or the professional weavers of the Surma Valley.

But the chief interest of these fabrics lies in their quaintness. The *kadisil* of the Garos, a band of cloth worn only by the heroic taker of a scalp ; the *jyngki* of the Lalungs and Syntengs, a sleeveless coat or rather a sheet of cloth passed over the head and worn to hang down in front and behind like the boards of a sandwich-man ; the mixed nettle and cotton fabrics of the Nagas, the boating costume of the Manipuris—coat, waistcloth, puggery and necktie; all these are quite unique. Many more examples might be cited, but there is one article which is especially worthy of attention, *viz.*, the bag or satchel. Some varieties of this are found among nearly all the tribes, and on many of them great skill and artistic taste are displayed. A collection of these satchels from all the hill tribes bordering on Assam would be of value, not only as curiosities, but as examples of the varieties of fancy weaving practised by these primitive peoples.

The peculiar nature of many of these fabrics renders a bare description of them of little use without an explanation of the way in which they are worn or used. To explain this, it is often necessary to describe the dress of the people. The arrangement and scope of this section are accordingly somewhat different from those of the two preceding. The fabrics have been grouped according to the tribe or tribes that make them, and, under each group, the description of the fabrics has been supplemented by all available information concerning the dress of that particular people.

Manipuri Fabrics.

The cotton fabrics of the Manipuris are far more numerous and far more varied than those of any other tribe within or bordering on Assam. This variety is partly in the texture and partly in the nature of the ornamentations. The puggeries of the Manipuris are among the finest fabrics of Assam, while the sheets made by these people for the Nagas are surpassed in stoutness only by those of the Nagas themselves. But the greatest variety is found in the ornamentations. Nearly every device is known to the Manipuris; the dyeing and stamping of cloth, the use of different coloured threads in warp and weft, embroidering by hand as well as the ordinary *jamdanee* work, the stuffing of cloths at the time of weaving, and the formation of ribs by varying the arrangement of the healds: all these are illustrated in the fabrics of Manipur.

Writing in 1835, Captain R. Boileau Pemberton in his "Report on the Eastern Frontier of British India" says: "The principal articles of manufacture in Manipur consists of coarse *khee* cloths, perfectly white; a very soft and light description of muslin, worn by the women as scarfs; a coarser description for turbans and jackets; and their silk manufactures, which are remarkable for their strength and the brilliancy of their colours, and are made up principally into petticoats, jackets and large scarfs, the last of which are worn only by the higher order of the male sex: some of these scarfs are very richly embroidered and though the work is coarse, they are highly prized in Ava." During the last sixty years the skill of the Manipuri weavers has increased. The rich embroiderings are not confined to silks, but are to be found on many of the better cotton cloths. The brilliancy and variety of the colours form a most noticeable feature of some of the cloths of Manipur.

In Sylhet, Manipuri cotton cloths are included among the chief manufactures of the district enumerated by Mr. Hunter in his "Statistical Account of Assam" (1879). To quote from this work: "*Manipuri khesh*, or cotton cloths, used as coverlets for beds, and at times for screens and tablecloths, are woven by the Manipuri women who reside in the district, from white or coloured country thread. They are generally made from 5 to 9 feet in length by from 3 to 6 feet in breadth, and are sold, according to size and quality, at prices varying from 1s./3d. to £1 each. The Manipuris also weave handkerchiefs, mosquito curtains and common dusters. They embroider the edges of the more expensive cloths very skilfully with silk. Handkerchiefs of fine quality are sold at from 4½d. to 6d. each."

In Cachar "all the clothes worn by Manipuris are manufactured solely by women. The usual dress of the men consists of a *dhotie* and short jacket called *foorithe*, but even more eccentric costume may be seen among the Manipuris than among the Bengalis of Cachar. The dress of the women is a coloured cloth tied tightly under the shoulders just above the breasts, fitting closely to the body and legs and reaching nearly to the feet." This was written in 1865 by Mr. J. Ware Edgar, who also gives an interesting calculation of the earnings of Manipuri weavers in this district. This calculation has already been reproduced and need not be repeated here. The dress of the Manipuri women is, however, more accurately described by Colonel Dalton:—"The chief garment of an adult female is folded over the bosom and under the arms, so as to press somewhat injuriously on the contour of the bust whence it flows to the feet, and is generally of gay colours with a neat border. Young girls are more becomingly clad in spencers or bodices, and the lower garment is folded round the waist."

Below are enumerated the principal cotton cloths made by the Manipuris. The list received from Manipur is very long, but unfortunately the description of the several cloths is extremely brief. It will be seen that *chadar*, petticoats (or rather women's waistcloths) and bedcloths are generally made on the smaller loom ; and *dhuti*, puggeris, mosquito curtains, satchels and cloths for special wear on the larger loom. The coarser cloths made on the smaller loom are said to be largely sold for local use. The finer fabrics appear to have suffered from European competition.

The list from Manipur has been supplemented by information received from Sylhet and Cachar, and by a description of some cloths received from all these places. In Cachar no fabrics are made in large quantities, but the Manipuri mosquito curtains, *gamcha* (*i.e.*, *iru khudei*), and *khesh* are made in greater numbers than any other fabrics in the district.

1.—Foijom.

This is a *dhuti* or loin-cloth for men. Several varieties of this cloth are made in Manipur, for all of which the four-poster loom is used. No description of these cloths has been received. An ordinary *foijom* costs from R 1 to 3. The following varieties are found :—

> (i) *Ashelang foijom.*—"Manipur cotton *dhuti*. Price R2 to 3."
>
> (ii) *Ureng foijom.*—"Green *dhuti*. Price R2 to 3."
>
> (iii) *Khamen chatpa foijom.*—"Silk *dhuti*—honorary dress. Price R20 to 40."

This would appear not to be a cotton fabric, but it is included in the list received from Manipur, and so is given here; as no specimen has been sent, it is impossible to say whether it has been rightly or wrongly included.

Waistcloths or *dhuti* called *fijong* are also included in the list of Manipuri cloths made in Silchar. Respecting them the Deputy Commissioner writes : "These are simply larger sized *iru khudei*" (No. 32) "but have altogether ceased to be manufactured, the *dhuti* of Manchester manufacture having driven them completely out of the market. When manufactured they were sold according to size and quality at prices varying from 8 annas to R1-8-0."

2.—Ning kham.

"A boat race *dhuti*. Price R5 to 10" (Manipur). This too is made on the four-poster loom.

This and fabrics Nos. 21, 23 and 28 form a complete boating outfit.

3.—Fanek.

This is a petticoat woven in Manipur on the smaller kind of loom from English or country made thread. Its price varies according to the quality. The following varieties are named, but no descriptions are given :—

> (i) *Langhou fanek.*
> (ii) *Golap machu fanek.* } Price R5 to R15.

> (iii) *Kumchingbi fanek.*   Ditto.   There are two cloths bearing this name in the Indian Museum, *viz.*, Nos. 38 and 39, received from the Shillong Museum. No. 38 is a blue and white striped cloth with red borders at the sides. (The white stripes are very narrow.) It measures 5 feet 2 inches by 3 feet 1¼ inch and is made up of four strips of widths varying from 9 to 10½ inches. The border on one side is 2 inches in width and that on the other side 1¾ inch. Between the red and blue is a blue-black stripe, and the red is toned down by a few blue lines. At the end of the cloth are plaited lines in red. The ends are sown up. The price of this cloth is R2-8.

No. 39 also is a blue and white striped cloth in which the white stripes are merely lines. It measures 5 ft. 7 in. by 4 ft. 1 in., and is composed of two strips. It has a red border on each side containing patterns of oval design worked in rose, yellow, heliotrope, dull yellow, blue and white. The style of the ornamentations on each side is the same. Price R3-4. This cloth was exhibited by the Political Agent of Manipur as No. 3024 in the International Exhibition held at Calcutta in 1851.

> (iv) *Chambrei mapal fanek.*
> (v) *Kokfai fanek.*
> (vi) *Kabo napu fanek.*
> (vii) *Makong fanek.*   } Price R5 to R15.
> (viii) *Hangam mapal fanek.*
> (ix) *Lourang fanek.*
> (x) *Tong kap fanek.*
> (xi) *Leirel fanek*

(xii) *Pungou fanek.*　　　　　Price R1 to R1-8.
(xiii) *Hikok fanek.*
(xiv) *Kombrei fanek.*　　　⎫ Price R5 to R15.
(xv) *Awa napu fanek.*　　　⎬
(xvi) *Urei rom fanek.*　　　⎭
(xvii) *Pumthit fanek.*　　　　Price R10 to 30. An old pattern not now used.

A specimen of this cloth received from Manipur measures 5 feet 6 inches by 4 feet 2 inches. It is a very handsome cloth of medium texture made up of two pieces of equal size stitched together at the sides. These two strips of cloth are exactly similar in design, and the border patterns are identical. The outer edge of each strip has a border about 2¼ inches wide. This border consists of a central stripe of green (1¼ inch wide) with a white stripe about one-third of the width on each side, the remainder being made up of very narrow stripes of dark blue and green and lines of white. The central green stripe has a handsome design woven on it in silk. This design consists of yellow ovals forming a framework with a diamond shaped opening in the centre containing a star of many colours. The ovals are joined by yellow loops, and in the intervals is filligree work of many colours. The colours used are red, salmon, dark blue and white. Except at the extreme ends, the stripe is uniform throughout but there are two different arrangements of the colours in the stars and filligrees, and these succeed each other alternately.

The two white stripes have pretty floral patterns worked upon them in red, yellow and green silk, the two patterns are not alike. They are simple but very difficult to describe.

The thin dark blue stripes have each a double broken line of white cotton thread running along them, but are otherwise quite plain.

The body of the cloth consists of white and green stripes, the former about ½ inch wide and the latter of half that width. The white stripes contain pretty patterns woven in red and salmon silk, similar to, but not identical with, that on the inner white stripe of the border. The green stripes are plain except for a double broken line of yellow silk running along the centre.

At each end of the cloth is a border, one rather more than an inch deep and the other about ¾ inch deep. Unlike the end borders of Assamese cloths, these are the plainest part of the whole cloth, for they contain no ornamentation, except a single looped line of white cotton thread running across them. There is at one end a similar looped line of thick maroon coloured thread marking the division between the end border and the body of the cloth, and at the other a cross stripe formed of two such looped lines side by side.

This cloth has no fringes, but at one end the loose threads project for about ⅛th of an inch; at the other end not only the loose threads but also a portion of the cloth has been cut off, so that there is absolutely no fringe—the cutting is very uneven.

One of the most noteworthy features about this cloth is the closeness of the weaving. The weft is entirely of white, but, owing to the closeness of the weaving, it nowhere comes to view so that the colour of the background is decided solely by that of the warp. The excellence of the weaving is perhaps even better shown by the fact that there is no tendency to fray at the end that is cut off flush.

The manufacture of this cloth must have involved an enormous amount of labour. The whole of the patterns are separate from the background—the cloth itself. The pattern on each stripe has been worked independently. These patterns may possibly have been formed at the time of weaving, but they are more probably of needlework.

The price of this cloth is R15, which does not appear excessive considering its quality and the amount of labour involved in making it.

(xviii) *Kumnang fanek.* An old pattern, not used. Price R10 to R30.
(xix) *Khendra fanek.*　　　Ditto　　　　　　　　ditto

Besides the above varieties of *fanek* there are two others in the Indian Museum, *vis* :—

(xx.) *Lei fanek.* — — Price R7. This may be the same as the *Loirang fanek* No. (ix) but without a description of that cloth it is impossible to say.

A very strong and well woven cloth bearing this name is to be found in the Indian Museum (No. 19 of the Shillong Museum series). It is made up of two equal strips fastened together at the edges and measures 5 feet 6 inches by 3 feet 11 inches. The body of the cloth is striped pale and dark blue (almost black), six stripes going to the inch, and the pale blue being rather wider than the dark. The weft seems to be all pale blue, but it nowhere appears at the surface, as the weaving is so close.

At each side of the cloth is a handsome border, one 2 inches and one 2½ inches wide. The former border consists of a stripe of white nearly 1 inch wide with a narrower stripe of light blue on one side and one of dark blue on the other (or outer) side. The pale blue stripe is edged on each side by lines of dark blue and itself contains a simple floral pattern in green and yellow, green being the more prominent colour. The dark blue stripe has a rather more elaborate pattern consisting of rose buds in floral frameworks of yellow, which colour is more prominent than the rose. The extreme outer edge is white, and near the edge appear a few white lines. The wide stripe of white forms a background for an exquisite floral design in dark blue, green and rose which cannot be described without an illustration. The body of the design is dark blue, but the centres of the leaves are bright green and an occasional blossom appears in a delightful tint of rose. The harmony of colouring is perfect.

The border at the other side is similar in its arrangement. The central stripe is more than an inch wide and the design is rather different from that described above. The centres of the leaves are pale green, there are no rose buds. The pattern on the inner stripe is red and green, a length entirely red being succeeded by a length entirely green. The pattern on the outer stripe is dark yellow throughout, and is not so elaborate as the corresponding pattern on the other border. The designs appear to be of needlework. Across the cloth, near either end, runs a plaited line in red, beyond which the side borders do not extend, and there is therefore no ornamentation besides the stripes, except a single thin plaited line in white running across the cloth at two-thirds of the distance between the red line and the end.

(xxi) *Saloo hekok fanek.*—Price R5-12. This may be the same as the *hikok fanek* No. (xiii).

Two examples of this cloth are to be seen in the Indian Museum, *viz.*, Nos. 21 and 22 of the Shillong Museum collection.

The first (No. 21, Shillong Museum Collection) is strong and closely woven, but is a lighter fabric than the *lei fanek* just described. It is made up of two narrow strips and measures 5 feet 9 inches by 4 feet 3 inches. It has lengthwise stripes of dark and light blue, six to the inch, the dark stripes being slightly the wider. The dark blue is almost black and the light blue is of a peculiar shade, but not so pale as that in the *lei fanek*. Each dark blue stripe is followed by a red line, and each light stripe by a line of white. The weft is wholly red.

At each side is a border, one 2½ inches, the other 2¾ inches in width. They are similar but not identical in design. Starting from the inside, first comes a white stripe (about ½ inch wide) with a pattern in crimson, rich green and yellow; this is followed by a wide dark blue stripe with a bold design in ovals, the framework being entirely yellow, and the larger leaves inside rose with centres of dull yellow, while the small branch leaves are black with white centres. In between the ovals is a filigree of red, yellow, black, white and dull yellow. Beyond this comes a second wide stripe rather wider than the first, with a pattern in black, red and yellow. Lastly, there is an edge of dark blue with occasional black lines.

Each end of the cloth has a cross stripe of plaited lines with a single plaited line of white half way between it and the end. There are no fringes.

This is a very pretty cloth. The decorations appear to be of needlework.

The other cloth (No. 22, Shillong Museum Collection) is very strong and rather coarse; it is made up of two equal strips joined together, and measures 5 feet 5 inches by 4 ft. 2 in. The body of the cloth, which consists of black or rather very dark blue stripes about ½ inch wide divided off by lines of white, is very plain, but the border designs are very handsome. The ends are plain and are devided off from the body of the cloth by a red plaited stripe; one end only has a white cross line.

The borders are on the same principal as those in the last cloth as regards style and background. In that at one side the inner pattern is alternately wholly heliotrope, wholly red and wholly bright crimson. The central design, of oval shape, has the framework of bright yellow, and the centres of crimson, white and dull yellow; these three colours, and also a very dark green, are used for the filigrees between the ovals. The outer pattern is alternately dark blue and rose.

In the border at the other side the inner pattern is nearly all heliotrope with a trifle of yellow, the central design is of the same colour as that on the other border but with heliotrope substituted for red, the outer pattern is of crimson and dark green.

The weft in this cloth is all dark blue.

In Hailakandi the *fanek* is described as a cloth worn by females, size 6 feet by 4½ feet. Price from R2 to R6.

From Cachar comes the following interesting description of the *fanek*: "A kind of cloth similar to the *khesh*" (No. 4) "in texture but of finer quality, the edges of which are embroidered skilfully with coloured cotton or silk thread. The designs are generally of various nondescript flowers and are worked by means of ordinary sewing needles, there being hardly any difference between those of the present and the past. The *fanek* is a sort of petticoat in various striped colours, the prevailing colours being green and dark blue with red and yellow stripes, worn by women tied loosely round the breasts and hanging something like a tunic half way to the ankle. Girls under puberty, however, wear it from the waist to the ankle, the upper part of the body being covered with a species of quarter-sleeve jacket generally of dark blue or green velvet. *Fanek*s are made up of two pieces stitched together lengthwise and are of different sizes varying from 3 feet by 2 feet 3 inches to 6 feet by 4 feet 6 inches to suit girls and grown up women, and are sold, according to size and quality, at prices varying from R2-8 to R7. Those imported from Manipur, however, fetch a higher price up to about R10 on account of their superior finish." This description of the petticoat worn by Manipuri women in Cachar at the present day is almost identical with those of Mr. Ware Edgar and Colonel Dalton written in 1865 and 1872.

A *fanek* received from Silchar measures 5 feet 5 inches by 3 feet 10½ inches, being made up of two pieces closely fastened together. The stripes are of dark blue and white (edged with red on one side). The borders are about 3½ inches deep and consist of a central design in large ovals on a background of dark blue with a narrow stripe of white on either side containing a pattern in red and blue cotton thread.

Beyond the outer border is another stripe of dark blue, broken with white lines. The ornamentations in the central design are in silk coloured yellow with red, white, dark blue and bright blue.

The ends are as usual plain, being divided off from the body of the cloth by cross red plaited lines and one end of each strip * has one thin cross plaited line of white. There are practically no fringes. The weft is green, but does not show. Price R7-8.

A Manipuri petticoat called *ponek* has been received from Sylhet. It measures 5 ft. 8 in. by 4 ft. 2 in. and is a strong cloth of medium texture, made up of two equal strips which are fastened together very loosely, *viz.*, only at points about 9 inches apart. The cloth is similar in design to those already described. The stripes in the body are dark blue (nearly black) and yellow (edged on one side with red), the former being rather the wider, *viz.*, nearly ¼ inch. The side borders, which are almost identical, are about 3 inches wide and consist of one central design on a dark blue background 1¾ inch wide with a narrow stripe of pale blue on each side containing a floral pattern. Beyond these outer pale blue stripes is another background of dark blue with no pattern but broken by very thin light lines. The central design is coloured mainly orange, with crimson, dark purple, white and medium blue; it is of the usual oval shape, but not very elaborate. The narrower patterns are coloured crimson, dark blue, dull green and yellow. Each end has a plaited stripe of red and a thin plaited line of pale blue; this line is however missing from one end of one of the two strips forming the cloth. The ornamentations are all in silk except the plaited lines and stripes across the ends which are of cotton. The weft is of red, and the weaving not being so close or good as in similar cloths from Manipur, it is visible to some extent on the surface.

It is evident from this specimen that the Manipuri weavers residing at Sylhet are not so skilful as their fellow countrymen at home, as this cloth is said to be a specimen of the superior cloths woven by the Manipuris of Sylhet.

(*5*) *Ngaubong*—(Manipur and Silchar) or *khesh* (Silchar and Sylhet).—"A *chadar*, made on the smaller loom. Price R1-8 to R2 in Manipur.

In Silchar "the *ngaubong* or *khesh* is a thick cloth either plain in white or colours, or variously striped, used as coverlets for beds and at times worn by the men as a

---

* Opposite ends.

chadar and by the women as a *fanek*. Europeans and Indians of the upper classes also sometimes use it as a screen or table cloth. They are generally made from 5 to 9 feet in length by from 3 to 6 feet in breadth, and are sold, according to size and quality, at prices varying from 8 annas to R 3. The *ngaubong* like the *fanek* is invariably made up of two pieces stitched together."

In Hailakandi the *maubong* appears to be the same cloth; it is a sheet worn by the males, measuring 9 ft. by 6 ft., price from R2 to R3.

A specimen *khesh* received from Sylhet is a green cloth of medium texture, measuring 8 feet 8 inches by 4 feet 1 inch. It is made up of two narrow strips sewn closely together. The ornamentations consist of stripes only. At each end is a red stripe, edged with white, between two very narrow red and yellow stripes. At one end are three indistinct stripes, all white on one strip and two white and one yellow on the other. The peculiarity about these three stripes is that each contains one line near the centre showing up prominently on the right side of the cloth and two lines near the edges showing up on the wrong side; this is effected by a variation in the weaving. At the other end is a stripe about one inch deep, made up of nine thin stripes coloured yellow, red; white, red; yellow, red; white, red; yellow. This stripe runs across both strips of the cloth and is woven in a most peculiar way, so that the red stripes are hardly visible except one line in each, which is thrown into bold relief; and the yellow and white stripes are dim except for one line in each, which is more distinct, but not so prominent as the red lines. Beyond this stripe is a line of white, formed by three white threads shot in the weft in the usual way. All these stripes are formed at the time of weaving. The cloth has a fringe at each end, one 1¼ inch long and the other 3 inches long.

In Watson's "Textile fabrics" two cloths from the Surma Valley called "*Kass* or scarf, men's garments" are described as follows:—

"(*a*) *IV 125*. Cotton—Something like a small diaper pattern. The only attempt at ornamentation is in the narrow fringe at the end of the piece, in which red cotton is introduced at intervals of 1 inch. Length 3 yards, width 1 yard 18 inches, weight 1 lb. 5oz. From Sylhet.

"(*b*) *IV 126*. Cotton.—Bleached. Somewhat like the duck used for military summer trousers. No special borders or ends. Good example of a favourite plain warm material. Length 2 yards 18 inches, width 1 yard 9 inches, weight 1lb. 3oz. From Cachar."

The name would seem to be the same as the *khes* of Manipur.

5.—Lui.

"A *khes* made of *lui* texture. Price R 1." A specimen received from Manipur is a white ribbed cloth made up of two strips and measuring 7 ft. 6 in. by 3ft. 9 in. Apart from the ribs, which run diagonally across the cloth, there is no ornamentation except a border formed of three stripes and two lines of black at either end, the whole being about 2¼ inches deep. The ribs in these borders do not run straight but form zig-zags.

The fringes at both ends are rather over two inches long.

This cloth is of peculiar interest, as being an example of fancy weaving. The ribs are evidently formed by a peculiar arrangement of the healds, which however has, unfortunately, not been described. The price of the cloth seems very cheap, considering that the cloth is ribbed.

6.—Warumit.

A *chadar* or shawl, made on the small loom. Price R1-8 to R2-8 (Manipur).

A specimen of this cloth, received from Manipur, and described as a *khes* of towel texture, appears to be a large bath towel. It is made of two pieces strongly joined together and measures 8 ft. 6 in. by 4 ft. 4 in. It is entirely white except for a narrow green stripe along either side at the extreme edge, and 3 yellow cross stripes near each end. It has a plain fringe at either end, one 1¾ inch and one 2¼ inches long. This cloth is another example of fancy weaving, the process of which has unfortunately not been described. The pattern is formed of bold ribs or rather ridges running straight across the cloth, with the intervening hollows honeycombed by threads of the warp crossing them at moderate intervals. This is the pattern in the body of the cloth, but it is slightly varied at the ends, between the fringes and the borders. Price R1-8.

7.—Pondel.

A *chadar* or shawl made on the smaller loom. Price R1-8 to R2-8 (Manipur).

8.—Heiri maku.

A *chadar* or shawl made on the smaller loom.   Price ℞ 1-8 to ℞ 2-8 (Manipur).

9.—Musumfi.

A *chadar* or shawl made on the smaller loom.   Price ℞ 1-8 to ℞ 2-8 (Manipur).

10.—Odah.

A *chadar* made on the small loom.   Price ℞1-8 to ℞2 (Manipur).

There are two specimens of this cloth in the Indian Museum.

No. (i) No. 64. (Shillong Museum Collection). Exhibition No. 3034. This is a blue and white *chadar* from Manipur, a single strip measuring 7 feet 4 inch by 2 ft. Price 12 annas. It is a plain coarse cloth, a kind of check formed by blue alternating with white in both warp and weft, the blue patches in each case having two blue lines on either side. The weft is only indistinctly seen. Across each end runs one blue and white plaited line. There is a 2-inch fringe at one end, the other end being simply rough.

No. (ii) No. 98. (Shillong Museum Collection.) This is almost exactly like the last but larger, being formed of two strips and measuring 7 feet 8 inch by 4 feet 4 inch. Price ℞1-6.

11.—Phee arangba.

This is the name of a cloth in the Indian Museum, received from Manipur. It is not mentioned in any of the district reports.

This cloth (No. 23, Shillong Museum Collection) is a single piece measuring 7 feet 6 inch by 2 feet. It is very coarse but warm. Price ℞1-2. The pattern is a plaid, the colours of the warp being in order as follows :—white, brown, blue, red, blue, the whole repeated, and lastly white ; then comes a border 5 inches wide made up of thin stripes and double lines, the colours, which are mixed up, being white, red, yellow, brown and blue. The weft contains only brown and salmon which alternate with each other.

Between each main stripe are 2 to 4 thin stripes of the same or different colours. The width of the main stripes varies from 1 inch to 1⅜ inch.

At each end is a fringe and the usual plaited band running across the cloth 1¼ inch from the fringe. The colours of this band are brown and white.

12.—Lamphi.

A *chadar* made on the four-poster loom.   A dress of honour.   Price ℞15 to 60 (Manipur).

13.—Inaphi.

A kind of fine muslin shawl or *chadar* worn by Manipuri women and rarely by men as a *pagree.* This description has been received from Cachar but *inaphi* are said to be not woven there, but invariably imported from Manipur. No cloth of this name is included in the list from Manipur. There are, however, two specimens of this cloth from Manipur in the Indian Museum.

(i) *Leichutpa Inaphi* (No. 88, Shillong Museum Collection.) Price ℞3.

This is a very light, muslin cloth made up of two strips and measuring 14 feet 8 inch by 4 feet 8 inch. The cloth itself is white and quite plain except for double threads at the ends and edges, but it bears a pink pattern which has evidently been produced by stamping.

(ii) *Inaphi Poongai.* Price ℞4-8.

This is a heavier cloth than the last but not coarse. It is in two strips and measures 8 feet 6 inches by 5 feet 4 inches. It is plain white with five black borders at each end ⅜ to ½ inch wide and containing designs of long and short rectangles. At each end there is a slight fringe.

14.—Moirangphi.

Specimen from Manipur.—This is a white *chadar* of very fine muslin-like texture, measuring 8 feet 6 inches by 4 feet 3 inches and consisting of two strips joined together. Along the edge on each side is a black stripe of thicker texture, and from this black border, designs in the shape of besoms jut out into the body of the cloth, their length being 1¼ inch. At each end is a plain white fringe about 3 inches long ; there are also two double lines of coarse thread, one black, one white, three narrow stripes of black, and a patterned stripe of black about ⅜ inch deep. This last stripe consists of a pattern woven in on the background of white muslin. The other ornamentations are all a portion of the actual cloth. Price R4.

This cloth is of peculiar interest as exhibiting yet another variety of Manipuri weaving. For the whole length between the borders at each end, the side borders are entirely black, in both warp and weft, but the black weft does not extend into the body of the cloth except where required to form the besom-shaped patterns, and there only to a short distance. Similarly the white weft in the body of the cloth ends at the side borders and besom-shaped patterns. At the point of juncture the white weft and the black are inter-locked and then shot back in opposite directions. It appears, therefore, that three shuttles must be used simultaneously, two containing black thread to form the black portion of the weft on either side, and one containing white thread to form the white portion of the weft in the centre.

In the end borders the weft, whether white or black, runs entirely across the cloth including that portion of the borders at either side.

The warp is entirely white except at the sides where it is black to the width of the side borders. In both warp and weft the black thread is of medium texture and the white exceedingly fine.

15.—Marang Phi.

This may be the same as the last. It is a *pagri* made on the four-poster loom. Price R4 to R6 at Manipur.

16.—Koyet athek pi.

Specimen received from Manipur. Price R2.—This is a *pagri* measuring 8 feet 6 inches by 4 feet 6 inches. It is of exceedingly fine muslin-like texture and is entirely white. It has absolutely no ornamentations except a plain fringe 2 inches in length at either end, and the stripes and lines of thick thread to strengthen the cloth at the sides and ends. The arrangement of these is exactly like that in an English handkerchief.

This cloth is very similar in size and texture to the last and there seems no reason why it should not be used as a sheet as well as a *pagri*.

17.—Chadar athek pi.

A *pagri* made on the four-poster loom. Price R2 to R3 in Manipur. Probably the same as No. 16.

18.—Khudei.

A *pagri* made on the four-poster loom. Price R2 to R5. The following varieties are found in Manipur :—

    (i) *Lamthan khudei*. Price R 1·8 to R4
    (ii) *Leichatpa khudei*. „ „ 1 8 „ 3
    iii) *Ngaunbong khudei*. „ „ 3 „ 8. This is made on the smaller loom. It may be the same as the *inaphi* (No. 13).

In Cachar the word *khudei* is used as identical with *iru khudei* which is a different cloth (*cf.* No. 32).

19.—Lamthang khulhat.

A *pagri* made on the larger loom. A dress of honour given by the Rajahs. Price R5 to R15 in Manipur.

20.—Waikhu matha.

A paggri made on the larger loom. Price R3 to R6 (Manipur).

21.—Samjil.

A boat-race paggri. Price R5 to R10. (Manipur). Made on the larger loom.

22.—Khadang chit.

A boat-race paggri (tie). Price R3 to R8. (Manipur). Made on the larger loom.

23.—Ebla kooki pagri.

Eight specimens of this cloth were exhibited by the Political Agent of Manipur at the Calcutta International Exhibition (No. 3069). Price R12 for eight pieces. I have seen five of these pieces now in the Indian Museum (Nos. 9, 10, 11, 13, and 16 of the Shillong Museum Collection).

No. 9 is a fine cloth formed of two pieces, measuring 7 feet by 4 feet 2 inches. The colour is a shade of purple-brown. It is quite plain except for the thick edges at the sides and ends. Nos. 10 and 16 are exactly like No. 9 except for the colours which are, respectively, red and dark green. Price 10 annas each. Nos. 11 and 13 are similar, but of much finer muslin-like texture, very soft, and coloured respectively pink and salmon. Price 10 annas each.

24.—Kajek phisang.

A plain purple cloth of muslin texture in one piece, measuring 5 feet 10 inches by 2 feet 11 inches. (Indian Museum, No. 14 Shillong Museum Collection, probably one of the eight pagris exhibited by the Political Agent of Manipur.)

25.—Puggri.

A cloth from Manipur in the Indian Museum (No. 35 Shillong Museum Collection). The local name is not given but the cloth appears distinct from any of those described above. It is a plain white cloth with a dark blue edge on each side. Two plaited white silk lines, with a plaited blue cotton stripe between them, run across the cloth at either end, the fringes are also made into tassels by the addition of silver foil. The cloth has a silky feel. It measures 8 feet 1 inch by 24½ inches. Its price is R3-12.

26.—Lasing thaba furit.

A coat, price R1 to R3 (Manipur). Made on the four-poster loom.

27.—Ningthow phi.

A coat, a dress of honour, price R10 to R20 (Manipur). Made on the larger loom.

28.—Hiyang furit.

A boat-race coat, price R5 to R10 (Manipur). Made on the larger loom.

29.—Jagoi polloi.

A nautch dress, price R10 to $50 (Manipur). Made on the larger loom.

30.—Luhongba potloi.

Marriage dress, price R10 to R50 (Manipur). Made on the larger loom.

31.—Pana khao.

A betel-nut bag, price 4 annas to R1. (Manipur). Made on the larger loom.

32.—Iru khudei.

A towel, price 8 annas to 10 annas (Manipur.) Made on the larger loom.

In Silchar the *iru khudei* or *khudei* is described as " a common towel or duster; a species of rough cloth manufactured quite plain, but occasionally with a red border at the two ends or at both the sides and ends, and used as bathing towels and also as waistcloths by men engaged at work in the fields or other similar work. These are also sometimes worn by very little boys, and measure from 8 feet 9 inches to 7 feet 6 inches in length by from 1 foot 6 inches to 2 feet 6 inches in breadth; and are sold, according to size and quality, at prices varying from 2 annas to 8 annas."

33.—Mompak fidak.

A bed-sheet, price 12 annas to R1-4 (Manipur). Made on the smaller loom.

34.—Kangthol fida.

A counter-pane, price R1 to R2 (Manipur). Made on the smaller loom.

35.—Dolai fi.

A *chadar* used chiefly for tying bundles; price R1 to R1-8 (Manipur). Made on the smaller loom.

There is a specimen of the *dolaiphee* from Manipur in the Indian Museum (No. 40 of the Shillong Museum Collection) which was exhibited as No. 3037 by the Political Agent of Manipur at the Calcutta International Exhibition. This must be the same cloth as the *dolai fi*, but it is a counterpane and not a *chadar*. It is made up of two strips and measures 6 feet by 3 feet 8 inches. It is of very coarse cotton and is very variegated in colour, the colours in the warp being red, yellow, white, and blue, mixed up, and those in the weft red, blue and yellow, then red and blue with a thin stripe of yellow in between. The width of the red and blue in the warp varies. Some of the stripes have patterns on them. The cloth has rough fringes at the ends. Price 10 annas.

36.—Lashing fi.

A quilt, price R2 to R2-8. (Manipur). Made on the smaller loom.

A specimen received from Manipur, measures 8 feet 4 inches by 4 feet 4 inches being made up of two narrow strips. It exhibits still one more variety of Manipuri weaving. The warp is in stripes, alternately green, red, yellow, and white, the red and white stripes being only half the width of the green or yellow—and one set of 4 stripes going to the inch. But the upper and lower threads of the warp are not continuous as is usually the case, for where the upper threads are green the lower are yellow and where the upper threads are red the lower are white and *vice versâ*. The weft is entirely yellow. The weaving in both warp and weft is double, *i.e.*, the threads are woven in pairs. After the first 15 or 16 threads of the weft have been shot a tuft of cleaned cotton wool is laid in between the upper and lower threads of the warp, extending across the whole width of the cloth, then another 4 threads are shot and another tuft introduced and so on, a tuft of cotton wool being woven in after every four shots of the weft. At the extreme end of the cloth the plain weaving again contains 15 or 16 shots of the weft. Each end of the cloth is doubled over and then over again and loosely hemmed. A twisted cord of red thread is then sewn on around all four sides and the counterpane is complete. The result is a very pretty warm and serviceable bed-quilt. The price is R2 which does not appear excessive.

37.—Maithap.

" A kind of *pari* or rug in which rolled cotton forming cross threads or woof are shot in between the main threads or warp, which as a rule are of various colours." (Cachar). The cloth thus described is said to be imported to Cachar from Manipur, but not made there. No cloth of this name is reported from Manipur, but from the description, which is hardly intelligible, this cloth would appear to be the same as the *lashing fi* of Manipur (36).

In Hailakandi a cloth called *maitha* is described as a bed-sheet, size 9 feet by 6 feet, price from R2 to R3.

38.—Kantha.

A quilt, price R2 to R10 (Manipur). Made on the larger loom. The name sounds rather Bengali than Manipuri.

39.—Phibong.

A cotton *darei*, price R3 to R7 (Manipur). Made on the smaller loom.

Variety- *Phibong jamiba*, " a cotton *darei* for bed, price R3 to R5 " (Manipur).

40. Kangkhal.

Mosquito curtain, price R2 to R5. The following varieties are found in Manipur, all made on the larger loom :—

(i)	*Kangkal doria*.	Price R3 to	R 8	
(ii)	,, ahutpa.	,,	,, 8	,, 15
(iii)	*Lam jeng kangkhal.*	,,	,, 1	,, 2
(iv)	*Kangkhal asuppa*.	,,	,, 8	,, 15
(v)	,, hikok.	,,	,, 5	,, 8

In Cachar the *kangkhal* are described as mosquito curtains, plain, coloured, parti-coloured or white, made of a sort of fine net manufactured by the Manipuri women. They are of different sizes and very cheap, being sold at from 8 annas to

R1-4 each. They are used chiefly by the menial servants of the rich and by the lower class Hindus and Mahommedans. The mosquito curtain received from South Sylhet may possibly be of Manipuri manufacture.

41. Ukhal.

A purdah, price R2 to R15 (Manipur). Made on the larger loom.

42. Fagang.

A purdah or curtain made of different colours.

A specimen received from Manipur is a strong coarse cloth of many colours measuring 7 feet 9 inch by 7 feet and made up of 7 strips varying in width from 1 foot 3 inches to 8½ inches. The strips or panels, are alternately mainly green and mainly red. The green panels, which are comparatively wide, have a wide central strip of green broken only by two lengthwise lines of red, yellow and white; the remainder consisting of narrow red and green stripes alternately, most of these green stripes being varied by broken lines of white or yellow which are not a part of the background or cloth itself. The red panels are much narrower and are entirely red except for two narrow stripes on either side, one green and one yellow. The weft is green throughout but does not show.

This forms the body of the cloth, but at either end there is a border about 10 inches deep, in which a simple pattern is worked on the background with red and yellow thread. Beyond this border is a length of plain weaving to the fringe which is plain and short. The border is divided off from the body of the cloth and the plain end by two thick cross plaited lines of dark blue and white cotton; and two more such lines divide the central or main portion of the design itself from the outer or subsidiary portions.

The price of this cloth is R10.

43.—Mej phida.

This is a coloured table cloth. One specimen 8 ft. by 4 ft. has been received from Manipur, and another of nearly the same size but slightly wider was bought by me from a Manipuri at Golaghat. The two cloths are almost exactly alike. Both consist of two pieces of rather thick cloth with lengthwise stripes of orange, red, blue, yellow, purple and dark blue harmoniously blended. The dark blue stripes are broken by a double line of white running down the centre. The other stripes are either plain or varied by each successive warp thread being of a different colour from the one before. Beyond this there is no ornamentation except a plaited band of red and dark blue running across near either end, and the fringes, which are about 5 inches long at one end and two at the other. The weft is red throughout but hardly visible.

The price of the cloth from Manipur is R4. For that purchased at Golaghat I gave R7. The man who sold it to me said it was not used by the Manipuris themselves, but was made specially for Europeans.

44.—Ilh.

A fishing net thus described in Cachar. "The Manipuris manufacture a kind of square net with cotton thread, measuring from 6 to 15 feet square. These are sold according to size and quality at prices varying from 8 annas to R1-8, and are used after being fitted on to bamboo frames."

This is hardly a cotton fabric.

45.—Leiroom.

Chadar or shawl made on the smaller loom and used chiefly by Tankuls. Price R2 to R3.

Concerning the cloths made by the Manipuris for the Nagas of the Naga Hills, no detailed information has been received, and no specimens of such cloths have been sent.

The following cloths are made by Nagas living in the Manipur State for their own use. They are included there instead of among Naga fabrics in order that all the cloths made in Manipur may be kept together. These Nagas appear distinct from any of Assam.

46.—Koupui Lenglol (Naga name).

A Koupui dhuti, price R 3. (Manipur). A specimen of this cloth received from

Y

Manipur measures 4 feet 8 inches by 1 foot 11¼ inches. It is a thick, strong and very closely woven cloth made up of no less than four narrow strips very closely and strongly bound together. In colour it is a reddish-brown with three white stripes edged on each side with black and blue. The 3 seams of the cloth run along the centre of these white stripes. The weft is all white but does not show. At each side of the cloth is a border about 2¾ inches wide, marked off from the body of the cloth by a narrow blue and yellow stripe. The two side borders are alike. Down the centre of each border runs a narrow stripe of white on which are zig-zag lines of red and blue at intervals. Besides this white stripe there are several · parallel lines of blue or white and one double broken line of blue. There are also a number of cross lines of different colours, red, blue, orange, yellow and green, some in pairs and some in stripes, arranged regularly along the whole length of the border. These are worked on the background. The extreme outer edge of the border is white.

At each end of the cloth is a border about 3¼ inches deep, made up of cross lines and 2 patterned stripes, worked in different colours on the background; and near this border at each end some simple triangular designs in red and blue are found on the main stripes of white. The two end borders are alike.

The ends of the cloth are strongly bound and have no fringes, but six tufts of different coloured threads are fastened on each end to form tassels.

47.—Langupui feisoi (Naga name).

Koupui petticoat for females.   Price R5 (Manipur).

Specimen from Manipur.—A cloth in six pieces measuring 4 feet 6 inches by 3 feet 4¼ inches very similar in style to the last, but the four central pieces are black instead of red, and the main white stripes have no ornamentations beyond the end borders. The side borders extend over the whole of the outer pieces, but the cross lines in these borders extend only about ⅔rds of the way across from the inner edge. The weaving is not so good or close as that of the last cloth so that the white weft is exposed in many places. There are 8 tufts at each end.

48.—Fungfei   (Naga name).

A *Koupui chadar* for females.   Price R2-8.

Specimen from Manipur.—A cloth, in two strips, measuring 6ft. by 1ft. 5 in. Plain dark blue with a 2½ in. border at each end, consisting of 7 cross lines with a very simple pattern between one pair of these and a row of stars between the next pair. The innermost line is like a chain, made up of simple crosses. The colours used are red, white and yellow. The fringes at each end are twisted into tassels with a blade of bright yellow straw and a tuft of red or green hair tied at the ends. This cloth is not so thick as the last two.

49.—Feingao (Naga name).

A *Koupui chadar.*   Price R5 (Manipur).

Specimen from Manipur.—A thick, heavy and closely woven cloth, measuring about 6ft. 6in. by 3ft. 9in. in 6 pieces or panels. The four centre pieces are white and quite plain except for a border at each end and a few red and blue plain triangular patterns at the seams ; these patterns are in sets of eight, 6 red and 2 blue at intervals along the seams. The border, which extends across all 4 pieces, is in red and blue and of no particular interest. The two side pieces have borders mainly red and similar to those described in the *koupui lenglol* (No. 46), but having fewer cross lines and those all coloured black and red. The fringes at each end are twisted and knotted.

50.—Karouphi.

Tankul *chadar*. Price R4-8 (Manipur).

Specimen from Manipur.—A stout and strong sheet measuring 8 feet 6 inches by 4 feet 10 inches made up of 4 pieces. The two outer pieces are red with very dark blue stripes at the edges, two thin dark blue stripes and a central broken stripe of blue. The extreme outer edge of each stripe is red, and the stripes have all single lines of yellow running parallel and near to them. At each end is a cross plaited band of white. This band and the central broken stripe are worked on to the background, the other stripes forming part of the cloth itself.

The two middle pieces have 3 stripes of red bordered by white and divided from one another by two broader stripes of blue. Across each end run three plaited bands of red, the middle one being wider than the other two and bordered with blue.

Parallel to these stripes and about 2 feet from those at each end is another cross plaited band of red. The fringes at both ends of the cloth are plain but long and bushy.

There are no other ornamentations.

The following descriptions are given of some cloths in the Indian Museum coming from Manipur, and very similar to those just described.

(a) " No. 1917 Naga sheet or *choombary chadar* ornamented with coloured jute fibres and sticks. From Political Agent of Manipur. "

This is a plain blue cloth made up of two strips 19¼ inches and 19½ inches wide, but otherwise just alike. The only ornamentation consists of 4 lines with stars running along the cloth and a very plain border and a fringe at each end. The two outer lines are yellow and 3 inches and 17½ Inches, respectively, distant from the left edge of the cloth ; the two inner lines are white and about equi-distant from the outer lines and from each other. The stars are white or faded yellow and have from 13 to 15 rays. The end border consists merely of 8 shots of weft repeated thrice at equal intervals. The threads of the fringe at each end have sticks attached with straw wrapped round them, and some of these curious appendages have red hair projecting from the ends.

There is another unlabelled cloth just like this.

(b) No. 29 (Shillong Museum Collection). Blue and white, length 5 feet 1 inch breadth 4 feet 1 in. This is made up of nine narrow strips, the two outer strips being alike and the remaining seven being of two varieties which alternate with one another. The outer strips are 11 in. wide of which 10 inch are blue and 1 inch white, but the blue has on it three ¾ in. stripes of white. Of the other stripes one kind is plain blue, 5¼ inches wide and the other plain white 1½ inch wide.

At distances varying from 5 to 7 inches and greater near the ends of the cloth than near the centre, the two outer pieces have two red lines running across the blue part and a design on the white part.

At the corresponding places on the white strips are designs formed by red and blue cross lines.

Both ends of the cloth are bound with white and have no fringe.

(c) No. 26 (Shillong Museum Collection). This is made up of two strips and measures 7 feet by 3 feet 6 inches. The body of the cloth is white with a dark blue edge about 1¾ inch wide of which 1 inch is plain and the rest ornamented. Each end of the cloth has a border 1 foot or more deep composed of cross stripes alternately red-brown and dark blue with white lines in between. This cloth is very coarse, strong and warm.

(d) No. 30 (Shillong Museum Collection) Aimol *chadur* or *Heik ikphee*. Made at Manipur by an Aimol Naga woman. Exhibition No. 3060. Price 11 annas (this seems very cheap).

This is a coarse, warm cloth, measuring nearly 8 feet by 4 feet 2 inches and made up of two strips. The body of the cloth is brown with a simple diamond pattern in white, the sides are plain brown 1¼ inch wide. Near one end of the cloth is a yellow cross, border on a white background with a few red threads running parallel to it on either side, and between this border and the end of the cloth the white appears in zig-zags and not in diamonds. At the other end one strip ends off abruptly.

(e) No. 31 (Shillong Museum Collection).

A duplicate of No. 30 but both ends have the yellow border.

(f) No. 44 (Shillong Museum Collection).

A sheet measuring 5 feet by 4 feet 5 inches made up of four strips and coloured blue red, yellow and black. It has a cross plaited border of some width near one end and a thin cross border beyond it. At this end the fringe is very long, at the other there is a shorter fringe. Price R 4. The cloth is very similar to the *loha* from the Naga Hills (No. 42 Shillong Museum Collection).

(g) No. 97 Shillong Museum Collection. *Heikoi phi.*

This is almost exactly like No. 30 (d) but the brown border is only ¾ inch wide and neither panel ends off abruptly. Price 15 annas. The names of these two cloths should, in all probability, be the same.

NAGA FABRICS.

In interest the Naga cotton fabrics fall little short of those of the Manipuris. The Nagas are divided into many tribes, and each of these, like the Scotch Highland clans, uses a peculiar pattern of cloth, so that any individual can be easily identified by his tartan. Though Naga cloths have often attracted attention and formed the subject of many interesting notes, yet even now there is unfortunately little information available regarding the distinctive colours and patterns adopted by the various tribes. The Census Report of 1891, however, contains a very valuable note by Mr. Davis which deals with a few tribes only, and from this note the following has been extracted.

Ao Nagas. " They wear a loincloth and small apron. The pattern of this last varies from village to village. All wear a cotton cloth thrown lightly round the shoulder, the commonest colours being dark blue or dirty white." Speaking of the women of the Chungli and Mongsen tribes Mr. Davis writes : " The clothes of both are similar. They consist of a dark blue petticoat, sometimes ornamented with red stripes, reaching from waist to knee, and a dark blue or dirty white cloth thrown loosely round the shoulders".

Naked tribes, Tamlu and Mesong —" The women wear a white petticoat, in some cases striped with red. This petticoat is only about 12 inches wide, and only just long enough for both ends to meet when being worn, and is a garment that leaves-very little to the imagination."

Semas. " They are practically naked, as the small flap they wear dangling from their waists cannot be said to in any way hide their nakedness. In addition to this flap they wear the large cloth common to all the Naga tribes. The commonest pattern among them is a cloth with alternate broad stripes of white and dark blue....... The women wear a very scanty black petticoat and leave their breasts bare."

Lhotas.—" The customs of this tribe present no marked differences from those of the Rengmas on the south. Their dress is, however, slightly more decent, and consists, for the men, of a small loin cloth and apron, of either light blue or white, striped horizontally with lines of red, or for the lower villagers, of dark blue, striped with broad lines of red. A cloth of alternate broad lines of white and dark blue is worn round the shoulders and reaches to the knee.......The women wear a scanty black petticoat and leave the breasts bare."

The tribe which has attracted most attention is that of the Angamis. As early as 1839 Mr. E. Grange noticed their tasteful dress, the men's blue kilts faced with cowries and their coarse grey or blue shoulder cloths tied in so curious a way in time of war. " The poorer classes, " wrote Mr. Grange, " make their cloths from the pith of a nettle which is procurable in great abundance and which makes a very fine fibred hemp. " But a much more detailed description of the costume of this tribe is given by Captain John Butler, Political Agent to the Naga Hills, in his " Rough notes on the Angami Nagas and their language, 1875." This account is so interesting that it is quoted at length.

" As regards the dress of the Angamis, I do not think we could find a more picturesque costume anywhere than that of the men, but it requires to be seen to be understood, and I am afraid no amount of description can adequately represent the vivid colours and general get up of a well-dressed Angami warrior, flashing about in all his gala war paint......

" The Angami's chief article of attire, and one which distinguishes him from most other Nagas, is a kilt of dark blue or black cotton cloth of home manufacture, varying from 3½ to 4½ feet in length, according to the size of the man, and about 18 inches in width, decorated with three and sometimes, though very rarely, with four horizontal rows of small white cowrie shells. This kilt passes round the hips and overlaps in front ; the edge of the upper flap is ornamented with a narrow fringe, whilst the overlap, having a string attached to its lower corner is pulled up tightly between the legs, and the string, which generally has a small cowrie attached to it, is then allowed to hang loosely a few inches below the waist belt, or is tucked in at the side, and thus the most perfect decency is maintained, forming a pleasant contrast to some of their neighbours, " who walk the tangled jungle in mankind's primeval pride." I do not think that any dress I have ever seen tends so much to show off to the very best advantage all the points of a really fine man, or so ruthlessly to expose all the weak points of a more weedy specimen as this simple cowrie begirt kilt. Thrown over the shoulders are generally, loosely worn, from 2 to 3 cotton or bark home-spun cloths, according to the state of the weather. Some of these cloths are of an extremely pretty pattern, as for instance, the very common one of a dark blue ground, with a double border of broad scarlet and yellow stripes on two sides, and fringed at both ends. When out on the war trail, or got up for a dance, these cloths are worn crossed over the breast and back, and tied in a knot at the shoulder......

" The dress of the women, though neat, decent and picturesque in its way, is not nearly so showy as that of the men. The most important perhaps, though least seen portion of a woman's dress, is of coarse the petticoat, which is usually a piece of dark blue home-spun cotton cloth, about 2 feet in breadth, which, passing round the hips, overlaps about 6 inches. This is partially, if not entirely, covered by the folds of the next most important article of clothing, a broad cotton cloth whose opposite corners are taken up and made to cross over the back and chest, thus covering the bosom, and are tied in a knot over the shoulders. Finally, a second cloth is worn, either thrown loosely over the shoulders or wrapped round the hips and tucked in at the waist. In the cold weather they generally add an extra cloth, whilst in the warm weather, or when employed in any kind of hard work, such as tilling their fields, etc., they generally dispense with these and drop the corner of the other; or in other words simply strip to the waist."

The curious way in which Angami Naga men and women tie their shoulder cloth is very interesting. That adopted by the men was noticed by Mr. Grange who said that the cloth in war time is tied up in such a manner as to allow of a bamboo being inserted to carry the person away should he be wounded. That adopted by the women is no less interesting, for it is peculiar to them and the Jaintia women alone of all the tribes on this frontier. This fact, Captain Butler says, had some 13 years before been referred to by an intelligent Hill Kachari as conclusive proof of the truth of a legend regarding the origin of the Angami Naga tribe. According to this legend the youngest brother of the Jaintia Rajah fell in love with the Rajah's daughter and carried her off by force. He fled first to Dimapur and then to the neighbouring hills where he settled down with some Kacharis and his own followers and so established a colony which is the Angami tribe of the present day. Captain Butler, however, never found any confirmation of this strange story and expresses doubt as to its truth.

Of the Nagas living near Banpara Mr. S. E. Peal has written. " The chiefs often wear a dark blue cloak like a dressing gown not tied, that contrasts strongly with their usually nude condition. Assamese cloths are also bought and worn by the Nagas who can afford the luxury during the cold season, but those who cannot, wear the little scrap commonly seen at all times and about the size of foolscap. Women wear an equally scanty morsel, which, in some tribes, I hear, is often dispensed with......As far as I can see, the women wear no head gear at all."

In another passage, alluding to some women and girls in Banpara, Mr. Peal says : " Costume, as usual, was at a discount, and as is often said a pocket hand-kerchief would make four suits."

Considering the scantiness of their clothing, it is surprising to learn that the Nagas have a comparatively valuable wardrobe ; yet in 1881 Mr. McCabe said that almost every Naga owned cloths worth R 10 to R 30. Naga cloths are, however, very expensive.

The passages quoted above refer to the Nagas of the Naga Hills. A still further variety of cloth is found among the Nagas of Cachar. Writing in 1866, Mr. J. Ware Edgar described the clothing of these people as follows :—" The dress of the Nagas consists of a triangular piece of cloth tied round the waist and hanging down in front, leaving the back almost bare, and I have been informed that the costume of some Nagas is even slighter than this, being simply the fibula of the Romans. The women wear a wrapper extending from below the navel to the knee and un-married girls wear another cloth tied over the breasts."

Apart from the variation of pattern from tribe to tribe, there is another peculiarity about the Naga cloths, viz., that they are made in very narrow strips which are fastened together to make a wide cloth. This characteristic was noticed as far back as 1841 by Mr. Robinson and holds good to the present day. The joining to-gether of two or more strips to form a wide cloth is common to the plains of Assam and most hill tribes, but the peculiar feature here is that the strips might be woven much wider than they actually are, and though each strip in a cloth is sometimes of a different colour or pattern from the rest, yet sometimes two similar strips are joined together where one wider strip might easily have been woven and used instead.

The following is a list of some of the Naga cloths, with descriptions wherever possible. The list is, of necessity, imperfect, but it will suffice to show the main features of the cloths worn by the Nagas. Besides the characteristics above mentioned the main features of these cloths are their coarseness and great durability and the distinctive nature of the designs upon them. The arrangement of the list n this case is according to the places whence the cloths come.

Angami cloths from Kohima in the Naga Hills.

The cloths here described are those made by the Angami Nagas at the present day. The general descriptions are those given by the Deputy Commissioner of the Naga Hills, and the detailed descriptions are of cloths received from Kohima. The following information regarding these cloths is also given by the Deputy Commissioner :—

" Most cloths have a fringe at one end. This is composed of the loose yarn left over at the end after the cloth is finished. The loose threads are twisted together three or four at a time, by hand and knotted at the end ; they thus form a fringe 2 to 3 inches long.

" Small conventional patterns are often woven into white cloths during the process of weaving, they are usually in red or blue yarn.

" No cloths are made except what are used as articles of wearing apparel by men, women and children.

" The material, workship and durability of the Naga home-made cloths are good. They are of no artistic value. The dexterity of the workman does not appear to improve or deteriorate. No steps are necessary to improve or maintain the quality of the fabrics made.

" I am quite unable to give, in detail, the cost of the chief cotton fabrics made in this district. Imported goods do not come into competition with them at all. The quality of the home-made article is much better than that of the imported goods. The price is also higher.

" None of the cotton fabrics can be said to be manufactured in large quantities. The industry being entirely a domestic one and the trade being small, scarcely any cloths, except those actually required for use, are manufactured." All Angami cloths are very rough to the touch.

1.—Menni.

" Kilt worn by the men. These are small black cloths about 18 inches broad by 42 inches long. They are worn round the waist and are all of the same pattern. Price R 1 to 8 annas."

Specimen.—A strong, closely woven cloth of thick texture, measuring 3 feet 10½ inches by 1 foot 4½ inches and made up of two narrow strips. One end has two thick cross lines and a plain fringe. The other end has no fringe and is tightly bound. Each strip has one thick line running down its centre, otherwise the cloth is quite plain. The thread is all black. Price 12 annas.

2.—Chipha.

Waist belt and purse combined, generally white, with various small inserted patterns. About 3 feet long by 4 inches wide. Price 8 annas.

3.—Mehat 4.—Kwemho and 5. Chicha.

" The waistcloth used by women. These are of various patterns but they all serve the same purpose. They vary in length from 3 feet to 3 feet 6 inches or 4 feet by 2 feet to 2 feet 6 inches broad and reach from the waist to the knee. They are worn round the waist. Price R 5 to R 2-8. "

Specimen.—Kwempu, woman's waistcloth. Price R 4-8. This is a cloth of the same texture as the *menni* or rather thicker, measuring 4 feet 11 inches by 2 feet 5½ inches and composed of 4 strips. The two outer strips are dark blue with three narrow stripes at the outside, and three near the middle, a single stripe of red ⅜ inch broad near the inside and a rather broader white stripe at the extreme inner edge ; all these stripes run lengthwise. The two inner strips are plain white with 3 narrow lengthwise stripes near the centre, the two outer stripes being blue, and the central one red. Besides this the white stripes have five small designs in red and blue, one in each panel of one strip and one in the outer and 2 in the inner panel of the other strip. These designs are all in zig-zag lines or diamonds and triangles, but each is distinct from the other. They are situated almost at the centre of the cloth, but slightly nearer the fringed end.

The weft of the outer strips is entirely dark blue and that of the inner strips entirely white, and the threads of the weft show through here and there but not to any great extent.

One end of the cloth is bound with a twisted cord of red cotton, sewn on with white cotton thread, the other end is fringed and has two plaited cross bands, one of red and white and one of red and yellow.

6.—Kwehi.

"The *chadar* or large wearing cloth worn by both men and women. This cloth is made in various colours, but all are used for the same purpose. Each different coloured cloth has a different name. The size of this cloth is about 2½ yards long by 54 inches wide. It is used to cover the whole body from the neck to the knees. These cloths are very durable and warm, and some of the patterns are handsome in appearance. Price from R8 to R3-8."

7.—Loha.

"Worn as a *chadar* by men and women. Price R 7-8. This is apparently one of the varieties of the last cloth *kwehi*."

Specimen —A very strong, closely woven and heavy cloth measuring 5 feet 6 inches by 4 feet and made up of 4 pieces. The two inner pieces are plain dark blue, the two outer pieces striped dark blue, red and yellow. There is a very narrow stripe of dark blue on the extreme outer edge, then a broad stripe of red (3½ inch) followed by eight comparatively narrow stripes (*viz.*, 4 blue with alternately yellow and red between), and lastly another blue stripe 2 inches wide.

The weft in all strips is dark blue. One end of the cloth has a red twisted cord sewn on with yellow, and the other end a long fringe and a border consisting of a central plaited band with a plaited line on each side—all in red and yellow. *C.f.* Specimen No. (ii) described below.

8.—Vatzi.

"Women's breast cloth. These are either all blue, all white or half blue and half red. The cloth is worn knotted over one or both shoulders. If over both shoulders, the opposite corners are knotted together so that the cloth makes a cross, covering the breast. These cloths are about 4 ft. long by 3 ft. broad. Price R2 to R3."

9.—Love.

Specimen.—Price R3-8. This is a nettle cloth, measuring about 6 ft. by 3 ft. 6 in. and made up of 4 strips exactly alike, *viz.*, of natural colour (dirty white), with a stripe of black down the centre, but otherwise quite plain. The extreme edges are of ordinary cotton in both warp and weft, the rest being of cotton in the weft and nettle in the warp. The ends are bound up and have no fringes.

This cloth is very heavy and strong. It is apparently a *chadar* or upper sheet, but its use is not stated. It is sent as an example of a mixed fabric,—cotton and nettle. The nettle is much rougher to the touch than cotton. The word *love* means nettle.

There is a cloth almost exactly like this in the Indian Museum, *viz.*, No. 57, (Shillong Museum Collection). *Love kwa* price R3; size 5 ft. 10 in. by 4 ft. This was exhibited as No. 3185 by the Deputy Commissioner of the Naga Hills.

Cloths from Mokokchong in the Naga Hills.

The following are the cloths made at the present day by Nagas residing in the Sub-division of Mokokchong. Concerning them the Sub-divisional Officer says :— "The general quality of the fabrics is coarse and the ornamentations rough. They cannot be compared with the imported goods, the latter being never used by Nagas except when they go out to service with Europeans. White and black cloths are made in large quantities but only sufficient to supply local wants."

10.—Subu.

A white cloth, without any ornamentation, worn by the poorer classes. Prices from 8 annas to 12 annas. Lasts about 18 months.

11.—Saram.

A black cloth, the same as above. Price from 8 annas to R1-8. Lasts about 2 years.

12.—Subangvu.

A red ornamental cloth worn by the richer classes and costing from R2 to R10. This lasts about 10 years. They are several varieties of this cloth with different ornamentations, each village having a different way or ornamenting. They are worn by men only and only on special occasions. These cloths are about 6 ft. by 5 ft. The quality of all these cloths is more or less coarse.

13.—Sepeti.

A petticoat worn by women, price from R1 to R4.

14.—Langtum.

A cloth worn over the loins and private parts by men. Price 4 annas.

15.—Sijak.

A kilt worn by men about 18 in. long by a foot broad, ornamented with rows of cowries.

16.—Sokae.

An ornamented sash worn across the chest by Nagas on gala days, when dancing and when on the warpath. Price from R3 to R5.

Naga cloths from North Cachar.
17.—Inkum basi.

Sheet. Coarse white cloth about 8 feet by 5 feet.

Inkom baiee
Inkobaiee } Sheets. These would seem to be the same as the above.

18.—Bare kom.

Waistcloth. White or blue cloth about 3½ feet by 1 foot.

19.—Rikaosha.

Woman's cloth. Blue cloth bought from Kukis as a rule. From this description it would appear to be a Kuki cloth.

20.—Engenina.

Woman's dancing cloth, white or blue, much ornamented. (*Specimen*).—This is a small stout cloth, measuring 3 ft. 10 in. by 1 ft. 9 in. in four pieces. The two central pieces are white with a 2-inch stripe, brown-red in the middle and dark blue at the edges, about an inch distant from the outer side. At about the same distance from the inner side are two narrow stripes or lines, one blue and one red. The two outer pieces are similar to the inner ones, but the blue and red stripe is towards the inner edge, and besides the blue and red lines there is a third line, in blue, beyond which the cloth is not white but red-brown. In one of the outer pieces this outer blue line and the red-brown part beyond it end off irregularly, and do not extend to the end of the cloth, the continuation being white, as if the coloured threads in the warp had been too short and had had pieces of white thread joined on to make them of the proper length. In the other outer piece there is a series of designs on the white stripe between the coloured stripe and lines. These designs are of the usual kind peculiar to the Nagas, *viz.*, zig-zag lines and triangles in blue and red, and, as usual, each is different from the rest. They are found at intervals along the whole length of the cloth, except 3 or 4 inches at the two ends. The three seams of the cloth are ornamented with a line of red binding and the characteristic blue triangles which point upwards and downwards alternately. This ornamentation usually extends to within 2½ inches of each end of the cloth, but, at one end of the seam of the ornamented piece, they extend to within less than an inch of the end.

The ends of the cloth have no fringes, but are edged with a brown-red twisted cord fastened on by white threads, and at each corner and each seam at either end a bunch of blue and red-brown thread is fastened on to form a tassel. Price R3.

Naga cloths made in Cachar.

21.—Langthupai.

A species of sheet similar in every respect to the Kuki *paul*.

22. Phailah.

A species of towel or waist cloth similar in every respect to the Kuki *lukom.*

23. Phaisoi.

A species of petticoat similar in every respect to the Kuki *punreh.*

These are all the Nāga cloths reported from the different districts, but there is a very good collection in the Indian Museum, most of which are from the Nagas Hills, but some from Manipur and the Khasia Hills. Those from Manipur have been already noticed among Manipuri cloths. The following are some of the Naga cloths in the Museum:—

From the Shillong Museum Collection.

(i) No. 25. *Chadar* from the Naga Hills. Length 5 ft. 2 in., breadth 3 ft. 1 in. A coarse cloth made up of four strips, the outer two of which are red and about 6 in. wide, and the inner two blue and about 1 ft. wide, all are quite plain except at the ends, where there are fringes and big a plaited cross line in red and white between 2 other plaited lines of red and yellow. The fringe at one end is long, that at the other short.

(ii) No. 42. *Loha* from Naga Hills. Price R5. (Exhibit No. 3192. Angami cloth, *loha*, exhibited by Deputy Commissioner, Naga Hills. Exhibition price 8 annas.) A coarse warm cloth, length 5 ft. 4 in., width 3ft. 7in., in four strips 10 to 11¼ inches wide. The two centre strips are plain blue, the outer strips are alternately blue, yellow and red, the first and last colours predominating,—the edges are blue. One end is sewn up with blue, the other is fringed. At the fringed end is a band of four plaited cross lines, the outer 2 yellow and the inner two red, between two thin yellow and red plaited stripes. The broad stripe fringes out at the sides.

(iii) No. 43. Like the last except that the plaited cross band is deeper consisting of 4 red lines between 4 yellow lines on either side—in all 12. There are fringes at both ends. Size about the same as the last.

(iv) No. 46—*Chudder* from Naga Hills. Price R4. Length about 6ft., width 3 ft. 9 in. in 4 strips, of which the 2 centre ones are plain white and the outer ones half white, the other half being in stripes blue, white and orange-red; of these the widest is the outer stripe which is orange-red and measures about 2 inches. Beyond these stripes is a thin blue line and then the edge which is white. Otherwise this cloth is like the last. It is made of coarse cotton.

(v) No. 47. *Chudder* from Naga Hills. This cloth is torn, its width is 3 ft. 5 in. (in 4 strips). The body is striped blue and red, with a white line running down each red stripe; the blue stripes are broader than the red. The side borders are red (width 2½ to 3 in.) with a few blue and white lines to relieve the monotony. The extreme edges are white. Between the stripes and red borders on each side runs a green and dull yellow stripe. This cloth has no fringes, both ends being bound. There is a thin red and a still thinner white plaited line across each end. A coarse cloth.

(vi) No. 49. *Kevemho* or petticoat from the Naga Hills. Price R6. Length 4 ft. 9 in., width 3 ft. 2 in. in 4 strips. The 2 central ones are white with 3 lines (blue, red and blue), about 1¼ in. from the outer edge. In the space between the lines and the edge rectangular patterns are woven in at intervals. The two outer panels are dark blue with a few red stripes to relieve the monotony. A coarse cloth.

(vii) No. 51. *Mushe kue* from Naga Hills. Price R9. Length 5 ft. 10 in., width 3 ft. 8 in. in 4 panels, of which the two centre ones are white and the two outer ones are striped red-brown, white and dark blue. The outer edges are dark blue. One end is bound up and the other fringed—at the fringed end are the usual plaited cross stripes.

(viii) No. 52. *Serna cloth* or *kitsee kwa* from Naga Hills. Price R5. Exhibited at the Calcutta International Exhibition by the Deputy Commissioner, Naga Hills. Local and Exhibition price on the ticket illegible. This is a very coarse cloth, measuring 5ft. by 3 ft. 8 in. in four strips. The two outer strips are black having on the outside two, and on the inside one red line running lengthwise. At each end is a knotted line in white running across the strip; one of these strips, is 11¾ in. and the other about 14 inches wide. Of the inside strips, one is black and similar to the last two, except that it has only one red line at each side, it is rather more than 1 ft. wide. The other strip is only about 6 in. in width and is white. At each side there are two black lines at a short distance apart, those on the right being about ¼ an inch and those on the left about ¾ of an inch from the edge. Between the two inside lines is a pattern in black running the whole length of the cloth and uniform throughout. This pattern consists of fancy cross bands of a curious pattern difficult to describe without an illustration but very characteristic. Outside the black lines the cloth is plain at each end but has a simple pattern of zig-zag and cross lines in the centre. This pattern begins at about 21 in. from one end, is itself 22 in. long and ends about 17 in. from the other end. At each end is a pretty red and blue cross border of simple pattern. Each end of the cloth has a two-inch fringe in which the threads are twisted together and knotted at the ends.

(ix) No. 53. *Kirhani* from the Naga Hills. Price R1-8. Length 3ft. 11in., width 1 ft. 8 in. in 4 panels. This is a coarse cloth striped in red, white and blue, red being the predominating colour. The weft is all white. The ends are bound and quite plain but for some blue bunches of thread or tassels fastened on at the outer edges and each seam.

(x) No. 54. *Vakwa* from Naga Hills. Price R7. Length 4 ft. 7in., width 2 ft. 4 in. A coarse white cotton cloth fringed at both ends, and made up of four strips. The two centre strips are plain white, but the two outer ones are striped and have an outer edge of brick-red, 2 in. in width, with a black and white line down its centre, and an black stripe (touching it) on the inside ; beyond this is a white stripe, then one of brick-red, then one of white and then one of black. Along each seam is a line with red and black triangular designs. The vertices of all the triangles in any one seam point the same way, but those of the middle seam point in opposite directions from those of the others. The two ends of the cloth are alike, and have a plaited line between two broken cross lines.

(xi) No. 55. *Vakwa.* Size 4 feet 6 inches by 2 feet 1 inch ; a duplicate of the last.

(xii) No. 56. *Moshe kwa* from the Naga Hills. Price R9. Length nearly 6 ft. by 4 ft. This cloth is like (iv) No. 46, except for the colours being black and brick-red and the ends having only two small cross stripes with no stripes between them.

(xiii) No. 57. *Love kwa* cf. No. (9) above.

(xiv) No. 58. *Moshe kwa* from the Naga Hills. Price R9. Length 6 ft. 2 in., width 3 ft. 9 in. This is similar to (iv) No. 46, and of the same colours except that the blue is of a darker shade. The texture of this cloth is rather finer and one end only is fringed, the other being bound. At the fringed end the cross lines are smaller and closer together. In this cloth there are at intervals ribs in twos and threes across the central plain strip and the white portion of the outer strips.

(xv) No. 59. *Gaimho* from the Naga Hills. Price R6. Length 5 ft., width 3 ft. 4 in. This is a coarse but soft cotton cloth in four strips, of which the 2 outer ones (6½ in. wide) are plain red and the 2 inner ones plain blue. At each end are plain fringes 4¼ in. long and a thick plaited cross line.

(xvi) No. 60. *Gaimho* from Naga Hills. Price R6. Exhibited by Deputy Commissioner, Naga Hills (No. 3186). Similar to the last but having only two strips. The edges are 5¼ in. wide, and the cross lines are smaller.

(xvii) No. 61. *Padi* from Naga Hills. Price R4. Length 5 ft. 8 in., width 3 ft. 8 in. Red, white and blue. Almost identical with (iv) No. 46.

(xviii) No. 62. *Mosi kesha* from Naga Hills. Price R7. Length 4 ft. 9 in., width 3 ft. 5 in. A coarse cotton cloth in four strips, of which the two central ones are plain white and the two outer ones striped, with a white edge. The coloured stripes are four in number and alternately (1) dark blue, ¾ inch wide, and (2) dark blue with a red band down the centre, 1 in. wide. One end of the cloth is bound and the other has a 4-inch fringe with the usual three cross plaited stripes.

(xix) No. 66. *Jevimbo* or loin cloth from the Naga Hills. Price R4. Length 5 ft. 4 in., width 3 ft. 2 in. This is a like (xv) No. 59, but the red and white plaited stripes at each end lie between the small yellow and red plaited lines. The width of the red strip is 5¼ in. and 5¼ in.

(xx) No. 67. Like the last.

(xxi) No. 68. *Mukro* from the Naga Hills. Price R4. Length 6 ft., width 3 ft. 8 in. This is labelled as a check but it is not a check. It is a cloth in four strips of which the 2 central ones are white and the outer ones striped. The stripes are white (5) followed alternately by blue (3) and red (2), then beyond the last blue stripe is a red stripe 2¾ in. wide, then a blue line before the edge which is white. The white stripes are wider than the coloured ones. The ends of the cloth have a small plaited cross line and short knotted fringes.

(xxii) No. 69. *Chudder* from the Naga Hills. Length 14 feet 6 in., width 3 feet 2 in. in two strips. This is a highly variegated plaid, the warp and weft being alternately red, blue and white. The blue is very dark ; red is the most prominent colour and white the least prominent, being only in narrow stripes or lines. The full colour is seen only in squares and rectangles, for the weft shows through. The one end has a one-inch tassel, the other is merely rough. There are no ornamental designs. This cloth is of a different nature from those just described, and is of thinnish texture.

(xxiii) No. 70. *Mute* from the Naga Hills. Price R3. Length 5 feet 2 in., width 3 feet 8 in. This is a coarse cloth made up of four white strips with a black stripe down the centre of each. The 2 outer strips have a border of two thin stripes, blue on the outside and red in the centre. One of the central strips has two similar stripes inside. Across the two central strips run four small diagrams, one in each of the 4 divisions of white; but these are not in a line. The two outer diagrams are in red, white and black, and the 2 central ones, which are longer than the others, are in black, red, white and yellow. The ends of the cloth are bound.

(xxiv) No. 72. *Lengti* or cloth band from the Naga Hills. Price R1. Length 4 feet 8 inches, width 7½ in. This is a dirty white cloth quite plain except for a claret coloured line across each end. The fringes are 5½ inches long.

(xxv) No. 73. Similar to (iv) No. 46.

(xxvi) No. 74. *Lerha* or waistband from the Naga Hills. Price R3. Exhibited by Deputy Commissioner, Naga Hills (No. 3197). This is very similar in size and shape to No. 1606 described below, (No. xxxvi), but the designs are not identical. There are 7 designs, the first 3 being all different and each deeper than the one before; the next 3 like the third and the last like the second. These designs are in red and black and show only on the face of the cloth. It requires an illustration to explain them, but they are of the usual zigzag, diamond and triangular pattern. The fringes are the same as in No. 1606.

(xxvii) No. 75 *Lerha*, size 2ft. × 5in. Like the last but the designs are different and larger; though of the same style. There are three distinct designs, very much alike. The pattern starts 7 inches from one end of the cloth and finishes 10 inches from the other. There are two pigtails at the ends, one at each edge.

(xxviii) No. 86 Shirt (?) from Naga Hills. Length 5ft. 5in., width 1 ft. 9in. (in one piece). This is a thick board like-cloth with ribs across it at intervals throughout the whole length. It is plain white with a long fringe at each end (8 to 10 inches).

(xxix) No. 91 *Sama*. An Eastern Angami Naga cloth. Price R2. Length 5ft. 1 in., width 3ft. 4in. It is a coarse cloth made up of four strips each black with a thin blue stripe down the centre and a still thinner white stripe at the edge. The outer strips have a white edge with a very thin red stripe separated from it by a line of blue. One end of the cloth has a fringe near which is a plain red cross band (¼ inch deep) edged on the inside with a line of white; between this band and the fringe a white and red line runs across the cloth, The other end is bound.

Besides those in the Shillong Museum Collection there are many other Naga cloths in the Indian Museum, among which the following are some of the more interesting,

(xxx) No. 76 (Indian Museum). A coarse Naga cloth from the Kassyah Hills, received from Lieutenant J. Gregory in 1867. Length 4 ft. 7 in., width 3 ft. 10 in. This cloth is in three strips; the centre one is dark blue and rather narrower than the other two; the outer ones are striped blue, red and yellow, blue being the most, and yellow the least prominent colours. There fringes at each end of the cloth, that at one end 4 inches and that at the other 3 inches long. At the former end there is, in the central strip, a cross band ¾ inch deep made up of four red lines between two yellow lines. In the right hand strip is a similar band ½ inch deep, and in the left strip a band of red and yellow in which the colours alternate as follows:—red (1 line), yellow (2 lines), red (2 lines), then yellow (1 line). At the latter end the bands are all alike consisting of 3 red lines between 2 yellow lines. They are of the same depth as at the other end. The threads of these borders project on either side and are formed into a kind of tassel.

(xxxi) No. 2064 (?). A blue Koropa Naga head cloth from the Naga Hills. Length 6 feet, width 1 ft. 10½ in. A cloth of fine texture, quite plain. At one end is a ¼-inch fringe, the other is merely rough,

(xxxii). No. 1571. A cloth very similar to the Serna cloth (viii) No. 52, but in 5 strips, and with more ornamentations, the outer edge on both sides having plain patterns at intervals all the way along. Length 5ft. 6in., width 1ft. 9½in.

(xxxiii). A Naga cloth, measuring 7ft. 4in. by 4ft. in 2 strips, plain blue, but with an 8½in. border at each end, red with white spots; the main portion of this border is 3 inches deep.

(xxxiv). No. $\frac{662}{15.6}$. Angami Naga cloth. Length 3ft. 8in., width 1ft. 7in. in 3 strips, 8, 4 and 7 inches respectively. The cloth has no tassels or fringes, but is merely bound with red at each end. The two outer strips are plain black with red edges. The central strip is white with a red line down the centre and two black lines down either side. Between the inner black lines are 10 rectangular designs at intervals along the cloth in red and blue. The first three designs at one end are only $\frac{3}{4}$ inch deep, but after this they gradually increase in size to the seventh, which is $1\frac{1}{2}$ inch deep; from this point they again gradually grow smaller, the tenth being $\frac{3}{4}$ inch wide. The first and the tenth designs are at the extreme ends of the cloth, and the other at irregular intervals varying from 3 to 4 inches apart. They are all 2 inches wide and consist partly of coloured lines on a white background and partly of white lines on a coloured background. The lines are either straight or in the characteristic ziz-zag and diagonal formations. Most of the designs are different from one another.

(xxxv). No 2068 (Indian Museum) A scarf with small doodhia beads in the fringe from the Naga Hills. This cloth consists of two equal narrow strips and measures 3ft. 2in. by 8in. It is plain blue except for a little red at the sides, down the seam and on each side of it and in the end borders. The peculiar feature about this cloth is the fringe which has some curious things called doodhia beads near the end of the seam and at regular intervals on either side. Some tassels have 3 such beads, some one. Towards the edges are some ordinary beads instead of the doodhias. It it probable that many of the doodhia beads have fallen off, as the cloth is very old.

(xxxvi). No. 1606. A cloth from the Naga Hills, Assam, quaintly labelled " Lota Angami or the shoulder band." Length 3ft. 8in., width 5½ in. It is entirely white except for the designs which are in blue (nearly black) and red. There are six such designs and, the two ends of the cloth being uniform, the three patterns at one end are like the three at the other. Starting from one end there is 4½ in. plain white, then comes pattern No. 1, one inch deep; then $\frac{3}{4}$ in. plain white, then pattern No. 2, 3½ in. deep; then $\frac{3}{4}$ in. plain and pattern No. 3, 5½ deep. Pattern No. 1 consists of five coloured isosceles triangles with the vertices downwards and a narrow coloured stripe parallel to the outer sides of the two outer triangles. The intervals are white. Of the coloured portion the first $\frac{1}{4}$ in. is red and the next $\frac{1}{8}$in. blue, i. e., the bases of the triangles and the ends of the stripes are red and the rest blue. The second pattern is more complicated, and consists of 4 portions, alternately red, $\frac{3}{4}$ in. deep, and blue, $\frac{7}{8}$ in. deep. The first portion, $\frac{3}{4}$in. deep, is a row of 5 isosceles triangles with their vertices upwards and a narrow stripe on each side parallel to the outer sides of the outer triangles, and of the same length. The next portion consists of four rather larger isosceles triangles with their vertices downwards. These triangles are on the same base line and together occupy the whole line—except a short length at either end; each of these short lengths forms one end of a stripe, the outer edge of which is a continuation of the outer side of the end triangle of the first portion, and the length of which is equal to the side of a triangle of the second portion. The outer stripe is continued from the first portion and is therefore parallel to this fresh inner stripe. The designs in the 3rd and 4th portions are the same as those in the first and second respectively, but upside down. Pattern No. 3 is still more complicated, but after exactly the same style. It consists of six portions, of which the 3rd to 6th are exactly like the four portions of pattern No. 2, and in the same order; and the first and second are like the 3rd and 4th portions of pattern No. 2. The portions as before are alternately red and blue, but the latter are one inch deep instead of $\frac{7}{8}$ in. as in the last pattern.

Along each side of the cloth run 2 black lines. The ends of the red and blue threads form wide fringes at the side of the cloth, and at each end of the cloth is a long white fringe plaited into the form of Chinaman's pigtail, 12 inches long. This is a most interesting cloth.

The following cloths are all adorned with cowries, and are of particular interest on account of their uniqueness. Some hardly conform with the orthodox ideas of clothing.

(xxxvii). No. 1687. Naga lota armlet. Size 6 inches by 3 inches. This is a piece of dark blue cotton cloth fastened round a piece of bamboo at each end, with four rows of cowries on one side. Three of these rows contain large cowries very close together and the fourth, at some interval, smaller cowries not so closely packed.

(xxxviii). No. 1687. Naga lota armlet. Similar to the last but larger. Size 6 inches by 4 inches. The arrangement of the cowries is :—first 3 rows, then 4 cowries, then 5 cowries, then a fourth row.

(xxxix). No. 690. Naga lota kilt. This is a double cotton cloth, size 16 inches by 10¾ inches. It is fastened round a piece of bamboo at one end, and bound with white at the other end, which has no bamboo. Two red lines run down the centre of the cloth. At the bound end are two broadish white lines, then two patches of cowries extending over 4½ inches, then a slight gap beyond which are two more similar patches, and then 3 cross rows of cowries. From these rows to the bamboo end is plain. The patches each contain eight lengthwise rows of cowries, the number in each row varying from 17 to 19, according to the size of the cowries. On the reverse of the cloth is a looped tassel at the centre of the bamboo end.

(xl). No. 691. Naga lota kilt. Length 13 inches, width 12 inches at the bamboo end and 10½ inches at the plain end. This is similar to the last, but the patches, though consisting of 8 rows of cowries, are shorter, the first two being 2¼ inches long, 11 cowries in a row, and the second two 2½ inches long, 10 cowries in a row. The outer rows are rather longer as the cowries are larger. Beyond the last cross line of cowries and near its centre are 4 cowries fastened parallel to one another so as to form a rectangle. Down the centre and along each edge of the cloth runs a red line between two white lines.

(xli). No. 688. Naga lota kilt. Length 13 inches, width 10¼ inches, at the bamboo end, and 10¾ inches at the plain end. This is like No. xxxix, but the first patches of cowries consist of 8 rows, 2 inches long (8 in a row) and the second of 8 rows, 2¼ inches long, (8 large or 9 small in a row). There are no red lines. The bamboo end has a handle.

(xlii). No. 692. Naga lota kilt. Size 12 inches by 11½ inches. A cloth similar in pattern to No. xxxix, but the patches of cowries consist of 9 rows 2 inches long, each row containing 8 cowries. Beyond the last cross line of cowries and close to its centre are four cowries close together which radiate from a central point so as to form a star or cross. The length of the plain portion at the bamboo end is 5¼ inches. There are no red lines. To the bamboo end a handle is attached by means of string.

(xliiij). No. 689. Naga lota kilt. Similar to the last. Length 12 inches, width at bamboo end 10½ inches and at the other end 11 inches. The patches of cowries consist of 8 rows, and are only 2 inches long (8 cowries in a row). The cowries are smaller towards the centre. There is a star of four cowries as in the last cloth, and the bamboo end has a similar handle.

(xliv). No. 588. Naga woman's waistcloth. Length 4 feet 2 inches, width 1 foot 4 inches. This is a black cotton cloth made up of two narrow strips of equal width. Of these, one is quite plain, and the other has a cross row of cowries (side by side) at one end, and three rows running lengthwise for 32, 33, and 34 inches respectively. The row near the outer edge is the longest and that near the inner edge the shortest.

(xlv). No. 7283. Naga cotton cloth or keshuni. Length 3 feet 10 inches, width 1 foot 4 inches. A plain black cloth in two strips. One strip has two rows of cowries, and the other strip one row which is broken by a gap of 2 inches after 17 cowries (4½ inches). Each row is about 31 inches in length. At the cowry end is a fringe, the other end is merely bound.

(xlvi). No. 79 I.M. Naga woman's waistcloth from Lieutenant J. Gregory, Naga and Khasia Hills, Assam. Length 4 feet, width 1 foot 3 inches, in 2 equal strips. Similar to the last, but of the three rows of cowries one is 35½ inches, and the other two are 33 inches long, and at the end of each line are two cowries endwise on. Between the left and central rows are four designs, the two end ones being a star of three cowries, and the two centre ones two cowries forming an angle. Between the centre and right rows are two three-rayed stars of cowries.

The Naga cloth described below is perhaps more interesting than any of those in the Indian Museum.

(xlvii). Kacha Naga woman's breast cloth from Ledo. Price R 3. This is a white cotton cloth, measuring 4 feet 11 inches by 8¾ inches, made up of two very narrow strips of equal size. Along each side of each strip run two narrow stripes of blue. The ends of the cloth are fringed. At each end is a border about one inch deep which runs entirely across both strips.

The border at each end is followed by a length of about two feet which contains a mass of designs of different shapes and sizes on the white background. These designs are packed close together, but are arranged in rows. At one end of the cloth there are 35 such rows on each strip, and at the other end there are 33 on one strip and 35 on the other. Each row contains either four or five designs, but the distribution is irregular. The variety of these designs is really wonderful; almost every row contains at least one new design.

The remainder of each strip, *viz.*, a length of about 9¼ inches between the two end borders, is covered with a central cross stripe and five small fancy, but simple, borders on each side of it. The central stripe is three inches deep and contains a pattern of blue and claret diamonds. The borders on one side of this stripe are like those on the other, except for a slight difference in colour.

The colours of the ornamentations on one strip of the cloth are dark blue and claret throughout; those on the other are dark blue and claret or red, *viz.*, claret for the first foot at one end, then red up to the central stripe which contains both red and claret, then claret to the ninth border and beyond that red.

Khasia Fabrics.

In his " Notes on the Khasia Hills and People," 1844, Lieutenant H. Yule, R.E., gives the following interesting description of the dress of these people:—" The characteristic dress of these people is a short sleeveless shirt of thick cotton cloth, either of the natural colour unbleached, or striped partly with blue and red and always excessively dirty. It has a deep fringe below and is ornamented on the breast and back with lines of a sort of diamond pattern embroidery, from the edges of which hang certain mystic threads to the length of which they attach some superstitious importance in purchasing the garment. The shirt closely resembles one figured in Williamson's Ancient Egyptians, Volume III, page 346. Over this a few wear a short coat of cotton or broadcloth, and many wrap a large mantle striped or chequed with broad reddish lines. The latter is their most picturesque costume. Some have a strong *penchant* for articles of European dress, and their potato merchants generally bring a small invoice of these from Calcutta on their return voyage........A very large turban covers the head of the better class, others wear a greasy cap with flaps over the ears or go bareheaded........The women are generally wrapped in a shapeless mantle of striped cotton cloth, with its upper corners tied in a knot across the breast. The Khasias are utterly unacquainted with the art of weaving; nearly all the usual articles of their dress, peculiar as they are, are made for them by other tribes bordering on the Assam Valley......

The great festivities of the people are funereal—" They (the men) are all clad in the most brilliant finery that they possess or can hire, richly embroidered outer shirts of broadcloth, silken turbans and dhoties, large bangles, " etc., etc. " In the centre are the village maidens. They are swaddled in a long petticoat as light as the clothing of a mummy, with an upper garment, like a handkerchief, passing tight under the right arm and tied in a knot on the left shoulder."

The equipment of a Khyee or Khasia chief was described in 1840 by Captain Fisher as " martial and striking in appearance; a tunic of strong cloth, bordered by particolours without sleeves, well adapted to muscular exertions, sits close to his body above the waist."

In would appear that about 1879 some of the Khasias did practise weaving to some extent, as in Mr. Hunter's " Statistical Account of Assam " cotton cloth is included among the manufactures of several of the Khasia States, *e.g.*, Khyrim, Nongstain, Ram-brai and Ji-rang. At the present day, however, the Khasias apparently do not weave, at any rate not those of the Jowai sub-division, for the Sub-divisional Officer writes :—" The only tribes in the Jowai sub-division who manufacture cotton cloths for their own use, wholly or in part, are those inhabiting the northern part of the sub-division on the Nowgong borders. These are the Mikirs and the Salungs, and also a few Kukis, all of them migratory tribes. The Syntengs of Mynso and Sutuga also manufacture cotton fabrics, but on a smaller scale."

Kuki and Tipperah Fabrics.

The Kuki and Tipperah fabrics produced in Assam are of little interest, for they are generally plain and indifferently woven.

The dress of these people in their native place is thus described by Mr. Hunter who follows Captain Lewin.

Kukis.—" The only clothing worn by the men is one long homespun sheet or mantle of cotton cloth. This mantle is sometimes of very good manufacture, the best description being dyed blue and interwoven with crimson and yellow stripes. The women wear a strip of thick blue cloth round the loins, about eighteen inches in breadth."

The reason given by the Kukis for wearing such scanty clothing is that if they wear much in this world, they will be given none in the next. The Tipperahs do not share this fear and so provide themselves with a rather more ample outfit.

Tipperahs.—"Their dress is of the simplest description. Among the men a thick turban is worn, and a narrow piece of homespun cloth, with a fringed end hanging down in front and rear, passes once round the waist and between the legs. In the cold weather a rudely sewn jacket is added. The dress of the women is equally inornate. The petticoat is short, reaching a little below the knee, and made of very coarse cotton stuff of their own manufacture. It is striped in colours of red and blue. If the woman be married this petticoat will form her whole costume, but the unmarried girls cover the breast with a gaily dyed cloth with fringed ends. The women never cover their heads."

The Kukis of Assam, says Captain Dalton, "wear a turban which the more wealthy decorate with the red downy feathers of the *hathe pakee* bird and red ribbons of dyed goat's hair."

In Sylhet, according to Mr. Hunter, the Kukis "go about perfectly naked when at home, and only wear a piece of loose cloth when they leave their villages, not so much for the sake of decency as to avoid ridicule." The dress of the Kukis in Cachar is described by Mr. Ware Edgar (in 1866) as commonly consisting "of a coarse cloth tied round the waist, and hanging down in front as far as the knee. Those who have lived much in the plains, however, have adopted the *dhutt*. The women wear a cloth tied loosely round the breasts and hanging something like a tunic half way to the knee. Young women wear coloured, elderly women white cloths." These cloths are all woven by the Kukis themselves, but the most interesting article woven by them is a rug which is described in full hereafter. This rug is very similar to that made by the Miris. As already shown, its manufacture was, in Mr. Ware Edgar's time, a profitable occupation.

In the Naga Hills the Kukis seem to dress more decently. The men wear "a large cotton shawl or sheet (*chaddar*) either wrapped round the loins, or hanging down from the shoulder to the knee. The women wear a short petticoat reaching from the waist to the knee, with generally a second petticoat tied under the armpits, but this is frequently discarded for a small cotton shawl thrown loosely over the shoulders." (Hunter).

From the above it will readily be understood that the cloths of the Kukis exhibit few marked varieties. Below is given a list of those reported from different parts of the Province, to which is added a brief description of some Kuki cloths in the Indian Museum.

Kuki cloths from Cachar.

1. Paul.

A species of cloth similar to the Manipuri *khesh* (Manipur No. 4), but of a stouter make. They are generally used as wrappers for the upper part of the body, and are sized from 6 feet 9 inches to 7 feet 6 inches in length by from 3 feet to 4 feet in breadth, two pieces being stitched together sideways. They are sold, according to size and quality, at prices ranging from R 2 to R 4. They are mostly made of white thread, but some are black with or without a few narrow red stripes, and have fringes (? end borders) woven with red and yellow threads, and sometimes also green.

2. Punneh.

A species of petticoat, in texture similar to the *paul* (No. 1), but of various patterns, the prevailing colours being dark blue with red and yellow stripes, and brown with black stripes. The stripes are generally very broad. Some cloths are plain black or white with or without a few narrow red and yellow stripes. The women wear them loosely round the breasts reaching to the knee; but old women living in the hills generally wear one from the waist to the knee with a second tied under the armpits; this is however frequently discarded for *lukom* (No. 3). The size of these cloths is generally 4 feet 6 inches long by from 3 feet to 4 feet 6 inches wide; they are made up of two pieces stitched together sideways. The price varies, according to size and quality, from R 2 to R 4.

3. Lukom.

A species of cloth serving the double purpose of towel and waistcloth, not unlike the Manipuri *iru khudei* (Manipur No. 32), but of stouter make and having fringes like those of the *paul* (No. 1). They are generally 6 feet long and about 1 foot wide, and are worn by the men round the waist, hanging down in front as far as the knee. The price varies according to quality from annas 12 to R 2.

4. Paunri or pari.

A kind of rug made of lumps of raw cotton (cleaned) woven into a coarse, stout cloth and knotted tightly between the weft. The sizes range between 7 feet 6 inches by 4 feet and 9 feet by 4 feet 6 inches; the price varies, according to size and quality, from R 3 to R 7. These rugs are made up of two pieces stitched together sideways.

Specimen from Silchar. Price Rs. 5.—This is a rug measuring 7¼ feet by 4 feet, and made up of two narrow strips of almost equal size. The face has a thick nap or fleece, and the reverse has a ribbed appearance. At each end is a plain fringe about ¼ inch long, and about an inch of plain cloth (without a nap), across the centre of which runs a thick plaited line of dark blue thread. At each side the nap comes right up to the edge and extends even slightly beyond.

The backing or body of the cloth is made of coarse white cotton woven in the ordinary way except that the thread is laid double in the warp and shot double in the weft. The fleece is formed by inserting tufts of white cotton wool at regular intervals between two successive shots of the weft. These tufts are arranged in rows across the whole width of the cloth in such a way that two double warp threads pass over each tuft, and the ends of each tuft stick out above the warp. The tufts in one row do not overlap, but are all entirely separate, being divided from one another by four double warp threads. There are generally three shots of the weft between each row of tufts, but the number varies occasionally.

Kuki cloths from North Cachar.

5. Paikong.

A *dhuti.*—A white cloth about 9½ feet by 1¼ foot.

6. Lakum.

A *puggri.*—White with red embroidered ends, about 12 feet × 2 feet or less. From the name it might be thought that this cloth was the same as No. 3 from Cachar, but the descriptions do not tally.

7. Boonbam.

Body cloth, about 7 feet by 2¼ to 3 feet. Sold largely to Nagas also.

8. Shal.

Dancing cloths.—White cloths, heavy and well embroidered in red, blue and yellow and with fringes attached. Size varying from 6 feet to 10 feet by 1 foot to 2 feet.

Specimen.—A plain black closely woven cloth of medium texture measuring 8 feet 3 inches by 4 feet, and made up of two strips. At each end is a border in red with some yellow about 8¼ inches deep, the central portion is about 5 inches deep, and the pattern is very simple but distinctive; it is also very faint. This border must be very tedious in the making as the designs are formed of coloured threads woven in between shots of the weft, and each is separate from the others, though the pattern runs across the whole cloth. It contains also some cross lines of red, which of course are of one continuous thread across the strip. The seam is bound with red along the portions which cross the borders. One end of the cloth is plain, the other has a fringe about 3 inches long, twisted and knotted at the ends; between the fringe and the border is a small plaited line of blue.

9. Thangnangbara.

Specimen.—A rather coarse white cloth in one strip measuring about 9 feet 3 inches by 10¼ inches. Each end has a border and a short fringe knotted close to the cloth and twisted beyond the knots. The border at one end is 4 inches deep and that at the other 3¼ inches. Each consists of three patterned stripes, and 2 rows of very simple *phul* between broken coloured lines. The colours throughout are claret and blue, the patterned stripes are formed of threads running more or less across the cloth and woven in between the shots of weft; the small designs are formed in a similar way, but the thread of each seems to be separate. The broken lines are merely coloured threads of weft shot in the ordinary way; they are rather indistinct. There is nothing very distinctive about these borders. But for them the cloth is quite plain.

The use of this cloth is not stated. It is probably a *puggri* and may be only a variety of the *lakum* (No. 6).

10. Jangjenatuan.

Specimen.—A thick dark blue cloth in one piece measuring about 5 feet 9 inches by 13¼ inches at the centre, but the ends appear to be drawn tighter together and are only 12¼ inches wide. The body of the cloth is covered with cross patterned stripes, at irregular but short intervals, and of different sizes, varying in depth from 1¼ to 2¼ inches. The pattern on these stripes is very simple, being merely rows of diamonds. At one end is a border 8¼ inches deep, the central and main portion being 5 inches deep; beyond the border is a plaited line of dull red, then at a slight interval is a short looped fringe; the other end is similar, but the border is only 9¼ inches deep and the fringe is plain. The pattern of these borders is very simple. Both borders and stripes are formed of dull red and white threads woven in between shots of the weft; the blue background shows in all of them.

The use of this cloth is not stated.

11. Vaijete.

This is a thick and closely woven cloth, 6 feet by 2 feet 5 inches, made up of 2 strips. The body is white, but along the extreme outer edge on each side is a 2-inch stripe of dark blue, and at short intervals from it another blue stripe rather more than an inch wide but broken by two lines of white into 3 almost equal portions. Each end has a border woven in red and blue on the white background, one about 8 inches and one about 9 inches deep. There are practically no fringes. The end borders are very simple and call for no remarks. Where it crosses these borders the seam is bound with a thick plaited red cord; in the body of the cloth it is bound with blue thread. The peculiarity about this cloth is its side stripes. The outer stripes are dark blue in both warp and weft, but the blue weft does not generally extend beyond this stripe, but is turned back and interlooped with white weft which crosses the inner stripes and the body of the cloth. Some of these dark threads in the weft extend beyond the outer stripe to different distances, the longest reaching the inner edge of the inner blue stripe. A regular pattern is in this way formed by means of these dark threads, but owing to the closeness of the weaving, it is but dimly seen where the warp is white, and is quite indiscernible where the warp is blue.

The use of this cloth is not stated. The price of the 4 specimen cloths just described is Rs. 12, but the *shal* is very old and ragged.

Kuki and Mikir cloths from Jowai in the Khasia Hills.

The Kukis and Mukirs or Jowai are famed for their *juprap* shawl or *chadar*.

12. Juprap.

Chadar used by men as garments or bed sheets. Two pieces of cloth are joined together to make a sheet size 6 feet by 8 feet. Price R0-12-0 to R1-4-0.

Specimen.—A thick but rather closely woven cloth, measuring 5 feet 10 inches by 2 feet 11 inches and made up of two strips closely bound together. Plain white with no ornamentations but 3 blue lines across each end and a very simple blue border on each side. This border consists of two sets of 3 blue lines, the central one in each set being thinner than the other two. Between these two sets of lines is a white stripe ¾ inch wide divided into squares by cross lines of blue thread.

2 s

These cross lines are all formed of one continuous thread which, starting at the inner edge of the white stripe, appears double on each side of the cloth where it crosses this stripe, then passes (out of sight) across the inner set of 3 blue lines and re-appears beyond on one side of the cloth only, as a broken line running about ¼ inch into the body of the cloth, then turning back at a slight interval it returns to the inner blue line from which it started, being again invisible where it re-crosses the 3 blue lines. It then runs along this blue line (on the face of the cloth) for a short distance when another double cross line, etc., is formed as before. Running in this way the thread extends from the one end border to the other. At one end of the cloth is a short looped fringe, at the other a longer plain fringe. The price of this cloth is Re.-1-8.

13. Jusem.

Sheets or *sari* used by women (chiefly Mikirs and Lalungs) size 5 feet 3 inches by 3 feet. Price Rs. 2-8.

Specimen.—A thick and closely woven cloth (in two strips) size 5 feet 6 inches by 3 feet 1½ inch. Quite plain black with no fringes and no ornamentations except a narrow simple patterned stripe in yellow and claret running down each side and a very narrow cross stripe in claret and yellow and a single line of yellow, at each end. Price Rs. 2-8.

14. Thohnai.

A tape or kind of waist band used by women for supporting the *sari*; size 6 feet by 3 inches; price 3 annas. Used chiefly by Mikirs and Lalungs.

Tipperah Cloths from Sylhet.

15. Bingnai.

Cloth worn by Tipperah women.

Specimen.—A rather closely woven cloth, of medium texture in one piece measuring 4 feet 6 inches by 1 foot 5 inches. For about 5 inches at one side it is quite plain white, then comes a strip of the usual tint of dull red, edged with white and blue, thence to the other side the cloth is white, with blue lines running along it at irregular distances, averaging about ¼ inch. At either end are three cross lines in dull red but dimly visible. There are no designs and all the coloured lines and the broad stripe are formed in the weaving, being part of the cloth itself.

16. Bisha.

A cloth used by Tipperah women to cover their breasts.

Specimen.—A coloured cloth similar in texture to the last, measuring 4 feet 10 inches by 1 foot 1 inch. The centre of the cloth is of a faded tint of red, and the sides (2½ and 3 inches) blue. Of the red portion 1½ inch on each side is plain and the rest has lines running down it alternately blue and dirty white. The blue portions have each a stripe of faded dull red, dirty white and blue mixed running down them near the outer edges. Across each end of the cloth are several dirty white stripes, woven in on the usual back-ground, and beyond them a plaited line of the same colour which fringes out at one side. There are ten such stripes, covering 9 inches at one end, and 11 inches at the other. The fringes are short and uneven. The cloth is of very inferior workmanship and the width varies considerably; apparently no temples have been used. The weft is entirely of the reddish colour. The cloth appears to be an old one, the colours have a very washed-out appearance. It is impossible to say whether the dirty white stripes were originally coloured or not.

These two cloths are "specimens of a good class, prepared only by Tipperah people that live in the range of hills lying within British territory round the southern border of this District. These people have settled more or less permanently within the District and so the specimens possess a local interest."

Kuki cloths from Assam in the Indian Museum.

There are many Kuki cloths in the Indian Museum. Several are plain white sheets of different sizes with slight ornamentations at the ends. The wider ones are all made up of two strips joined together. All are coarse. The following are brief descriptions of some of the more characteristic or interesting specimens :—

(i) No. 2119 I.M. *Dhoti* worn by Koru Kukis. From the Chief Commissioner of Assam. A white cloth, measuring 4 feet 1 inch by 2 feet 9 inches, in two strips. It has borders of blue at the sides and thin, red borders at the ends.

(ii) No. 2118 I.M. *Dhoti* worn by the Cheeru Kukis. From the Chief Commissioner of Assam. A white cloth, measuring about 10 feet 8 inches by 1 foot 4 inches with red and blue borders.

(iii) No. 2111 I.M. *Dhoti* worn by the Korm (? Koru) Kukis. From the Chief Commissioner of Assam. A white cloth, measuring 5 feet 4 inches by 1 foot 10¼ inches, striped red with a little blue at the sides and having a deeper straggling border of brownish red and blue. One end is tasseled and the other rough.

(iv) No. 1944. *Lengti* worn by the Kukis round the loins. A perfectly plain white cloth, measuring about 9 feet 6 inches by 1 foot 10½ inches. The ends are bound. Price, R1-6.

(v) No. 1248. *Dubra* worn by the Kuki women of Assam A coloured cloth 4 feet by 1 foot 7½ inches. The warp is all of a dirty pale blue colour and the weft partly of that colour, but chiefly of dark blue. The only ornamentation consists of cross lines and stripes 3 inches deep.

(vi) No. 1963. A cloth used by the Kukis of Assam to cover the body. It is in two *short* pieces fastened together end to end and not side by side, and measures about 7 feet 4 inches by 1 foot 6 inches. The point of interest in this cloth is the variety of colouring. Each piece is made up of four coloured stripes which are divided off by bands of yellow and dull brown with light blue and white margins. There are similar bands at the outer edges of the cloth. The patches are as follows :—(1) dull red, 8 inches wide ; (2) dark blue, 3 inches ; (3) dull brown and dull red stripes, 4 inches ; (4) like (3), but 3 inches wide.

(vii) No. 1954. A breast cloth worn by the Kukis, measuring 4 feet 2 inches by 10¼ inches. It is a coarse cloth, plain white, with a 12-inch border at one end and an 11-inch border at the other. The borders, which are of the usual reddish hue, differ slightly in pattern, but all contain four cross bands, each very simple, but different from the others. The widest band at one end is 2¼ inches, and that at the other 2 inches. Beyond the bands is a plaited cross line. One end of the cloth has a slight fringe, the other has practically none.

(viii) No. 65. *Saukon.* A cotton scarf worn by the *Kaukhal* Kukis when fighting. Price 6 annas. This is a very coarse and bad woven cloth, measuring 5 feet 4 inches by 1 foot. It has cross ribs in pairs at short intervals all along the cloth. At each end is a 5½-inch border consisting of a central portion, 3 inches deep, of diamond pattern in red and blue, with filligree work on either side. The coloured threads which form the margins of this border are brought out on one side only and made into a fringe. Each end of the cloth has a very short fringe, knotted.

(ix) No. 1937. *Pagri* or turban used as a head dress by the Kukis of Assam ; woven in a hand loom by the Kaukhal Kukis in all their villages. Price, R2.

This is a coarse cloth measuring 9 feet 9 inches by 10 inches. Plain white, but with slight ornamentations at the two ends, 3 inches and 3½ inches deep respectively ; these are very poor.

(x) No. 2. A turban ornamented in front with a tuft of feathers of the holapakee bird, used by the Kukis or Thadows. Presented to the Asiatic Society of Bengal by Lieutenant Stewart of Cachar in September 1856. The tuft stands out in the front of the forehead. This is a plain white cloth measuring 9 or 10 feet by 11½ inches. The tufted end is double and has two cross bands of claret colour ; the other end has merely plain ribbed lines. The feathers are threaded on a kind of bristle and sewn on to what looks like the end cut off another turban and loosely fastened on to the end of this turban. This is formed into a roll with the bristles wrapped up in it and the feathers projecting at the top.

No. 2113 I. M. is a perfectly white turban of the usual length, and about 7½ inches wide. There are also some coloured sheets very similar to the Gaimho and Kevemho of the Nagas, but none of any special interest.

Mikir Fabrics.

The following interesting account of Mikir clothing by Mr. E. C. Baker, S. D. O. of North Cachar, is extracted from the Assam Census Report for 1891:—"The women weave the necessary wearing materials. The dress of the men is most distinctive, and consists of a jacket formed of one piece of cloth; this is doubled and sewn together down the sides, merely having large armholes; the hole for the head to pass through is then cut out, the borders being securely tied down and hemmed. This jacket is of either a red or blue colour, sometimes, though rarely, all white, but in any case it is most elaborately worked with embroidery of various colours and patterns, principally angular. In addition to this, a cloth is worn which passes between the legs, and is retained in its position by a string round the waist, the ends hanging down behind and in front. In some cases the cloth is extremely small, and in some rather voluminous. A few of the advanced Mikirs now wear *dhoties* instead of this cloth. The women dress in a long cloth fastened round the breast under the armpits, but during work they seem to generally double the cloth and merely wear it from their waist downwards." Unfortunately no Mikir cloths have been included in the list received from North Cachar, nor have any specimens been sent from that sub-division.

In his account of the Naga Hills, Mr. Hunter states that the Mikirs of that district have adopted the dress of the Khasias.

In Jowai, a sub-division of the Khasia and Jaintia Hills, the Mikirs and Kukis are classed together, and they appear to weave the same fabrics. (*cf.* Kuki cloths Nos. 12 to 14).

Among the plains districts of Assam the Mikirs are found in Nowgong and Tezpur. The following account of Mikir fabrics has been received from the Deputy Commissioner of Nowgong.

" The Mikirs can weave only a few varieties of cloth, and the cloth woven cannot be usually larger than 4 cubits by one. The cloth which the Mikir women usually weave is called *pelu*. Two pieces of *pelu* cloth stitched together make a *maku* cloth, which is used either as a bed sheet or a wrapper. Another kind of cloth they make is called *bankok*, which is 2 to 3 inches broad, and is used as a waistband by the females; their own thread being very coarse, they often purchase coloured thread in the bazar. The *mekhela* (*pini*) of a Mikir woman is made up of two pieces of *pelu* cloth stitched together and is generally made of coloured thread. The Mikirs cannot work out any flowers or other designs. They never sell cloth, but largely depend on others for their requirements. They cannot make *eri* or silk cloth and cannot mix these with cotton."

The following account comes from Tezpur:—" The Mikirs have no ornamentation for their cloths, except some red or black lines at both ends of some of them, and they cannot weave cloth broader than about half a yard. Their fabrics are called *mako kapor* by the Assamese.

" The Mikirs of the sadr sub-division have the following fabrics peculiar to their tribe:—

" 1. Rikong.

" *Rikong* is called *lengti* by the Assamese. It is a long piece of cloth put on round the waist by the Mikirs; size about 2 or 3 yards long and 8 inches broad. Price 4 annas; lasting for about three months.

" 2. Pelu.

" *Pelu* are the *chelenge* of the Assamese and used as such by the Mikirs. They consist of two sheets of cloth sewn together, such sheets measuring 4 yards by ½ yard; thus the size of a *pelu* is 4 yards by 1 yard. Price R 1 each, lasting for about four months.

" 3. Jambilee.

" *Jambilees* are bags made of pieces of cloth 1 yard by ½ yard each. Price 8 annas, lasting for about six months.

" 4. Choy.

" A *choy* is a coat made of a sheet of cloth 1½ yard long and about ½ yard broad, with long fringes at both the ends. Price R1, lasting for about six months. Used by males only.

" 5. Pilee.

" *Pilees* are small *mekhelas* put on by the Mikir females only from waist to knee joint. Four sheets of cloth, each measuring 1 yard by ½ yard are sewn together lengthwise with openings at both the ends. Price R1, lasting for about three months.

" 6. Jiso.

" This fabric resembles the *gatlowz gamcha* of the Assamese, described above" (*cf.* Assamese No. 21) " size 2½ yards by ¼ yard. It is used by females around the breast, and lasts for about three months. Price 8 annas."

" 7. Bankok.

" It is a belt used by both the sexes ; size 2 yards by 2 inches, and lasts for about four months. Price 4 annas."

It will be seen that the same cloths are made in both Nowgong and Tezpur, but there appear to be a few differences in the use of the Mikir names.

The following are some of the most interesting Mikir cloths in the Indian Museum :—

(i) No. 1688, *Lengti.* Mikir cloth from Assam, price R 1.—This is a coloured cloth, measuring 2 feet 7½ inches by 11½ inches. The weft is all brown, but does not show, the warp is blue, brown and white, the blue and brown forming stripes, and the white only lines and very narrow stripes. The ends are bound and quite plain.

(ii) No. 1669, *Langoti* (*Lengti*). A striped Mikir cloth from Assam. This cloth measures nearly 3 feet by 1 foot and is similar to the last, but the white stripes occasionally form a pattern, and at each corner of the cloth are two tassels or ropes knotted at both ends, those at one end of the cloth being 8 inches long and those at the other 9 inches.

(iii) No. 1723, Mikir *langoti* from Assam.—This is a plain white cloth measuring 9 feet by 9¼ inches, and having a 2-inch border at each end. This border is of claret colour and is quite plain, except that it is divided into four parts with white and blue lines. The cloth has fringes twisted and knotted at the ends.

N.B.—There is another cloth like this, but about 6 inches longer.

(iv) No. 1722, " Shoulder cloth, made of cotton twist, woven in the hand loom by Mikirs in all Mikir villages in Cachar, Assam."—This cloth measures about 10 feet 3 inches by 10 inches, and is just like the last, except that the border at each end is double, one part being 1½ inch deep and the other ⅜ inch. These borders are of claret colour, but have blue and white edges.

(v) No. 1715, " Blue shoulder cloth worn as a sheet hanging over the shoulder. From the Mikir Hills, Assam. Price 8 annas."—This is a rather coarse cloth, measuring 7 feet by 1 foot 7 inches. It is plain blue with two very dark blue cross bands at each end, between which are tufts of dark blue cotton.

(vii) No. ? Mikir body cloth from Assam.—A plain white cloth with claret coloured borders, very roughly made of coarse cloth, size about 8 feet by 3 feet 1½ inch, in two pieces. At each end is a cross band of claret about 1½ inch deep, followed by three thin bands, beyond which come first three lines, and then, at some interval, two more lines, all of the same colour. At each end is a false fringe.

(viii) No. 1726, " Mikir cloth with parallel stripes and broad border, green striped, from Assam."—This is a coarse cloth 5 feet 6 inches long and 1 foot 5 inches wide. The main colour is white, but there is a broad green border on each side. These borders are 4½ inches and 4½ inches wide respectively, but they are broken up by stripes of yellow, red and white ; some of the stripes are plain red or plain white, the rest are of mixed colours. The central (white) portion of the cloth has cross lines and bands of various sizes, the largest being 6 inches deep, and containing a diamond shaped pattern of blue, red and dull yellow (or amber). The rest of the bands and lines are blue and red, with an occasional touch of the same shade of yellow. One end of the cloth is bound up by the looped fringes being inter-looped (like the ropes fastening the walls of a tent) and secured at one side of the cloth. The other end has a 6-inch fringe plaited, as it were, into ropes. The cloth is of no artistic value.

(ix) No 1713, " Mikir cloth or *Mekhla* worn by the women around the waist as a covering, received from the Deputy Commissioner of Nowgong, Assam. Price R 2-14."—This is a coarse cloth, stiff and rough, with no ornamentations. measuring 4 feet 8 inches by 2 feet 1 inch. The main colour is a shade of red, but at each side is a border, about 5¼ inches wide. This border is made up as follows : Starting from the inside first comes a brown-black stripe ⅜ inch in depth, bordered on each side with white, then two very thin stripes similarly bordered, one red, one brown, then a stripe of claret rather less than ⅜ inch deep, the thin stripes are then repeated, and beyond them to the edge is brown-black. One end of the cloth is rough, the other fringed with two double white cross lines, a couple of inches from the fringe.

(x) No 1714, *Kigu*, or female waistcloth, received from the Mikir Hills, Nowgong. Price ₹ 1.—This is a coarse cloth, 4 feet long and 2 feet 5 inches wide, in two pieces, joined together. It is plain blue, the monotony being broken only by a few lengthwise stripes. The ends are bound up.

(xi) No. 1712, " *Tangali*, a cloth tied round the waist by Mikir females as a girdle to support their *mekhla* or waistcloth, from the Deputy Commissioner, Nowgong, Assam."—This band measures 5 feet by 2¾ inches and is white with blue cross stripes containing a slight design, the edges are of claret. At each end is a plain twisted fringe.

N.B.—This and No. (xii) seem to be the same as the *bankok* of Nowgong and Tezpur.

(xii) No. 1670. " Belt made of cotton twist from the Mikir Hills."—This is like the last, but the cross blue stripes are plainer. It is of coarse cotton and measures 5 feet 4 inches by 2 inches.

(xiii) No. 1716, " *Pagri* or head covering for Mikir chiefs, from Assam."—A claret coloured cloth of medium texture, striped with yellow in cross bands of three pairs each. The ends are similar to one another and have a 2-inch border containing rectangular designs, the frames being blue and the outside and inside lines yellow. This would appear to be needlework, but, the cloth being very old, it is difficult to say. Size 8 feet by 1 foot 5 inches.

(xiv) No. 1073, (?) *Jaban*, used by Mikir men as a purse, from Assam. Price 2 annas ; length 1 foot 10½ inches, width 1 foot 9 inches.—This is a square of red cloth with dim white stripes, simply doubled and sewn together at the corners only. Inside, a still coarser white cotton cloth 12½ inches long and 14 inches wide is sewn as a lining.

(This would seem to be the *jambilee* of Tezpur).

Cloths of the Lalungs and Syntengs.

The Syntengs of Sutuga are famed for sleeveless coats called *Jyngki* or *jymphong*, those of Mynso for scarves or *gamsha*.

There are no specially artistic designs for borders.

The fabrics made by the Syntengs of the Jowai Sub-division are :—

1. Jyngki or Jymphong.

A sleeveless coat, used by men and boys covering their body from shoulder to waist and having a long hanging fringe extending to the knees. Size 2¼ by 1¼, two fold ; price 5 annas to ₹ 3.

Specimen (i)—This is a ribbed cloth, 3 feet 10 inches long and 1 foot 7 inches wide. It is made of very coarse home-spun cotton, the ribs being formed by 3 weft threads of still coarser cotton, the number of ordinary threads in between the ribs being sometimes three, sometimes four. This cloth is almost entirely plain. It has two thick, red brown threads at each end, one running entirely across the cloth, and the other only a portion of the way, the thick line however being continued in white thread. Besides this, the only ornamentation consists of 3 sets of 4 lines in the body of the cloth. These lines are of the same colour, *vis*, brown-red ; they do not extend right across the cloth, but are less than 7 inches long and are almost, though not quite, equi-distant from each side. Each set is formed of one continuous thread, introduced between the shots of the weft, two lines in each being on opposite sides of one triple rib of the cloth, and these two being themselves separated by one plain white weft thread. Two of these sets of coloured lines are about 6 inches from the centre of the cloth, one on either side ; the third is about 9 inches from one end of the cloth. At this end there is a fringe nearly 6 inches long, at the other end the fringe is less than 4 inches in length ; both fringes are looped. This cloth is not sewn in any way, but is merely a plain sheet, so at first sight it is difficult to see how it can be called a coat. But between the first two sets of short coloured lines there is what at first looks like a flaw in the weaving, *vis.*, a line in which there is a gap between two threads of the warp. This line is nearly equi-distant from each side of the cloth and extends almost up to the 2 sets of coloured cross lines at either end. There is a similar flaw or line of weakness similarly situated between the third set of coloured lines and the coloured border lines at that end of the cloth. For the rest, the weaving is all uniform. These lines of weakness are evidently intended to be cut through. The first would then form an opening for the head to pass through, and the cloth would hang down over the body like a coat, with 2 coloured portions and the long fringe in front and 1 coloured portion and the short fringe behind. The object of the second hole is not clear, but from its position on the cloth, it may be presumed that it is intended to allow of the garment adapting itself to the figure of a somewhat portly gentleman.

Specimen (ii). The second is a much larger and more handsome specimen than the first. It is a thick board-like cloth, measuring 4 feet 6 inches by 1 foot 10 inches. The colour is mainly red, with lengthwise stripes of dark blue varying greatly in width, some of which have white lines running down the centre or along the sides. The weft, which is hardly visible, is entirely blue. At each end are fringes about 11 inches long and a border design consisting of a patterned stripe in white and blue edged with red and white, lying midway between two narrow and plain stripes of red and white. The threads of all 3 stripes fringe out at one side of the cloth. Near the centre of the cloth there is a slit, one foot long, which is formed by the weft being shot not right across the cloth in the usual manner, but only half way across from each side and then shot back. At one end of this slit there are three patterned stripes, the central and largest one in red, white and blue, and the other two in red and white. These stripes are 6 inches long and run across a portion of the cloth midway between the two sides. At the other end of the slit there are 5 patterned stripes alternately narrow (¾ inch) and wide (2¼ inches), in red, white and blue at intervals of about ½ inch, with one plaited line of red and blue close in front of the first, and another close behind the last stripe. These stripes are situated like those at the other end of the slit, and, like them, are 6 inches long. Altogether they cover a depth of about 10 inches. Beyond them is another slit extending to the end of the cloth, and formed like the first, with this exception, that where the end border stripes occur, the weft is continued right across the cloth, the loose portion at the centre being ½ inch long at the inner border stripe and 1 inch long at the outer. The cross-wise stripes, patterned or plain, are all woven on to the background, the length-wise stripes are all a portion of the background itself.

The price of these two *jyngki* is R1-12-0.

2. Gamsha.

A scarf used by men as a turban or a *lengti* (waistband), or for carrying children on the back. Size 7½ feet by 1 foot. Price 4 annas.

A specimen received from Jowai is a plain white cloth made of coarse and stiff cotton, with no ornamentations except three brown stripes at either end. The fringe at one end is looped and about an inch long, that at the other, plain and 4½ inches long. The size of the cloth is as stated above. The thread is very peculiar and evidently home made. Price 6 annas.

3. Munajim.

Bags or small sacks. Size 3 feet by 1 foot. Price 4 to 6 annas.

The Lalungs manufacture *chadar* and the *jyngki* or *jymphong* and *jusem* as already described (*cf.* Synteng No. 1, Kuki No. 13). They generally use no cloths but those of their own make.

Fabrics of the Kachari, Rabha, Mech, and Pani Koch tribes.

The following interesting account of the clothing of the Cacharis is extracted from Mr. B. H. Hodgson's Account of the "Koch, Bodo, [*] and Dhimal people" 1849. Of the last two tribes Mr. Hodgson writes:—"Clothes. With both people they are made at home, and by the women. The Bodo women wear silk. The Bodo men and Dhimals of both sexes wear cotton only. Woollen is unknown, even in the shape of blankets. The manufactures are durable and good and not inconveniently coarse, in fact precisely such as the people require; and the dyeing is very respectably done with their own cochineal, morinda or indigo, or with madder got from the hills, but all prepared by themselves. The female silk vest of the Bodos possessed by me is 8½ feet wide by 7 feet long, deep red with a broad worked margin of cheque pattern and of white and yellow colours, beside the groundred above and below. This garment is called *do khana* by the Bodo, and must be a very comfortable and durable dress, though it somewhat disfigures the female form by being pressed over the breast as it is wrapped round the body which it envelopes from the armpits to

---

[*] *i.e.*—Kachari.

the centre of the calves. The female garment of the Dhimals differs only in material, being cotton. It is called *bouha*. The male dress of the Bodos consists of two parts, an upper and a lower, the former is equivalent to the Hindu *chadar* or toga. It is called *shuma* and is 9 to 10 cubits by 3. The latter, styled *gamcha* and which is 6 cubits by 2, is equivalent to the Hindu *dhoti*, and after being passed between the legs is folded several times round the hips and the end simply tucked in behind. The male dress of the Dhimals is similar : its upper portion is called *pataka*, its lower *dhari*; the whole *dhaba* with this people, *hi* with the Bodo. All cotton cloths, whether male or female, are almost invariably white or undyed. Neither Bodo nor Lhimal commonly cover their heads, unless when the men choose to take off their upper vest and fold it round the head to be rid of it."

"The Rabhas and Hajongs of the Goalpara district are also branches of the Kachari race and connected with the Garos." The costume of the Rangdoniya Rabha famales is peculiar ; they are at once distinguished in the markets by their dress. The dress is a turban of dark brown cloth worn very much over the head, and as a scarf a cloth of the same colour and material folded round the bosom. The petticoat, like that of the Garo women, encircles the body below the hips, instead of round the waist, but it flows decently to the feet, while the Garo apology for a robe does not reach half down the thigh. The males of the race are not in costume distinguished from the Bengalis." (Dalton.)

"The clothing of the Pani Koch," says Mr. Hodgson, " is made by the women and is in general blue, dyed by themselves with their own indigo, the borders red, dyed with morinda. The material is cotton of their own growth, and they are better clothed than the mass of the Bengalis." Captain Dalton further tells us that "the dress of the women is put on like that of the Rabha women, but is scantier and of different colour."

Mr. Hodgson's account is nearly 50 years old, and Captain Dalton's of half that age; nowadays little is heard of the Dhimals and Pani Koches who have practically become absorbed among the Assamese. I made some enquiry about these people when stationed at Goalpara, the district in which they lived, but could find no trace of them. The only people whose clothing is of interest at the present day, therefore, are the Kachari and the Rabhas and Meches, two kindred tribes. The distinctive fabrics made by these races are described below.

Cotton fabrics of the Kacharis of Cachar.

(1) Gainthao.

A species of waistcloth or *dhuti*, similar to the Manipuri *fijong (cf.* Manipur No. 1), the manufacture of which has altogether ceased, as is the case with the *fijong.*

(2) Righu.

A species of petticoat similar in all respects to the Manipuri *fanek (cf.* Manipur No. 3), except that it is invariably made quite plain, with either green or white thread. These are sold at prices varying from R1-8 to R4 according to size and quality.

(3) Rimsao.

A species of *khesh* or *chadar*, almost similar to the Manipur *ngowbong (cf.* Manipur No. 4). These are, however, made quite plain, but rarely with green thread throughout

(4) Rihsa.

A species of towel similar in every respect to the Manipuri *iru khudei (cf.* Manipur No. 32).

Cotton fabrics of the Kacharis of North Cachar.

(5) Gaintao.

A *dhuti* or white cotton sheet about 9½ ft. × 3 ft. Evidently the same as (1).

(6) Rijubo.

A waistcloth, white, about 7½ ft. × 2½ft. [Possibly the same as (2).]

(7) Rimshao.

Sheet—a large white cotton sheet about 10 ft. × 6 ft. [The same as (3).]

(8) Gamsha.

Puggree—a white cloth, 9 ft. × 2 ft. [Probably the same as (4).]

(9) Rajampai.

(?) Body cloth. A women's blue cloth, 7½ ft. × 4½ ft.

Specimen.—Cachari woman's dancing cloth. This cloth measures 5 feet 10¼ inches by 2 feet 6 inches. It is of rather fine texture, closely woven and delightfully soft to the touch in comparison with the cloths of the Nagas, Kukis, Lalungs and Mikirs. It is not blue, but plain white with borders at one side and both ends. The side border is 2 inches wide, 1 inch being a plain stripe of dark blue with little oval flowers of red and orange (alternately) worked on the dark blue background; the other inch is divided off from the body of the cloth by a narrow stripe of dark blue, and contains a succession of besom shaped figures shooting out across it from the blue design to the stripe within. The marginal stripe is blue in both warp and weft, and the designs shooting out from it are blue in the weft only, the blue weft interloping with the white weft of the body of the cloth just as in the case of the Manipuri *moirangphi* (Manipur No. 14). The narrow inner stripe is coloured in the warp only. The borders at both ends are mainly of brown-red colour (in the weft alone). One is 3 inches deep and consists of narrow stripes and lines of different colours. On the inner edge are two such stripes of blue divided by a line of red and having lines of yellow on the edges. Then comes nearly 2 inches of plain red-brown, beyond which the blue stripes and coloured lines are repeated as before; then a narrow stripe of white, followed by a broad stripe of claret with a blue line across the centre, and lastly a yellow stripe edged on each side by one line of red and another of blue. The yellow stripe is the only one containing any designs, and these designs are very simple buds in dark-blue and red-brown. The border at the other end is larger and more elaborate. It is 5 inches deep and is made up mainly of cross stripes of black and dark-brown. These stripes are not (as at the other end) formed merely by a change of colour in the weft, but are woven in coloured thread on the ordinary background. Between these stripes there are (1) A very narrow stripe of orange weft on which a row of small flowers is woven. (2) A white background containing a row of large flowers alternately orange with red or blue centres, and blue with red centres; (3) two rows of designs shaped like bottles in light green on a background of claret weft, and lastly (4) a number of cross lines one white, two orange, and one blue and white. Beyond these stripes is a row of blue and brown flower-buds on a background of yellow just like that in the border at the other end. The cloth has no fringes, and the ends are not rough but finished off by a blue thread apparently sewn on. The body of the cloth is not of the usual nature but is very slightly ribbed by rather thicker threads being shot in pairs at slight intervals along the weft. The cloth is altogether of very superior workmanship. It is a single piece and so would appear to be made on the four-poster loom. Price Rs. 2.

Cachari cloths from the Goalpara district.

The Cacharis of the Goalpara district, and especially those living on the South Bank, are celebrated for their *gamcha*, the other cotton fabrics made by them being like those made by the plainswomen of the district, and already described among the cloths of Assam Proper. It is therefore only their *gamcha* which remain to be described. Being stationed at Goalpara for some months while preparing this monograph I had ample opportunity of seeing these *gamcha* made and worn. I took descriptions of many of the more interesting specimens. In nature the *gamcha* of the Cacharis are like those of the Assamese, but they are distinguished by the vast profusion of coloured ornamentation; the body of the cloth is also usually coloured, the more common shades being red and blue. The thread is not home-made but bought from the bazaar ready dyed in the colours required. The uses to which the *gamcha* are put are various; the Cacharis use them themselves either as waist bands in place of the *dhuti*, or as sheets like the *chadar*. Most Cacharis when at work in the house or the fields can be seen carrying a very dirty *gamcha*, often profusely ornamented, thrown loosely over one shoulder for use as a duster or for any other purpose as occasion may require, from securing a thief to drying his own hands and feet. When not likely to require it for any of these purposes the happy owner gets rid of it and at the same time adds to his stature and personal appearance by winding it round his head; it is not however in its nature suited for a puggri. The Garos living near the plains are also fond of buying up the more gaudy specimens of these *gamcha* and using them in place of their own *lengti*. Passing them once between the legs and round the waist they allow the two embroidered ends, to hang down to full view in front like an apron often extending well below the knees. The effect is most striking and is heightened by the fact that this is the only stitch of clothing worn. Thus attired, a sturdy Garo carrying his basket of cotton from the hills down to the plains for sale in the weekly market is a sight well worth seeing.

The profusion of ornamentation on these cloths will be realised from the fact that a *gamcha* seven feet long often has 3 feet at one end, and 2½ feet at the other, closely covered with patterns and designs of great variety in shape, size and colour; leaving only some 18 inches of plain white or, more usually, uniformly coloured cloth between them. The patterns and designs are almost all woven in between the weft and do not form part of the background itself.

A few characteristic *gamcha* are described below.

(i) A dark yellow cloth of medium texture, measuring 7 feet 10 inches by 1 foot 4 inches with borders and fringes at both ends. The border at one end is 11 inches deep and is made up as follows starting from the fringe—

1 inch	plain dark yellow.
	Two lines of red weft.
5 inches	rectangular pattern in blue.
	Two lines of red weft.
1½ inch	a row of five coloured designs, the last, which is different from the rest, is a white square design standing on one corner, the other four are coloured as follows :—(1) red with blue centre, (2) blue with yellow centre, (3) white with yellow centre and (4) red with blue centre.
	Two lines of blue weft.
1½ inch	diamond pattern in white.
	Two lines of blue weft.
½ inch	a row of seven designs, coloured (1) red with blue centre, (2) blue with white centre, (3) white with red centre, (4) red with white centre, (5) blue with red centre, (6) white with green centre and (7) red with green centre.
	Two lines of blue weft.
½ inch	a diamond-shaped pattern in red.
	Two lines of blue weft.
¾ inch	a row of seven designs, coloured red, white, blue, white, red, white, blue.

The border at the other end is 9¾ inches deep, and is arranged as follows; starting from the fringe :—

	5 threads of white weft.
½ inch	plain dark yellow.
	threads of white weft.
2½ inches	blue pattern of diamonds, etc.
	2 threads of white weft
1½ inch	a row of seven circular designs coloured as follows :—(1) red with blue centre, (2) blue with red centre, (3) white with blue centre, (4) red with blue centre, (5) white with red centre, (6) blue with white centre and (7) white with red centre.
	2 threads of red weft.
1½ inch	white diamond pattern.
	2 threads of red weft.
1 inch	a row of seven circular designs, coloured (1) white with blue centre, (2) blue with red centre, (3) red with white centre, (4) white with blue centre, (5) blue with red centre, (6) red with white centre and (7) white with blue centre.
	2 threads of blue weft.

Nearly 1 inch	red diamond pattern.
	2 threads of blue weft.
¾ inch	a row of seven designs of uniform colour, circular in shape but having a diamond inside and again within that a central spot; colours red, white, red, white, blue, white, blue.

(ii) A red cloth of moderately coarse texture measuring 7 feet 1 inch by 1 foot 6 inches and fringed at both ends. The borders at each end are very extensive, the one being 2′ 11½″ and the other 2′ 7″ deep, leaving only 1′ 6½″ of plain red cloth in between. The borders are made up of rows of designs alternating with patterned stripes and coloured lines. Starting from the fringed end, the arrangement of these in the deeper border is as follows:—

⅝ inch	plain red.
	Coloured lines.
1¼ inch	a row of five designs, one on one side being dark yellow and all the others yellow.
	Coloured lines.
	A wavy line of dark yellow.
4⅜ inches	a diamond pattern in yellow.
	A wavy line of dark yellow.
	Coloured lines.
1½ inch	a row of six designs, three (alternate ones) being yellow and the other three respectively blue, dark blue, and blue.
	Coloured lines.
4½ inches	an open design in dark yellow.
	Coloured lines.
2¾ inches	a row of four designs at intervals coloured, in order, blue, yellow, blue and dark yellow.
	Coloured lines.
4½ inches	a pattern in yellow, the frames being like mis-shaped diamonds.
	Coloured lines.
2½ inches	a row of four small diamond-shaped designs (*phul*) respectively blue, yellow, dark yellow and yellow.
	Coloured lines.
	A narrow dentilated stripe of blue.
8½ inches	A pretty diamond-shaped pattern in yellow.
	A narrow dentilated stripe of blue.
	Coloured lines.
	A row of six mis-shaped diamonds, coloured, in order, dark yellow, blue (with a yellow patch) yellow, dark yellow blue and yellow, the outer pairs being close together and the others far apart.
	Coloured lines.
	A thin dentilated stripe of yellow.
3 inches	a pretty diamond-shaped design in blue.
	A thin dentilated stripe of yellow.
	Coloured lines.
1¾ inch	a row of 6 pretty designs in diamond frames; these are rather far apart and coloured respectively blue, dark yellow, yellow, blue, dark yellow and blue.
	Coloured lines.
	A chain line of blue.
1½ inch	a pretty diamond-shaped pattern in yellow.
	A chain line of blue.
¾ inch	A row of seven designs alternately yellow (4) and dark yellow (3).
	Coloured lines.

The border at the other end is made up as follows, starting from the fringe:—

¾ inch	plain red.
	Coloured lines.

4 inches	Four large and pretty rosettes close together coloured, in order, yellow, blue, dark yellow and yellow.
	Coloured lines.
	An uneven line of yellow, alternately thick and thin.
3½ inches	An elaborate and pretty pattern, blue specked with yellow and dark yellow.
	An uneven line of yellow, alternately thick and thin.
	Coloured lines.
1½ inch	A row of 6 diamonds at intervals, all yellow, but the 3rd and 6th are dark, and the others comparatively light in shade.
	A wavy line of yellow.
2½ inches	An elaborate pattern, containing also rosettes, in dark yellow.
	A wavy line of yellow.
1½ inch	A row containing two small rosettes one above the other, followed by 5 diamonds far apart, the first and fourth being dark yellow and the others yellow.
	Coloured lines.
3½ inches	Elaborate diamond-shaped pattern in yellow.
	Coloured lines.
3½ inches	A row of 5 elaborate square designs, coloured, in order, dark yellow, yellow, blue, yellow and dark yellow.
	Coloured lines.
	A wavy line of dark yellow.
2½ inches	A diamond-shaped pattern in yellow.
	A wavy line of dark yellow.
1½ inch	a row of 5 oval shaped designs coloured blue, yellow, dark yellow, blue and yellow.
	A narrow dentilated stripe of blue.
1½ inch	A pretty rectangular pattern in dark yellow.
	A narrow dentilated stripe of blue.
1 inch	a row of 7 oval designs, coloured alternately dark yellow (4) and blue (3).
	Coloured lines.

(III) A white cloth measuring 7½ feet by 1 foot 3 inches. Both ends are fringed and have similar borders composed as follows, starting from the fringed end :—

A row of 6 designs alternately blue and red.

A succession of crosses (two diagonal lines crossing one another) between two straight lines. Depth nearly one inch ; colour red.

A row of 6 designs alternately red and blue.

A rectangular pattern in red and blue, 2½ inches deep.

A row of three diamonds (red, blue, red).

(IV) A yellow cloth measuring 7½ feet by 1½ foot having the side edges made of blue warp threads laid in pairs. There are fringes and borders at both ends. These borders are almost alike, and are made up as follows, starting from the fringe.

One line of red weft.

1½ inch	plain yellow.
	1 line of red and 1 of blue in the weft.
½ inch	a row of seven designs alternately red (4) and blue (3). The designs in one end border are merely hollow diamonds with a spot in the centre, those in the other are very pretty rosettes formed of lines radiating from a central oval and ending in knobs, the resulting figure being of diamond shape.

1 line of blue weft.
3 inches—a diamond pattern, red with blue at the centre of each design. This pattern is not identical in the two end borders.
1 line of blue weft.
1½ inch—a row of 4 designs alternately red with blue centre, and wholly blue.
1 line of blue weft.
1 inch—a diamond pattern in blue
1 line of blue weft.
½ inch—plain yellow.
½ inch—a rectangular pattern in red.
A row of designs alternately red and blue.

(v) A blue cloth measuring 5 feet 10 inches × 1 foot 5 inches with fringes at both ends. At one end is a border 1 ft. 2¾ in. deep made up as follows (from the fringe) :—

1½ inch—plain blue.
Two lines of red weft.
Dentilated stripe (or line) of light yellow.
(A) 3½ inches—a pattern of complicated design, dark yellow specked with red and light yellow.
White chain line.
Two threads of red weft.
(B) 2¼ inches—A row of three designs on a background of plain white, the designs are diamond frames enclosing three diamonds one above another, the colours are alternately red in yellow frames and yellow in red frames. Between these designs are dotted small and medium-sized rosettes, red, yellow and white.
Two threads of yellow weft.
White dentilated lines.
(C)2½ inches—a diamond-shaped pattern in red with white and yellow borders.
White dentilated line.
Two threads of yellow weft.
(D) 3½ inches—a row of five square designs standing on one corner, coloured alternately dark and light yellow. Above and below these designs are five light yellow rosettes.
Two threads of yellow weft.
Red dentilated line.
(E) 1½ inch—a pattern of crosses yellow with red at the centre and at the extremities of the four arms of each cross.
Red dentilated line.
Two threads of yellow weft.
At the other end is a border similar to the above but differing in size, the depth of the main portions being as follows :—A 4½ inches, B 3½ inches, C 2⅜ inches, D 1½ inch and E 1½ inch. Moreover A is dotted with specks of white and light yellow.

(vi) A blue cloth measuring 7 feet 7 inches × 1 foot 3 inches and having ¼ inch woven double at each side, the warp consisting of 7 pairs of threads alternately white (4) and red (3). Both ends have fringes. The border at one end is as follows, starting from the fringe :—

¼ inch—plain blue.
(A) { Two threads of white weft.
 { A red line dentilated on both sides.
 { Two threads of white weft.
(B) nearly 5 inches—square diamond pattern in white interspersed with red lines and dots.
(A) repeated.
(C) 2¼ inches—a row of three large diamonds with two small diamonds (one above the other) between them. The small diamonds are wholly white, and the large diamonds are alternately white interspersed with red (2) and red interspersed with white (1).
(D) { Two white lines.
 { One blue line.
 { Two white lines.
(E) nearly one inch.—A full red pattern containing rosettes, etc.
(D) repeated.
 Nearly 1 inch—a row of designs (páwl) alternately white and red with centres of the opposite colour.
 Two white lines.
 One blue line.
 Two red lines.
 ¼ inch—white diamond square pattern.
 One red line.
 Two white lines.
 ⅜ inch—a row of six designs (páwl) alternately red and white.

The border at the other end is almost the same, but there is a slight variation in the small diamonds in (C), and the depth of (B) is 4½ inches and of (E) 1½ inch.

(vii) A white cloth measuring 4 feet 2 inches × 1 foot 2 inches with a fringe at one end only. The border at the fringed end is 14½ inches deep and composed as follows :—

1½ inch—plain white.
Two blue lines.
6½ inches—main pattern in two large rectangles with filligree at the right.
Two blue lines.
2½ inches—a row of four diamonds alternately blue and yellow but all containing red also.
Two blue lines.
3½ inches—a row of five circular designs (páwl) alternately red (3) and yellow (2).

The border at the other end is of the same depth and is practically the same, but with slight variations throughout, thus :—

1¼ inch—plain white.
Two blue lines.
5¼ inch—main pattern as in the first border.
Two blue lines.
2¾ inches—a row of four circular designs (*phúl*) alternately blue and red.
Two blue lines.
3¾ inches—red diamond pattern.
Two blue lines.
1¾ inch.—A row of designs.

(viii) A white cloth measuring 7 feet 7 inches × 1 foot 2 inches with a fringe one end and a false fringe at the other. The border at the latter end is 1 foot 1 inch deep and is made up as follows :—

1¼ inch—plain white.
Two blue lines.
5¼ inch—red pattern made up of two rectangles with filligree at the left.
Two blue lines.
Two white lines.
Two thick red lines.
4¼ inches—a blue diamond pattern.
Four yellow lines.
3 inches—red pattern containing designs like 3 thick Maltese crosses one above the other.
Two yellow lines.
Three inches—a row of three diamond squares alternately blue (2) and red (1).
Two yellow lines.
2¼ inches—red diamond pattern.
Two yellow lines.
1¾ inch—a row of five designs (*phúl*) alternately red (3) and blue (2).

The border at the end with the plain fringe is 2 feet ½ inch deep and is of the same nature, *viz.*

1¼ inch—plain white.
6 inches—red pattern of 2 rectangles.
5 inches—blue diamond pattern.   ⎫
3¼ inches—red Maltese cross pattern.   ⎬ with coloured
3¼ inches—row of diamond squares as above, but having blue instead of   lines in be-
   yellow.   tween as be-
2 inches—red diamond pattern.   fore.
1¼ inch—row of 4 designs alternately red and blue. ⎭

(ix) A red cloth fringed at both ends and measuring 6 feet × 1 foot 1 inch. The border at one end (1 foot 9¼ inches in depth) is made up thus :—

½ inch—plain red.
(A) ⎰ Two white lines.
    ⎱ Two red   ,,
    ⎱ Two white ,,
1¼ inch—4 yellow diamond squares far apart.

(A) repeated.
Blue dentilated line (teeth upwards).
4 inches—main pattern in two rectangles with filligree at both ends, yellow and blue.
Blue dentilated line (teeth downwards).
Two yellow lines.
3¼ inches—a row of 3 yellow square designs.
Two blue lines.
Two red   ,,
Two blue ,,
Three red ,,
4 inch—yellow diamond pattern.
Two blue lines.
Two red   ,,
Two blue ,,
1¼ inch—a row of 3 oval yellow designs far apart.

(A) repeated.
Blue dentilated line (teeth upwards).
2½ inches—pretty yellow pattern with rosettes.
Blue dentilated line (teeth downwards).

(A) repeated.
2½ inches—a row of three yellow trees far apart.
Two white lines.
Three red   ,,
Two white ,,

The border at the other end is 1 foot 11½ inches deep, and is made up as follows :—

¼ inch—plain.
1 inch—a row of four oval-shaped designs.
4-inch—main diamond pattern yellow and blue.
3½ inch—3 large yellow diamond squares.
3¼ inch—3 diamond squares rather different from those in the last line.
Blue dentilated line.
3 inch—yellow pattern, pretty.
2¾ inch—a row of designs.
with lines in between as in the border at the other end.

The above descriptions are sufficient to give a general idea of the nature of the ornamentation on the Cachari *gamcha* of the present day. The characteristic features are *two, viz.*, 1st, the minute sub-division of the borders with the consequent rapid changes from point to point; and 2ndly, the wonderful variety resulting from a judicious combination of few materials. In other cloths the borders, even when made up of several parts, are almost invariably centralized; there is one main stripe which overshadows all the others and to which they are merely subsidiary. In the *gamcha* just described this is not the case, some of the stripes, and some of the designs are larger and more brilliant than the rest, but all are small and insignificant in comparison with the size and brilliancy of the entire border. Then, again, the designs and stripes all bear a strong similarity to one another in their general form, and the colours used are ordinarily none but red, blue, yellow (of different shades) and white with an occasional green, but the way in which these stripes and designs are intermixed, and the changes rung on the different colours relieves the border of any suspicion of monotony and teaches a striking lesson in permutations and combinations.

Four specimens of Cachari *gamcha* were purchased by me at Darrangiri in Goalpara. Of these, three call for no special notice, but the fourth, for which I gave the comparatively high price of R2-8, is larger than usual and more embellished. This cloth is red, it measures 8 feet 3 inches × 1 foot 6 inches, and has borders respectively 2 feet 9 inches and 3 feet 4 inches deep. The borders are marked by an unusual variety of colouring, by the absence of any rows of rosettes or similar designs and by the existence at the inner end of each border of a row of elephants, and, above it, a row of men driving camels with the reins and a pankha in one hand and an umbrella in the other. It is not usual to find natural objects depicted in Cachari *gamcha*. No. (IX) above described contains, it is true, a row of trees, but the representations are hardly natural.

The Cachari cloths from other districts resemble those of Goalpara.

The Rabha cloths of the present day call for no special remark being like those made by their neighbours. The following description of a Rabha *gamcha* is given not because it exhibits any peculiarities of its own, but rather to show its likness to Assamese *gamcha*. This *gamcha* was seen by me at Krishnai in Goalpara. A blue cloth measuring 6 feet × 1½ foot made of country thread of ordinary texture. Price 8 annas. The border at one end consists of a diamond-patterned stripe in white, 2½ inches deep, with a row of five rosettes beyond, alternately yellow (3) and white (2); beyond these rosettes are 3 double white stripes. The border at the other end is made up in a similar way, but the patterned stripe is only 1¾ inch deep and of a slightly different pattern, and the number of rosettes in the row beyond is only 4; they are coloured white, white, red and white.

Of the Mech cloths now made one only is sufficiently distinctive to be described, namely, the *patani* or cotton cloth worn by the Mech women as a petticoat. These, like Cachari *gamcha*, are distinguished by their variety of colour. None are plain ; they are either checks or else adorned with patterned stripes which run the whole length of the cloth. These stripes extend either over the whole width of the cloth or else to a considerable distance from each side, leaving in between them a comparatively narrow panel plain or striped. The favourite colours for the background are red or red and blue mixed. The effect of this mixture is to make the cloth appear purple when seen from a distance. The favourite colours for the patterns worked on this background are white and yellow. A description of four of these *patani* is given below.

(i) *Pachrangi patani.*—A cloth woven by a Mech woman and brought by her husband for sale at the Chapaguri hat in Goalpara District. Price R4. Worn only by women as a petticoat. It measures 8 feet × 4 feet and is made of imported thread of medium thickness. There are short fringes at each end, but no borders except a very narrow stripe made up of 2 blue, 4 yellow and 2 blue, lines in the weft ; except for this the weft is entirely red. There are, however, very wide borders on each side of the cloth and extending the whole length. These

two borders and the plainer portion in between them are of almost
equal width. This plain portion is divided into 11 main stripes alternately red (6) and blue (5).* The stripes vary in width, but the red
are much wider than the blue. Down the centre of the four interior
red stripes runs a very narrow stripe of yellow edged with blue, the two
outer red stripes having instead a rather wider central stripe of blue,
yellow and red. The two side borders contain each five patterned
stripes alternately white on blue background (3), and yellow on red
background (2); between each of these patterned stripes and outside the
last one are plain stripes alternately red (3), and blue (2). Further,
between the plain and patterned stripes are very narrow stripes made up
of lines of red, white and blue, or red, yellow and blue. The pattern on
the stripes is rectangular and very simple. Of the patterned stripes the
inside white one is one inch wide and the rest 2 inches, the plain stripes
vary in width from $\frac{1}{4}$ to $1\frac{1}{4}$ inch and the parti-coloured stripes from
$\frac{1}{4}$ to $\frac{3}{4}$ inch.

(ii) *Pachrangi kapor* of *dinga-dinga* pattern from the Sadr Sub-division of
Goalpara. Price R4-8.

A cloth measuring 7 feet 9 inches × 4 feet and much resembling the last;
the borders at the sides are, however, much wider, and so are the
patterned stripes in these borders. On the contrary the plain and
parti-coloured stripes are much narrower. The designs in the pattern are
squares containing diagonal rows of small diamond square frames
each having a similar but smaller frame within it. The designs are
divided from one another by bars (cross stripes) and lines. The central
portion between the two side borders is a single red stripe $7\frac{1}{2}$ inches
broad with one very narrow blue and white stripe near one edge and two
near the other. In this cloth, as in the last, the weft is of red throughout,
except for a few threads near either end. The fringe at one end is much
longer, and that at the other shorter than in the last cloth.

(iii) *Pachrangi kapor* from the Sadr Sub-division of Goalpara. Price R4.
This measures 7 feet 9 inches × 4 feet 3 inches, and its peculiar feature
is that the patterned stripes extend continuously across the cloth, there
being no plain central portion at all. The patterned stripes are rather
more than 2 inches wide, and are alternately white on blue and yellow
on red as before. The pattern consists of squares containing concentric
diamonds with lines parallel to the sides to fill up the corners. The
intervening plain stripes are also alternately blue and red, and are about
$\frac{1}{2}$ inch wide except those between the two outer patterned stripes on
each side, these being about 1 inch wide. The fringes are both short,
and the weft entirely red, except for a few threads at each end.

(iv) *Patani kapor* of *dinga-dinga* pattern. From the Sadr Sub-division of
Goalpara. Price R2-8.
This cloth measures about 8 feet × 4 feet; it contains no patterned
stripes at all but is a simple check of red and blue which alternate in
both warp and weft, and so, form squares about $\frac{3}{8}$ inch in size. This
check forms the body of the cloth, but there is a border about 13 inches
wide on each side. In these borders the weft is as in the body of the
cloth but the warp consists of parti-coloured stripes of red, white and
blue (in lines) divided from each other by plain stripes alternately red
and blue. These stripes all vary in width, but the average width of the
parti-coloured stripes is 1 inch and of the plain stripes $\frac{3}{8}$ inch. At the
ends are no borders, but only a line made up of two blue threads
between two white ones in the weft. One fringe is about double the
length of the other, which is very short.

These four cloths are very characteristic of the fabrics now made by the Meches,
and they exhibit very clearly the principal varieties among them. The doubt as
to the exact meaning of the terms *patani* and *pachrangi* has already been referred to
in the description of the Assamese cloths. Of the three Mech cloths from Dhubri, the
patani is quite distinct from the *pachrangi*, but these latter appear to be called
patani also, and the cloth from Goalpara, which is almost exactly like the *pachrangi*
from Dhubri, was called *pachrangi patani* by the husband of the woman who wove
it. This would go to show that *pachrangi* as used by the Meches signifies a cloth

---

* That is, in the warp, for the weft is entirely red.

with this particular arrangement of coloured stripes. The word literally means " of 5 colours," and this epithet is not altogether inapplicable to the two cloths abovenamed. The word *patani* would appear to be applied generally to cloths used by women as waistcloths instead of the petticoat (*mekhela*).

Garo Fabrics.

The clothing of the Garos is distinguished chiefly by its scantiness, and has, on that account, frequently attracted attention. The earliest reference to it seems to be one by Robinson, who in his " Descriptive Account of Assam," 1841, says :— " The Garos, men, women and children, go literally naked. A narrow girdle about the middle constitutes the whole of their dress. The women's dress, like that of the men, consists merely of a small girdle seldom more than a foot wide of a very coarse striped cotton cloth, all the other parts of the body are left exposed." Capt. Reynolds, in 1849, alludes briefly to the clothing of the Garos in practically the same terms, and adds that the women's girdle encircles the waist and reaches only half way down the thighs. Describing the Garos in 1872 Capt. Dalton says he was struck with the " pretty, plump, nude figures of the girls. Their sole garment is a piece of cloth less than a foot in breath that just meets round the loins, and in order that it may not restrain the limbs, it is only fastened where it meets under the hip at the upper corners." Capt. Dalton also relates that many of the Syntea Garos may be seen unadorned, by which he probably means naked. " The head gear is arbitrary; some appear with turbans, some without, and some wear round their heads a single band of coloured cotton. The Garo males, on the whole, become their nudity better than the females. Their sole garment is a long and narrow strip of cloth, which is worn as a girdle round the waist, and, passing from behind between the legs, is brought up again to the waist from which the end as a flap about six inches in breadth and often highly ornamented, hangs down in front."

Mr. Hunter, in his " Statistical Account of Assam," 1879, says that the Garo chiefs (or *laskar*) of Goalpara wear a somewhat more elaborate costume than other Garos and a turban as well. He describes at some length the costume of the ordinary Garos in their own Hills :—" The hair of the head is worn long and is never cut, but either tied up in a knot or kept off the face by a piece of cloth or *pagri* worn round the head and called by the Garos *kotip*. Their dress, if such it can be called, is of the simplest description, and consists, for the males, merely of a band of home-spun cloth about a yard and a half in length, which is passed round the waist and between the legs, and then tied at the back. Although small, the cloth is dexterous-ly worn, and serves all the purposes of decency. It is called *ganda bara* and is as-sumed at an early age. The dress of the women is somewhat more extensive, but still very scanty, and consists of a cloth tied round the waist called *rikung*. No-thing is usually worn over the bosom. Both men and women carry a small blanket or overall, made from ordinary cloth for the more well-to-do, and from the bark of a tree for the poorer classes. The Garos of the Eastern Hills resemble the Khasias in their dress. Many of them wear the small fringed jacket which is the Khasias' ordi-nary dress. The women dress much the same all over the hills."

In 1885 an anonymous writer, under the pseudonym of Esme contributed a very interesting article upon " The Garos, their customs and mythology " to the *Calcutta Review*. This writer describes the loin cloth of the Garos as five inches wide, and after explaining the way in which it is tied, she says :—" This cloth is of native manu-facture, and is generally red and dark blue, and the frontpiece that forms the apron is frequently ornamented with rows of white beads. .... Many of the men wore a small piece of cloth wrapped round their heads. .... If they " (the women) " have an abundance of ornaments, they have very little else to boast of. Their cloth-ing consists of a strip of dark red and blue cloth, about a foot wide and long enough to reach round the loins ; a sort of diminutive petticoat that they fasten below the hip-bone on the left side. Those who had babies, and I noticed there were very few who had not, had them slung in a cloth across their shoulders, so arranged that they could sling them round from the back to the front at pleasure, and with as little concern as if they were bundles of cotton." The writer then goes on to notice the extent to which cheap imported fabrics of gaudy patterns are supplanting the aboriginal costume. This taste for the glaring and trashy fabrics of the West is unfortunately growing day by day.

A specimen of each cloth made by the Garos at the present day has been sent by the Deputy Commissioner of the Garo Hills together with a most interesting descriptive note, which is reproduced below.

1.—RIKUNG.

" The *rikung* or women's petticoat is worn round the hips, the upper edge only is fastened, the rest is open, permitting an extensive display of leg. The price of the cloth varies from 6 to 12 annas, according to the pattern. A bead and shell ornament is often added which may cost up to R40.

Above the *rikung* round the waist is often tied a belt of white beads called *senki*. The effect is rather pretty. A *senki* costs from R3 to R15."

Specimens.—

(i) A cloth measuring 2 feet 11 inches × 12¼ inches, and like the *ganda* made of Garo thread, but not so closely woven. Price 8 annas. The weft is entirely reddish brown, but it hardly shows; the warp is mainly blue, but is striped with four plain reddish brown stripes and with six-lined stripes of reddish brown, white and blue; of the plain stripes the two outer ones are wide and the other two narrow. The two outer varicoloured stripes on each side form the borders of a simple patterned stripe of white on a background of blue; the two central ones are wider and farther apart, but between them lies another patterned stripe (similar in design to the first but not identical), which is bordered by plain lines of reddish brown. The centre of all these six stripes is a broken line of white. The extreme edges of the weft on either side are white. There are practically no fringes, but at one end the loose threads are cut off short and tied in bunches with a knotted white cord running across the cloth. At the other end the threads appear to be plaited and then sewn firmly on the cloth.

(ii) A cloth very similar to the last, but an inch narrower and about two inches longer. It is made of imported thread which is softer and rather finer than the Garo thread used in the last cloth. The weft is of blue instead of red, and the warp is blue striped with red. There are four such stripes each rather over ¼ an inch in width, and down the centre of the cloth, instead of a fifth red stripe, run two lines or rather very narrow stripes of red ⅜ inch apart, and between these on a background of blue a dotted line of white. The blue stripes are much wider than the red, but down their centre runs a broken line of white between two red and white lines. The red in this cloth is of the ordinary bright shade found in imported threads, it is very different from the dull reddish brown of the Garos. The peculiar feature of this cloth, however, is the beads. Along the side of the cloth runs a row of beads, these beads are of the same size as those on the *ganda*, and are fastened in a similar way, but they are threaded in pairs, end to end, instead of singly, and stand out, not from the face of the cloth, but from the edges, so as to have the effect of adding to the width of the cloth. At each end a similar row of beads, but single instead of double, runs across about 7½ inches, the short fringes here being doubled down on to the cloth; the other side of the cloth and the remaining four inches of the ends have no beads. In each of these rows besides the beads forming the rows themselves, there are two additional beads of about half the length, threaded one at each end of the upper cord to which the larger beads are secured. On the face of the cloth are no beads of this nature, but each side of the two central narrow stripes of red has a row of very small white beads at intervals from one another, running along the outside. The price of this cloth is R3.

(iii) A Garo *mekheli* from Gaolpara. Size 3 feet 3 inches × 1 foot 4 inches. Price 8 annas. This is a cloth which I saw woven by a Garo woman at Bhandara in the Goalpara sub-division. The weaver called it a *mekheli* (a corruption, no doubt of the Assamese *mekhela*), but it is the same as a *rikung*. The cloth is blue with red and white, all the thread being imported. There is a border along one side of the cloth, consisting of a narrow stripe of red between two lines of white, and a broken stripe of white on a background of blue edged with red and white. This border is followed by a broad stripe of blue (5½ inches wide), then come two patterned stripes of white on blue divided from one another by a plain red stripe; the patterned stripes are edged with red and white, and the plain stripe with blue; they are respectively about 1 inch and ¼ inch wide. Beyond these stripes comes another broad stripe of blue (5½ inches wide) which reaches to within ¼ inch of the other side of the cloth. This stripe, however, is not plain, but contains 15 lines of red at varying distances apart, the distances increasing towards the centre of the cloth. This broad stripe is followed by a very narrow stripe of red edged with white, beyond which the cloth is plain blue to the side. The weft is blue throughout, and the weaving being loose at the centre of the cloth and comparatively close at the sides, the central stripe of red shows an almost equal amount of blue, but the narrow red stripes at the edges show practically none. The two ends of the cloth have short fringes and two pairs of white lines running across at a slight interval.

A *senki* has been received from the Deputy Commissioner of the Garo Hills. It consists of 12 strings of beads like those on the *gonda*, but of only half the length; these strings of beads are formed into a belt by being passed through flat pieces of cane about ⅛ an inch wide. There are four such pieces, two at the ends rather over three inches long, and two at the middle 3½ inches long. Between the two central pieces are four yellow glass beads on each string. Beyond the two outer pieces one bead is threaded on each string, and then the cords holding the beads are tied and twisted together in pairs. The whole length of the belt so formed is about 2 feet 5 inches. The price is R12. It is, as the Deputy Commissioner says, the only pretty thing worn by the Garos.

2.—SALSAK.

"The *salsak*, or woman's headdress, is worn tied round the head, often in the form of a cap. The price varies from 4 annas to a rupee. Beads are sometimes threaded into the strings at each end, but not sewn into the cloth like the *rikung*."

Specimen—

A cloth measuring about 3 feet × 8½ inches, made of imported thread. Price R1. The weft is of brown, but does not show, as the weaving is very close; it is much thicker than the warp, and so gives the cloth a sort of ribbed appearance. The warp is mainly blue; down the centre runs a stripe of white and red lines dividing the cloth into two symmetrical strips, each of which contains a central patterned stripe of white, with a touch of red, on the blue background, also two minor stripes of plain red, one narrow stripe of red, white and blue (towards the outside) and one red and white line (towards the inside). At the extreme edge of each side of the cloth is a single pair of white threads in the weft. The ends of this cloth are like those of the *rikung* (No. 1). The four corners of the cloth have cords of cotton twisted and knotted at the extremities. At one end of the cloth both corners have two blue cords, but those at the one corner are nearly 5 inches long, those at the other being only slightly over three. At the corresponding corners at the other end of the cloth are one white cord (8¼ inches long), and 2 cords (1 white, 7 inches; 1 blue, 3 inches), respectively. These cords are probably required for fastening the puggry.

3.—GANDA.

"The *ganda* or man's loin cloth is tied round the waist, and the end is passed between the legs and brought over the part round the waist, a foot or so hanging down the front. This flap is often ornamented with rows of beads. The price is about 4 annas. The beads are called *rippok*, and appear to be made of some shell or other. They are not locally produced but are imported from Bengal."

Specimen—

A cloth measuring 7 feet 1 inch × 4 inches, closely woven of rather coarse Garo thread. Price 6 annas. The weft, which does not appear, is entirely reddish brown. The warp is mainly blue but has two stripes of reddish brown towards the outer edges, and has two lines of red near the centre, which is a broken line of white. At one end are four rows of beads sewn on across the cloth. The rows are about an inch apart and contain respectively 15, 15, 16 and 17 beads, the last row being at the end of the cloth. The beads, which are ⅜ inch long and fairly thick, are as close together as possible, and stand out from the cloth on end; they are sewn to it by a thread which, starting from the back of the cloth, is threaded through the bead, passed over a piece of string at the top, and then again threaded through the bead and through the cloth. The string at the top passes over all the beads of the row and is knotted at both ends.

4.—KADASIL.

"The *kadasil* is a narrow fillet of cloth with a row of beads (*rippok*) down each border, worn over the forehead and tied at the back of the head much in the same fashion as the ancients wore wreaths. Nobody who had not taken a head could wear one. Now-a-days they are rarely, if ever made, and I have never seen a man wearing one. They are rather rare."

The Deputy Commissioner sent a specimen which he had procured with some difficulty. This specimen is indeed a curiosity. It consists of a narrow band of cloth, about 4 feet 6 inch × 1 inch, which is double and sewn together at the side and ends. On this band, in a central position, are sewn 15 plates of brass, each studded with two rows of three bosses. These plates are rather more than an inch long, and, being fastened close together side of side, cover nearly 14 inches of the band. To each end of the band is fastened a row of single beads. These beads extend over that portion of the band that has the brass plates and about ¼ an inch beyond at one end; being fastened like those of the *rikung* (No. 1), they increase the width of the band at this place to about 1¾ inch. This central portion of the band is finished off by a thin hollow tube at each end through which the band is threaded sideways, a portion of the tube being cut out on each side with this object. The outer cord fastening the beads, after passing along the row on one side, is threaded through the hollow of the tube at one end, and then runs along the row of beads on the other side, and is finally threaded through a single bead before being knotted at the extremity.

This band would form a very handsome ornament for the warrior's head, and would afford him some protection against a downward cut from a *dao* or similar weapon. The price of this band is R5.

"Of these four cloths the first two are worn only by women and girls, and the last two only by men and boys. Beside these no other cloths are made by Garos from cotton. Shirts, sleeveless coats, paggaries, etc., are all imported from the plains, or from the Khasias. The only other home made article is :—

"5.—DOKKABA.

"A small bag used for carrying odds and ends. It is called *dokkara* or *jolung a* and its price is about 6 annas to a rupee."

A specimen received from the Garo Hills is 10¼ inches deep and 9 inches wide. It is made of a single piece of cloth about four times this length, and of about the same width. This cloth is doubled over, and then again doubled over and sewn together at each side. The bag thus made has really two pockets, but probably only the central one is intended for use. A band of white cloth nearly 1 inch wide and 8 feet long is sewn on to form a handle. The cloth of which this bag is made is very pretty. The background is plain white with a thin stripe of red between two similar stripes of blue near each edge. But on this background are woven red and blue cross stripes extending over one half of the cloth, *viz.*, that half which forms the outside of the bag; the other half, forming the inside or lining, is quite plain. The decorated part consists of 5 broad bands each 2 inches deep, and rather more than an inch apart. At each end are three narrow bands at slight intervals, and between each broad band are two similar narrow bands. The broad bands are alternately blue edged with red, and red edged with blue and are so woven that the white warp threads of the background appear in diagonal lines running 4 one way then 4 another and so on across the cloth, the intervening space between each set being filled up by three white lines, in opposite directions meeting one another and forming three v's one within another. The narrow bands are all alike, *viz.*, one red line between two blues, and are so woven that the white warp lines cross them not diagonally but straight, appearing singly on the blue portion, and in pairs on the red. The coloured threads are woven in several strands, and so form broad and thick lines. The ends of the cloth, as might be expected, have practically no fringes, the rough ends of the thread being tied in bunches by means of a red and white twisted cord running across the cloth and knotted round each bunch. The whole forms a very serviceable and pretty bag, not dear at the price, one rupee.

This completes the list of Garo cloths with the exception of Garo *lengti* and *phali* referred to in the report from Dhubri, but these are not described and are said to be the same as the *yanda* and *rikung,* respectively.

Miri Fabrics.

The Miris of the hills are said to be altogether ignorant of the art of weaving. As may be expected, then, cotton fabrics do not constitute a very material portion of their clothing, which will be seen from the following description written by Capt. Dalton after a visit to the Hills near the Soobansiri in 1845 :—

"The costume of the women is peculiar, a sort of petticoat extending from the loins to the knees is secured to a broad belt of leather, which is ornamented with brass bosses ; besides this they wear round their middles an infinite number of rings made of filaments of bamboo embroidered with the fibres of another plant. A band of similar material, from which a bit of cloth is suspended in front, is suspended tightly round the breasts under the arms. This is their travelling and working dress; but at other times they wrap themselves in a large cloth doubled, brought over the shoulders and pinned in front like a shawl.

"The males also wear a profusion of blue beads. Their costume is simple enough, a band round their hips composed of rings of bamboo, the same as worn by the women, but not so numerous, an apron attached thereto, before and behind, and a cloth wrapped round their body and pinned so as to resemble a shirt without sleeves, a cap of cane or bamboo work, with turned up peak, which however is worn behind; and over their shoulders as a cloak, which also serves as a pouch or knapsack, they throw a covering made of the black hairy fibres of a plant, which at a little distance resembles a bearskin."

Even these few cloths are not made by the Miris themselves, but are imported, and Mr. Hunter states that the women are often seen with nothing but the canework, cloth being altogether dispensed with.

The Miris of the plains, however, have learnt to weave. "The women weave their own petticoats of coarse cotton in stripes of gray colours wrought with dyes obtained, as they say, from the Khamptis. Another article of domestic manufacture is the Miri rug (Jim) made of cotton ticking on a backing of thick cloth." (Census report, 1881). For their petticoats they use the four-poster loom, and the Assamese process ; for the rug, which is by far the most interesting thing they make, they use the beny or primitive weaving sticks; the process of manufacture of this rug has been already explained in detail. When at Golaghat I visited a Miri village and there saw the women weaving ; they were using only the four-poster loom, but that in nearly every house, and they were making, not only petticoats, but also gamcha, for their own use, and not for their husbands. I purchased some specimen cloths and a description of these and of the rug is included in the list below. No other specimens have been received, and the Miri cloths reported from Tezpur and Jorhat appear to be of the same nature as those from Golaghat.

1.—CHURIA.

The Miris of Jorhat are said occasionally to make and wear a churia like the phaloi of the Noras and Turrungs (Cf. Nora No. 1).

2.—MEKHELA.

The Miris of Jorhat and Golaghat make mekhela of two kinds, the first very like the Assamese mekhela, and usually white with a small coloured border at one end, the second more like the patani but smaller; it is a plain sheet, and not a made-up garment, and is usually coloured. The two kinds will be fully understood from the general description and the description of particular specimens given below, the former being from Jorhat and the latter from Golaghat.

(i) Egie.

"The plain mekhela of the Assamese does not find much favour with the Miri women, who appear to be fond of coloured raiments. They therefore prepare check-ed cloths of various patterns with European yarn of different colours, and the plain mekhelas made by them have at least the lower end ornamented with coloured thread. This variety of mekhela is called by the Miris egie, the form and size of which are the same as the Assamese mekhela, but the price is higher, viz., from 12 annas to R1-8-0, owing to the employment of coloured yarn, which is more expensive than yarn of natural colour."

(Specimen)—

This is a small mekhela measuring 3 feet 2 inches in length and 5 feet 4 inches in circumference, being made up of two pieces each 3 feet

2 inches × 2 feet 8 inches or rather longer, allowing for the join at the sides and the hems at the top and bottom. The hem at the bottom end is ¾ inch and that at the top only ¼ inch deep. This garment is made of rather coarse imported white yarn, loosely woven and is quite plain, except for a ¼ inch border at the, bottom end just above the hem. This border is very simple, consisting of rosettes in blue and red on a background of yellow. The rosettes occur in triplets, at intervals of about 3 inches. There are six such triplets on each piece of the cloth and they consist alternately of one blue between two red, and one red between two blue. Each rosette has a bar on each side of it of the same colour as itself. I paid R2 for this *mekhela*, but the correct price, I subsequently learnt, was 8 to 10 annas which about represents its value.

(ii) *Mategape*.

" The Miri women make another variety of waistcloth for their own use which they call *mategape*. The thread is of red and blue colour obtained from the Khamptis of Lakhimpur at R2 to R3 per seer. The *mategape* is not sewn as the Assamese *mekhela* but is merely a sheet about 5 feet long and 3 feet broad, made up of two narrow pieces stitched together at the edges. This cloth is of a beautiful red colour with blue stripes lengthwise, and a few cross stripes in blue and white. This kind of garment is worn by adjusting it round the waist, or above the breast, the free end of the cloth being in front. Its use is confined to the women of the richer class, who wear it on high days and festivals. Its price is between Rs. 3 and 4."

The specimen described below does not correspond to the above description, but it is of the same shape and used in the same way, so it may be included under this head. It is a much less elaborate cloth than the above, and is used by all classes and is not the monopoly of the rich.

Specimen—

This is a cloth measuring 4 feet 4 inches × 2 feet 4 inches, made of rather coarse cotton thread, which looks as if it were home-spun, but the woman from whom I purchased it said it was imported. It is at once marked as being made on the *beng* by the nature of the weaving, and by the fact that it is in two narrow strips. The weaving is close, so that the weft, which is of dark blue, does not show. The two strips are alike. The outer edge is dark blue; then comes, first a stripe of brown ¼ inch wide edged on each side with a line of white, next a stripe, 6 inches wide, in which the warp threads are alternately dark blue and brown, and lastly a succession of 6 brown and 5 blue stripes alternating with one another to the inner edge of the strip, which is plain blue. These brown stripes are, like the first, plain brown edged with white, the first of them is nearly ¼ inch wide, the next three about ⅜ inch, and the last two about ₁⅟₆ inch; the blue stripes are broken with brown lines, the first three being about 1½ inch wide, the fourth 1 inch wide, and the fifth, which is between the two narrow brown stripes, of the same width as those stripes. There are no fringes, the loose ends of the threads being cut fairly close at one end and tied in bunches by a knotted white thread, and very close at the other end, which is sewn up by a similar thread of eight strands. The only ornamentation on this cloth is a row of eight stars of 6 rays, alternately red and white, between two cross lines of red and white, but these lines appear only on the reverse of the cloth, and the designs appear on that side, not as stars but as a confused mass of thread like an X in shape. The row of stars runs across only one strip of the cloth, and is situated about midway between the two ends of that strip. For this cloth I paid R2, the true price being annas 12 or R1.

3.—RIHA.

As in the case of the *mekhela*, so in that of the *riha* there are two distinct varieties, woven by the Miris of Jorhat.

(i) *Rie*.

This variety is of the same size as the Assamese *riha*, but is distinguished by coloured stripes in either weft or warp or both. It sometimes has, and sometimes has not, fringes and broad ornamental borders at the ends. It is worn about the waist and breast with the *egie*, being wound several times round the breasts, and having the end tucked in between. The price is 12 annas to R1-8.

(ii) *Beebie.*

This is about 6 feet by 2½ feet, and is worn about the breast with the *mategape*, and is, like the *rie*, striped with different colours. Price 12 annas to R1-8.

From Golaghat a cloth called *methani* is reported, measuring 9 feet × 3 feet, and worn by Miri women wound round the breast. Price 8 annas to R1. This is probably the same as the cloth described below, which is the only kind of *riha* I saw in Golaghat. It will be noticed, however, that the dimensions do not exactly correspond. The cloth described below was called a *gamocha* by the women from whom I bought it, but it is evidently a *riha*, though it is difficult to say to which of the two classes of *riha* found in Jorhat it corresponds. I saw it being worn by Miris with both kinds of *mekhala* indiscriminately.

Specimen.—

A carefully woven cloth of medium fine texture measuring 10 feet 6 inches × 1 foot 7½ inches. The weft is entirely of red, the warp is of red, yellow and white. From one side a width of about 8¼ inches is red and yellow with white lines about ¼ inch apart, then comes a width of about 5½ inches of white with red and yellow lines similarly situated, then an inch in which the red and yellow and white lines alternate in pairs, then 1½ inch plain red, after which the cloth has very narrow stripes alternately white and red and yellow. The red and yellow are so nearly of the same shade, that it is rather difficult to distinguish between them, the yellow thread, which does not always accompany the red, is, however, rather thicker than the red or white. The narrow stripes vary in width at places. The loose threads at each end are cut off rather short, but are twisted together and knotted. Every alternate cord so formed has a bunch of several coloured threads tied at the end to form a tassel, the colours being red, white, blue, yellow and green variously combined. At each end is a border woven across the cloth in green thread on the ordinary background. The main portion of this border, which is of a simple diamond pattern, lies between two narrow fancy stripes on each side, the inner one being white and the outer green. Beyond this border, on the far side from the fringe, is a row of small designs in the shape of diamonds and fancy X's alternately. The colours of these, yellow, green, white, and dark blue, are irregularly distributed. This is a very nice cloth and by no means gaudy; it forms an excellent cummerbund or sash, for tennis, and I have seen it being used for this purpose. The price is about R1.

4.—MIRIJIM OR PARI.

This is a rug peculiar to the Miris, who make it whenever they are settled. Curiously enough it is called by a slightly different name in each of the places from which it is reported. In Sadiya it is called a *pari*, in North Lakhimpur *jimkapor*, in Dibrugarh *mirijin*, in Sibsagar *jin* cloth or *tulapari*, in Golaghat *mirijin*, in Tezpur *mirijhim*, and in Jorhat *gabor*, but here the name *mirijin* is also used.

This rug which is made by a special process, already fully described, very much resembles the Kuki *pari* (Kuki No. 4), the main difference being that the backing is much rougher and appears stronger, and the thread is very thick, and woven single instead of being comparatively fine and woven double; the fleece, too, is made not of tufts of cotton, but of rolls which overlap one another. The Kuki rug is, on the whole, superior to the Miri rug, it is much more downy in the fleece, and probably warmer, but not so durable.

Three specimens have been received, one from Dibrugarh, one from Sadiya and one from North Lakhimpur. They are very similar in appearance but differ considerably in size. That from North Lakhimpur is in one piece, 7 feet 9 inches × 2 feet 5 inches. Price R8. Those from Dibrugarh and Sadiya are both in two pieces sewn together; they measure respectively 8 feet 4 inches × 4 feet 4 inches and 7 feet 4 inches × 5 feet 4 inches. Price R7-8 and R12. The rolls of cotton vary considerably in thickness in each rug, but they are on the average thickest in the specimen from North Lakhimpur, and thinnest in that from Dibrugarh. Each roll passes under two warp threads, then over two and then under the next two, about an inch sticking out at either end. The second pair of threads under which one roll passes is the first pair under which the next roll passes, so that the rolls overlap one another. The fleece reaches to each edge of the rug, but does not protrude far if at all beyond. It does not quite reach either end of the rug. In all these rugs the backing is quite plain and is woven of very coarse homespun thread much coarser than any imported from Europe; that in the rug from North Lakhimpur is particularly coarse. From the method in which the fleece is woven into the backing, this backing appears ridged on the reverse. No colours are used in any part of these rugs and no ornamentations except a fringe at one or both ends.

These rugs are used to put on the bed, or as carpets. In Golaghat they are said to be used as a winter dress, and the S. D. C. of Tezpur says, that in some places, but not in Tezpur, coats for winter use are sometimes made out of them. In North Lakhimpur there are two sizes of rugs made by the Chutia Miris, the one measuring 12 feet × 3¼ feet, price R10, the other measuring 9 feet × 3 feet, price R8. Both are comparatively fine and are called *mihi* to distinguish them from those made by the Abors, which are called *mota*. The specimen received is of the smaller size. In Dibrugarh these rugs are made to order in various sizes, the price being sometimes as high as R20. In Jorhat the price varies from R3 to R10.

There is a cotton cloth from Upper Assam, described in Watson's "Textile Fabrics" (page 132) as "No. IX 434. Sleeping rug with looped pile of bleached cotton. The rug from which the samples have been cut was formed of two pieces sewn together. Length 2 yds. 8 in., width 1 yd. 24 inches, weight 6℔s. 2oz." It is probably a *Mirijim.*

PHACHU OR TALATPARA KAPOR.

The Miris of Jorhat sometimes make bedsheets like those of the Noras (of Nora No. 3).

MONA OR JOLONGA.

This is a bag made by the Miris and Morans of Jorhat out of a rough piece of cloth 2 feet × 1 foot, doubled over and sewn up at the sides. It is hung over the shoulder by means of a rope, specially made for the purpose, or by a strip of cloth about 6 inches wide, the ends of which are sewn on to the edge of the purse. To make this kind of *mona* the *set kapah*, *i.e.*, the dark variety of cotton is generally used. Price 4 annas to 6 annas."

6.—Abor Fabrics.

When making a survey of Assam and the neighbouring countries in 1825-8, Lieutenant Wilcox noticed the costume of the Abors. He found the chief article of clothing to consist of a waist cloth of bark, and the rest to be of wool. "Almost every man had some article of woollen dress, varying from a rudely made blanket waistcoat to a comfortable and tolerably well-shaped cloak. One of these, of a figured pattern, was made with sleeves; it was said to come from the country of the Bor Abors; the texture was good, though coarse, as was that of a red cloak worn by the chief of the village." Speaking of the Abors of Membu, Lieutenant Wilcox says:—"The purpose of the primary article of their clothing (which consists of a triangular piece of coarse cloth 6 inches long and 4 or 5 broad at the end, by which it is suspended to a string tied round the loins) is vitiated every time they sit down, but of this they seem perfectly careless. All the more wealthy Abors have cloaks of Thibetan woollens." The material out of which the triangular piece of cloth is made is not stated, but in all probability it is cotton, and it is not improbable that the blanket waistcoats above referred to were not really of wool, but of cotton, and that the woollen cloaks were imported from Thibet. That the use of cotton has been long known to the Abors is shown by the following account written by Captain Dalton after his visit to Membu in 1855 :—"For savages the adult females are decently clad. Their dress consists of two cloths, generally tinted green and red, manufactured by themselves from cotton grown in their own farms. One round the loins forms a petticoat just reaching to the knees; it is retained in position by neat girdles of cane-work; the other is folded round the bosom, but this is often dispensed with, and the exposure of the person above the waist is evidently considered no indelicacy. In regard to male costume the smallest particle of covering is all that is considered necessary for purposes of decency, but when full dressed an Abor is a very imposing figure. Coloured coats, without sleeves, of cotton of their own manufacture or of the manufacture of their neighbours, the Chulikatas, are commonly worn. Some wear long coloured Thibetan cloaks with loose sleeves of woollen cloth obtained from Thibet, and they make themselves warm jackets of, and use as wrappers and blankets, white cotton cloths of their own manufacture, with a long fleecy nap."

The cloth with the fleecy nap is evidently the *jimkapor*. The Abors of North Lakhimpur at the present day make two sizes of this *jimkapor*, *vis.*, one 12 feet × 3½ feet, price R7; and one 9 feet × 3 feet, price R5. They are coarser than the Miri rugs, and are consequently cheaper. In Dibrugarh, too, the Abors make this *jim*, but it is not so strong as that of the Miris. They also weave a kind of cotton cloth in blue and red stripes, called *Mako kapor*, of which the women's clothes are made.

Mishmi Fabrics.

About the cotton fabrics made by the Mishmis at the present day no fresh information has been received, and so it will serve no useful purpose to describe at length the cloths made by them in the past. Wilcox (1825—28), Griffiths (1836), Rowlatt (1845) and Cooper (1873) have all recorded their personal experiences of the Mishmis and their clothing. The cloths they wear are inferior, but they are of their own manufacture and of cotton. The men's dress consists of two parts (1) a very scanty loin cloth passing between the legs and fastened in front, and (2) a coat of blue and red or brown striped cotton cloth which, from the description, appears in shape to resemble very closely the Lalung *jyngki*; it is, however, sewn together at the sides, armholes being left, and is, according to Cooper, worn open in front. It reaches from neck to knee. The women's dress similarly consists of (1) a sleeved jacket or bodice, buttoning in front, barely covering the breasts and reaching half way to the waist, and (2) a tight fitting plaited cotton skirt reaching from waist to knee. The chiefs wear long woollen cloaks from Thibet, and, when at home, a red strip of muslin round the head. Their wives wear petticoats brought from the plains.

The Chulikata Mishmis are comparatively skilful in weaving, they are noted as probably the first people of Assam to learn the use of the rhea fibre, and other nettles for weaving purposes. The jackets of the women are often tastefully embroidered and are generally worn open, exposing an ample bust.

Singpho Fabrics.

The Singphos appeared on the Assam frontier for the first time about a century ago, but little information is available about the clothing of those who have settled in Assam. In 1836 a brief allusion to it was made by Dr. Griffiths, who noticed that the men's clothing resembled that of the Burmese, but the women's was more distinctive and consisted chiefly of a kind of gown. The clothing worn by the Singphos in their native land has been fully described by Captain Hannay in his "Sketch of the Singphos or the Kakhyens of Burmah," 1847. The men wear a scanty nether garment or a chequered patso and a jacket made either of dark blue cotton or of a stout yellow-coloured cloth made from a cotton of the same colour produced on their hills. They have also a substantial cloth or plaid, of a picturesque brown and red pattern, or a piece of coarse dark blue or red broadcloth. Some of the Singphos living near China wear a jacket and short drawers of a dark colour. Of the women the poorer classes wear a *tomien* or open petticoat of cotton stuff, sometimes in checks, sometimes in broad bands of Indian red and deep blue; this, their sole garment, is fastened round the waist, leaving the breasts usually bare. The better class of women dress like the Shans, but retain their own peculiar dark colours. Even when Capt. Hannay wrote, however, this dress was giving way to long cloth and fine *chadar* of Bengal muslin. The Singpho women of the Hukong valley, both married and single, wear white muslin turbans.

The cloth woven by the Singphos is of coarse but strong texture. The cotton is produced by themselves, and spun by their women, and dyed by them before being woven. The dyes used have been described by Mr. Duncan in his monograph on "Dyes and Dyeing in Assam."

No specimens of Singpho cloths have been received, but the Deputy Commissioner of Lakhimpur says that coloured and chequered cloth is still woven by the Singphos for making jackets.

Two of the Singpho cloths in the Indian Museum may be noticed :—

    (I) No. 7621.—A Singpho *dhuti* from Sadiya. Length 24 feet, width nearly 1 foot 7 inches, in one long strip doubled in two and sewn together at the ends and sides. The colour is mainly green with red, white and yellow forming a check. Some of the green threads in the warp are of darker shade than the rest.

(II) No. 7624.—A Singpho *chadar* from Sadiya. Length 14 feet, width 3 feet 10 inches, in two strips. The cloth is white with blue and brown lines forming a check, one end has a fringe, the other only the rough ends of the thread.

Daffla Fabrics.

Though backward in most arts, the Dafflas weave the cotton cloths they wear. Their ordinary dress consists of " a short, sleeveless shirt of thick cotton cloth, some-times of the natural colour, but more frequently striped gaily with blue and red and always excessively dirty. Over this is thrown a mantle of cotton or woollen cloth fas-tened about the throat and shoulders by means of pins made of bamboo. The women are generally wrapped in a shapeless mantle of striped or plain cotton cloth, with its upper part tucked in tightly over the breast, and enveloping the body from the armpits to the centre of the calves ; another cloth is also thrown over the shoulders, answering the purpose of a cloak, the upper corners of which are tied into a knot sufficiently low to expose the throat, which is invariably cased in a profusion of bead necklaces of all varieties of colour."

This description was written by Mr. Robinson in 1851. No more recent information can be found. The following cloth is to be seen in the Indian Museum :—

No. 2657.—A cloth worn by the Daffla women. This is a coarse cotton cloth measuring 4 feet. ×1 foot 7 inches in four strips. It is striped length-wise with stripes of red-brown, white and dark blue, and thin stripes of black. Down the central seam runs a red-brown line, and at inter-vals along this line triangular spots of blue occur in pairs. One of the white stripes near the edge has a very crude pattern. The ends of the cloth are plain and bound up, but there is a bushy tassel on each strip of the cloth.

Nora and Turung Fabrics.

The Noras and Turungs form a small community living in the Jorhat sub-divi-sion, and the following descriptions of cloths made by them at the present day are all derived from the report and the cloths themselves received from Jorhat. No other information is available regarding the fabrics woven by these people.

(1) Phaloi.

A variety of *churia* (man's waistcloth) with numerous stripes of different coloured threads both lengthwise and across. It is but rarely woven at the present day. Price between R2 and 4.

Specimen—This is a striped cloth of moderately fine thread measuring 12 feet 8 inches × 2 feet 11 inches. The stripes all run lengthwise, being formed in the warp. They are of red, yellow, dark blue, and light blue alternating in irregular order. They vary in thickness, but, except at the edges where they are narrower, average ⅜ in. in width. The weft is entirely dark blue, and as it shows through the warp it affects the colours of the stripes. The ends have a false fringe and a very short true fringe, but no other ornamentations except three narrow cross stripes, 2 red and 1 yellow at one end, and 2 yellow and 1 red at the other ; they vary slightly in depth. The thread is apparently home made and home dyed. Price not mentioned.

(2) Chinn.

A Nora woman's petticoat, the same as the Assamese *mekhela* with this exception that at a distance of about an inch from the hem at the lower end, another band of the same kind of cloth, and of the same breadth as the hem, is fastened on all round the garment. This sort of *mekhela* is invariably dyed blue or black. Price R1-8.

Specimen—A black, *mekhela*, 3 feet 6 inches long and 5 feet 6 inches in circumference, made up of three pieces of cloth. Two of the pieces are about 3 feet 5 inches long × 2 feet 9 in. wide, and are sewn together at the sides ; the top and bottom are hemmed, the hems being about 1 inch deep. The third piece is about 5 feet 6 inches long and 6 inches wide. This is turned down at each side (in opposite directions) and hemmed, the hems being about 1 inch deep. The ends being sewn together, this piece forms a narrow band of the same circumference as the petticoat formed by the first two pieces. This band is sown on to the bottom of that petticoat, so that the hem on one side of the band overlaps that round the bottom of the petticoat. The cloth is of rather fine texture and dyed black.

(3) PHACHU OR TALAT-PARA KAPOR.

Bedsheets of different sizes are made of home-spun or European yarn with coloured stripes, which, however, are not as numerous as those in the *phaloi*. They are generally made on the *sam* loom in narrow pieces which are stitched together at the edges. Price 4 annas to R1.

(4) THUNG.

A bag. This is made by the Noras of a piece of cloth, about 2 feet long and 1 foot wide, which is folded in two and sewn together at the edges. It is hung on the shoulder by means of a cotton rope specially made for the purpose, the ends of which are sewn on to the edges of the bag. Price 4 annas to 6 annas.

Specimen—A bag about 14½ inches deep and 12½ inches wide made in the manner explained above. The cloth is woven by the special process already described in detail. The warp is of white thread and the weft of black, except for nearly 3 inches at each end where it is white. Two lines of dirty yellow nearly ¼ an inch apart run across the cloth at each end on the black portion near its juncture with the white. The ends of the cloth are rolled round and then sewn. The handle is made of a thick plaited cotton rope, about 3 feet long, which is sewn along each edge of the bag, leaving a portion of about 1 foot 9 inches long to form the handle. The thread is fine but woven double so that the texture of the cloth is rather coarse.

A small square of cloth has been received from Jorhat as a specimen of Nora and Turung cloth dyeing. The colour, dark blue, is good but rather patchy.

Khampti Fabrics.

The Khampti women are good weavers and skilled in embroidery, but this skill they display chiefly in the manufacture of an elaborate bag for their husbands. The clothing of both men and women is plain and neat. It is thus described by Captain Dalton:—"The men commonly wear tight fitting jackets of cotton-cloth, dyed blue, with a white muslin turban, so twisted as to leave exposed the top knot into which their long hair is twisted, projecting somewhat over the forehead. The nether garment is of coloured cotton of a chequered pattern, or of silk, more or less ample according to the rank of the wearer. The upper classes wear the Burmese *patso*, a piece of parti-coloured silk." The women "wear the hair drawn up from the back and sides in one massive roll which rises 4 or 5 inches so much in front as to form a continuation of the frontal bone. The roll is encircled by an embroidered band, the fringed and tasselled ends of which hang down behind. Their lower garment, generally of dark coloured cotton cloth, is folded over the breasts under the arms and reaches to the feet. This style of wearing the principal garment, common to the Shans and Manipuris, appears to have been introduced into Assam by the former, as the Assamese women of the lower classes have all adopted it, but the Khampti women wear in addition a coloured silk scarf round the waist and a long-sleeved jacket."

A very similar description was given by Mr. Cooper in 1873 :—"The costume of both men and women is extremely picturesque. That of the women, who are good-looking, is very becoming. A loose fitting jacket of white silk or cotton, with long full sleeves, and buttoned down the chest, covers the upper part of their body to the waist; a piece of striped silk or cotton cloth fastened round the waist falls like classic drapery to the ankles, displaying the outlines of their well-shaped limbs ; while their skirt-like garment, having a kind of open fold in front, occasionally affords a glimpse of a rounded limb of the most perfect symmetry. The costume of the men consists of a close-fitting jacket of white cotton with tight long sleeves rolled up over the waists and buttoned down the chest. A piece of checked cotton cloth secured round the waist, and several yards in length, is looped up between the legs, giving somewhat the appearance of Turks' trousers, while a very white strip of cloth is twisted and tied round the head in the shape of a puggaree, with the ends sticking up over the forehead, the hair being twisted into a knot on the top of the head ".

At the present day the Khamptis of North Lakhimpur make *mekhela* and *mona.* The *mekhela* is a cloth, from 9 to 10½ feet long by 3 to 3¾ feet wide, used as a waist cloth or petticoat by the women. It is dyed black by the Khamptis themselves, and is quite plain, but for occasional designs (*phul*) at the ends. A specimen received from North Lakhimpur measures only 7 feet 4 inches by 2 feet 7 inches. It is perfectly plain black and of medium texture. Price R1-8.

The *mona* is a bag used for carrying betelnut ; it measures 1½ foot by 1 foot. There are two kinds now made in North Lakhimpur ; one plain, with designs at the mouth price 4 annas, and the other of black and white check, price 8 annas. No specimen has been received from North Lakhimpur, but a very handsome Khampti bag, costing R10, has been received from Dibrugarh. This bag is 12 inches deep and 10 inches wide. It is made up of two pieces of cloth, one forming the outside and the other the lining. The former is about 2 feet 3 inches by 10 inches, and the latter about 1 foot 10 inches by 10 inches. Both pieces are doubled in two, and then about an inch and a half at each end of the larger piece is again doubled over, and the ends of this cloth sewn on to the corresponding ends of the lining. The two edges of both cloths are then sewn on to a rope which forms the handle. This rope is very thick and is plaited of red, white, green and dark blue cotton thread of many strands ; it is about 4 feet 3 inches long, and, the two ends being sewn along the edges of the bag, the central portion forms a handle about 2 feet 3 inches in length.

At the bottom corners of the bag this rope is bound round with white thread, and the ends form enormous bushy tassels.

The outer cloth is of muga silk, and, except for a depth of about 1¼ inch at either end, is entirely covered with exceedingly rich and handsome embroidery. At one end the narrow strip is entirely plain, but at the other there is a coloured stripe made by substituting yellow cotton for muga thread in the weft.

The pattern of this embroidered portion is made up as follows :—Starting from either end, first come four patterned stripes in which the pattern is worked in coloured silk. Each of these stripes is bordered on both sides by cross lines of coloured cotton. The stripes vary in size but cover altogether a depth of 3 inches. The patterns on these stripes are exquisite and the colouring is perfect. Next come four cross stripes of plain maroon worked in cotton with a thin patterned band between the two inner stripes, and still thinner parti-coloured bands between the others, the colours in these bands being green, maroon and yellow. These stripes are almost equal in depth, and between them cover 3½ inches.

These stripes at either end enclose between them the central figure of the embroidery, *viz.*, a large square mosaic of hexagonal designs. This figure is in light green silk, and is bordered on the sides by 3 stripes of different widths and very different patterns, and at the ends by narrow patterned stripes.

The designs in this silk embroidery are distinctly classical, the colouring is at once brilliant, varied and harmonious ; every colour of the rainbow and many intermediate shades are found in the brightest tints. The whole effect is truly dazzling, such as can be produced by nothing but the perfect combination of skill and art.

The lining is of cotton cloth, one half of which is plain white and the other striped with equal stripes of white and brown ¾ of an inch deep, the colour being in the weft alone.

No other cotton fabrics in Assam are so tastefully and richly embroidered as this Khampti bag, but this bag itself is hardly a cotton fabric, for the outer covering is of muga silk, and the embroidery of pure silk, and it is only the lining and the plainest portions of the outer covering that are of cotton.

In the Indian Museum can be seen a very fine specimen of this bag and many other cotton fabrics of the Khamptis. The bag needs no separate description, but a few of the other fabrics may be briefly noticed :—

(i) No. 1755.—*Phanovy dhuti.*—A cloth of moderately fine texture, measuring 26 feet by 1 foot 7 inches, folded in two and sewn together at the sides. The colours are blue, yellow, pink and white, forming a large check.

(ii) A Khampti cloth from the Shillong Museum, like the last in texture and similarly sewn. It measures 23 feet 4 inches by 1 foot 7 inches, and the colours are light green, rose, dark-blue and white, forming a large check. The white is also found in stripes, and the dark-blue in thicker stripes.

(iii) A Khampti *dhuti* having a check of light green and white only.— At each end is a cross yellow border, and at about one foot from each end two narrow yellow lines. In other respects it is like the last but one foot longer.

(iv) A Khampti cloth from the Shillong Museum of moderately fine texture, and measuring about 23 feet by 1 foot 5 inches. The colours, which form a small check, are green, yellow, red and white. It is sewn together at the sides.

(v) A Khampti cloth from the Shillong Museum, measuring 22 feet by 1 foot 6 inches sewn together at the sides and ends. The colours, which form a check, are yellow, purple, green, dark-blue and white. The texture is like that of the last cloth.

(vi) No. 1754.—A Khampti *dhuti* worn by men.—This cloth is 24 feet 8 inches in length, and is coloured dark-blue with light-green stripes in warp and weft forming a plaid. The texture is rather thick.

(vii) A Khampti cloth, evidently a puggary, measuring 10 feet 8 inches by 1 foot ¼ inch. This is a pretty cloth, but not a check, the warp being entirely dark-blue, the weft is composed of rose, light-green, yellow, dark-blue and white. There is a short fringe at each end. The texture is moderately fine.

Fabrics of other Shan Tribes of Assam.

I.—*Pakhial Fabrics.*

The Phakials or Phake are a branch of the Shan or Tae nation which is characterised as a lively, merry people, fond of dress, especially the women. This branch of the Shans is conspicuous above others of the nation in Assam for their coarse cotton manufactures, and for their skill in dyeing both in the piece, and in the thread. The methods and materials employed by them in dyeing have been explained by Mr. Duncan. "The dress of the women", writes Captain Hannay, " is after the style of the Eastern Shans, and consists of a kind of loose jacket, very short-waisted and common to all the nation in Assam. The Phake, however, in their knowledge of the art of weaving and dyeing are perhaps the most characteristic of the whole in dress. The Khamptis appear to keep to one colour, the blue, whilst the Phake assume the dark check, which appears peculiar to the whole race, and has also extended to the nations of the entire Eastern Archipelago."

(ii) *The Khamjangs.*

" As an agricultural people, they are superior to the Phake or any of the frontier inhabitants. They do not, however, excel in the art of weaving or dyeing, and manufacture but little beyond the cloths in use among themselves, coarse white cotton garments are more common with them than the coloured habiliments of the other Shans."

(iii) *The Itongs.*

"In their dress they have generally adopted the white of the Assamese, although the fashion of their garments is Shan."

Bhutia Fabrics.

It is only the coarser cotton cloths worn by the Bhutias that are woven in the country, and the manufacture of these appears to be confined to the villages near the plains; the quality is poor. "Their dress," says Captain Dalton, "is a loose woollen coat reaching to the knees, bound round the waist by a thick fold of cotton cloth." The full front of the coat is used as a pocket or general receptacle for everything from a betel nut to a putrid fish. As the bare skin forms one side of this pocket, the arrangement is not of the nicest. These woollen cloaks are for winter use, the material used in the summer being a coarse cotton. The belts used by the chiefs from which the *dao* is suspended are embroidered and have a rich appearance. The dress of the women is described by Captain Dalton as a long cloak with loose sleeves, and by Captain Pemberton as a loose garment, very similar to that worn by the Hill tribes to the eastward of Assam. The material of which this garment is composed is not stated.

The priests were found by Dr. Griffiths to be the best clothed of all the Bhutias. Their dress consisted of a sombre jacket with no sleeves, with either a yellow or red silk back ; over this a sombre scarf.

Captain Pemberton considered the Bhutias inferior to the naked Nagas, and Captain Dalton remarked that the Bhutia women appeared to take less care in adorning themselves than any other Hill lasses he had met, their clothes being dirty, clumsily made and awkwardly put on.

Other Tribes.

The above account includes most of the Hill tribes residing in or bordering on Assam. The cotton fabrics of the few that remain appear to possess no peculiar interest, for little information is available concerning them. One tribe, perhaps, deserves notice, *viz.*, the Lamas, who live in the plains beyond the Mishmi country. These people, Captain Neufville says, are described as being clothed something after the European fashion, in trousers and quilted jackets; and Lieutenant Rowlatt, who visited the village of Tuppang in 1844, says that they were dressed in a loose robe that falls in folds around the waist.

H. F. SAMMAN.

APPENDIX I.

Jail Manufactures.

Some of the convicts in Assam jails are employed in weaving, and the fabrics they produce, though not of much artistic value, are, at any rate, distinct from most others made within the Province.

Owing to the scarcity of labour in Assam it was, until quite recently, the policy of Government to employ convicts as far as possible on extramural work. Hence weaving like other industries has never held an important place among the employments to which the prisoners are put. Moreover, to make it at all profitable, weaving requires some skill on the part of the workman, and so this form of labour is of necessity restricted to two classes of prisoners, viz., those that know the art on entering prison, and those whose terms of imprisonment are sufficiently long to allow of their having time to learn the art and practice it. Female convicts appear never to have been largely, if at all, employed in weaving, and the professional weavers of the Surma Valley are not a criminal class. Hence the cotton industry in the jails of Assam has been almost exclusively confined to the three central jails of Gauhati and Tezpur in the Assam Valley and Sylhet in the Surma Valley. When Dibrugarh was a first class jail the long-term prisoners were often employed in weaving jangis and dusters, but this manufacture ceased with the reduction of the jail to a subsidiary jail in 1879. In the Sibsagar jail a few cloths were woven by the prisoners in 1894 and 1895, but no other subsidiary jail appears to have tried weaving.

From a statistical account of the District of Sylhet it appears that, as far back as 1867, the prisoners made a few cotton fabrics, for the following are mentioned :—

Colored table cloths 6 feet by 5 feet, price R5. Bathing towels, price R9 per dozen. Table napkins, dusters, etc., price R3 per dozen.

The following is a brief sketch of the weaving industry in the jails of Assam compiled from recent administration reports together with a note on the present state of that industry in the three central jails.

In 1880 Captain Williamson was deputed to study the working of Bengal jails, but he recognised the impossibility of introducing into the jails of Assam any of the manufactures then being carried on in Buxar, Bhagalpur and Alipur. As regards weaving, he considered that the manufacture of satringis and good carpets might perhaps be introduced as a remunerative and light form of labour when the demand for extramural labour should have slackened, but that, in the matter of jail and police clothing and blankets, it would be impossible to compete with the steam power looms of the Bengal jails.

Accordingly, for the next ten years, weaving was not encouraged in the jails of Assam, though the Gauhati jail did turn out a few cloths for use by the prisoners confined there, and in some of the subsidiary jails and look-ups of the Assam Valley. In 1881 the average daily number of prisoners employed on weaving in Gauhati was only 21, in 1882 it fell to 13, and in 1883 to less than 10. In 1882 cloth weaving was included among the minor industries carried on in the Sylhet jail, and in 1883 nearly the whole of the receipts from weaving were from the jail at Tezpur. It was in this year, 1883, that receipts from different industries were first shown separately in the annual returns. Henceforward the receipts from weaving, though fluctuating largely, diminished from R580 (in 1885) to R199 in 1891, the lion's share always coming from Tezpur, and the small balance entirely from Gauhati and Sylhet. From 1891, however, these receipts rose by leaps and bounds, till in 1895 the comparatively large amount of R2,748 was realised. In Gauhati the industry still takes an insignificant place, but in Sylhet it has rapidly developed and become far more important than anywhere else, the receipts from Sylhet in 1895 being nearly double those from Tezpur. In 1894 weaving was started on a very small scale in the Sibsagar subsidiary jail, but it did not prove a success, and has had to be abandoned.

The following table shows the rapid development of the cotton weaving industry from 1891 to 1895. The figures for 1885 are also given for sake of comparison over a period of ten years. It may be noted that these figures show the gross receipts only and not the profits.

Receipts from cloth weaving in Assam jails.

Year.	Sylhet.			Tezpur.			Gauhati.			Sibsagar.			Total.		
	R	a.	p.	R	a.	p.	R	a.	p.	R	a.	p.	R	a.	p.
1885 .	26	14	6	359	12	3	32	9	0	......			419	3	9
1891 .	17	6	3	152	10	8	29	5	0	......			199	5	11
1892 .	63	2	3	421	5	6	35	15	0	......			520	6	9
1893 .	139	5	6	520	6	0	26	0	0	......			685	11	6
1894 .	1,164	2	6	390	12	6	83	12	9	3	6	0	1,642	1	9
1895 .	1,730	11	6	972	10	4	44	7	6	1	2	0	2,748	15	4

.The cause of this rapid increase is an attempt to produce police and choukidari uniforms in the central jails. Such a proposal had been abandoned as impracticable in 1880, and it is therefore not surprising to find that twelve years later, when the conditions in Assam were practically the same and progress had been made in Bengal, the effort did not prove very successful. In reviewing the result of the experiment in 1894, the Inspector General of Jails remarked :—" So long as we can find remunerative outdoor labour, the result does not matter, but it would be different if we had to find more work inside our jails." That necessity has now arisen, for in 1896 extramural labour in all but the smallest jails was almost absolutely prohibited. It will be very interesting therefore to watch the progress of the industry in future years. That weaving by the handloom can ever prove a success financially can hardly be expected, but there is no reason, on that account, why it should not continue to hold an important place among jail industries, as it is eminently adapted to convict labour ; it forms an excellent occupation, the work is capable of exact measurement, and any scamping is impossible without immediate detection.

In 1890 the Chief Commissioner was of opinion that a move should be made in the direction of adapting jail industries to the requirements of the consuming departments of Government. Accordingly, in 1891 the Inspector General intended to introduce into two of the central jails the weaving of khaki for the Assam Police, but exceptional circumstances prevented any new industry from being started that year. The project, being approved by the Chief Commissioner, was carried into effect the following year. The results of that year's work are thus stated by the Inspector General of Jails :—" Since, my last report I have endeavoured to introduce the weaving of khaki cloth. I have not succeeded in Tezpur, but in the Gauhati jail I have met with more success. The texture has to be improved before the cloth can be used for the Military Police. I have had more success, however, in turning out blue jumpers and *dhotis* and red puggris for the Civil and Armed Civil Police. Sample suits have been made at both Tezpur and Gauhati, and at both stations committees composed of the Deputy Commissioner, the Superintendent of the Jail and the District Superintendent of Police have examined the articles. The reports are favourable regarding the cloth, but the blue colouring is considered inferior. This will have to be improved. Six suits of clothing manufactured at each of the two jails will be issued to policemen, and further reports made in due course. The jails are able to turn out this clothing cheaper than similar articles now supplied by the contractors. I have every hope that, with careful supervision, the experiment will be successful, and that the industry, when fully developed, will be beneficial to both the police and the jails."

These hopes, however, were not to be realised. In 1893 the manufacture of clothing for the Civil Police was confined to the Tezpur jail, but the results were not altogether satisfactory. " We made and issued during the year the following :—

	Number made.	Actual cost.			Number issued.	Sale price.			Profit.		
		R	a.	p.		R	a.	p.	R	a.	p.
Red puggris . .	397	483	13	6	397	496	4	0	12	6	6
Blue jumpers . .	8	10	8	0	8	11	0	0	0	8	0
Blue *dhotis* . . .	19	15	7	0	19	17	13	0	2	6	0

" The profit to the jail is very small. We have issued the clothing at rates below the contractor's rates and the police have likewise saved the cost of carriage to Assam. But the manufacture will have to be improved and the colour made more fast and lasting before we can call the experiment a success." During this year in Sylhet some of the prisoners were employed in making clothes for the Manipur State Jail, and the manufacture of uniforms for rural choukidars was commenced.

In 1894 the only articles of police uniform manufactured were red puggris, and these only on a small scale ; 466 were made at a cost of R582-8-0 and sold at a profit of R20-6-0 only. The financial result therefore was not satisfactory. In Sylhet the manufacture of uniforms for the village chonkidars was continued during the year, and this accounted for the large receipts shown in the table given above. The profits derived from the sale of these uniforms are not stated.

The present state of the industry in the three central jails will be seen from the following particulars received from the Deputy Commissioners of those three Districts :—

Gauhati.—The following cotton fabrics are made by the convicts in the Gauhati jail :—

    (1) Dusters.
    (2) Prisoners' uniform.
    (3) Towels.
    (4) Red turbans.
    (5) Darris.

These are all made of imported thread bought from the bazaar, white or ready coloured red or green as required. There is no account of the profit derived from the manufacture of these fabrics, as the object in view is rather to keep the prisoners employed than to acquire a pecuniary profit. It is estimated, however, that a sheet of cloth measuring 42 yards by 1 yard gives a net profit of R2 after deducting the cost of materials and labour. From darris no profit is derived.

The process of manufacture, which is said to be the same as that followed by the Assamese, is taught to the convicts ; men and women of all castes are employed on this work, but chiefly Naga men.

Tezpur.—The following is a list of all the cotton fabrics made in the Tezpur jail :—

1 Prisoners' clothing of all sorts.
2 Uniform for paid warders of the jail.
    The prices of these cannot be compared with bazaar rates; the charge is adjusted by book debit.

3 *Jharan*—Dusters.

(i)	Blue and white checks	.	Price 3 annas,
(ii)	Red and white checks	.	Do.
(iii)	White with black borders	.	Price 2 annas and 3 pie each.
(iv)	„ „ red „	.	Do.

4 *Barkapor*—Sheets . . . Price 8 annas a yard.
5 *Darri*—Floorcloths . . . Price R2 per yard,
    The sizes are not stated.

This jail manufactures the cotton cloths required for the prisoners by itself and the jails of the upper districts of Assam. The dusters are sold to the public and the darris are sometimes made to order.

. The process of manufacture is the same as that followed by the Assamese. The thread used is and always has been imported yarn bought from the bazaar ready dyed or plain.

All classes of male prisoners are employed without distinction of caste or creed, but especially long term prisoners. Naga men make good weavers, but it has been found that the most skilful weavers are Bengalis who have been previously convicted in Bengal, and employed on this work in the jails of that Province.

There is nothing in the records of the jail from which a history of the industry can be made out, but it appears that weaving has been carried on on a small scale ever since the opening of the jail.

Sylhet.—The cloths usually made consist chiefly of prison clothing, but comprise dusters, coarse bedsheets, dhuties for the use of female prisoners, and coarse sheetings.

As for the most part this jail supplies the Sub-divisional lockups in the district, and the subsidiary jails of Cachar and Manipur with all prison clothing, the sale of cloths to the public does not take place to any considerable extent, and no figures are therefore available to show the profit or loss arising from the manufacture.

The yarn used for weaving is purchased in the bazaar, which is in turn supplied from Calcutta.

Last year (1895) an attempt was made to produce a stuff made of cotton mixed with Cawnpore wool for winter coats, but the article proved inferior to cloth of the same sort sold in the bazaar. Some time back uniforms for the rural police (village choukidars) were made in this jail, but when the experiment was being made, no statistics were systematically kept. Hence the result of the experiment cannot now be stated.

Only handlooms are used, and these are of the same description as those of the weavers of Sylhet, and the method of manufacture is the same.

As a rule male convicts of all castes, including Assamese, are employed in weaving. A certain amount of preliminary training being necessary, it is the practice to employ long-term prisoners on this work.

Weaving is not the only stage of the industry carried on in the jails of Assam. Experiments have also been made at cotton ginning and even at the cultivation of cotton. For some years a cotton gin was worked with considerable, though fluctuating, success at the Tura lock-up in the Garo Hills. In Mr. Darrah's "Note on Cotton in Assam" some interesting particulars have been given regarding the working of this gin. Beyond this there is no information available, except the following figures which show the gross receipts on account of ginning in the Tura lock-up from 1886 to 1893. No figures are available for years previous to 1886, and, though the gin afforded capital hard work for the prisoners, it has now been abandoned :—

Gross receipts on account of cotton ginning in the Tura Lock-up.

								R	a.	p.
1886	.	.	.	.	.	.	.	464	1	11
1887	.	.	.	.	.	.	.	1	1	6
1888	.	.	.	.	.	.	.	126	9	6
1889	.	.	.	.	.	.	.	836	14	10
1890	.	.	.	.	.	.	.	205	12	3
1891	.	.	.	.	.	.	.	182	11	3
1892	.	.	.	.	.	.	.	99	13	0
1893	.	.	.	.	.	.	.	93	3	0
1894 and 1895	.	.	.	.	.	.	Nil.		

Another gin was for some time working at Goalpara, but not for long. The gross receipts on account of ginning by it in 1887 were R93-6-6. Figures for other years are not available.

Except at these two places, cotton ginning seems never to have formed a substantial item of manufacture in any of the jails of Assam. In 1892 at Dibrugarh the receipts on account of ginning were R15-2-9, and at Nowgong R5-8-3; and in 1894 in Tezpur R1. No other instances have come to notice.

The only instance of experimental cultivation of cotton in the jails is one recently made in Tezpur. The following particulars have been received : 1*l*. 1*l*. 5*l*. of land was sown with four seers of Bhoko or Garo cotton. The land was first ploughed and then the seeds were sown broadcast in April 1896. After this the land was harrowed once. The plants began to yield in September, and are expected to continue yielding till the end of April. The outturn up to 28th February 1897 was 1 maund 20 seers 8 chattacks of uncleaned cotton, which was found to contain an equal quantity of fibre and seed. The quality of the cotton obtained was good. The cotton was not sold, but kept for use in the jail. The value of labour expended was R33-12-0. On the whole, the experiment may be considered a success in spite of the partial failure of rain when it was much wanted.

APPENDIX II.

The following information about dyeing among the Noras and Turungs of Jorhat has been received and is given here as supplementary to the account contained in Mr. Duncan's Monograph (page 49).

"The Turungs and Noras of this sub-division dye cotton thread and cloths with the rum plant to a very large extent. The process adopted has been very fully described in Mr. Duncan's monograph on "Dyes and Dyeing in Assam," page 49. By this method light or dark blue colour is obtained as required. This colour is again converted into black by the bark of a large creeper which is very common in the jungle and is called by the Assamese *Barasi akora lata*, and by the Turungs *Tungataru*. It has hooked thorns like the *Barasi*, *i.e.*, fishing hook.

"The bark is obtained and cut into small pieces. It is then either slightly boiled or steeped in cold water in an earthern or metal vessel till the water attains a reddish black colour. The blue cloth is then put into the liquid for some minutes. The cloth is then dried in the sun. It is put into the liquid once or twice according to the depth of the dark colour required.

"They also dye blue or black longcloth in the above way from which they make shirts, coats, etc."

APPENDIX III.

A good deal of information has been received from the various districts concerning the varieties of cotton grown and the methods of cultivation. It contains little new matter and so has not been embodied in this monograph. The following points, however, may be noted.

In *North Lakhimpur*, there is only one variety of cotton grown, but it is called *dhanua* when grown as a mixed crop with *ahu* paddy, and *bira* when grown as an independent crop.

In *Jorhat*, there are two kinds of cotton grown, *viz.*, one with white flowers called *boga kapah* or simply *kapah*, and one with khaki flowers called *set kapah*. The *boga kapah* is sorted into two classes for sale, *viz.* (1) *Jola bachha* which contains the more perfectly opened and woolly pods and sells at from 5 to 8 seers for a rupee; and (2) *Kanria* (round like the *keroo*), which contains the imperfectly opened and less woolly pods, and sells at from 7 to 10 seers for a rupee.

In *Nowgong*, there are two varieties, *viz.*, the *bar kapah* and the *saru kapah*. The cotton is sorted into two classes for sale, and sometimes into three. The best quality is called *joha* and sells at R5 per maund, the worst quality is called *rai* and sells at R3-8 per maund. An intermediate quality called *rabrab* sells at R4-8 per maund, but the sorting is not usually carried so far as this.

In *Mangaldai*, only one kind of cotton, called *baria kapah*, is said to be cultivated, but *chemti kapah* is found in the homestead.

In *Gauhati*, three kinds of cotton are grown, *viz.*, *bhoka*, *chepti* and *rangi*.

In *Silchar*, the *khungajas* variety mentioned by Mr. Darrah and described as pale khaki is said to be reddish-white.